LOST

On

CHERRY STREET

Willow River Press is an imprint of Between the Lines Publishing. The Willow River Press name and logo are trademarks of Between the Lines Publishing.

Between the Lines Publishing
1769 Lexington Ave N, Ste 286
Roseville MN 55113
btwnthelines.com

First Published: June 2024

ISBN: (Paperback) 978-1-958901-88-5

ISBN: (eBook) 978-1-958901-89-2

Library of Congress Control Number: 2024934282

LOST
On
CHERRY STREET

Jack Donahue

For my father, Jack, a father's son

and

Joan Lehnert, dear friend and brave spirit

Prologue

Imagine the insignificance of the life of a man that took a rapid descent to the bottom, well on his way to an ignominious death in the gutter where he lay fallen, left unclaimed by family or friends. What could anyone say about someone who vanished into the dark shadows of a life lost?

Long before this man sat like a ghost in a room full of people who talked about other people they knew and cared about; there was a time that mattered. Almost by accident, some information did surface about this man's life, and an effort was made to make sure, at long last, that the record of his existence would come into full view. Enough information had been pieced together about his time on earth that had fallen to pieces, more than enough to enable someone to not so much tell his story exclusively, but rather to examine his life in terms of the larger narrative. The story that is being told here is the saga of his family, those who came before him from Ireland, and those who made a life for themselves within the Irish American enclave on the Lower East Side of New York City. It was the failures and successes of the individuals in this previous generation that contributed significantly to this man's rise and fall.

This is the story of the Callaghan family, reaching back three generations, looking at their lives stream by like a rush of water over the promontory's edge. The flow of Jim Callaghan's life cannot be distinguished from the other minute particles amongst the waterfalls' mist. From the rise and fall cycle of that mist, springs forth the ephemeral fabric of lives that created Jim's life, that bore the stamps of failure and success, spreading the Irishness of it all through succeeding generations. This is not about what his life could have been but what his life was. Telling this man's story was made possible through the assemblage of birth and employment records, ship logs, family records, police reports, court records, hotel registers, newspapers, family letters, marriage certificates, and official documents. Even fragments of cryptic, seemingly random notes dropped to the floor, found in pants pockets and worn-out purses turned out to be helpful. Fortunately, I gained much from the gathering and organization of personal anecdotes told by those who knew him and were willing to tell me, the narrator, what they knew. Some of the individuals sat in that very room where Jim was always marked present but nevertheless might as well have been absent, for he was regarded less important than the family dog. Whatever paper trail and anecdotal information happened to be passed down from generation to generation over the hedges or through the gossip mill, contributed to the story that follows. It is a story of lives lost, lives destroyed, and lives lived fully.

The coffin ship

It began with nine-year old blonde-haired, blue-eyed Peggy O'Rourke, born in Collooney Town, County Sligo, Ireland. Growing up, Peggy often stood at the edge of the woods near enough to the breathtaking Mills Falls to have her face fully spritzed by the mist. It was her favorite place where the Owenmore River courses over multiple, staggered rocky ledges. She enjoyed the thunderous power, the rushing sound, and the purifying smell at the edge of the woods. With her nostrils opened wide, she inhaled the fresh air, damp moss, and the atmospheric drifts rising from the stumps of fallen trees that pushed forth new growth.

Peggy delighted in swimming directly into the chaotic white-capped rush. It was the same force of water that turned the mill's paddle wheel that turned the shaft, that propelled the gears, that moved the belts to make candles, felt and wire. As the water rushed over the edges and converged into the vortex of dedicated propulsion, she thrust her wiry body full force into this faucet of power, if only to see which was stronger.

But the days of her delight came to an abrupt end in 1847 during The Great Hunger that infested every corner of Ireland during an especially harsh winter. Mrs. O'Rourke had been forced to witness her penniless neighbors thrown out of their cabins into the bitter cold, where many died and were buried in shallow graves.

It came as no surprise when a judgment with a notice to appear was handed to the O'Rourkes for non-payment of their rent, resulting in the imprisonment of Mr. O'Rourke. They faced eviction from their cottage unless every coin of back rent was paid. There existed no possibility for that outcome. Soon afterwards, the silver-tongued landlord, who had engineered the father's imprisonment, offered to pay the passage of Mrs. O'Rourke and her two daughters on the British ship *Echo*. The rickety ship was scheduled to sail from Dublin Harbor to British North America three weeks hence.

It would be a life better than any she could find in this blighted land; the landlord told her convincingly. It would be a new life filled with safety, shelter, and numerous employment opportunities. This is what awaited the family in a land predisposed to welcome Irish emigrants. Furthermore, one of his agents would be on the dock to greet them the moment they alighted from the ship.

Facing a grim prospect like that of her evicted neighbors, Mrs. O'Rourke lent a receptive ear to these ambitious promises. However, should she decide to leave Ireland, it would be without her husband, for there was no date set for his release nor funds available for legal assistance. In an attempt to appease Mrs. O'Rourke's agonizing sense of guilt over the abandonment of her spouse, the landlord promised to make every effort to free her husband. She believed him.

With little time to spare, the three O'Rourkes, dressed in threadbare clothes, hiked over the hardscrabble terrain, picking up a night of shelter here and there and some portions of grub that would keep them going another day, on occasion catching a free donkey cart ride. They were unaware of the challenges that awaited them, but what could be worse than starvation and freezing to death next winter?

Mrs. O'Rourke was unaware passengers in steerage would be packed like cattle on the way to slaughter, shoulder to shoulder with other famine refugees, malnourished, penniless, dressed in rags, some of them stricken with typhus and other diseases. She knew other families whose ship passage was also underwritten by the same landlord. The O'Rourkes saw these neighbors and friends leave under duress, yet never learned of the ultimate outcome, or if indeed the landlord's promises came to fruition.

Peggy did not arrive at the dock with an embroidered bag with wooden handles full of her belongings. She did not come with a change of clothes for the six-week voyage. She was consigned to wear the same rag calico dress, undergarments and what was left of her hooded cloak. She did not come with a host of dreams, hopes and expectations.

Under protest, Peggy refused to climb the boarding ramp with her mother and younger sister. She had been dragged by her mother every step of the way against her will to the last brig sailing out of Dublin that day, a barely seaworthy, poorly built, overcrowded vessel. They were the last to board and would face a fight for sleeping space in steerage.

Mrs. O'Rourke, desperate to catch any passage out of Ireland that offered even the slightest chance of survival for herself and her daughters, gripped the top of Peggy's cloak with one hand and held the hand of Colleen with the other.

"We can't leave Da. Not ever," Peggy said.

"Da is in prison," Mrs. O'Rourke explained, keeping an eye on the British sailors lowering ropes to lift the ramp. The ship was already packed with over one hundred desperate Irish refugees, none with grand illusions about where they would be sailing to, "We have a judgment but no money, dear Peggy. We have a judgment but no food. We have a judgment but no home. Come with your Ma, while I still have a bit of fight left in me."

Peggy was pushed to the ramp by the sailors and fell in behind her mother and sister. "I will hate you forever for this, Ma," Peggy said, "I certainly shall."

Colleen held Peggy's hand. "I don't want to die with strangers, Ma," Peggy said, "I want to die with Da, if die I must."

Mrs. O'Rourke whispered, "I pray to our Father in heaven that you will live. That is all I can do. I wish your mother herself had more to offer, my dear little ones, but I have not a thing. That is the truth so help me God with Mary the mother of Jesus as my witness."

The *Echo's* captain was skilled in navigating the brig through rough waters and was planning to sail into Quebec harbor in sixty days. He was adept as a seafarer, vigilant about his crew and the ship under his command. He was a keen observer of currents, high waves, and strong winds. It was this intentional focus that prevented him from paying close attention to sick passengers, rendering him personally unable to alleviate overcrowded conditions on board. The captain set his sights forward and never looked back.

The O'Rourkes were the last to descend into the hold, leaving them with the worst accommodations — a sliver of space on the hard plank floor, barely room enough for their emaciated bodies.

Small groups of passengers were allowed topside on the foredeck daily, one hour at a time. Adults were apportioned one pound of oatmeal and biscuit for the week. The children were provided with rations half that amount. By the end of the first week, an opportunistic and hungry Peggy taught Colleen how to sneak around the makeshift stoves to steal food. Wait for my signal, Peggy told her. While the adventurous older sister created a momentary distraction, the little one snitched bacon. They shared what they stole with their mother, no longer strong enough to make the daily trip to the foredeck to breathe fresh ocean air.

By the second week, more passengers remained below deck, having fallen sick. They huddled in the dark, unventilated space, side by side with other malnourished and sickly passengers. There was no room for Mrs. O'Rourke, Peggy, and Colleen to move away from the steady stream of vomit, urine and feces emanating from the passengers infected with typhus, dysentery, and repetitive fever. The pots used for toilet facilities were seldom emptied as frequent storms at sea required the hatches to be battened down. Passengers needing to relieve themselves found the nearest corner to empty their bladders and bowels.

"I need to wash myself," Peggy said.

"Give your Ma a kiss now. You will always be a sweet-smelling flower to me," Mrs. O'Rourke said.

"I would give love and affection to you Ma, but the smell is so bad."

Making the sign of the cross, Mrs. O'Rourke closed her eyes and said, "Tis like swine in slop, it is dearest Peggy, so don't be expecting miracles until we land."

There was no relief from the stench in the confined lice-infested space. The atmosphere was dense, close, and foul, overbearing and unrelenting for the scores of men, women and children forced together on the cold, bare wooden floors. All sense of privacy and decency were abandoned. Too ill to move, some unfortunates lay in their own filth the entire voyage.

Only the strongest had any chance of fighting off invasive, contagious diseases. Ultimately, those chances dwindled so that even the strongest succumbed to serious illness. No medicine was available, and the meager biscuit portions were barely enough to sustain them. The drinking water was not potable, drawn from wooden barrels that had previously stored vinegar, oils, even chemicals. Personal cleanliness was no longer a consideration. If anyone was fortunate enough to possess a bar of soap, it could only be moistened with seawater. No clothes were cleaned and hung on a line to dry. Only the most fortunate passengers had a change of clothing.

By the end of the third week, pure water was scarce and put aside for the captain and crew.

Mrs. O'Rourke had lost the ability to walk or stand and started to experience the onset of high fever and diarrhea. With no control, lacking strength to rise to a sitting position, she joined the ranks of others forced to lie in their own filth. She felt dizzy and nauseous day and night. The meals Peggy and Colleen tried to feed her were burnt to a crisp on the outside yet raw within.

Peggy rarely slept more than a few hours at a time, keeping a close vigil on her mother. Late one night, Peggy slipped over to a neighboring passenger's side and picked up the yellow tallow candle guttering to its end over the lip of the copper candlestick. There were but a few minutes of light left before it burnt out, giving Peggy just enough time to wander to the furthest corner of the hold where she stealthily removed another passenger's blanket. She returned to her mother's side and covered her shivering body and Colleen's tiny frame cradled inside the contour of her mother's body. As the candle burned down to within an inch of light, Peggy pulled back the blanket for a moment to take a closer look at her mother. Mrs. O'Rourke's face was swollen, and her legs appeared larger than normal, marked with black splotches around the ankles and soles.

Stirred awake by her daughter's attention, Mrs. O'Rourke removed a silver cross and chain from her neck and handed it to Peggy. "Come closer my child so I can put a whisper to you."

Peggy placed her ear against her mother's mouth, "I will listen to every word."

"This cross and chain were given to me by my mother. It is only right that you accept it from me."

"I will do that now, Ma. I want no share of hating you. I will fill my heart only with love for you."

"This cross is worth far more than the silver, Peggy dearest. Promise me you'll always remember that. Wear it for your protection and Colleen's. It will remind you that Jesus is always with you. Even to the end of days," Mrs. O'Rourke said as she closed her eyes and fell back to sleep.

The noxious piles of bodily discharges grew as each day passed. Acidic urine soaked through the floors, causing the hard planks to become sponge-like. There was no escape from the foul stench. It was not a living hell. It was a dying hell. Into the fourth week of the voyage, numerous passengers showed signs of high fever, consumption, cholera, typhus, and dysentery. The suffocating air inside the hold was a thick porridge of contagious disease.

Despite the horror in the hold, those immobilized below deck were spared the daily witness to the grotesque, dispassionate dumping overboard of dead bodies. The poor souls were wrapped in sailcloth and tossed to their burial place in the sea, without the benefit of a religious service, not even a prayer to fortify them on their journey to eternal life.

British ships did not require a physician to be on board and the quality and quantity of the medicines were inadequate for the volume of deadly pestilence that pervaded each corner of the brig's hold. Peggy was sickened at the sight of her mother's fever which had entered a dangerously delirious phase. The blotches on her skin became watery and odious. Peggy and Colleen could not escape being witness to their mother's rapid decline. At first, Mrs. O'Rourke complained of swelling in the throat, then groaned with severe, debilitating aches that afflicted every bone in her body.

Peggy examined her mother's feet, now swollen to twice their normal size, the skin cratered with putrid, black spots, oozing pus. Mrs. O'Rourke's head was so hideously puffed up, Peggy thought some monster had invaded her mother's body. Mrs. O'Rourke's initial dizziness turned into a fiery fever, causing such severe pain that she thought her head would explode.

Many passengers were starving to death. Unable to hold down food, they were stricken with diarrhea. Sharks followed the brig, sinister beneficiaries of bodies thrown overboard in mid ocean, ominously aware that there was more to feast upon by staying on course with the ship. There was a constant wave of moaning and raving by the sick, coupled with shrill, desperate cries for water, even though its foul contamination would make the poor, suffering souls even sicker. The hold was a hideous gathering place for the dying and near dead, marked with swollen faces and sore-infested bodies, looking like ghosts of leprous whiteness, with painful, oozing sores unattended to. Yellow and withering ghastly black streaks encircled the eyes of the walking dead. What drove the pain and suffering to the point of cruel, mad hysteria were the incessant moans and cries, the ravings of the delirious, the caterwauling shrieks of frightened children being torn from parents, unaware the adults had already died.

Peggy and Colleen could not sleep as the hellish cries of their fellow passengers announced the solemn nearness of death. Those writhing in pain were afraid to move. The simple action of placing one foot over another tormented their bones and limbs, while their insides convulsed in unrelieved agony. It was a scene of desolation with no relief.

There occurred a momentary lapse in the hold, a moment of eerie silence, allowing Peggy and Colleen to fall into a deep sleep. They were unaware their mother had given up her spirit after an effort, seemingly beyond human endurance, that drove her to get her daughters on a ship with at least a glimmer of hope they would someday own futures worthy to suffer for in the present. Although surrounded by the sounds of anguish and the passing of many Irish souls, mere inches from where they gathered, the daughters had deliberately ignored the smell of near death emanating from the one who had given them life, so focused were they on their own desperate situation. They could not bear to look at the outward signs of their mother's withering spirit, brought about by sheer exhaustion of mind and body, as well as poor health insinuating itself into her emaciated body. Finally, her spirit seeped out of her body in a noxious vapor, like a final hiss of steam lifting off a pot. In the days leading up to this moment, Peggy knelt by her mother to witness the protest of her mother's organs against any further work. The hostile resistance of her body's feeble functioning, no longer assigned the task for which they were originally designed, failed at last to be a worthy and hospitable home for a gentle, resplendent soul.

As the girls slept, two men with lanterns approached. Without a word, they lifted Mrs. O'Rourke's dead body and carried her to the deck above.

No physician was available to determine whether an unresponsive passenger was either dead or near death. It did not matter. Mrs. O'Rourke had been tagged with typhus and showed, over a period of several days, the delirium of constant, unremitting fever.

Therefore, Mrs. O'Rourke was thrown overboard, without so much as a warning to her daughters, without a sheet to cover her, without a priest to bless her journey to eternal life, without a prayer to honor her life on earth. Only a splash - barely heard on this night on the sea - which gave way to announce her journey to the deep, her body destined to tumble about on the bottom of the Atlantic Ocean.

Peggy and Colleen did not wake up to an open area next to them as the neighboring passenger quickly occupied the newly available space. Peggy awoke and walked up and down the rows of the near dead inquiring after her mother. She turned over a few bodies that might have been her mother. She inspected each corner of the ship, suspecting that her mother needed a private space to relieve herself, although she had never so much as moved a limb for weeks. Peggy walked upstairs, to seek information.

The captain had commanded the crew to keep their distance from the deadly diseases surrounding them. Healthy passengers were allowed the one-hour respite on the foredeck but were forbidden to cross the line into the afterdeck, with the deprivation of rations as punishment for foolishly doing so.

Displaying no fear, nor any regard for British authority, Peggy crossed into the forbidden afterdeck seeking news of her mother's whereabouts. She stopped every sailor, but no one answered her questions or directed her to anyone in authority. When she demanded to see the captain, she encountered the ship's mate who told her that if she made a nuisance of herself, he would not hesitate to feed her insolent Irish body to the sharks.

Peggy tried to sidestep the mate but the large, rough-looking man with a thick, unruly beard grabbed her shoulder and drew her in close enough that she smelled his repulsive tobacco breath. "Get back in the hold or I'll have you join your mother at the bottom of the sea. I'll feed you to the sharks, I will." The mate then directed Willie, the cabin boy, to escort Peggy back across the line.

More than four years older than Peggy, Willie stood eye to eye with the tall Irish lass. He looked behind him to see if it was safe to talk. As he walked Peggy across the line, he took off his cap and held it to his chest, "I'm afraid Miss that your Ma is here no longer. I'm sorry for your loss, Miss."

"How do you know that for sure, cabin boy?"

"You can call me Willie if it makes no difference to you," he said, "I been seeing you and your sis snitch bacon right out of the pan. Well done! Anyhow, I came downstairs part way with my lantern when the sailors took your Ma. I saw you and your sis asleep next to her the moment before. That's all I can say."

"Well, I suppose that's proof enough ... Willie."

"What's your name?" he said, staring at the cross around her neck.

"Peggy O'Rourke."

"Are you a Christian girl, then?"

"Catholic is what I am."

"Miss Peggy, are you an orphan now?"

"Don't know what to say on that subject, Willie. Mind you, I might not be if my Da still be alive."

"I'm an orphan as well."

"Where are you from?"

"London."

"What kind of dread was there on your Ma and Da?" Peggy said.

"Dunno. Never had any to speak of. I roamed the streets and the captain gives me a job on the ship."

"There's a wonder on you, Willie."

"You think so?"

"I do. I must take leave of you now. My sister was foot to foot with Ma. I have to go."

"If you need more food, just tell Willie. Fresh water too. If I can sneak it away. Whatever you need. You want no more messing with the mate. He's the meanest man on this ship."

Grateful for Willie's warning and offer of assistance, Peggy headed back to the deepest part of the vessel.

On the forty-second day of the voyage, after three thousand nautical miles on the open sea, the captain steered the *Echo* to within sight of Quebec. Small ships came alongside and directed the captain to join the queue on the St. Lawrence River where the sick were to be removed and quarantined on Isle de la Grosse Pointe. Forty-five bodies out of the original one hundred fifteen passengers had already been committed to the deep.

The clinics and fever tents on the Isle were barely able to handle the hordes of the gravely ill. Fifteen ships were in the queue. To add to the sorrow, more passengers died while desperately awaiting medical help. The captain was obliged to follow strict orders from the authorities that stipulated no bodies were to be tossed into the sea. The *Echo* had to wait its turn for the inspecting doctor to board the ship to examine the passengers and determine who needed to be quarantined. The healthy would be released and transported to Montreal and other cities for further disposition. Any newly deceased were to be wrapped in excess sailcloth and meal bags, loaded into rowboats, and transported ashore where they would be placed in coffins.

When the physician got around to boarding the *Echo*, word came to the captain that not all the sick would be allowed ashore due to a severe shortage of beds in the field hospitals. The deceased could be sent ashore first. Their number was added to daily.

Peggy noticed a rash of yellow, watery pimples on Colleen's thin legs. The blisters were spreading up her bony shins and thighs, onto her pelvis and chest. Distressed, she felt Colleen's head, which burned with a high fever. She wrapped her sister in a blanket and carried her up to the foredeck. She pushed her way forward through the crowd, determined to find Willie so her sister could have fresh water to drink and untainted food to eat. She saw Willie helping the sailors wrap the corpses in sailcloth and lowering them to the rowboat tethered below. He had the task of tying rope around the ankles. The sailors then looped rope through the binding and lowered the deceased.

Peggy waved frantically to Willie. As the sailors guided a corpse over the edge, Willie ran over to Peggy, observing that Colleen was gravely ill. Peggy guided her sister to the deck, took the cross off her neck and said, "Willie, we don't have any bit of time to waste. You said I could ask you anything."

"I did say that Miss."

"You must wrap Colleen and myself into one of those cloths and lower us into that boat. I need you to do it now, Willie. Right now. I beg you. You must do us this grandest favor."

"The mate will throw me to the sharks for sure."

Pressing the cross and chain into his hand, Peggy said, "You are the only one who has been kind to us. The cross is worth something. See the mark on the back. It is real silver."

"You shouldn't give this to me Miss Peggy. No need for that."

"Take it now, Willie. Hurry!"

Pointing to the rowboat below, Willie said, "Those bodies have disease. You will catch it and die."

"Colleen will die if we wait another day. Suppose the doctor doesn't choose Colleen. Please, my fellow orphan. I will remember you in my heart forever."

"Lie down and be still." Willie said as he put the cross and chain over his neck. He tied the sailcloth loosely around the sisters, dragging it along the deck. He placed the bundle between two adult corpses. Willie and one of the sailors then lowered the three bundles into the boat which headed for the Grosse Isle shore.

With the rower's back facing her, Peggy poked her head out to see how far they were from land. She eyed the spot where the coffins were stacked on the hill. To her left, she saw the long row of huts and white tents. The sailor looked over his left shoulder, steering the boat toward the hill. They were twenty-five yards from land. When he put his muscle to the oars, Peggy undid the binding. She opened the cloth and rolled over the bow into the cold water. With Colleen clinging to Peggy, the O'Rourke sisters descended a few feet below the surface.

Rising to the surface, Peggy said, "Come on, little sister. Hold on to me. Push your legs just a wee bit more." Peggy side-stroked with her left arm while holding her sister. They rode the current as it pushed them onto the muddy bank. Peggy lifted her head to see a bit of a rise beyond the reeds. She turned Colleen to a supine position.

Exhausted, the sisters slept for a while and awakened when Peggy felt water lapping against her feet. She knew she must get to the copse of small trees on the plateau beneath the hill, lest they come this far only to drown in a pool of water.

"We must go a little farther, Colleen."

"You go on ahead. I'll be all right here," Colleen said.

"We stay together, precious sister. We will always have each other."

"Ma and Da?"

"In our hearts forever."

"In heaven then?" Colleen asked. Her eyes closed as she sighed.

"We have to go farther. A wee bit more. Can you be of any strength to do it, Colleen?"

Peggy knelt beside her and helped her to her knees, coaxing her frail body away from the water. "See that little tree over there?"

"Yes. I see it. It is much too far for me, Peggy."

"We are going there. Colleen and myself."

Colleen pointed to the hill landscaped with rows of huts, "Not there, Peggy."

"Later, little one. Just to that tree for now." Peggy said.

Weighing no more than four stone, Peggy gathered all her strength and pulled Colleen to a standing position. She then lifted her onto her shoulder and supported her backside with both hands. Peggy's feet sunk deeper into the damp earth with each step. Her mouth was dry, her stomach empty. She could not remember the last time she ate.

Peggy made it to the small tree, dropped to her knees and let Colleen's body slither to the ground. She propped Colleen against the tree, closed her eyes and fell asleep. When she awoke, she noticed Colleen's body was about to tip over. She felt her sister's cold hands. She looked into her eyes, now vacant and still. Peggy brushed back the hair off Colleen's face and cradled her in both arms, as the stench of death claimed another O'Rourke.

Several bodies from other ships washed ashore. A young man walked cautiously over to Peggy as she clutched Colleen's body.

"Is that your sister?"

"She is that, sir."

The man looked up to the hill and pointed, "Would you let me help you get to that place? That is where we need to be."

"I must stay with my sister, sir. Thank you all the same."

"Your Ma and Da taught you good manners, wean. Did they also teach you to be a stubborn Irish lass? Tell me the truth, now, for your sake and mine."

Peggy held her sister tightly. The man knelt on the ground in front of the O'Rourke sisters and prayed, "Father in heaven. It has been a cruel journey so far for these, your little ones. We might question you, Lord, why it has to be such a difficult time for us Irish. I now ask that you give me strength to complete our journey up this hill. We have come this far, Father. Would you please in your infinite mercy help us the rest of the way." The man looked at Peggy, her hair knotted with dirt and bits of marsh reeds, her weary eyes closed, tears flowing over sunburnt cheeks, "For reasons known only to you Father, you have allowed this young lass and myself to survive. We are thankful for that."

The man bowed to the ground, placed one hand on Colleen's bare feet and prayed fervently, "Father, would you send your holy angels to this sacred ground. May they escort this little one's spirit back to you. I beg you Father, Holy Ghost, and Son Jesus to allow her brave big sister to let go and take my hand, I pray. Amen."

Peggy did not accept his extended hand. She looked at him and said, "Are you finished your share of prayers?"

"I will do more than pray, little one. Come with me now, lass. Some of the bodies that washed ashore with me are no more. Like your sister. Take my hand, please."

"And let my sister be eaten by rats. I will not."

"Your sister, God bless her, is now in heaven. Right at this moment, I tell you the truth as I know it. Now take my hand while we still have some life left in our bodies."

Peggy dropped to the ground and sobbed, "I want to die right here. And be with Colleen. Be with Ma. What is there left to live for? Can you tell me that, foolish, praying man?"

The man stood, making his final plea, "I cannot answer that. I sometimes question the God I just prayed to. I ask, 'Why did this happen to us Irish? What terrible things have we done as a people to deserve this?' But I do know this, brave lass. Your story and my story are not finished. I do believe there is a purpose for what is happening to us. I do not pretend to know the future. But I do know this. I am after life itself. I did not come this far to be a quitter. Let the Gaelic take over. Now, take me hand and climb on me back. Let you, sweet lass, and me, foolish praying man, see how long we can last."

"I thank you, sir. You are a kind man in an evil world."

"Take me hand and climb on me back now."

Peggy did so. They made it to the medical huts and never saw each other again. He must have been an angel, she thought, as she awakened from her delirium. She was kept in the clinic for several months where she was treated for malnutrition, typhus, and dysentery.

Word spread among the survivors that life in America would be better for the Irish than life in British North America, where the Irish in general and the Catholics in particular were not held in high regard. Peggy accompanied several emigrant families as they crossed the border into America. Along the way, portions of the caravan split off en route to towns in New England and New York, where their Irish relatives had settled after surviving their own journeys to America.

Peggy was invited to tag along with Emma Kennedy, a woman in her twenties, whose brother and scores of other Irish emigrants were the principal laborers who built the Croton Aqueduct, providing water for Sing Sing, surrounding communities, as well as New York City. As Emma and Peggy headed toward the village of Sing Sing, they and others were given hot meals, as well as packages of breads and biscuits. When the group gradually dispersed, dwindling down to just Emma and Peggy, they were able to make several one-night stops, often in the homes of other Irish immigrants who were fully aware of their own hardships and the kindness shown them when they had first settled in America.

At one of the Irish American homes along the way, a woman was so taken with Mrs. Kennedy and the ragamuffin Peggy, she rummaged through her attic chest to provide an outfit for Emma and went to town to shop for Peggy. Afterwards, Peggy was able to leave her rags behind and continue her trek dressed in a brand-new straw bonnet and a bright calico dress.

Emma's brother had started a family in the Hudson River village of Sing Sing and had written to Emma, praising the land, the people and the job opportunities. Peggy and Emma were welcomed at the boarding house on Dale Street owned by Mrs. Kennedy's elderly aunt. It was there that Peggy was sheltered, fed, and clothed and where she worked for her keep, doing laundry and house cleaning.

One day, Peggy was introduced to a prominent visitor and friend of Emma's aunt, Matthew V. Flaherty, a New York State Congressman who represented their district.

Mr. Flaherty removed his big black hat, shook Peggy's hand, and said, "Miss Peggy O'Rourke, I was told you survived against all odds. You will go far in this country. I trust America will be kinder to you than Ireland. Had I known of your abilities and fierce determination beforehand, I would have sponsored your journey myself."

"Thank you, Mr. Flaherty. I hope America will be kind," Peggy said.

The Congressman chatted with Emma Kennedy and the other boarders for several minutes. As he was about to leave, Peggy asked, "Could you help me find my Da?"

"Mrs. Kennedy can bring you to my office. After you give me all the details, I promise to look into the matter."

"I can give you all the details right now, Mr. Flaherty," Peggy said, "And there's one more thing, if you don't mind."

"And that is?"

"If you find out that me Da is not living, can you look for someone else instead?"

"And who would that be?"

"The landlord. I can tell you sure enough his name and where he lives."

"Why would we be interested in finding that man?"

"To dispose of him, Mr. Flaherty."

"Dispose?"

"May I speak plainly, sir?"

"Please do."

"To honor the O'Rourke family name and the people of Collooney in the County of Sligo, and in fact, all Erin," Peggy said, looking with her piercing blue eyes at the man who held great power and authority, "For them, *he* must be killed for his lying tongue and murdering hand."

"I'm very familiar with the history of British cruelty toward the Irish, not the least of which are the false promises they make of free housing and good wages," Mr. Flaherty said as he placed his hand on Peggy's shoulder, "They've had a habit of speaking those lies for hundreds of years. I imagine they made similar promises to the O'Rourke family. We'll talk on the subject when next we meet."

Devil s Bit

At a glance, the Callaghans of Tipperary were no different than other Gaelic families during the time of The Great Hunger. Their desire to leave the motherland they loved for America was driven by unrelenting deprivation and death. After all, the streets in the big country across the ocean were lined with gold, its rivers and streams gurgled with fish that jumped right out of the water into waiting nets. Furthermore, the pastures that flowed across the vast land were not covered with rotted plants and fruits nor littered with the carcasses of horses and cattle.

What separated the Callaghans from most of their neighbors and became the formative tale of their fortune or misfortune, was the promise of guaranteed employment and a place to live in New York City for their eldest son, Stephen. The assurance of food, shelter and a job would help the young man acclimate readily to a new life in a strange land. Stephen was eager to sail to the land of opportunity. However, his settling would not take place on the prairies or great plains where Americans worshipped the land and rode wild stallions bareback, but rather in the gritty pit of the Lower East Side of New York City. This corner of the country was rife with gangs committing vicious crimes in and around the dance halls, brothels, and dives.

Stephen loved what Ireland used to be and loved his family but what he dreaded most was parting with his one true love, Bridget, (Biddy) O'Dwyer of the parish Glenkeen in Borrisoleigh. Soon after they became attracted to each other, Biddy had the notion that her first true love and she would walk hand-in-hand through one of the many idyllic romantic spots overlooking the Cloiagh River in the ravine known as the Valley of the Robbers. All the young couples from Borrisoleigh, Templemore, and Thurles eventually claimed their favorite patch of emerald-green in and around that part of the country. There, lovers explored the natural beauty during the bright light of day, holding hands in awe of the inspiring spread of the vast Irish landscape.

Stephen Callaghan decided to introduce Biddy to a different kind of beauty, which could only be discovered on Devil's Bit; the oddly shaped mountain loomed over the landscape. It presented such a spectral sight that it gave Irish fathers the opportunity to scare their disobedient sons into submission with the threat of an unaccompanied overnight visit. Not that Stephen was more mischievous than other Irish boys, and no less fearful of his father's wrath, he nevertheless one day in his early teens decided to visit Devil's Bit Mountain. By doing so, he could either debunk the legend but still pretend to be scared or withstand the obligatory hellish punishment from the Father of Lies himself.

What Stephen found at Devil's Bit pleased him, a fissure in one of the big rock formations that led to a secret cave. At its southern end, it appeared that a sizable portion of the mountain had been extracted, giving it the name "Devil's Bit", a stretch of mountain divided by a plateau between Big Rock and Little Rock. The fissure, located at the base of Little Rock was accessible only by squeezing behind a massive boulder that rested against the rock's face. This was Stephen's discovery and his alone, as he never heard anyone else speak about its existence. He visited the cave often and never told another soul of his discovery, until he shared that discovery with Biddy. Soon, this spot became Stephen and Biddy's secret rendezvous.

On the day of their parting, Stephen took Biddy's hand and began the climb to the pinnacle. The flattened grass trail winding up to the summit was slippery and muddy as small streams spilled over the trail. The climb was steep. A thick cluster of pine trees along the left side of the trail rose to just beneath the rock formation. This forest of evergreens created a forbidding doorstep into nightfall even on the brightest day. The gentle murmur of streams did little to mitigate its fairy tale spookiness.

Stephen held Biddy's hand, guiding her over moss laden logs and slippery rocks, ducking under branches. Songbirds flitted ahead of them on the trail, a grassy, shaded valley of gnarled trunks and shimmering, scimitar shaped leaves, leading ever higher to the ramparts of Little Rock. As they climbed, hand-in-hand, they turned around every few meters to look below at the vast landscape decorated with slated-roof farmhouses, most of which were sand and limestone structures now relegated to famine house status. The panoramic view of rolling hills and gullies receded as they climbed higher to the summit.

Stephen and Biddy knew the land close-up, the craggy parts with pockets of rocks spread amidst the hills and farms, and the freshwater brooks and flowing streams. Growing up, they frequently visited the ancient cemeteries dotted with Celtic crosses and simple stone markers bearing family names similar to their own. They hiked the winding dirt roads that led them to their neighbors', once vibrant farmhouses. Now, at the tail end of the potato famine that devastated their land and their lives, many of the homes were vacant and in the early stages of decay, spoiled by the all too recent reality of death or eviction. Although the brunt of the famine had passed there were still many children who were starving and near death. What was left of their beloved country foretold a dismal future.

Stephen knew he needed to seek a better life for himself before he too would be counted amongst the dead.

When Stephen and Biddy reached the plateau of Devils Bit, they saw the Rock of Cashel in the midst of what remained of a Romanesque 13th century cathedral, its distinctly round shape standing in stark contrast to the church's two rectangular towers. Also within view was the less ancient round tower, a folly built by the land-owning Carden family of Templemore. It was used as the site for a meeting in 1834, when Daniel O'Connell addressed a crowd of 50,000 people as part of his campaign against the compulsory payment of tithes to the Anglican Church. The land and the people never forgot the meeting held during the Tithe War. As the years passed, huge crowds enthusiastically and rebelliously embraced the spirited music, song, and dance on "The Rock". All that was wrong about the Anglican imposition of an unfair tax still lingered in their Gaelic souls.

Climbing higher, Biddy and Stephen saw views of Lough Derg and the Slieve Bloom Mountains, while to the south they gazed across the plains of Tipperary, bounded by the Galtee, Comeragh and Knockmealdown Mountains. As they climbed higher still and got closer to the cave, they stopped frequently to catch their breath in the thinning air and reminisced about their previous visits to their secret place. Biddy felt intimidated during their initial visit, when Stephen introduced her to the primal beauty of total darkness. At first, she hesitated, not sure she could trust him so early in their relationship. Before long, the experience heightened her sense of smell, touch, and taste. She learned firsthand what Stephen tried to explain about the music of silence heard inside the womb of total darkness, their heartbeats the only sounds. Inside, Biddy felt as one with Stephen.

During each visit, it was Biddy who suggested they explore the intimacies of each others' bodies. Within the cave they could kiss and embrace while the rest of the world ceased to exist. Stephen always brought a few sprigs of mint so that their breaths would be pleasant, masking the bad odors that inevitably flowed from empty stomachs.

Stephen and Biddy crawled into a corner of the cave where not even a sliver of light invaded the darkness. At Stephen's urging, Biddy waved her hand in front of her face and saw nothing. Stephen ran his fingers through Biddy's long, auburn hair. She kissed his lips, playfully biting the bottom of his ear, whispering, "Must you go, Stephen?"

"I must take to the road, Biddy. I have my ticket and the ship sails two days hence. Soon the Callaghan family will have their visitors. Everyone is coming, Biddy. Every family, except the Carneys. As you know, me, Ma, and Da have had their troubles with them. When the hour comes for their own son to go, the Callaghan family will not be paying them any respect."

"Be the forgiving one Stephen. Don't be holding grudges," Biddy said.

"It's not me. I would mend the fences if it were up to me. The Carney and Callaghan parents had their dispute long ago. It was never settled."

"Still, would you be the one trying now, Stephen? It is a small village. Aren't we all hurting enough, each one of us?"

"Of course, you're right, Biddy. I'll make the case with Da. He holds the biggest grudge."

"Sometimes it's so long ago the hurt took place. Maybe the families don't even remember how the trouble started."

"That's true. There is a deep rift between them. You are right and wise, Biddy. I only wish I had a fair share of your wisdom and care for others. It's time to build a bridge. I will visit the Carneys on your advice. I believe I know the trivial cause of the breach. I'll bring Ma and Da into the conversation as well. They will listen to their eldest son, especially now that I am about to leave forever for a foreign land."

"I am already proud of you, Stephen. I think the world of you."

"I know, Biddy. I feel the same about you."

"I must tell you that my parents will be visiting. I cannot be there as I know I will surely faint. The Callaghans' mourning their son is burden enough."

"This time belongs to only us. It is very soon we must part."

Biddy grabbed Stephen, holding him tightly.

"Da has no money, Biddy. You know that. We're poorer than poor. Our family is starving, just like yours. I wish there was another road open to me. Then surely, I would take it. A certain benefactor man in America sent me passage on the *Swan*."

"Will himself be beholding to this benefactor man, Stephen?"

"Himself for some time, I imagine."

"Be careful then. This man might ask you to be doing things you should not do. Better you be paying your own way than paying him back," Biddy said, holding Stephen's face between her delicate hands, "Will you be seeing other girls in America, Stephen?"

"My only love is Biddy O'Dwyer. You must know that by now."

"Suppose you meet an upclass lass?"

"I'll pay her no mind."

"If I give meself to you now, would you consider staying behind, Stephen?"

"You can't make this more painful than it is already. It is the only opportunity the Callaghans have. For me to go first, being the eldest. I will find my opportunity and send passage for James to sail … and you, of course. We will be together forever."

"I will die before we see each other again," Biddy said.

"Don't you be speaking nonsense. As soon as I can afford your passage, we will be together."

"The ground is cold Stephen, but I don't feel cold. What I do feel is a strong desire for you. Will you take me now, Stephen? While me body is warm and ready for you."

Stephen grasped Biddy's head with both hands. He kissed her forehead, then took a deep whiff of her hair and held on for several minutes. He trembled when he moved one hand slowly along her neck, then her shoulder, down along her soft, smooth arm. She moved closer to him, nestling her head on his chest, just beneath his chin. Stephen continued to explore every inch of her body. There was no turning back. He got the invitation he desired for so long.

As they kissed, she guided his hand along her side, then over the slight curve of her hip. She held his face, kissing him deeply with an open mouth and exploring tongue. Stephen placed his free hand under her dress and felt the soft, warmth of her creamy smooth legs, moving up from the ankle, slowly along the calf, then on to the flesh of her thighs as she freely parted her legs.

They made love in the darkness on the fleece she brought from the cottage. She knew that she would have to leave the stained blanket behind, littering what now became the sacred ground they would remember the rest of their lives.

As they emerged from the cave, shielding their eyes from the bright sun, they embraced again. Holding each other close, they looked at the vast expanse of the countryside, several Tipperary counties within view. It was once a land good for pasture and tillage but now barren and dry, a forlorn landscape surrounding the tall spires of Saint Ann's Cathedral. Each dwelling, though appearing sturdy, had been ravaged inside by the famine. If that was not cause enough for deep sorrow, no dwelling was spared the loss of the family's eldest son sailing to America for survival and opportunity in a foreign land.

Holding hands, Stephen and Biddy gazed upon each other, feeling as one within the fullness of their consummated love. Biddy removed a jackknife from her dress pocket. She cut a lock of her auburn hair, folded it inside a small muslin cloth and handed it to Stephen.

"Now what would you be doing that for?" he asked, taking the gift, and placing it in his pants pocket.

"I need to know that each night we are separated, you will have part of me self with you," Biddy said, weeping.

"I will caress this each day and night, Biddy," Stephen said, "Now, I must call on the Carney family. I'll do this for you and for the peace of both families. Then, I must help Ma and Da make the preparations for tonight's gathering … for me own wake, no less."

The American wake

Christy, next in line in the O'Doul clan for passage to America, carried his Da, Ely, to Stephen Callaghan's wake. Christy's older brother, Thomas, was one year in America. Thomas's last letter home boasted abundant opportunities yet failed to contain funds for Christy's passage. Christy's Da was a fixture at every wake in their community. Old Ely was the local bard and pre-eminent seer, a beloved spinner of legendary yarns.

Although Ely weighed little more than six stone, Christy got weary on the upward climb to the Callaghan farm. At a crossroads they met the remnant of the O'Brien family, the widow herself and daughter, Mary, a blessed wisp of a ten-year old who every day scrounged for food to keep the two of them alive. Mary had placed teabags for Stephen inside the pocket of her patchwork dress. Daughter and Mum were grateful to the Callaghans for supporting their family when the father and two brothers were dying of starvation.

As the dirt road leveled near the dried-out brook, and the seven o'clock hour for the gathering approached, Christy felt Ely's warm, labored breathing on his neck. Separated by just two thin shirts and Ely's tattered jacket, Christy felt the irregular rhythm of his Da's beating heart. The caravan stopped near a cemetery of freshly dug graves, bearing names all too familiar to them. Three members of the Keogh family approached from the opposite direction. Old Ely slipped down off his son's back to greet Mr. and Mrs. Keogh, and their eldest son Patrick.

"Are you not goin' to the Callaghans?" Old Ely said.

"We wouldn't miss it, Ely. Your tales are good for me heart, especially in these troubled times," Mr. Keogh said.

"Well, the purpose is sad," said Ely, "But we have to make it lively for the Callaghans."

"I heard that Stephen has a sponsor in America. Can ya tell me the truth of it with any authority?" Patrick said to Christy.

"I know it's true as we're standin' here but I'm not sure Stephen will speak about it. The sponsoring man's name is Flaherty."

"From County Cork, is he?"

"A fair number of folk say originally from hereabouts," Ely said.

"Tipperary, you say?"

"I do. And more particular, Templemore," Ely said," That is what is being told."

"How come we don't know him well?" Patrick said.

"Made his mark in America. Here he was just a sly fox. Know what I'm getting at?"

"The moment Stephen steps on American soil, he'll be workin' at a good scale."

Mr. Keogh addressed Christy and Patrick, "Maybe Stephen will arrange an introduction so you lads can sail."

"The subject won't be mentioned this night," Ely said, "Unless, of course, it fits into one of me stories."

Pointing to Patrick, Ely said, "You know your Da and I would sell everything we own to send you boys along but ..."

At that moment Patrick stepped up to Christy, "Let me carry your Da the rest of the way."

"Thank you, Patrick, but I still have some steps left for me Da."

Mary O'Brien moved ahead of the group with her Ma, who asked of Mrs. Keogh, "What do you have in that sack, Emma?"

"Breads for Stephen, to take on his sail." Emma said, as the weary survivors of the great hunger trudged along.

With Stephen's encouragement, Liam and Margaret Carney came to pay their respects. Neighbors waiting outside the limestone cottage moved aside a to allow them access to the farmhouse. When Thomas Callaghan opened the door, his wife Ellen ran past him and hugged Margaret Carney. They were the dearest of friends. Thomas stood right up to Liam and said forcefully, "Man to man, I want to ask for your forgiveness, Liam Carney."

Liam grabbed his old friend with both hands and said, "If forgiveness is what you want, it is forgiveness I give to you, Thomas. Do you even remember why we fought?"

"I do, Liam," Thomas said, holding his friend, "You told me I wore ill-fitting clothes. After all these years, I must agree with you. I still wear ill-fitting clothes, but that is not enough to keep two handsome Irishmen apart from each other, is it now?"

"I believe I was trying to be funny at the time, Thomas," Liam said, "But, I missed the mark by quite a distance. By the way, you can thank your son, Stephen, for bringing about this peace. He takes no credit though. He told me he only spoke the kind and wise words Biddy told him to say."

The two Das laughed and shook hands vigorously as they led the others inside. The neighbors occupied every inch of space. While the men found a place to sit, the women helped Mrs. Callaghan with her preparations.

During the early part of the evening, married couples, widows, widowers and two or three orphans being cared for by their nearest neighbors, came to pay their respects. Several neighbors brought chairs and left them behind to accommodate those who followed.

Stephen greeted each man, woman, and child, politely answering every question. Where will you stay? What will you eat? Do the fish in America really jump out of the rivers into the fishermen's baskets? Will you make friends with folk who are not Irish? When there was a lull between questions, Stephen reminded everyone the *Swan* was set to sail out of Queenstown in less than twenty-four hours with him aboard. The finality of that statement brought forth a flood of tears.

Mrs. O'Dwyer stepped forward and kissed Stephen on the cheek and addressed him affectionately as the wee lad she knew for so many years. "Steveen, me husband and I tell you right now how proud we are that such a fine young gentleman as yourself is courting our Biddy. When you settle in America and call for our daughter, we would be liars if we said we would not miss her. The Good Lord knows we will have our share of joy knowing you have each other." While Mrs. O'Dwyer spoke, Stephen squeezed the muslin pouch Biddy had given him. The O'Dwyer's had planned a short stay. They knew how meager the portions were in such hard times. They did not want the food to run out before the other mourners were properly served. They exchanged heartfelt greetings with Stephen's parents, the four of them knowing Stephen and Biddy would someday marry and bring them together as one family.

Mrs. Callaghan removed the large pot of soup from the hearth as bowls and spoons were set in place at the long, rectangular table. "Thanks be to God for His bounty," prayed Mr. Callaghan, adding words of praise for his loving wife and family. He asked his youngest son to make an accounting of the family's gratefulness for their friends and neighbors. James Callaghan acknowledged each person by name, including the little ones, and thanked them for being caring friends and good neighbors who enriched their lives.

The broth was little more than flavored water, yet no one complained. When the meal ended, the table was pushed against the wall, opening up space for entertainment. When everyone was settled, Mr. Callaghan passed around clay pipes, the bowls filled halfway up with good tobacco he bought on the tick.

Stephen listened with pride to each story told about him. He had helped neighboring farmers milk their goats and cows from the time he was eight. When he finished the work he did with his father, he often went door to door to see if anyone needed him to run errands. He worked with the village carpenters, tinsmiths, and stoneworkers, learning each trade. He never asked for money, yet never turned down a meal in return for his labors. He soon became the stoutest lad in all of Templemore.

Mr. Keogh called out, "Steveen, you mastered whatever trades there are in this part of Ireland. Somehow Flaherty learned thorough about you lad. He will put you right to work in America."

"That he will," said Old Ely, "That crafty phantom heard all he needed to know. I'd be a liar though if I said I ever set eyes on him – even when me eyes were seeing as they should."

"Don't forget to tap on the door of the Cobh Relief Committee, Steveen. They will give you some maize for your journey," Peter Collins said, "and may the devil never be told where you live in America."

The widow O'Brien said, "I will always remember dearest Steveen, how you helped me work our farm for so many months after me beloved Dermot was pushing up daisies. God rest his soul. He loved you even more than I did if that's at all possible. You helped the O'Briens keep the landlord at bay." The widow then looked directly at each one of the Callaghan men, "You lads and your da stood up to the Queen's men. Stared them down until they ran like roosters who lost their peckers." Everyone laughed.

The aroma of good tobacco filled the room. More stories were shared, often with a touch of humor and questionable veracity. The effects of the homemade alcohol became apparent, as the deepest regions of hearts, minds and spirits began to unlock. A dead silence followed the insouciant bonhomie. Family, friends, and neighbors avoided looking directly at

Stephen, knowing before long, he would leave them, and they would never see him again.

The silence and the mood were broken by heavy pounding on the door.

"They're here," Mr. Callaghan announced as he ushered in two men and a woman, old friends from his previous parish.

"Meet Tipperary's musical queen, Bridie Quigley, the lass with the golden voice and a gift for playing every instrument known to the world," Mr. Callaghan preened, "And her brother Mickey, the greatest fiddler in all of the Erin Isle. And Mr. Tin Whistle himself, Colin McGahran."

"Keep your rumps right where they are," Thomas Callaghan said, as he ran into the bedroom. He returned holding aloft a bodhran and tipper. He held the instrument up high so that everyone could see it. Thomas Callaghan held the drum close to his ear, hit it a few times with the wood stick and proclaimed, "I made it meself. Sadly though, me missus is missing one of her piecrust forms."

Caressing the bodhran close to his chest, Thomas said, "You may remember me blind pig, Sally. We kept her and a few goats in the house on the coldest nights. Do I have to tell you how warm they kept us? Before Sally gave up her spirit in these hard times, she gave me permission to stretch her skin over this drum. Doesn't it sound good? Go on, admit that it does." He handed the bodhran and tipper to Patrick Keogh, "Would you do us the honor, Patrick?"

"Certainly, I will, Mr. Callaghan. I know me downstroke fairly well and me upstroke very well. I might be having some trouble with me instroke. These professionals must promise to drown out me mistakes." With the tin whistle, fiddle, bodhran and Bridie playing the jaw harp, no one had to be reminded to pound the floor in a continuous movement of jigs and reels. For forty-five minutes the music lifted them off the floor and out of their inhibitions.

Ellen Callaghan and Stephen remained seated. Mother and son clung to each other outside the circle of dancers and musicians, holding on for dear life on their last night together.

When the music stopped, the dancers took a deep breath. Thomas Callaghan poured more poteen, giving extra portions to the musicians. Bridie Quigley placed her harp on a table, took one sip and sang a ballad, the words and melody painfully familiar throughout the Erin Isle.

> *The night before leaving they are bidding goodbye*
> *And it's early next morning their heart gives a sigh*
> *They do kiss their mothers and then they do say*
> *Fare thee well, dearest father, we must now go away*
> *Their friends and relations, their neighbours also*
> *When the trunks they are packed up all ready to go*
> *The tears from their eyes they fall down like the rain*
> *And the horses are prancing going off for the train*

Bridie announced they would play *Skibbereen*, named after a small town in County Cork, where 9000 men, women and children were buried in a common grave at Abbeystrewry. As soon as Bridie began to sing, Stephen left his mother's side and stood alongside his Da. Everyone knew the song took the form of a discussion between a father and son. Bridie sang the first two lines, then asked everyone to join in.

As notes of *Skibbereen* wafted up to the stucco and wood beam ceiling of this once thriving farmhouse cottage, silence reigned for several minutes while Stephen and his Da walked hand-in-hand to the center of the room. Stephen kissed his Da on his cheek. Da returned the kiss. Stephen placed his left hand on Da's waist and his right hand on his shoulder. Da held on to his son.

Thomas asked the musicians to play *Skibbereen* again. Only heartfelt whispers would be sung between father and son.

The dance began, and in step with the music, Stephen placed his mouth close to his father's ear:

Da, my dear, I love to hear

You speak of this Erin Isle

Da moving in sync with his beloved son, whispered:

I do, Steveen, it was once

So bright and beautiful,

So rich and rare the soil

Stephen looked directly into his father's eyes, as he stepped to the music:

You say it was a bounteous land,

Where a prince may dwell

Da moved closer to Stephen and whispered:

You are that prince my son, my everything,

Though I could never be a king

Stephen held his father closer, seeing that he was growing weary:

I will always remember in forty-eight

You stood against eviction

Da would have surely fallen had it not been for the strength of his son's embrace:

We the Callaghans stand as one, Steveen,

And we must fight with total conviction

Stephen and Da moved as one to the music, never missing a step. Stephen sighed,

I will never forget you, Da.

I am stronger because of you.

With the final words of the song, Da took a handkerchief from his pocket and wiped his eyes and brow, saying softly:

I will cry each night you are gone my boy.

Don't ever give the devil his due.

As it was nearing midnight, the parents of the younger children got up to leave, offering their deepest condolences to the Callaghans, barely able to look directly at Stephen. As they filed out, a new visitor arrived, Margaret Lenihan, known throughout Tipperary as a professional keener. She was as necessary an ingredient at a wake as Old Ely. Margaret had lost her husband several years before The Great Hunger and has been keening ever since.

A voice cried out: "Old Ely, tell us a tale."

Yet another voice demanded, "Tell us how St. Patrick killed the devil. Tell us the truth that only you know, Ely."

"Patrick fought the devil. He gave him a good fight. He killed some rotten snakes, but Satan is still here in Tipperary," Old Ely said, "Look around if you don't believe me. I see limestone famine houses with slated roofs. Horses dead on the road. Cows and goats too. I see the twin mountains. Instead of rolling hills of green, I see pits. Druid ceremonies. Pagan sacrifices. I see graves, winding dirt roads, craggy rock outcroppings, dried up brooks and streams, and ancient cemeteries filled with the old dead and the new dead. I see that crosses have no power over death."

Old Ely rocked in his chair. His body shook. When he shut his eyes, his vision became clear. His voice dropped several octaves, "St. Patrick wanted to save everyone but only Jesus saves. Patrick is a warrior. He grabs the devil by the tail and flings him. Patrick looks at his hands. They are blistered. Smoking hot. The devil fears that Patrick will trap him, so he bites a chunk out of the mountain and escapes through the gap. The devil has a bad taste in his mouth. He spits out the rocks. Some land in the middle of Tipperary."

Old Ely stopped rocking, wet with sweat. It seemed he was at peace with his vision until he started rocking again, faster, and faster. The seer continued, "The devil does his work in the dark. God is light. Satan is darkness. Darkness will hide me, but the light of the Lord will show the way."

"That is in the Good Book, Ely," one mourner shouted.

"Not all the rocks are spit out in Tipperary … there are more … big as boulders. The devil puts them in his apron … Satan is big, but God is bigger … the devil crosses the big sea … he drops them in another country … Split Rock … Split Rock," Ely said again and again, his voice descending into lower octaves, devolving into a barely audible stream flowing through the tunnel of his mind.

At that moment, Margaret Lenihan aroused everyone with cries of anguish. Deep wailing spread like a contagious fever. The mournful cries bounced off the stone walls and thick beams. No one held back, keening for the loss of Stephen, soon to be dead and gone to them, though he stood not five feet distant from the cluster of mourners. Many keeners fell to the floor, pounding the broad wood planks in their unrestrained grief. The banshee was let loose to inhabit their forsaken souls. It was frightening to hear and witness with crying eyes. Whenever there was a tamping down, a cry turned into a whimper, a mere sideways glance at Stephen sent the mourners into renewed paroxysms of grief. This went on for hours. Some mourners passed out from sheer exhaustion, while those who managed to stay awake, keened until there were no tears left.

As dawn broke, Stephen placed his bags and gifts outside the front door. One bag contained a few articles of clothing. Several other bags were filled with breads, hard rye, and oatmeal biscuits that could be softened in a cup of strong tea. The Callaghan's neighbors, the poorest of the poor, gave generously out of their poverty. The older mourners began to leave, embracing Thomas and Ellen. They tried not to look at Stephen, lest one whimper trigger the next round of uncontrollable weeping.

The younger lads and lasses stayed behind to help Stephen carry his belongings to the livery station. They stood to the side, allowing the Callaghan parents private moments with their son.

From the start, Stephen knew this final farewell would be the most difficult part. He approached his parents, whose swollen eyes made the depth of their agony apparent to everyone. Thomas and Ellen held on to each other as they had throughout their marriage. Stephen looked at his father and said, "I don't want you to worry about paying your debts. The first money I earn will be sent to you and Ma for the tobacco and other incidentals. If there's anything left, use it for James's sail." Thomas shook his head and wrapped both arms around his son.

As Stephen turned toward his mother, she lowered her head. Stephen kissed her on the cheek, then gently lifted her chin until they made eye contact, "From the deepest part of me heart I say to you, Ma, I love you more than life itself."

"I know you love me, son. The truth is always in you. Be careful in America. I hear it is a strange and dangerous place," she said.

"I will be careful, Ma. You can rest on that promise. I will write a long letter every week."

Stephen lifted a bag and turned to face the road ahead. Thomas patted him on the shoulder and gave him a slight nudge forward. Stephen took two steps and felt the grip of his mother's hands on his free arm. Though she clung to him tightly, Ellen's knees gave way, forcing Stephen to crouch down and catch her before she hit the ground. Although Stephen's plan to emigrate to America was well known to the family for at least a year, Ellen never before this day truly considered that she would lose a child. Not until this moment. Crying out to the heavens she said: "Jesus, Mary and Joseph, save me."

The local parish priest, Father Patrick McCray, resplendent in his vestments, arrived to witness a mother's futile effort to prevent her son's departure. This scene had become all too familiar to him during the hard times. He walked directly over to Ellen and asked, "Do you have any holy water in your house, Ellen?"

"I do, Father. You blessed it yourself. Remember?"

"Indeed, I do," said Father, "Why don't you bring it here so we can join together in a blessing for your son."

Thomas and Ellen entered the house and returned with a small, white bowl containing the blessed water.

Stephen knelt before the priest. Father McCray motioned for all the mourners to gather around him. "Ellen and Thomas, would you be feeling true now to stand behind your son, and place your hands upon his head," then, turning to the others, "Put a hand on the shoulder of the person nearest you, as we prepare to receive the Lord's blessing."

The priest sprinkled the bowed heads. He dipped again and sprinkled the top of Stephen's head, praying, "I bless you Stephen Michael Callaghan on your journey to America. I ask that our loving and merciful Father provide you with traveling mercies," Father McCray sprinkled Stephen three times more, praying "In the name of the Father, and of the Son, and of the Holy Ghost. Amen"

Ellen and Thomas Callaghan stood arm in arm at the door of their house, watching the young residents of this diminishing parish escort Stephen as they took to the road for a one-hour journey by foot to the livery station. There, a horse and trap would be waiting to transport Stephen and his baggage to the railroad station. The train would be the last leg of his journey on Irish soil before he boarded the *Swan*, now sitting in Queenstown harbor on the southern end of Ireland, County of Cork.

As he approached the first bend in the forested road, Stephen turned around and saw his parents standing arm-in-arm outside the house. He waved to them one last time. They waved back. He placed his right hand in his pants pocket and squeezed the muslin pouch, as the slow yellow haze of sunrise glowed on the horizon. Its irregular beams shone on the path ahead, as a whisper surrounded each tree.

Welcome to America

"Just got word the *Swan* is within sight of the harbor, gentlemen. Go and fetch that Gael, Stephen Callaghan," Matthew V. Flaherty said to his trusted associates, John Aubrey and Charlie Poole.

Poole, the Tammany Hall ward heeler for Mr. Flaherty's office, boasted he could accurately identify the region in Ireland where a particular dialect was indigenous to, however small or obscure the locale, upon hearing a mere three sentences spoken in Gaelic. Charlie was also conversant in German, Yiddish, Italian, and Polish, all useful to Mr. Flaherty who represented those immigrant groups that populated New York City's Lower East Side. Their allegiance to Mr. Flaherty was the cornerstone of his strength throughout the 5th District, where he wielded political power. Like his boss, Charlie favored his Irish kin above all others.

John Aubrey was an indispensable jack-of-all-trades who anticipated Flaherty's needs before the boss himself knew of their existence. John performed a variety of duties for Mr. Flaherty the Congressman and Mr. Flaherty the businessman, shifting back and forth fluidly behind the scenes in matters most secret. His latest task necessitated frequent trips to his native Barbados, where he negotiated with local authorities to release prisoners incarcerated for minor crimes, mainly drunken revelry, or petty theft, so that they could work as laborers on undeveloped property Mr. Flaherty owned in Rockland County, New York. In a large, forested area west of the village of Sloatsburg, Flaherty envisioned converting one hundred acres with a bounty of brooks, streams, and a small lake, into a 'Little Ireland' vacation spot for homesick Irish workers. As the overseer, Aubrey arranged to clear the land, making it arable for a small 'tater' patch.

The first wave of Barbadian recruits leveled much of the rocky terrain and enriched the soil with a special mixture of highly fertile compost formulated by Aubrey, a man with many interests, ranging from those of a base nature to those that aspire to the loftiest heights.

As Poole and Aubrey got ready to leave the office, Charlie asked Mr. Flaherty, "How will we recognize Stephen?"

"Look for a tall, handsome, blue-eyed Irishman with broad shoulders and a shock of black curly hair," Flaherty said, "There might be several Irishmen on board who fit that description. I'm counting on Stephen to recognize you,"

"How so?" John inquired.

"Stand close to each other on the dock. I alerted Stephen to be on the lookout for the long and short of it."

John and Charlie eyeballed each other and laughed. Half a man shorter and a full man wider than Charlie, John's physical appearance was especially noteworthy. He was short and stout, bent over with a broad, moderately humped back, rounded shoulders, with long, muscular arms ending in large, stubby claw-like scoops for hands. Charlie was tall, his lanky body topped by a large cranium, made more pronounced by the egg-shaped prominence of his forehead. His narrow shoulders barely wider than his neck, dropped into skinny arms. His caved-in chest accentuated a hard-knot potbelly above narrow hips connected to stem-like legs, a stick-figure body supported by small feet.

Before Poole and Aubrey exited the Cherry Street office, Mr. Flaherty said, "After you get Stephen settled, come back to the office. I have something to tell you about fruits and vegetables."

As Stephen disembarked, he spotted his escorts among the throng of stevedores and onlookers.

Rather than the hardy young lad of nineteen years Charlie and John expected to meet, Stephen appeared less than robust, marked by sagging shoulders and an overall lean and haggard look. The voyage from Queenstown took its toll on the Callaghan lad.

John Aubrey took the sack out of Stephen's hand. "On behalf of Matthew V. Flaherty, welcome to America, Stephen. My name is John Aubrey, and my associate here is Charlie Poole. As per the instructions from our employer, we are going to ditch the contents of this sack and outfit you with brand new apparel."

Charlie extended his hand, speaking in Gaelic, "I see that we need to fatten you up. I don't think we need to ask about the food on your sail. We know all about that slop."

Stephen shook Charlie's hand, then John's. "Excuse me one moment gentlemen, there's a stirring in me to take this all in." Stephen swiveled around, looked at his surroundings, took deep breaths, and absorbed the fullness of his first steps on American soil. He dropped to his knees and kissed the ground. Near tears, he said, "To me, this is heaven. I smell freedom. I smell opportunity. I smell a new life." He took another wide-eyed look around and noticed passengers queuing up for customs. He turned to Charlie. "Should I get in line?"

"No need to. It's all been taken care of by Mr. Flaherty," Charlie said as he and John moved away from the crowd. Stephen lingered behind. The men turned around and watched as Stephen fumbled in his pants pocket. He removed the muslin pouch, ceremoniously cupped it in his hands, held it to his face, sniffed it deeply, then placed it back in his pocket.

Before introducing Stephen to his new quarters, the men arranged to have the young Irishman deloused and freed of every thread of rank cloth hanging off his body. Charlie carried a sack containing a basic wardrobe of shirt, pantaloons, and undergarments.

The men escorted Stephen to a basement shop on Rivington Street. "This is the first stop made available for Mr. Flaherty's most favored Irish friends," Charlie said, "Our very own delousing and fumigation station." Stephen was led down into the dark, barren space, dimly lit by streaks of daylight entering through the open door. The furnishings consisted of a small wooden cabinet, a stool, and a stove set against the far wall. "What are you planning to do with me?"

"Don't be alarmed, lad," Charlie said, "Mr. Flaherty's methods are foolproof. After you strip naked. John will throw your rags into the furnace. While he's busy with that task, I will lather up some cream and shave your head. After you have a brand-new bald head, the three of us will go shopping on Orchard Street for brand new clothes."

After they finished shopping, Stephen, carrying several bags of flannel shirts, trousers, and brogans, said, "Is there any mail waiting for me?"

"Mr. Flaherty put it aside," said Charlie, "He'll deliver it personally."

"I'm starved," Stephen said, "Do you think I might be able to line me stomach sometime soon?"

"Of course. Let's get you some meat and fresh bread," Charlie said, "Then lower a pint or two."

"That will warm me heart and me stomach."

After having been deloused, clothed, fed, and sheltered, Stephen fell asleep on a soft feather bed in his Cherry Street quarters, allowing him to put aside the memory of the thin, hard mattress in the first cabin on the *Swan* that he slept on throughout his eight-week voyage.

When Matthew V. Flaherty was first elected to the U.S. Congress representing New York City's 5th Congressional District two years earlier, having previously earned his political stripes upstate in the New York State Assembly, he began to affect a more flamboyant air. People took note of him whenever he made a rare public appearance, wearing gold, platinum and silver rings on three fingers of his left hand; a black Kossuth hat, with its slouch brim falling rakishly over his right eye; high-heel black leather boots; black velvet scarf; white silk shirt festooned with diamond buttons ablaze; and a black cloth talma that he put on and took off with the greatest aplomb, each element of his dress accenting his very upright and athletic physique.

Despite living in the shadows, the U.S. Congressman and Tammany Hall boss ruled lower Manhattan by providing a better life for his constituents in the 4th, 5th 6th and 8th wards.

With Tammany Hall backing, Flaherty experienced a mercurial rise as one of the highest-ranking dispensers of favors in New York City, providing a constant stream of cash flowing into his private coffers. His publicly funded largesse ranged from granting building permits for the construction of much needed housing for the daily hordes of new Irish, Italian, and Jewish immigrants, non-competitive government contracts, and licenses to open and operate dives, dance halls, and casinos, many of which the Congressman procured for himself.

Flaherty greeted his lieutenants upon their return to his office. Resting his hands on his desk, he spoke in Gaelic: "Let me say that every human being has a certain rotten spot inside of him. That spot germinates naturally, spreading further rot. From all my years of interacting with all manner and kind of the human species, I know this to be true. People are simply like so many banana peels, melon rinds, coffee grounds, eggshells, apple cores, and lettuce spines. Tell me, do either one of you know what ultimately happens to these vegetables and fruits, metaphorically speaking?"

Poole translated Flaherty's Irish verbatim to Aubrey, whose understanding of Gaelic was limited. Even though Charlie possessed a rare gift for foreign languages, the nuances and subtexts of what Mr. Flaherty communicated often escaped him. John, on the other hand, had more of an open mind, accented with a vivid imagination. He possessed an uncanny gift that intuited Flaherty's innermost thoughts and customarily coded, abstract speech.

"May I be so bold as to say …" Aubrey said.

"Go on," Flaherty said.

Charlie interrupted, answering Flaherty's original question in an enthusiastic, knowing, and confident manner, "I do, Mr. Flaherty. I certainly do. These organic materials become a most efficacious compost."

"Exactly, Mr. Poole. I knew I could depend on you," Flaherty said, leaning back in his plush high-backed leather chair, ridged with leather buttons, "What happens then to this efficacious compost?"

"It enriches the soil, I imagine …" Charlie said.

"That is true," Flaherty said, "Therefore, it follows that everything rotten has a purpose. Rot is turned into something good. Noble even. More good springs from rot."

Aubrey said, "I truly believe, Mr. Flaherty, that your work is exclusively designed for the advancement of the Irish race. The Irish are not dogs as some have claimed. They are not inferior. They are not savages or beasts. Our boys in Barbados will do a handsome job digging and splitting rocks. They will compost just as diligently. Although the hideous cruelty of slavery ended for them many years ago, there continues to be a group of Irish who are unfairly imprisoned on that island. The poor souls are forever seeking their own release. Not so much for the freedom to get drunk or steal again but to seek a more prideful freedom from the tedium of uninteresting work. They need excitement, adventure, and a personal challenge to occupy their mundane lives. Under my direction, they will be particularly savage in their devotion to the most challenging assignments."

"Well spoken, John," said Mr. Flaherty, "No disrespect, Mr. Poole, but I think Mr. Aubrey has a firm grasp on the fundamentals here."

Aubrey further illumined his understanding of his boss's nuanced directive, "I humbly request that we give this group of workers a distinctive identity. One that will encourage them to be proud of their fulfilling work. Enable them to be most grateful for the privilege of serving you. I would like to call this new division of your business enterprise, the *Cherry Street Rotters*."

Flaherty unfolded his hands, leaned back in his chair, and said, "My only concern is *Cherry Street Rotters* sounds very much like a gang. It just sickens me that organizations like the *Dead Rabbits*, *Musk Rats*, and the *Gophers* and all those other brigands and blackguards go about shamelessly bludgeoning innocent people, in full view of the public. No decent citizen appreciates open acts of terror and barbarism. Perpetrated for all the world to see in the Five Corners by gangs of mostly Irishmen, brutalizing each other with clubs and knives, and slung shots. All done at the very same time we are trying so hard to fortify the reputation of the Irish race. These gangs are doing their dirty deeds right out in the open, giving the Irish a bad name."

Charlie spoke up, "You both know I am a very distant relation to Bill Poole, AKA Billy the Butcher. I swear no allegiance to him. I am sure Billy is not even aware of my existence, he being generally uninterested in family trees."

"Pay that no mind, Charlie," John said as he patted his friend's knee, "It's not like we're going to advertise in the newspapers or file court records for a new business. Knowledge of the *Cherry Street Rotters* will remain a closely held secret exclusively among the three of us. The *Cherry Street Rotters* will operate discreetly."

"Excellent, Mr. Aubrey. Well said. So be it then. *Cherry Street Rotters* it is. You can add the formation of this new division to your already distinguished resume," Flaherty said.

Charlie surmised that the *Cherry Street Rotters* would somehow ennoble individuals who otherwise served no good-will purpose in this world, yet he was grateful that this particular Flaherty enterprise did not fall within his scope of responsibilities.

Aubrey's domain required more physicality than Mr. Poole's diplomacy. The task ahead included recruiting and transporting laborers willing to get off the hot island in the middle of nowhere to work in New York City, albeit starting their careers in the grimmest of the city's slums. Aubrey already planned to use some of the Barbadian recruits to fortify election results, convinced they would prove themselves worthy.

Aubrey had strong connections in Barbados. He was one of them, a mongrel mix of Irish, British, and Maroon, a Barbadian of very tainted blood consisting of unknown percentages of black and white genes. The British portion of his ancestry caused him shame. Outside of the intimate circle of Flaherty and Poole, he was unwilling to reveal the true nature of his family lineage. Overall, despite his unusual physical appearance, the pale coloration of his skin allowed him to be taken for totally white.

In administering Flaherty's penal colony/compost enterprise, Aubrey was allocated an ample budget that allowed him to bribe prison officials. The men incarcerated in Barbados for petty crimes were direct descendants, ten generations removed, of the many Irish men and women who were either indentured or enslaved by enterprising British tobacco and sugar cane planters. The 17th century Irish were shipped to the island as part of the ethnic cleansing conducted ruthlessly by the British. The Irish girls deemed ugly by the planters were put to work in the fields alongside the men. Those young Irish girls considered pretty, wound up as sexual playthings for the planters. Frequent whippings, often administered by native blacks, kept every Irish man and woman in line. The practice of interracial marriages centuries earlier brought John Aubrey into the world.

Aubrey recruited strong-bodied Barbadian men. Not much would be asked of them. Most could not read or write, making employment applications unnecessary. The released prisoners were sent north to do whatever work was necessary for the efficacy of the *Cherry Street Rotters*. Flaherty was excited about the potential fruits of their labor.

Aside from periodic composting trips to Rockland County, the *Cherry Street Rotters* were consigned to work underground in New York City, their shadowy assignments allowing Flaherty's real estate business to flourish. In the foreseeable future, there would be no shortage of ships full of Irish immigrants sailing into the New York docks, each family on board needing work and housing.

Through his considerable Tammany Hall connections, Flaherty controlled the stocking and delivery of coal, vendor's trades, permits for pushcarts, and all varied and sundry aspects of the Lower East Side milieu. The future looked bright. The scale of varied revenue streams could not be estimated.

Flaherty called on Stephen the next morning while he was still asleep. He tapped Stephen's stockinged feet with a stack of letters. "Wake up lad. There's work to do."

Stephen, groggy, said, "Where are me keepers?"

"Poole and Aubrey?"

"Yes."

"I sent them on their way."

"Who are you, then, if you don't mind me asking?"

"Matthew V. Flaherty. Glad to make your acquaintance."

Stephen sat up. "Forgive me Mr. Flaherty. I have no manners. I did not know."

"Easy, lad. I'm just another Gael to you," Flaherty said, eyeing Stephen's shaved head, "What in the name of St. Patrick happened to your hair?"

"Left it on the floor with all the nasty nits writhing within it."

Stephen took note of his employer's dress, the slouch-brimmed black hat, a black silk suit with a black string tie, a royal dandy for sure. Stephen expected Matthew Flaherty to be a much older man, previously imagining a rotund politician, not recalling their encounter when he was a lad back in Ireland. Instead, he now came face-to-face with a man fastidious about his weight and appearance. He could see that the politician had a powerful physique, giving credence to the rumor back in Tipperary that the Congressman was once a champion boxer.

"Your hair will grow back. And the meat on your bones. I remember that shock of black hair when I met the youngster Stephen Callaghan, the handsomest lad in all of Tipperary."

"This lad that you see before you is a grateful lad. Grateful for what opportunity you provided for me … and my family. The situation is pretty desperate back home. I'm sure you're aware of that. You're doing great things for our people."

"You're all family to me, lad. I am certain you will make the Irish proud. You are a good investment, Stephen. I can spot talent a mile away, I'll have you know. That's my particular gift."

"I don't exactly know what you saw in the young Stephen Callaghan, Mr. Flaherty."

"Piss and vinegar. That is what I saw. And another ingredient that'll be put to the test over time … but not too much time."

"And what would that be?"

Mr. Flaherty handed Stephen the banded stack of letters. "I met the female version of you a few years back. Here in the states. Maybe even tougher Irish than you are."

"Do I know her then?" Stephen said as he hurriedly slipped into his pantaloons.

"Hardly. She's a Sligo girl. On her Ma's side. And a Mayo lass on her Da's. What counts is that she is from the Erin Isle. I doubt you know her. She came abroad two years ago. Quite a story she can tell. Just a wee lass when I met her. Maybe someday she'll work for me. You two would make a great match."

"I'm spoken for, Mr. Flaherty," Stephen said as he thumbed through the stack of letters, spreading them out on the bed. He picked out Biddy's letter, pushing the others aside.

"Would you like some privacy, Stephen?"

"No sir, I don't mind," Stephen said as he fingered the muslin pouch in his pocket, "I just need to read this one first."

"Go on, lad. Take your time," Flaherty said as he stood by the window overlooking Corlears Hook Park, and the East River.

Stephen sat on the edge of the bed and tore open the envelope. After reading the first page, he dropped back on the bed, letting the other pages fall to the floor.

Flaherty turned around to see Stephen flat on his back, clutching the page.

"Good news or bad?"

"Read it yourself, Mr. Flaherty."

"O shite! You're going to be a Da. Congratulations, lad. I had no idea you were married."

"We ... I ... we're not," Stephen said, "We ..."

"No need to explain anything to me, I'm not a priest," Flaherty said, "You need to get her over here, lad. And James."

"I don't know about my brother at this particular time, Mr. Flaherty. I don't believe I have the resources. It will be enough for me to pay passage for a woman and child. I have not worked one day for you."

"Listen to me, lad, and listen well. I will take care of everything. Do you understand? You are to post a letter to her tomorrow and write to your brother as well. He is to marry her ... what's her name?"

"Marry her? But ..."

"What is her name, Stephen?"

"Biddy."

"It will be an arrangement. To keep her honest. Without shame. Are you hearing me now? There is no judgment here, lad. Your brother will understand. He will not touch her, but he will honor her, as she deserves."

"Is that necessary?"

"I am seldom wrong in these matters. Tell James and Biddy it is to be a marriage of convenience. I will pay their passage. Write that letter now. It is to be your first job on the Flaherty payroll. Write it right now so it can be carried on the next ship. You don't want her to show too much, in front of the priest. Jesus, Mary, and St. Joseph, write the letter now! Some priests are more pious than others in these matters, lad."

"You are much too kind, Mr. Flaherty."

"Great things are in store for the Irish in this country. You will be a part of it. Now, get busy," Flaherty said.

Baby on board

Stephen Callaghan heard the rolling thunder as he paced back and forth on the dock awaiting the arrival of the *Infantry*. The ship had sailed out of Liverpool July 29, 1850, carrying his younger brother James, his sweetheart Biddy and his yet unnamed son, now four months old. What started out as a slightly overcast early October day suddenly turned grim, as heavy clouds moved in, unveiling a canopy of darkness over the harbor. The barking orders of dock workers combined with the shrieks of excited onlookers spotting relatives they thought they might never see again, the screeches of gulls fighting for rotted food being dumped overboard, and the rumble of steel wheels banging over the uneven cobblestones distracted Stephen. Husky stevedores pushed their loaded wheel barrels back and forth, determined to get the ship unloaded before the rain poured down in torrents. The workers crisscrossed in front of Stephen, blocking his view.

Stephen shifted his feet, alternately squeezing, then sniffing Biddy's muslin pouch. In a few moments, he could toss that Devils Bit Mountain relic into the trash and plant his nose on top of her head and inhale the fullness of his beloved.

Stephen saw his brother first amidst the horde of disembarking Irish immigrants. His eyes darted from person to person in James's immediate vicinity. Where is Biddy? Why is she not at my brother's side? So tiny, she must be standing behind my brother.

James held a swathed bundle in his arms. He waved to Stephen, then strode toward him, his visage as gloomy as the weather.

Stephen did not look at the infant in James's arms nor take note of the anguish in his brother's eyes. Instead, Stephen pivoted right and left, peering anxiously over the top of James's head, searching for his Biddy. All that came into his sight were streams of unknown faces and the hulking ship, rocking in its moorings after its long journey on the vast, turbulent sea.

James tried to embrace Stephen but Stephen stepped back. "Where is she, brother? Tell me why Biddy is not at your side."

This was the very question James feared. He had been rehearsing a speech about Biddy for several days, dreading his brother's reaction to the inevitable pronouncement.

"She died on board, dear Stephen," James said, "And may God rest her soul, now most blessedly in heaven."

Stephen glared at James with wild, frightful eyes. He refused to accept this devastating news. James wanted to console his brother. Instead, he held the motherless child closer, as if the infant needed protection from his own father. Although the heavy rain subsided, James sensed a storm of explosive rage about to burst from Stephen.

Stephen's eyes were full of judgment and scorn. He could not speak. James filled the dreadful chasm between them with more disquieting details. "She was weak, Stephen, too weak to eat or nurse your son. Her decline began soon after bringing him into the world. She took on a terrible illness with typhus and gave up her spirit just a fortnight past. God rest her soul and the souls of all the Irish."

"Where is her body, then? When will they return her to me?"

James shifted the infant to his other shoulder as he looked off into the distance.

"Look at me, James. Answer my question. Where is her body?"

"Our beloved Biddy lies at the bottom of the ocean," James said, with eyes cast to the ground.

"What are you telling me?"

"She was buried at sea. They feared the typhus would spread."

"This was not supposed to happen," pointing to the *Infantry*, "That is not a coffin ship. Was there no physician on board? Did they not have medicine for her?"

"They did everything they could, but she perished all the same."

Stephen took the pouch out of his pocket and inhaled deeply. "I'm trying to understand why my Biddy had no proper burial. Tell me they had the decency to give that beautiful saint a Christian service, at the very least."

"Are you after the truth?"

"I am."

"Truth be told, there was no service for dear Biddy. Many bodies were thrown overboard with not so much as a simple prayer. I prayed powerful prayers. To Mother Mary. I prayed to Jesus. And I prayed to our own St. Patrick. Not only did I pray. I protested loud, Stephen. I protested long. My efforts came to no avail."

"Tell me, did my Biddy mention my name before she passed into heaven?"

James extended his arms, offering the child to his father. "Look at your son, Stephen. This is Biddy's gift to you. Take him. He is yours."

Stephen recoiled. "Take him? It pains me to set my eyes upon him."

Stephen looked at the stones on the ground. He studied the pattern of how they were laid, tracing his foot on the horizontal and vertical separations. He stepped to the edge of the dock and stared at the water. The activity taking place all about him dissolved into oblivion. Passengers filed past. Crew members unloaded barrels and equipment, lining them along the wharf. Stephen blessed himself repeatedly with one hand and caressed the lock of Biddy's hair with the other.

One of the sailors tried to maneuver a hand-truck loaded with barrels as he came down the ramp. He tripped over a rope and lost his grip on the top barrel. "The devil I am," he cursed as the entire load tipped into the water. The splash startled Stephen and broke his reverie. He offered forgiveness to his brother with a kiss on his cheek.

As the Callaghan brothers waited in the customs queue, the infant started to cry, his wails swallowed by the strong wind coming in off the sea.

"This child needs to be suckled soon, Stephen," James said. For the first time since their arrival, Stephen pulled back the swaddling from the baby's face and torso, marveling at the width of his son's shoulders. He could not imagine how this child issued forth from Biddy's tiny body.

Charlie Poole had accompanied Stephen to the dock but stood off to the side, granting Stephen private moments with his family. He had expected to meet Biddy, yet surmised Stephen's joyful anticipation had turned to sorrow. Due to Charlie's Tammany Hall connections, a brief discussion between him and the Customs Superintendent resulted in James and the infant being allowed to step out of the queue.

"We have to hurry along now," Charlie said, as he put his arm around Stephen's shoulders. James, holding his surrogate son, took one last look at the *Infantry* before he caught up to the others.

They arrived at Flaherty's Cherry Street office and stepped into the dome-shaped structure located at the edge of Corlears Hook Park, its stark white stone edifice looming as an architectural oddity, out of character with the monotonous row of rundown clapboard buildings across the street.

"Where is the beautiful woman I've been hearing so much about?" Flaherty said as he looked from Stephen to James. Stephen lowered his head.

James stepped forward, "Sadly, I am the bearer of bad news."

"Don't tell me ..." Flaherty said.

"Yes, sir. I am afraid so."

"And where did they store her body, I need to ask."

"In the sea, Mr. Flaherty. Her final resting place."

Flaherty came alongside the inconsolable Stephen and gently raised his chin. "My deepest condolences, Stephen. May you find peace in knowing Biddy suffers no longer. She is in heaven, lad. Leave your work aside now. Take as much time as you need to properly grieve. This is a terrible loss. Let me know at once if there's anything I can do. Not so much as your employer, but as your friend."

Flaherty took James aside. "Did they throw her overboard like a sack of excrement?"

"They were afraid the typhus would ..."

Flaherty put his hand on James's arm while glancing up at the high ceiling, "They have no respect for the living ... no respect ... for the dead ... did you marry that unfortunate lass?"

"I did, sir. I swear on my family's name I never touched her."

"That's a good lad. It is so important to have honorable people working with us," Flaherty said, turning to Charlie, "Isn't that always the case, Mr. Poole?"

"Absolutely. We would not have it any other way," Charlie said, looking at the Callaghan brothers, "If this lad is as honorable as his brother, then our organization will be all the more Irish for it."

"Does this child have a name?" Flaherty said.

"Biddy and I exchanged letters on the topic. She asked me to wait until we were together, to properly name the child. I am thinking of a name ...

but first …" Stephen said, taking the infant from his brother's arms, "We must get him fed. Or no name shall be necessary."

"Yes, in due time you'll name him. Then we'll get him properly baptized," Flaherty said as he nudged the young, dark-skinned boy sitting cross-legged on a leather mat, "Get your mother."

The boy put down his clay pipe, grabbed a lantern and made his way through a trap door. James sat down beside the potbelly stove situated in the middle of the large, circular room. Mother and son returned fifteen minutes later. The Lenape woman, dressed in a deerskin garment braided with fine beadwork, was holding a female infant in her arms. She handed the baby to her son and took the boy from Stephen. She cradled him in her arms and opened a flap on her dress. She held her left breast while coaxing the baby's mouth onto her nipple. The hungry infant started sucking immediately.

"By fortune of the stars," Flaherty said to Stephen, "Your wee lad will be fine in a few days. Margie is presently breastfeeding her own baby girl so she has … how should I say it … a surplus flow." "How can she feed her own baby and mine?" Stephen said.

Flaherty and the mother looked at each other, smiling. "Have you ever noticed Stephen, that a woman has two teats, whether Irish or otherwise?"

The boy led Stephen, and his mother, with her cargo of two infants, into the maze of wormhole tunnels connecting several buildings beneath Cherry Street.

"You must be exhausted. The journey. The tragedy. We might have to let you sleep for three weeks straight," Flaherty said to James.

"I could fall asleep this moment on one of those mats. Might I add, though, I am ready to start working whenever you call upon me to do so."

"Good. You'll be bunking with your brother for a week until we get you settled in your new home. After growing up together in Templemore, I imagine you were accustomed to sleeping together in the loft above the hearth."

"It'll give me some time to comfort him. I feel a whole eternity's worth of terrible for Stephen. He truly loved Biddy."

"Tis a sad lot for the Irish. You're better off here in America with our organization. By the way, you need to put some decent food in your stomach, James. Charlie will share a meal with you, and a pint or two."

"You are a kind man, Mr. Flaherty."

"Not everyone thinks so but thank you all the same."

James regained his strength and met with Flaherty and Poole after a few days. "Are you any kind of curious about the position I have for you?" Flaherty said.

"I am more than ready for whatever you need me to do."

"Some years ago, my ancestors purchased a parcel of land upstate from members of the Lenape nation. Benefitting from that inheritance, I bought additional parcels from their ancestors. Are you familiar with Lenape history?"

"Can't say that I am, sir, only a few days in my new country."

"When you step outside, Charlie will escort you to the riverbank. There's a marker there that pinpoints the actual location where the Lenape landed their canoes in the seventeen-hundreds when Georgie Washington was just a wee lad. When commerce arrived, the Lenape got pushed out. Some headed north to the Ramapough Highlands, a forested area with rock outcroppings. Good hunting, fishing, and arable land. Remember the woman looking after Stephen's boy? The one with two teats?" Flaherty said, smiling.

James nodded. "She came to the rescue just in time."

"She certainly did. Her name is Margie. She's one of the Lenape who stayed behind. Her whole family works for us. They are a very docile people."

"A fine family," Charlie said.

"Thank you for the enlightenment, Mr. Flaherty. I don't believe we have Indians in Ireland. Tinkers are closest to it, I guess."

"Let me tell you where you fit into our situation here. The land we own is known as Pine Meadow. It sat vacant for many generations. I not only want to help our Irish brethren get settled in this city, I dream that Pine Meadow could be a nice vacation spot for them. A haven to remind them of our motherland. We did some clearing and created a potato patch. A little bit of Ireland just a three-hour carriage ride north of here. With rock outcroppings like Templemore. Beautiful streams. The cleanest air an Irishman can draw into his lungs. I need a manager for the property. That would be you, James. You'll be getting deliveries of compost from time to time to enhance the soil's fertility. We'll provide strong backs to till the land. We also have a trading business with the Lenape. Basket making, pottery and other crafts they sell in neighboring towns."

"I hope it reminds me of the Ireland I knew before the hard times."

"Indeed!" Charlie said, rising from his chair.

"I see Mr. Poole is ready to give you a tour of the riverfront. In a few weeks he will escort you to the humble cottage in the woods. Judge for yourself if it is worthy of being named 'Little Ireland'. Look it over and let Charlie know of anything you need. Furniture. Cooking utensils. Whatever makes you feel at home. He will introduce you to our Lenape friends. You will need to organize them for our little enterprise up north. How does that sound?"

"I want to make you proud you brought me to this country," James said.

"Good. You'll make your lovely Ma and Da proud of you as well."

James lowered his head and followed Charlie Poole out of the building.

The Baptism

Flaherty's long arm of power extended beyond the political, social, and business domains. It insinuated itself into the institution of the Roman Catholic Church.

Polish immigrants in the 5th District represented a small share of Flaherty's voting bloc, but were a fiercely loyal contingent. Ward heeler Charlie Poole oversaw this constituency, dealing with complaints of unfairness in obtaining housing or gainful employment and brought those issues to his boss. One beneficiary of Flaherty's intercession, was the brother of Father Stanislaw Majewski. The priest's brother was an earnest, hard-working immigrant who found it hard to support his family of five. Congressman Flaherty provided the man with a coveted vendor permit, enabling him to open a fruit stand on the corner of Essex and Rivington, one of the area's busiest intersections. While creating this opportunity for the Pole, Flaherty arranged for the removal of the corner's current vendor, a dispensable non-supporter.

Poole executed the necessary paperwork, arranging the attachment of a summons to the vendor's cart along with an order to vacate. To keep it legal on its face, clerks at Tammany Hall dummied up the summons with embossed, official-looking seals and stamps, listing egregious infractions of the rules. The document was processed by friendly court clerks enabling the police to carry out the removal with all due civic-minded authority.

Father Majewski was made aware of his brother's good fortune which inclined him to cooperate when Flaherty asked him to overlook the lack of a formal birth certificate for the Callaghan child who needed to be baptized. Flaherty explained that its absence was due to the chaos surrounding the hard times in Ireland. There was no official certificate in Templemore, because the afflicted hamlet was deprived of many resources. Hundreds of records had either been lost, never issued or destroyed. The child's Baptismal certificate would become his primary documentation.

The Christening took place at St. Mary's Church on Grand Street. Stephen chose his brother as godfather and chose the Lenape Margie, still nursing the Callaghan boy, to be the godmother. As Flaherty, Poole and Aubrey stood to the side, parent and godparents gathered around the baptismal font awaiting the priest's arrival. Margie cradled the boy in her arms.

Father Majewski strode into the narthex with deliberate, authoritative steps. His white linen surplus swished with each swing of his arms. He meticulously adjusted the white stole draped around his shoulders, making sure both ends dropped to equal lengths above his knees. Margie handed the child to the priest as he stood behind the baptismal font.

Father Majewski began the holy sacrament of Baptism by inquiring of Stephen, "What Christian name have you chosen for this child?"

Leading up to this day, Stephen agonized over how to appropriately honor Biddy in the naming of their son. Foremost in his mind, and etched deeply into his heart, was his gratitude for her contribution to his family's reconciliation with the Carneys. What also factored into his decision was the lasting memory of where the child was conceived.

"Carney Bit," Stephen said,

Father Majewski looked at Stephen. "Carney bit what?"

"Carney Bit Callaghan," Stephen said, relieved the priest did not inquire which Catholic saint was named 'Carney' and which other saint was named 'Bit'.

"Can I ask a question Mr. Callaghan and at the same time make a recommendation?"

"Yes, Father. I have the utmost respect for men of the cloth."

"Which part of the name you want to bestow on this child is more important, 'Carney' or 'Bit'?"

"They each have great significance, Father."

"I am concerned that when this child reaches school age, some boys and girls might ridicule him for the 'Bit' part of his name."

"My son will beat the stuffing out of them."

With his patience waning, the priest said, "He can beat every bully in class. But aren't we concerned, each one of us, parent, godparents, and close friends … for this precious Christian boy? That we, honored to be entrusted by God with his welfare, need to seize this very moment, to safeguard his future by preventing any suffering he will surely endure. Especially when he reaches the sensitive, impressionable age of adolescence. The harm that is done in malicious name-calling could damage him for the rest of his days. For that is the time of his life, at puberty, that the cruelest insults will pierce his Catholic soul. What say you Mr. Callaghan?"

Flaherty whispered in Stephen's ear. Stephen, in turn, said to the priest, "Let's stick with 'Carney'."

"Carney Callaghan is a fine name. Biddy is smiling in heaven, Steveen," James said.

Without further interruption, Father cupped the holy water in his hands and baptized Carney.

James and Margie followed the priest into the sacristy to sign the baptismal certificate. . James signed first. Margie took the pen and made a pictograph of two adjacent circles, placing a dot in the center of each. Father

Majewski breathed a sigh of relief. No more christenings were scheduled for the remainder of the day.

Peggy O Rourke comes to town

Consider this my application, Mr. Flaherty: Peggy O'Rourke, born in the Parish Kilvarnet, Town of Collooney, County Sligo. At nine years of age, I emigrated from the hard times in Ireland. I was a fortunate survivor of coffin ship passage to British North America. En route, I was stricken with typhus and dysentery, nearer to death than life from malnutrition, I jumped ship into a dead-body rowboat. I swam ashore, was rescued, and carried on the back of a kind, persistent, prayerful Irish lad. He convinced me to abandon the body of my deceased sister so I could be spared for another chance at life. This strong man took me up a steep, rocky riverbank to the clinic on Grosse Pointe Isle in Quebec Province. There I was held in quarantine inside a fever tent for several months.

I was orphaned by the deaths of my parents, Claire and Liam, who had lovingly nurtured me. I was made sisterless beneath the shade of a black willow tree, where the lovely Colleen whispered her last breath, her faint heart patting a dainty touch upon my chest.

My name is Peggy O'Rourke. You and I met some years ago when I was ten years of age in the Village of Sing Sing at the home of a relative of Emma Kennedy, a fellow refugee from Ireland and patient at the Grosse Isle clinic. You told me at the time you were familiar with my story of survival. Emma led me into the fold of a raggedy caravan of survivors. I was weary but hopeful, bound for the welcome arms of relatives and friends scattered throughout the northern region of the country promised to be a heaven on earth. Wishing the other stragglers well, Emma and I journeyed together mostly by foot to the modest home of her relatives, the elderly Kennedy couple owning a boarding house in Sing Sing, bordering the Hudson River in Mount Pleasant, Westchester County, New York. This is where Emma fed me, clothed me and sheltered me.

They had corresponded with Emma throughout the famine years, ending their letters with warm invitations of hospitality. Emma opened a chamber within her heart solely for me. Presently, I am eager to place my future into your hands.

In the Kennedy household, I was clothed, fed, sheltered, and provided with the opportunity to be formally educated. So grateful that I had clothes to wear, food to eat and a comfortable bed to sleep in, I shared household chores such as laundry and house cleaning. Wherever I saw the need, I contributed to the harmony of my new, expanded family. It was in the Kennedy house where I first met you when you were a New York State Representative.

I graduated with honors from secondary school, volunteered for church and community, and worked every afternoon at the green grocers. These are my qualifications, my background, my experience, my past, and my present. This is who I am and where I am at nineteen years of age. However, this is not where I will remain. This is my introduction to you, as you currently serve our country as a U.S. Congressman. I am prepared to serve the people of your district. Let me repeat, I am eager to place my future into your hands.

Peggy's letters of introduction and request for an interview were read with great interest by Flaherty. He wrote back: "No need to conduct any further interviews, Miss O'Rourke. I've had my eyes on you since you stepped foot into my district ten years ago. I remember meeting you and am well aware of your grit, your determination, and your resourcefulness. I was the one who alerted the local newspapers to feature your remarkable journey from Ireland, across the Atlantic Ocean, as well as your heroic story of survival."

Flaherty kept in touch with Peggy's surrogate family, always inquiring of her health and progress in school. However, when Peggy decided to strike out on her own and seek opportunity in New York City, Flaherty did not propose that she work alongside him in Congress, nor become part of the local Tammany Hall political machine. Instead, he suggested she embrace finding fulfillment in a career that maximized her considerable resourcefulness in the burgeoning building boom on the Lower East Side.

Flaherty never doubted she would succeed as he welcomed her into his growing enterprise, devoted exclusively to the betterment of the Irish people. Flaherty's grand plan to provide better housing for immigrants was executed in secret. If ordinary citizens in the 4th and 6th wards knew that a public servant profited handsomely from the city's construction boom, they might be inclined to vote that servant out of office. The project needed to be carried out through the auspices of numerous dummy corporations, structured by Tammany Hall administrators, making it difficult to connect the dots that Congressman Flaherty was the architect of an elaborate construction enterprise.

In theory, the acquisition of property was carried out surreptitiously. Once a parcel of land was purchased, weeks later, another one five doors down would be acquired through a different company. This process was repeated, until one day, the whole street belonged to Flaherty.

The master plan was explained to Peggy, outlining to her that the clandestine but legal venture was a natural byproduct of the congressman's desire to rid the city of shoddy, unsafe, firetrap clapboard buildings and replace them with sturdier dwellings.

Flaherty summoned Stephen to his dome and introduced him to the firm's newest employee, Peggy O'Rourke. When she offered her hand to Stephen, and his was not forthcoming, she grabbed his hand by the wrist and yanked it out of his pants pocket. She shook it vigorously, never diverting her piercing blue eyes from his. He placed his left hand lightly upon hers, caressing the long, lithesome length of her fingers.

Peggy moved closer to him with feathery grace. His eyes beheld her long, swanlike neck, rising to her face, delicately sculpted like Belleek china. Her full lips did not escape his gaze. He wanted to touch her delicate skin with the back of his hand and run his fingers through her long, blond curls. He released his grasp, took a step back, and eyed her head to toe, noting that the bulge pushing against the buttons of her blouse suggested ample bosoms.

Flaherty broke the spell. "Stephen, as we expand from Cherry to Grand to Catherine and beyond, we'll knock down the dives as we go. Turn the ghetto into a decent place to live for our Irish kin. I need you to concentrate on employing crews of skilled stonecutters, masons, and carpenters, backing them up with a team of sturdy laborers. Tell me now, do you understand what I am getting at?"

"Somewhat, Mr. Flaherty," Stephen said, casting sidelong glances at Peggy, "Would you spell it out for a simple man like me."

Flaherty motioned for them to sit in the chairs in front of his desk. "I want you both to pay close attention. Ships loaded with Irish immigrants come into the harbor every day. Immigration numbers are beyond estimation. Whatever the experts forecast, multiply it tenfold. This is rich, uncharted territory for us. Irish families need housing. Irish men need jobs. We need to be in position to give them what they need."

"Agreed. I am getting the fullness of the picture now." Stephen said.

"You'll continue as project foreman, Stephen. Organize teams at multiple sites. Oversee the work. Make sure we don't lose pace."

Flaherty gestured toward Peggy, "Peggy O'Rourke will be ... let's simply call her a liaison. Or Quality Control Supervisor for now. Titles don't matter. What does matter is that she will coordinate and manage all affairs with suppliers. Getting competitive bids. Assuring quality control. Facilitating on-time delivery. If you need a single tool, it will be Peggy

O'Rourke's job to procure it. If there's a need for a specific type of lumber, mix of plaster, bucket of screws, molding for ceilings or doorjambs, Peggy O'Rourke is the one who will know the cost and delivery date. Peggy O'Rourke …"

Stephen stopped listening. He did not appreciate being suddenly and unexpectedly yoked with a stranger. A moment earlier, Peggy stirred his virility. Presently, the object of his fantasy not only began to lose its luster, but also posed an imminent threat to his masculinity. He desperately wanted to change the course of the river of disheartening words rushing against him.

"Miss O'Rourke will make sure vendors don't overcharge us," Flaherty continued, "She will hold them to their agreed-upon quotes. To be fair, the businesses that profit from *our* vision will themselves enjoy bigger fortunes from the increase in the volume of materials we purchase. As we grow, they will also. I am confident Peggy will drive a hard bargain. You will form a dynamic team, working in harmony, freeing me to serve the community. Knowing that the construction of adequate, comfortable housing for these poor Irish is getting done gives me peace. Work that is done correctly. On time. At the best price. Not for the vendors, but for us. Okay, do you both get the picture now?"

Peggy nodded.

Stephen alternately stared at the floor, rolled his head, and looked at the ceiling. "With all due respect Mr. Flaherty, I am not entirely of the opinion this arrangement will work as well as you say it will. I have an honest share of doubt on the subject. I express that thought so that you know all of the truth that is in me."

"That is exactly what I do *not* want to hear, *nor* expect to hear from you, Stephen. Give me one good reason …"

Stephen raised an eyebrow and turned his open palm in Peggy's direction, presenting his objection by this simple gesture.

"What's that supposed to mean? Explain yourself."

"She's a woman. The ruffians in the building trades will eat her alive and spit her out, they will."

"You know, Stephen, I find myself respecting your opinion. You are entitled to it, as ignorant as it is. I do not mean to diminish you, but I say with full confidence that no man in this city, as rough as it is, has yet to meet a woman the likes of Peggy O'Rourke. Knowing what I already know, no man has more backbone than she. Don't let her beauty and youth fool you. I don't find it necessary to defend her. She is quite capable of doing that all on her own. Let that be a warning to you. I hope she overlooks how you misspoke. Ultimately, you will appreciate how her gifts will be of great help to you in your own work."

Flaherty stood up and placed both palms flat on his desk. He leaned toward Stephen. "Speaking of your work, you will soon have your hands full. I want you to keep an eye out for talent. I want our Irish in America to be like the Jews. I want them to have a legitimate trade. Instead of unskilled laborers. Make them *skilled* workers. Apprentice them. Make them proud of their work."

Peggy sat sphinx-like, looking straight ahead. She smiled at both men. Her pleasant, imperturbable expression remained constant throughout the meeting.

New things

Flaherty let it be known to Peggy and Stephen that the majority of any new construction of affordable housing would be reserved for the Irish, who kept pouring into the Lower East Side in record numbers.

To Stephen, Peggy was unnecessary. He viewed her as an insult to his already proven capabilities. During the first few days of their collaboration, Peggy was little more than window dressing. She became a major distraction for the workers, who wanted to know who she was and why she stared at them while they worked. By mid-week, it was getting more difficult for Stephen to ignore her. He told the men to keep their eyes, minds and hands on their work. While Peggy watched, the men stared back, finding it impossible to overlook her mysterious presence and beauty.

Despite the risk of incurring Flaherty's wrath, Stephen relinquished none of his former responsibilities. He continued to meet with suppliers and contractors while trying to supervise the workers' daily assignments. The additional hours and stress caused by the increased volume of Flaherty's acquisitions, created a constant demand for Stephen's presence at multiple sites.

Since Stephen feared interloper Peggy would snitch, he schemed to place the blame squarely on her for not being a team player. What boosted his confidence was his record as a trusted employee, regularly rewarded with accolades and pay raises as he climbed the organizational ladder.

Peggy's plan was simple. Show up early every morning at the Water Street construction site, ready to work. On this particular Friday, dressed in a calico shirred-yoke dress and knee-high boots, she stepped over drunks and prostitutes spilling out of the brothels and dives and parked herself against the rail of a sawhorse. She folded her arms, rocking back and forth to the cadence of black mammies dressed in multi-colored aprons singing 'Strawberries!' and 'Sweet steamin' hot yams'. She watched them wriggle their straw baskets in and out of the mass of sleepy-eyed street peddlers bumping pushcarts over cobblestone streets.

It was day five of being ignored. Peggy greeted Stephen with a hearty 'Good Morning'. As was his custom, he did not reciprocate. Peggy had seen enough. What puzzled her was how long it was taking for Stephen to accept that hers was a separate and distinct authority. The man who hired him could fire him. Calculating that Stephen's stubbornness might outlast her patience, she decided to confront him head on.

Peggy saw the preeminent purveyor of hardware and tools make an appearance. The businessman headed straight to Stephen. Peggy seized the moment and stepped between them. She addressed the startled businessman, "Good morning. My name is Peggy O'Rourke … and yours?"

The man looked at Stephen, then at Peggy and said, "Who are you?"

"I just told you who I am. Now it's your turn. Who are *you*?"

O'Neill looked at Stephen again. "Who is *she*?"

Before Stephen had a chance to answer, Peggy said, "I'll tell you who I am. I am the Quality Control Supervisor for this company. I speak to you with the full authority of the owner. I am the new liaison between him and you. So, let's not waste another fecking moment with introductions. I'll ask you once more for the last time … what do you call yourself?"

"Dermot O'Neill."

"I am grateful to make your acquaintance," Peggy said, extending her hand which Mr. O'Neill limply accepted, "You are the hardware and tool purveyor. We appreciate your service. There's no question about the quality of your products or your timeliness in delivering them ..." Peggy said, glancing at Stephen, "This construction project is growing fast. Our boss wants *me* to let *you* know that we expect to double if not triple the amount of merchandise we plan to order from your firm within the next few months. That means, Mr. O'Neill, that we have before us the mutually advantageous opportunity to renegotiate your prices. We need to do it today. Right now, as a matter of fact."

Perplexed, O'Neill looked at Stephen as Peggy spoke, "We have already made you a rich man. Now, you stand a good chance to get even richer. That's your share of good news. However, keep in mind there are many other quality tool and hardware purveyors waiting in line right behind you ... eager to talk to us about their fine products. I might add, their prices are much lower than yours. In other words, you need us more than we need you. Isn't it a better wish for you to work with me on this than not, Dermot?"

O'Neill nodded in the affirmative, stunned. "So," Peggy continued, "Why don't we take a short walk over to my office so we can talk business. How does that sit with your disposition at this moment?"

O'Neill gave Stephen one final incredulous look. Stephen shrugged his shoulders and walked in the opposite direction.

Forty-five minutes later, Peggy returned to the job site.

"There's madness on myself right now. I need to tell you I will not be responsible for my actions if you ever pull a stunt like that again. Am I clear on that subject, Miss O'Rourke?" Stephen said.

"It is just as good for me to tell you that I plan to do what I am paid to do. Negotiate," Peggy said.

"Negotiation is *my* job."

"That most certainly *was* your job. However that parcel of your former job now belongs to me."

They stood toe-to-toe for a full minute. Stephen blinked first, "If you consider yourself a wise woman, you'll take a path that leads out of my way."

"I will stay where I am and do what I need to do. Let's see if we can lower your madness by finding a way we can work together on this project," Peggy said, "And if that fails, I'm not of the mind to take any of the blame ."

"I can handle all that's needed like I've done these last eight years. Why don't you be a nice lady and take your lovely face southwards. Maybe you'd be better off working in Mr. Flaherty's Washington office."

"This is where I belong. This is where Mr. Flaherty wants me. This is where I will stay."

Peggy retrieved a piece of paper from her dress pocket and handed it to Stephen. "Put your eyes to the new price structure O'Neill wisely agreed to."

Stephen looked it over. "Female luck. With no hope of lasting longer than today."

"Oh, himself says it won't? Twenty percent reduction in cost! I plan to institute even better discounts with other suppliers. In advance, I can predict their response. Even so, Mr. Flaherty will be charmed by these numbers. I plan to squeeze them by their kaks if I have to. Every purveyor. Every contractor. Every man who hopes to do business with us."

Stephen rocked back and forth on his heels. Wanting to make sure what she said registered with him, Peggy leaned closer, blue eyes to blue eyes, "I have a certain ability. I am not certain exactly where I got it. Maybe the good Lord blessed me one night as I slept. But I have a certain gift of spotting a man's weakness. Any man, Irish or otherwise. It's like a light shines on a certain spot within that man's well constructed facade, and reveals to me his weakest point. I then seize upon that spot, Mr. Callaghan.

It works every time. I don't have to prove it to you. The results will speak for themselves."

Stephen made a fist and gritted his teeth.

"While we stand here and prattle on, Mr. Callaghan, I get the impression you are frightened to death of new things. For sure it appears that I am one of those new things. You will be making the better choice getting yourself used to this new thing rather than not."

"Don't get that pretty mouth started with me, lass. Mind your manners. I am no pushover like O'Neill. You had the luck of the Irish shining upon you in that moment. *I know* the other suppliers. They will not be as soft as Dermot. Take me word for it."

"I don't care how soft or hard they are. If they want to do business with us, they'll cave in like a lame mule."

"You're a tough one, are you Miss O'Rourke?"

"Tough enough to get the job done. That much I guarantee."

"You want to know how *I* got to be tough?" Stephen said, hands on his hips, "Do you want to know what share of suffering I had just to get to this county? To come to America with not a coin to me name? What I had to give up? What I lost in the bargain? Just to get here. Right here!" he said, pointing to the ground.

"You can put words to it if you think it will arouse my sympathy."

"I sailed on a ship for eight weeks on rough seas. Hardly any food to eat. If I didn't have the breads my kind neighbors gave me, I would've starved to death. I lost two stone on the voyage, sailing with passengers smelling like a cow's rotted corpse. Then I get here only to have me head shaved as it was a breeding ground for lice. That wasn't the worst of it. Almost a year later, waiting for me brother to come down the ramp, holding a bundle in his arms that should rightly have been held by the mother of me only son who, who ..." Stephen's voice trailed off as he stared at the ground, " ... was the love of me life. Me own brother holds me son as he tells me ... they threw me son's mother overboard just days before she would have rightfully been in me arms. Added to myself's pain and suffering, I learned dear Ma and Da both passed on to heaven in the weeks before me brother sailed to America, without me there to comfort them in their sorrow and grave illness. As we're standing here, I am telling you the whole part of the truth."

Peggy did not respond.

Stephen yelled, "Overboard I tell you!"

"Sorry about your wife, Stephen."

"She wasn't my wife. It was supposed to be ... my brother married her just to ... oh, never mind. I don't know why I'm even talking to you."

"You're talking to me because you have to get your heartache out into the open. How is your son now, by and by?"

"He made it alive. Barely. I've had to raise him by myself."

"I don't doubt your efforts in raising your son, Mr. Callaghan. It's only fair to tell you what Charlie Poole told me ... you had quite a bit more help from a Lenape. Margie Two Tits, I think her name is."

"You have a smart mouth, don't you, Miss O'Rourke? You'll need more than that on the Lower East Side."

"Like I said. I'm tough enough." Peggy looked around and spotted a metal pipe on the ground. She picked it up and shook it in front of Stephen's face, "Suppose I take this pipe and whack it against your backside and beat the living shite out of you? Then, when you're layin' on the ground, all pissin' 'n moanin', begging like a whimpering baby for me to spare your life, I shove it straight up your ignorant Irish arse. Would that make me tough enough for you?" she said as the carpenters lay down their saws to watch.

"Aw, put it down Miss O'Rourke, before I get to my boiling point."

Peggy grasped the pipe with both hands and held it chest high. Stephen turned sideways as Peggy swung the weapon full force, hitting his side. Stephen let out with a yelp. "Next time I'll be aiming for your testicles, you thick Mick."

As she lifted the pipe once again, Stephen held up both hands in surrender. Noticing that the men were standing on the sidelines, laughing, he yelled, "Get back to fecking work or I'll dock your pay for all the time you're watching this crazy Irish bitch."

Stephen pointed at Peggy, "Are you daft? Put down that pipe. We'll talk this through."

"I'm done talking. You don't want me to work here. You don't respect my point of view."

"I just felt your fecking point of view, woman. Now, get hold of yourself, will you?"

"Are we going to work together or not? Answer that for me, Mister."

"I want to know your story. Where in hell did you get training for this job?"

"I don't think you're ready to hear my story, Mr. Callaghan. I don't want to place an unnecessary burden upon your tender sensitivities. However, it is sufficient for me to say, as far as your story is concerned, it appears to me that your bowl o'tears is overflowing and is in danger of having more saltwater in it than the Irish Sea. I am truly sorry for your loss, although I don't show it as such. But all's I'll tell you right now is this. I did not come here ..." she pointed to the ground, mimicking Stephen, " ... by *first* cabin. End of story. Don't ask me any further questions or I'll put the pipe to your kaks, I will."

Stephen and Peggy let go of their differences and had no further confrontations that day. No words, civil or otherwise, passed between them. The matter of her responsibilities was not discussed. They started afresh, both determined to build buildings for the Irish and build them well.

On the following Monday, Peggy approached Stephen, "Where's your boy? The men tell me he likes to hang around construction sites. Say he's got an interest in building things."

"He's seven years this side of the womb and belongs in school. I've been trying to get him interested in reading and writing but that's not working well."

"Why not, if you don't mind me asking?"

"The lad is not much for sitting still in the classroom. I tried teaching him on my own. All we do is argue. He's a stubborn one, he is."

"If you get him back into school, the teachers will know what to do with him. He'll learn what he needs to from them. Don't give up."

"They told me he's so far behind, he'd have to sit with the we'uns to make up for time lost. He won't go for that. When he's at home, he stares out the window when I try to learn him the alphabet. I don't know what to do with him. He's on the deep side of miserable, he is. He's only happy when he's watching me and the men work."

"Well, himself will figure it out, I'm sure. Let me have an introduction to him when the time comes we can manage to be friends."

The continuing education of Carney Callaghan

Until Stephen fully embraced the mutually beneficial working arrangement between himself and Peggy, he had worked eighteen-hour days building tenements throughout the 4ᵗʰ ward. The partnership with Peggy reduced his workday to a less stressful twelve hours, giving him more time to be with his son. As Carney became more fascinated with construction, father and son began to bond. Like his father, Carney learned by watching the tradesmen work.

St. Mary's Elementary took Carney back, but he continued to behave as if he were serving out a prison sentence. He often skipped class, forcing the principal to speak to Stephen about his son's chronic truancy. The concerned father gave Sister Mary Veronica permission to "use the ruler on the boy as needed." The good sister did just that but ultimately advised Mr. Callaghan it was time to find another school for Carney. Stephen abandoned the whole idea and paid Margie to look after him.

Carney was drawn to every aspect of his father's work, admiring the grand building of things. He hung around with the stonecutters, carpenters, and plasterers. He was intrigued by the utilization of skills that made a pile of materials scattered on the ground magically transform into a three-story tenement. Day after day, he watched the carpenters work, asking many questions about the measurement and cutting of wood. Sometimes, they let him use their tools.

Carney took a special interest in the work of the master carpenter, Danny Fogarty. He asked the small, wiry man to teach him the refinements of hanging a joist. Each time Carney approached, Fogarty brushed him aside, too busy to pay attention to an annoying kid. Carney persisted. "If ya show me, I won't bother ya no more."

Danny continued working. "Just nigger-rig it," he said.

Carney was learning a lot.

July 13, 1863

A dark mood had been stirring for some time in New York City. It reached its boiling point when the anti-war and pro-slavery Copperhead political faction pressed their relentless racist campaigns that ignited the passions of the poor and working-class whites. Newspapers boldly proclaimed that hordes of blacks would invade the city and take jobs away from the whites. The pot boiled over when the Enrollment Act of 1863 passed, establishing the first national draft. For $300, rich people could buy their way out of the draft. The poor had no such choice.

Ten days after the Confederate Artillery blasted cannonballs and breached the Union line at Gettysburg, Pennsylvania, unrest stewed in a hot pot in New York City, from river to river, Midtown to the Battery. Gulls and crows fought for garbage on the docks, their scavenger cries ringing out while church bells pealed in synchrony with the cadenced stomping of soldiers' boots. The rush of iron wheels on horse-pulled wagons loaded with Springfield rifles and ammunition pounded the uneven cobblestone streets. The city sounds on this hot summer day throbbed in discordance, rendering the customary noise of hammer upon metal and saw upon wood quiet and still.

The push by Flaherty to build new tenements on Maple and Water Streets in his expanding real estate empire came to a complete standstill. He instructed Peggy and Stephen to halt construction and to offer double pay for workers willing to stand guard over his buildings. The marauders flowed southward in waves, heading toward his district.

As the brass band played *Hail Columbia* in Madison Square, Colonel O'Brien appealed to the men in the crowd, insisting enlistment in the Irish Brigade was the patriotic thing to do. "Thank you for coming out today ladies and gentlemen. A little more than one week ago, we celebrated the eighty-seventh anniversary of our beloved country's independence. Now is the perfect time, men, to sign up to wear the Union blue."

Danny Fogarty heard enough. He threw a stone at the cornet player's head, turned his back on the Colonel, dropped his pants and shouted, "Hey kernel, you can kiss me Irish arse. I ain't takin' no bullet for no nigga!"

The Colonel leaned into Fogarty's face. "Listen you little shite, I got off a boat too. Not more than ten blocks from here. Sick and skinnier than I ever was during hard times. This is my country now. And yours too. America. May she ever be free. Worth fighting for. Worth shedding our Irish blood for. Thousands of courageous Union lads have lost their lives for a righteous cause. If you had any idea how bravely our boys fought at Antietam, at Chancellorsville, and at Gettysburg you wouldn't be talking so disrespectfully. They have done their duty according to their lights. What have you done? Where is your patriotism, lad?"

Mikey Finn stepped close to the Colonel and spit on the ground. "Don't give us your shite, you monkey in a cap. Get the feck out of our neighborhood. We don't need no band and no conscription neither."

More friends joined them. Ultimately a small army of miscreants overran the musicians, grabbed their instruments, smashing them to the ground. The crowd cheered the protesters and joined in the fight, men and women pulling forage caps and shell jackets off the fleeing soldier musicians, costuming themselves in military garb.

In waves, New York City conscription rioters roared through the streets, starting uptown in the forties, spreading in number with each new wave swallowing up blocks, then whole neighborhoods, each moment gaining in strength and violence. As word spread, new groups of rioters gathered in the hundreds, then thousands. Shop windows were broken. Stores were looted. Liquor was stolen, gustily consumed by men, women, even children. Wealthy people's homes were invaded, their furniture tossed out on the street, then lit on fire.

Rioters overpowered the police at the armories, picking up weapons and ammunition. The entire city was under siege. In the poorest neighborhoods, colored people were targeted, chased out of their tenements, beaten, and stomped on.

"Hang that nigga from the nearest tree," Fogarty shouted. His friends complied. The ladies and some of the children in the crowd used forks and knives to cut open the poor soul's dangling legs.

> *The men will cheer, the boys will shout*
> *The ladies they will all turn out*
> *That joyful day when Johnny comes marching home*
> *Get ready for the Jubilee, Hurrah! Hurrah!*

"There's a colored boy tryin' to git away. Git him. Git him!" Mikey said, "He's a runnin' toward the river. Thow'im in! The damn niggers don't know how to swim."

They threw him in who could not swim.

A colored carpenter named Joseph, living in an alley shack on Jerome Street, heard the noise swelling from the angry mob. He took his two little daughters into his arms and ran from his home. Mother followed, slow of foot with third child in her womb. The slowest in the mob could catch her. And catch her they did.

The short fuse of anger and booze spread the word of trouble and revelry. The righteous cause of liberty had no meaning to the drunken fools who alerted their friends of the whereabouts of the asylum for colored children. "Get all the colored kids at once. Burn it down! Burn it down!" With fair warning, teachers and counselors led the children away but not all escaped. One little boy climbed a tree, pulling himself up, branch by branch.

> *We are climbing Jacob's ladder*
> *We are climbing Jacob's ladder*
> *We are climbing Jacob's ladder*
> *Soldiers of the Cross.*
> *Every rung goes higher and higher*
> *Every rung goes higher and higher*
> *Every rung goes higher and higher*
> *Soldiers of the Cross.*
> *Keep on climbing, we will make it*
> *Keep on climbing, we will make it*
> *Keep on climbing, we will make it*
> *Soldiers of the Cross.*

There were the Irish bandaging the wounded after Gettysburg, burying the dead who met their maker on that bloody ground, then gathering together and marching onwards to build ramparts for the next deadly battle. At the same hour, there were other Irish drinking, rioting, and killing innocent souls in the streets of New York City, both groups pushing upwards from the grass, the gutter and the dead.

On July 20, 1863, Flaherty called a meeting in the dome. Peggy O'Rourke, Stephen Callaghan, John Aubrey, and Charlie Poole attended. The Congressman was in an unusually buoyant mood as he strode back and forth in front of his most trusted employees. He asked each of them for damage assessment in dollars-and-cents terms counting the loss of bricks and mortar, tools, equipment, and all sundry collateral damage sustained during the five days of rioting. He turned to Charlie and said, "Tell the men who were arrested that we'll free them in a few days. They are to say as little as possible and must not, I repeat, they *must not* sign anything."

"How about those caught hanging the coloreds?" John said.

"I'll handle that personally. How many of them are under our employ?"

"One of them for certain is Danny Fogarty," Stephen said.

"Is he worth springing?" Flaherty said.

"He can saw apart at an angle and join together again two pieces of lumber with his eyeballs only. As if the beams grew out of the tree that way. He is a master carpenter … at least before the noon bell."

"What do you mean by that?" John said.

"At the noon bell he goes to the saloon for lunch. He is useless after that."

Flaherty turned to Peggy and Stephen. "Don't worry. Not for one moment. Your hard work did not go for nought."

Reading from his report, Charlie said, "We lost a two-story on Cherry."

"We'll build a three-story in its place," Flaherty said.

"They burned a four-story to the ground on White Street."

"We'll raise up a fiver in its place. Just think of it as a forest fire. Old, dead trees burn to the ground. Stronger ones grow in their place. Business will be better than ever soon enough." Flaherty looked at his employees, seeking a show of confidence in return.

The complete accounting of damages was given by Charlie, dollar-wise to the penny.

Walking with Peggy on the way out of the meeting, Stephen said, "What an inspiration is that man Matthew Flaherty. He's got everything under control. I am proud to be under his employ. How about you, Peggy?"

She gripped Stephen's arm. "I wish I could share your enthusiasm. I don't know what to say."

"That's not like you, Peggy. You're never at a loss for words. Share with me what troubles you."

Peggy stepped around the debris that littered every street following the riot, the air thick with smoldering fires. "I'm just bearing the thought that maybe I misjudged him."

Stephen held both of her hands in his. "What do we need to know? We came from dirt. Like these charred remains in the gutter. Flaherty gave each poor one of us an opportunity. We're doing well. Are we not?"

Peggy stared at the sky. Plumes of smoke rose from the ashes. "Is it all about balance sheets? Buildings? Bricks? Saws and hammers?"

"It was a terrible thing that happened. Mr. Flaherty shared no part in it. What is it you expect of him?"

"I just expect him to … to say … to be …" Peggy said.

"To be what?" Stephen said."

"To be … more human, if I am allowed to venture an opinion."

"He's a businessman. That's how businessmen think, I imagine. Myself not having any training or experience in that regard."

"It's not just him," Peggy said as she released her hands from Stephen's grip and pointed to a rope dangling from a tree, "The Irish did this, Stephen. And they are us."

The next question

Early one sultry August morning, Peggy turned the corner on Jerome Street and saw the charred remnant of an alley shack being framed with fresh timber. She recognized the broad back of Stephen as he tipped over a wheelbarrow filled with replacement shingles. He took a rag out of his back pocket and swatted mosquitoes feasting on his bare arms and neck. Peggy came up behind him and tapped him on the shoulder. Startled, Stephen said, "Are you spying on me now?"

"No. What you do on Sunday is your business but yesterday, the accountant …"

"Out of me own pocket. I swear."

"The invoice for shingles was made out to you instead of the company. He…" Peggy said and stepped aside when a tall colored man with his right arm resting in a sling bent over to examine the shingles.

"Meet Joseph. A carpenter, like meself," Stephen said.

"Would you be Peggy?"

"I am … heartbroken for your loss, Joseph."

"Maybe Melinda be carrying our son. I won't ever know. They both with God now," Joseph said, lowering his head, "But Mary and Elizabeth be my sunshine."

At the sound of their names, Joseph's half-naked daughters stepped shyly behind their father. Four-year old Mary, sucking her thumb, clung to her father's coveralls.

"Joseph, would you mind if I had a moment with Stephen?" Peggy said.

"I'd invite you inside but there ain't no inside yet."

"Tis a heavenly thing you're doing, Stephen."

"You're the inspiring one. If Joseph had a good arm, he'd rebuild it himself."

"I want to help."

"I'm almost finished. Two more days at most."

"Do you think Joseph would let me buy clothes for his we'uns?"

"I think he will. He's a proud man but seeing as the girls are missing their Momma, new outfits will pick up their spirits. That will convince him."

Ships continued to pour thousands of new immigrants into the New York harbor at the close of the decade following the Civil War. Full of hope, they came for the jobs in the workshops, warehouses, and stores. The new Americans needed places to live near where they worked. The housing crisis that resulted from this massive incursion allowed building owners to generate huge profits. Most of them rushed to build before permits were approved and further partitioned existing space already too small, using cheap labor and shoddy products.

Flaherty, with a soft heart for the Irish, deftly engineered his political power in Congress and Tammany Hall to seize opportunities for profit. Flaherty's connections gave him a distinct advantage over his rivals. Whereas his competitors paid him exorbitant bribes disguised as license fees for the privilege of owning and operating marginally legal dives, saloons, dance halls and brothels, he parlayed those same funds to benefit his own enterprise.

As droves of Irish moved into the Lower East Side, the city's aristocrats gravitated northwards. Before long, the riverside 4th ward became a slum. The rich sold their buildings at distress prices, anxious to park their wealth and genteel manners in neighborhoods bordered by parks and promenades.

Real estate speculators acted quickly, not wasting any profits on quality housing for what they considered a lower class of people. It was no secret the Irish were looked down upon as an inferior race, a sub-human species of dirty, drunken rowdies. Flaherty gobbled up real estate in his own 4th ward district. He preserved the impressive facades and gutted the interiors to create space for the maximum number of partitioned apartments.

When available space could not keep pace with the volume of new immigrant arrivals, Flaherty succumbed to an expedient approach to construction. Whenever one of his tenement houses on the left and another on the right became totally occupied with rent-paying Irish, he instructed Callaghan to build alleyway huts between them. The privies in the rear of these buildings were already beyond maximum capacity. Conditions became dangerously overcrowded and unsanitary in the box-like rooms. Although he typically used higher quality building materials than his competitors, Flaherty's master plan was to jam twelve people into thirteen square feet of living space. He had to do it that way for the Irish, he explained to Peggy and Stephen, not so much for profit, but to provide the opportunity for these poor unfortunates to have a warm bed at night. They need a place to call home, room enough for a mattress or two on the floor, which is a far more humane option than homelessness and vagrancy.

Not much had changed in New York City in the years following the draft riots of 1863. That violent episode in the city's history was characterized as an insurrectionist protest against involuntary conscription into the Union war machine, but just as deliberate and severe, it represented a protest the unventilated, unsanitary living conditions forced upon the Irish and other immigrant groups. The enactment of New York City's Housing Act decreed multi-faceted and wholesale construction regulation for tenement housing.

The new stipulations looked good on paper but were seldom enforced. It came as no surprise to city reformers that building inspectors fell into the same class as judges and police, mirroring their willingness to accept bribes for looking the other way despite the law on the books. However, there were notable exceptions.

On Cherry Street, just up the block from the dome, one diligent inspector, Horace Champlin, approached Stephen and issued a stop work order. As he handed the citation to Stephen, Champlin took a deep bow and smugly tipped his beaver top hat, accented with a wide purple ribbon above the brim. A like-color handkerchief was wrapped about his skinny neck, and beneath that a fancy frock coat and boldly checkered pantaloons.

"You are required to dismantle that illegal alley hut, Mr. Callaghan. I'll be back to see that space cleared. You have ten days to make it disappear. For each overdue day, the fine is doubled. All spelled out right there on the document," the foppish bureaucrat said, tapping his finger on the summons.

"And where will that family live once we tear it down? Can you tell me that, Mr. Building Inspector ..." Stephen said, looking at the document, "... Mr. Horace Champlin?"

Stephen was tempted to reveal he took his marching orders from none other than the powerful Tammany Hall official and U.S. Congressman, but the public man who lived in private shadows would not be pleased. Instead, Stephen handed the citation to Peggy, grateful for the opportunity to relieve himself of this responsibility.

Peggy wasted no time calling a meeting with Flaherty.

"We have to remove the hut on Cherry," she said as Flaherty placed the summons on his desk.

"That's too bad. We had a tenant family lined up for that unit. A lovely young man from Galway with his bride, three we'uns and one on the way. They already gave me a deposit. He's gainfully employed in a store on Essex. My work in two worlds is sometimes on a collision course. I was the chief architect of a federal bill for better housing conditions. Certainly, I would support it in my own city. Yet we have to take emergency actions when there is not enough housing … until more adequate quarters can be built. Of course, I want our own people to enjoy good living conditions, but we can't allow them to live in the streets," Flaherty said.

Flaherty examined the document closely. "Seems like an overambitious bureaucrat signed off on this. Tell Stephen to leave the structure as is. I'll have Poole meet with Champlin. Charlie's very persuasive. If he can't convince the inspector to leave this unit alone, I'll ask Aubrey to have a sit-down with him. We have to do our best to help our people. They certainly cannot do it on their own."

"Just curious, what role does Mr. Aubrey play in the organization?" Peggy said.

"He's a very trusted associate, Peggy. John does various things for several of my enterprises. I'll try to get you two together in the near future. I must tell you how fortunate I am to have you, Stephen, Charlie, and John. All of you work so hard. Don't tell the others, but a substantial pay raise is in store for my most trusted associates … the four pillars of the mightiest real estate enterprise on the Lower East Side."

"Thank you."

"Back to the subject at hand. It's only idle speculation on my part that we would need Aubrey's special expertise. Poole is very competent. He'll figure it out. Probably just charm that building inspector to tear up the summons and forget the whole matter."

Flaherty shoved the paper into the drawer. "I'll instruct Poole to inquire of Champlin what needs to be done to get everything up to code. Maybe it's just a matter of making some adjustments in ventilation and sanitary conditions."

"I believe the stop order is also related to the hut being on city property."

"Good point, Peggy. I'll have legal counsel deliberate on that. I would think that if one owns the house on the left and also owns the house on the right, wouldn't it make sense the same entity owns what's between them? I just need a day or two to find out if Horace Champlin has any leg to stand on. In any event, I am so pleased how well you and Stephen are working together."

The next day, Flaherty summoned Poole and Aubrey to his office, granting them separate appointment times. Poole was first up and came in through the front door. He spoke briefly about various translation assignments, meeting with different immigrant groups about housing, then reported on his trip upstate, "I met with James. The basket and pottery business is humming along, making a small but tidy profit," Charlie said, "The Lenapes turn out a fine product. They're satisfied with the workload, deadlines, trips to town markets, and very pleased with their share. James tells me the 'Little Bit of Ireland' tater patch is not producing the crop he was hoping for. The potatoes are small and rather soft. Barely edible. Not quite the blighted rot he knew during the hard times, but not worthy of consumption."

"I hope it doesn't remind him of how he suffered during the famine."

"Nothing could ever compare to that. He's like the rest of us. Wants you to be satisfied with his work."

Flaherty took the Building Department's summons out of the drawer and showed it to Charlie.

"Less good fortune in that department," Charlie said, "Champlin's a bit of a pompous ass. Dresses like a peacock. Got nowhere with him."

"The next time you see James, tell him to expect another delivery of compost. Hopefully, that'll help produce an edible yield," Flaherty said. He retrieved his hat and talma from the rack. "That's all for today, Charlie. I'm leaving for Washington early in the morning."

"Good day, sir. Have a safe and productive trip."

After a few minutes elapsed, Flaherty put his hat and talma back on the rack. Aubrey surfaced out of the conduits beneath the dome, entering through the trap door.

"Greetings, John," Flaherty said, removing the stop order from the drawer. He pushed it into Aubrey's waiting fingers. "Let's put together another shipment of banana, lemon, orange peels, and coffee grounds."

Horace Champlin failed to show up at the Cherry Street jobsite by the final date specified on the summons. Having received no specific instructions about demolition from Flaherty's office, Stephen left the alley structure as is.

On the afternoon of the eleventh day, Peggy said, "Do you think something happened to him?"

"Who are you talking about?" Stephen said.

"Champlin, the inspector," Peggy said.

"Who cares?"

"Don't you think it's unusual he didn't show up? Come on now, let's be realistic."

"I'm not his keeper."

"Are we guilty of looking the other way? Is that what poor Irish trying to rise up do?"

"What are you getting at?"

"Do we know enough about Flaherty? And this Aubrey character? I saw him come out of the dome a few days ago. He gives me the jitters."

"What do you mean by *enough*?"

"We should know a little more than the nothing we now know."

"Explain yourself, for my ignorant ears."

"We're both so damn grateful we don't have to stare at poverty the rest of our lives. We Irish had more than our share back home," Peggy said, "Flaherty has a lot of influence in this city. Haven't you noticed that every time he is faced with a problem, it miraculously disappears."

"He's helping us Irish. Can we at least admit that? Look at us. Who knew we would do so well?"

"Are we deaf, dumb and blind, Stephen?"

"Things are looking up for us, Peggy."

"When we look up, are we staring at the bottom when it comes to our pride, our dignity and the truth?"

"That's the truest thing you said today, Peggy."

"Is there anything you're afraid of?"

"Nothing I can think of," said Stephen.

"We can walk away from this."

"And be poor as piss all over again? I don't know you as well as I prefer to, but I can tell you're speculating mightily right now. Is that the truth of it?"

"I have no proof if that's what you mean. But there's nothing wrong with inquiring, is there? We don't want to be duped, Stephen."

"You're coming across as the worrying kind."

"I got reasons not to trust people so much," Peggy said.

"This much I do know about Flaherty. He's satisfied being a mystery man, don't you think?"

"I know Irish men. In my experience, they are only afraid of two things, mostly at the same time."

"Are you referring to Mr. Flaherty?"

"No, I'm referring to you."

"Then tell me, what are those two things?"

"Success. Failure. Either or both."

"At the moment, I have no fear of success."

"Are you telling me the truth now, Stephen?"

"I am. I have no fear of success because I have no idea what it looks like."

"True enough. We'll have this conversation again, I imagine," Peggy said.

"I'm finding I have my share of pleasure when you confide in me," Stephen said, moving closer to Peggy, "In a different way to say it ... getting to know you more intimately is one of the great pleasures in me life right now."

"I believe the workers are watching us. Do you agree?"

"I do," Stephen said.

"Follow me around the corner so we have a moment to ourselves," Peggy said, as she grabbed Stephen's hand and led him to the other side of the building. She leaned up against the façade as Stephen pressed against her.

"Are you after something now or are you playing the minx on himself?"

"I am doing no such thing, Mr. Callaghan. I must maintain my dignity I'll have you know."

Stephen felt the whisper of her sweet breath as she spoke. "I have a favor to ask of you, Stephen."

"I knew it. I was enjoying this quiet moment but here comes the hitch."

"The favor I want to ask of you will favor us both," Peggy said, touching his nose with hers, "I don't want to spoil this moment either."

"Go ahead then, you gorgeous minx."

"If you're not willing to do it, I will do it myself some day. I want to ask *why*, Stephen."

"Why what?"

"*Why* is the next question we should ask and not shrivel from it. *Why* did Mr. Champlin disappear? *Why* does Flaherty always get his way? Throw in a who question and a what question. *Who* is John Aubrey? *What* exactly does he do for Flaherty?"

Not being able to resist her any longer, Stephen placed his lips upon hers and gave her a long, deep kiss. As he withdrew, she said, "Let's promise each other we will not be afraid to learn the answers to our questions."

Stephen kissed her again. "I'll be a man about this. I'm curious too. It makes it easier that we're in this together."

"Maybe it'll amount to nothing. Who knows? There might be some benefit in finally knowing what we're curious about," Peggy said.

They began the walk back to the job site. "Will you always watch my back, Stephen? I have yours. That I can promise you."

"I'm watching your back right now, Peggy O'Rourke. A fine back it is. And a fine front. And a …"

"Just like every other man I know. Let's get back to work."

Stephen found the right moment to pursue the next question a few weeks later while meeting Flaherty in his office.

"Stephen, we're close to locking up the whole street. Another year or two and Cherry will be all ours."

"Ours?" Stephen said.

"The more we expand. The more your salary increases. Do you see how that works?"

"I do. I just don't know how *you* do it."

"What do you mean by that?"

"Being a U.S. Congressman must be busy work. Representing so many citizens with so many issues."

"How do *you* do it?" Flaherty said.

"Well …"

"Well, what?"

"I do my job."

"What is your job?"

"No one knows better than you, Mr. Flaherty."

"You do."

"I do what?'

"I don't know what you do every moment of every day, but you do."

"I am grateful that you gave me this job. I am grateful that you brought me to America and gave me a place to live. I am grateful you provided Margie to feed and care for my son. I work very hard, always aware of the gratefulness that is due you."

"So, what is your job, Stephen Callaghan? There's Charlie Poole. There's John Aubrey. There's Peggy O'Rourke. And there's you, Stephen Callaghan. Each one knows their job better than anyone else, including me."

Flaherty took off his big, black hat and patted it against Stephen's shoulder. "Do your job. After Cherry, we got our sights set on a few streets further uptown. Aristocrat row house folk will continue to bail. With even more Irish nibbling on the edges of their sanctuaries, they will sell their spacious properties at distress prices. They despise the Irish. We're going to need more carpenters, joiners, and laborers. Make sure they're all Irish. Apprentice them. They're not like the Jews over on Eldridge," Flaherty said, "The Irish coming off the boats are not furriers, watchmakers, tailors, bookbinders, tailors, hat, cap, or dressmakers. Face it, the Irish are peasants. A lot of people who don't know us or care to know us share a low opinion — saying all the Irish care about is getting drunk on cheap whiskey while feeling sorry for themselves because they lost their homeland and then spend the rest of their days lamenting their exile. We can't force the Irish to think more of themselves, but we can train them to be specialists, Stephen. Not just the hewers or luggers of wood and stone, but master carpenters, plumbers, stone masons, and other trades just as important as what the Jews do for their people. You can shape your world or let the world shape you. So, which is it?"

"I understand what you're saying, Mr. Flaherty," Stephen said.

"Good. Then go do your job."

The Proposal

Every Sunday morning following Mass at St. Mary's, Peggy and Stephen headed to Corlears Hook Park. While the rest of the world disappeared, they sat under a massive elm tree and listened to the turtle doves billing and cooing. Taking full advantage of their only day off from the hammer and nail banging of new construction, Peggy and Stephen delighted to the peaceful whispers of the East River breezes and the repetitious cheery-up, cheery-oh songs of red-breasted robins.

"Would you, Peggy dear, join me for a snack and a brew?" Stephen said after they did a rollover on the blanket.

"I haven't grown weary of our pleasure right here, Mr. Callaghan," Peggy said as she instigated another toss, winding up on top, kissing him repeatedly, "What fancy saloon did you have in mind?"

"One Horse Tavern."

"That dive? What kind of romantic are you?"

"It's just a short walk from here," Stephen said.

"I'd rather stretch my legs and a find a place that has cushions on the chairs and *welcomes* fine ladies, such as myself."

"They have the best Irish music this side of the ocean, Miss O'Rourke. Stirs the spirit, it does. Can you not enjoy some tin whistle and fiddle with meself while we get silly with happiness on a Sunday afternoon?"

"All right then," Peggy said, "But the first ruffian who looks at me dirty will be the exact time we leave. Agreed?"

"Agreed."

The musty smell of malt and wet hops invaded their nostrils the moment they crossed the threshold. One Horse Tavern was a bastion of male supremacy, mostly of the swarthy Irish kind, a non fancy place. It had a rustic charm with sawdust sprinkled on the uneven wood plank floor, a potbelly stove, and an assortment of plain, mismatched chairs butted up against random square, rectangular, and round pinewood tables. Over the years, the tabletops were crudely carved with initials and body parts, their edges chipped, gouged, and splintered.

Several customers sat at the bar. It was the kind of cozy gathering place for men who liked to share bawdy jokes and smell bad together. Most of the long tables were filled with regulars from the 4th ward. Several patrons recognized Peggy, a familiar presence at neighborhood construction sites.

As Peggy and Stephen took seats at a table in the back of the saloon, a diminutive Irish waiter dressed in a gray waistcoat and bowtie came by and rested his tray on an empty chair. He unfurled a red-and-white checked tablecloth and plopped down a bowl of chili, a small platter of raw onions, a basket of stone wheat crackers and a cutting board laden with chunks of sharp cheddar cheese.

"Dark or light?" the waiter said.

"We'll start with light," Stephen said.

The trill of a tin whistle, the hollow thump of the bodhran, the fluent bowing of the fiddle, and the push-and-pull bellows of the concertina turned out familiar Irish tunes that filled the hearts of all present, including the lovebirds. As they nibbled on their snacks, the waiter placed a pitcher of pale beer on the table. Peggy gripped it with both hands and filled their mugs. With a few shakes of her head, she let her blond, curly tresses dance back and forth like frills on the bottom edge of a window curtain. She shrugged when one of the bar patrons missed the rung on his stool and fell to the floor in a heap. Stephen snuck glimpses of Peggy whenever she turned her head. Whenever their eyes did meet, Stephen felt the judgement of her cornflower blue eyes. He knew he could never win a staring contest with her.

"What's on your mind, oh friend of mine?" Peggy said.

"A few impure thoughts, I have to confess," Stephen said.

"Are you flirting with me in a saloon, filled with besotted Irish rowdies? What are you after, Stephen Callaghan?"

"I'm after admiring you when you're not nose-to-nose with a screws and nuts distributor. Admiring and remembering."

"Remembering what?"

"Your long legs. Like the time you wore a light summer dress. The wind blowing against your body. I'm remembering getting a glimpse of what treasures and pleasures lie beneath the gauzy petticoat."

"So, you're doing some lusty remembering right now, are you?"

"It gets me juices stirred up, it does."

"You look at me when I'm not being so aware?"

"It's a healthy thing. I can tell you that."

Stephen finished his drink and poured another. He felt his heart beating faster. He threw back a large draft, "I'm just thinkin' I'd enjoy a tussle, wrasslin' with the wildcat from County Sligo."

"Didn't we just do a few rollovers near an hour ago? I'm gathering you're after something else altogether different."

"I'd have to say that's the truth of it," Stephen said, "I'm wonderin' if you wouldn't mind being a mother to me son."

"I love your boy, Stephen. He captured me heart a long time ago. But I can't be his ma. I only have a thirteen-year head start on Carney. We're more like brother and sister. He's just a month shy of seventeen. A man now, don't you think?"

"You are right Peggy. Carney's as big as an ox. Stronger than most men. I worry about him though, not being able to read or write."

"He seems to get by all right, being so personable and all. He's a good worker too. You know that better than anyone," Peggy said, as Stephen gazed at her lips, nose, cheeks, and eyes, moving his head forward, mouth agape.

"Are you trying to say something? Maybe it would be a relief for you to just say what you need to say and get it over with." Peggy topped off his beer, and her own, "Go on now, be the man from Tipperary and say what you need to say to the lady from Sligo."

"We got off to a bad start, but we've been making up for it. We seem to enjoy kissin' n' cuddlin' of late. Is that not all of the truth, Peggy? And don't you enjoy our working together as much as I do?"

"I take it you are asking me to be your business partner or something of that nature. Is that what you're after, then?"

"That's not what I'm thinking right at this moment," Stephen said, "I was just thinking, Peggy O'Rourke, that it would round out me little family if you would agree to be ... to be a stepmom to Carney."

Peggy took a swig, and said, "Probably not, Stephen. For all the reasons previously mentioned."

The waiter replaced the empty pitcher with a full one. Stephen filled his mug and headed over to the musicians. They stopped playing when they witnessed the sense of urgency in his eyes.

"Excuse me lads. Do you know the tune 'Angel Whispers in Fields of Heather'?"

"We do," said the fiddler, "Should we play it for you now?"

"If you don't mind, lads, I'm trying to ..." Stephen mumbled as he handed cash to the musician, "Can you direct it to a certain lady?"

"Seeing as that lovely lass seated at your table is the only lady here, we will make sure she hears it loud and clear."

As Stephen headed back to the table, the musicians asked all present to sing along.

> *As the sea laps the shore of Killala Bay*
> *And pink bells of heather peal in the autumn sun*
> *I see her eyes mirror the bluest sky*
> *As heavenly angels whisper she is the one*
>
> *Touching her hands as a breeze bends the willow*
> *The angels whisper once again before I sleep*
> *At night I dream our heads will share one pillow*

And one life together is a promise I will keep
Her voice coos sweet like a mourning dove
While her spirit soars wild as the Irish sea.
Her hair glistens bright as the stars above
I do promise my troth for all eternity

"What a lovely song, Stephen. The musicians played it well. Weren't we talking *around* a certain subject a moment ago? By any chance are you attempting to ask me to be your … Missus?"

Relieved, Stephen blurted out, "That's what I have a powerful desire to say."

"So, are you proposing or propositioning? I'll give you one shot to say it right."

"Here? I don't have a ring in me pocket at the moment."

"Buy the ring later. Do it proper - on one knee. What could be more romantic? In a saloon filled with rough-looking Irishmen and the handsomest man here asking me to … is himself ready to find one of his knees on the floor before me? Is *your* lady worthy of that?"

Stephen slipped out of his chair and dropped to one knee. "If I only had but one day to live or if the good Lord granted me one hundred more years this side of heaven, I would want to spend every one of those moments with you. Peggy, I look at you and see the wonder of you."

The fellows at the nearest table caught wind of the conversation and asked the musicians to hold up the music. Everyone in the saloon listened in.

"Don't make me spell it out for you, Stephen. For the sake of the Callaghan name, just say it."

Stephen put his other knee down and held Peggy's hand. "I loved you from the moment I laid eyes on you. I am full of sorrow that at first, I was not respectful. You are the most beautiful woman I ever met in my life. I would do anything to make you happy. Will you give me the great honor

… would you, Peggy O'Rourke, agree to take the name Callaghan? Would you be my wife 'til the day I die?"

"There are some considerations a woman like myself has to weigh in her heart first, Stephen Callaghan."

"Name them, Peggy. For the love of St. Patrick, just name them before I become the first nearly sober man to pass out on the floor of this saloon."

The musicians struck a few chords, and the fiddler said, "Name the considerations now, Miss Peggy, before the devil takes your man."

Peggy held Stephen's hand tight and said, "Will you walk the uphill road with me? Will you always be there for me even in the storms?"

"I will," said Stephen, "Even in the whirlwind of a hurricane I will be your protector."

"And will you, Stephen Callaghan, before all these handsome witnesses, hold me as close as two swans with necks entwined?" "Peggy dear, your beautiful neck is longer than mine. If I can figure out how to entwine with you like the swans, entwined it shall be."

"One last consideration, Stephen, but I must say it in private," Peggy leaned over and whispered, "Listen to me careful, now. Plentiful is my love for you. Plentiful is also my desire to have you rid your pants pocket of that lock of Biddy's hair. I want you to walk over to that stove, remove that muslin pouch from your pocket and throw it in the fire. Would you do that for me?"

Seeing his pained expression, Peggy said, "Biddy will live in your heart forever, Steveen. I am good with that. However, if I agree to marry you, I must have all of you - body and soul - so, let me be clear about this - I am not willing to share any part of Biddy that continues to occupy space in your pants pocket."

Stephen thought about taking one last whiff but did as Peggy asked. He tossed the pouch into the stove. He watched it smolder and become one with the ashes. He blessed himself, remembering his time with Biddy in the Devils Bit cave.

Stephen turned from the stove and shouted, "Drinks all around, bartender. On meself. I want every man here to know I am going to marry the loveliest lass in all America. She actually said yes. I say again she said YES." Stephen got back to his seat, blushing.

The man at the next table stood up, looked at Stephen and said, "We didn't hear her say yes. Would you make it public, lass? For the whole motley crew of us/"

Peggy shouted "YES! I will marry Stephen Callaghan!"

Some men in the saloon requested jigs and reels, then took to their feet, dancing with the nearest willing partner. One man raised his pint, spilling half on the floor, "Here's to two Irish fools! They have no idea what they're doing but have the guts to do it anyway."

Carney moves upstate

One snowy Saturday afternoon in December 1867, Peggy O'Rourke and Stephen Callaghan were married at St. Mary's. Father Francis Donnelly officiated. James Callaghan stood in as best man, and close friend Mary Moran attended Peggy as Matron of Honor. Carney Callaghan, dressed in the first suit that ever adorned his husky frame, had the honor of holding The Order of the Holy Sacrament of Marriage for Father Donnelly.

In attendance were Matthew V. Flaherty, Charlie Poole, John Aubrey and several construction workers and their wives. In the back of the sanctuary sat a few St. Mary's regulars, devout elderly ladies who seldom missed a Baptism, Holy Communion, wedding, or funeral, vicariously experiencing the entire ceremonial life cycle of their fellow parishioners.

When the ceremony came to a close, the newly wed couple joined hands and walked down the center aisle followed by Mary, James, and Carney. Charlie Poole stepped forward to greet the couple. He gave Stephen a hearty handshake and kissed Peggy on the cheek. Next in line, John Aubrey shook the groom's hand while Peggy deftly reached for the hand of a carpenter who stood behind Aubrey. Last in the greeting line, Mr.

Flaherty asked the couple to step aside so that he could present his wedding gift.

Flaherty handed an envelope to Stephen. "The second-floor apartment at 347 Cherry is yours, rent free in perpetuity. It has the extra space you will need when you bring other Callaghans into this world. It's the front unit with a window overlooking the park. Stick your heads out far enough, you'll see the boats on the river. I planned it so that you don't have to divvy up the space. Half the second floor is all yours. For as long as you want to live there. You can bequeath it to your descendants."

Flaherty looked over at Carney. "Your son can live there when he has a wife and we'uns. It is my gift to the new Mr. and Mrs. Stephen Callaghan. Your only responsibility is to collect the tenants' rents. That's it. The contract spells out all the particulars."

Peggy and Stephen were taken aback by Flaherty's generosity. They had ceased to speculate about any criminal activity on his part. They agreed to be mindful of the proven, but dismissive of the unsubstantiated.

"Thank you, Mr. Flaherty. This is a most generous gift," Peggy said, kissing him on both cheeks.

"You deserve it," Flaherty said, whispering to Stephen, "Take some time off in the spring and make some more Irish."

"Won't you join us for a little celebration?" Stephen said, "We'll lower a pint or two at McGuires. Drink and dance until the sun comes up. After all, if it weren't for you, we wouldn't be together right now, would we? A man doesn't get a chance to marry such a beautiful woman like this every day. You have to come."

"Drink all you want. Eat all you want. It's on me, Stephen. I told Aubrey and Poole to pick up the tab. I have some urgent business in Washington."

"You're the most generous man I ever met in my life. Peggy and I will be forever grateful."

Poole and Aubrey signaled for Stephen to join them at their table. "Your brother looks a little pale," Charlie said.

Stephen looked over at his brother, who sat next to Peggy at the head table. "I don't think he's faring too well upstate."

"He's lost considerable weight," John said.

When Mary Moran got up to dance with her husband, Peggy took James by the hand and led him to the dance floor. He only lasted a minute before he needed to sit down again. As more couples left their tables and took to the dance floor for the jigs, hornpipes, and reels, Carney seized the opportunity to hop from table to table, swallowing whatever ale was left behind. At first, he thought no one was watching, but Carney caught a glimpse of Uncle James looking his way through the crowd of dancers. He then nonchalantly walked over to his Uncle's table and sat down with him.

"Look at the size of you! I hardly recognized you today," James said, holding his nephew by the shoulders. Carney stood and gave his uncle a slobbering kiss. "You're getting a little too happy, lad. You need to slow down a wee bit. You have to be careful about how much you drink, so it doesn't make you silly. You wouldn't want to fall flat on your arse in front of these people, would you?"

Carney gave his uncle a big hug as he let loose a loud, long belch. "I love you, Uncle James," Carney said as he stumbled backwards into his chair.

Carney helped his dad partition the second-floor apartment at 347 Cherry Street. It made him feel grown up when he was given his own room. Every evening before dinner, Peggy knocked on his door and invited him to the front room for reading and writing lessons. True to form, distractions on the street below caught his attention more than Peggy's tutoring efforts, proving Stephen right that his son was not much for learning. Carney's construction skills continued to flourish, however. He worked full time for Flaherty's real estate firm, often at different job sites. When Carney failed to show up at his assigned job site one morning, Stephen assembled several workers and scoured the neighborhood.

After several hours, Carney showed up at home. Peggy greeted him at the door. Carney's shirt was ripped in several places and his forearms and face were marked with bruises and cuts. "Did you get into a fight?" Peggy said.

"I think I'm in trouble, Miss Peggy," Carney said, sitting in the kitchen while she attended to his wounds.

"Want to tell me why?"

"I'm sorry but … I've bin doin' somethin' befer I go ta work each day. I can't …"

"You can talk confidential like. I'm not going to judge you."

"Dad told me that …" Carney said, looking at the floor.

"What did Dad tell you?"

"When I asked him 'bout girls …"

"Don't be embarrassed. Tell me everything."

"Dad told me if ya like a girl, to talk to her sweet like."

"I know," Peggy said.

"I knows this girl from the park. Very pretty. Anyhow, we wuz getting into a mood, like, ya know. Talkin' was goin' pretty good. Mostly me doin' it. She jes kept smilin' at me, gooey-eyed. I remembered what Dad said - if you open a girl's ears, somethin' else'll be willin' to open up soon afterwards."

"You mean …"

"Yes," Carney said, nodding his head vigorously, "She opened her legs, Miss Peggy. We did it behind a big tree. We both got excited. Afterwards, we wuz holdin' hands like you and Dad do sometimes."

"Should I know the girl, Carney?"

"You might've seen her around. In Corlears, mostly. Very pretty … 'n dark."

"Dark like a colored girl?"

"Not that dark. She's an injin."

Peggy envisioned the Lenape girls she knew from their settlement in Corlears Hook, hoping it was not who she thought it was.

"You and she didn't fight afterwards, did you?"

"Nah. We's still sweet on each other."

"How did you get these cuts?"

"Two creeps see us holdin' hands 'n say some ugly words."

"Did they try to hurt the girl?"

"Nah. They wuz just madder'n hell at me."

"You fought two men?"

"Yeah. They's both about my size, but mean lookin'. Not nice like the carpenters. So, sizin' 'em up I did some quick calculatin'. When one of 'em takes a knife outta his boot, I had to act fast. I kicked him in the balls real hard. He doubled over, fell to the ground moanin' 'n holdin' his kaks. The other one, he come after me with his fists, so I knock his hat off 'n grab him by his long hair 'n swing him 'round. His feet wuz off the ground, and he wuz squealin' 'n hollerin'. With all that movin', it looked like a carousel ride. Anyhows, I kept swingin' him 'round a few times more til I git dizzy. When I let go, he went sailin' 'bout ten feet 'n landed with a thud. Befer ya know it, the guy I kicked gits up ta help his buddy. So, I grab his long hair 'n then, without thinkin' about it I swing their two heads together real hard. Then I let 'em go. Problem is …"

"Problem is what?"

"Problem is after I met their heads together, one of 'em dint git up even when the other guy nudged him. He just lie real limp like a dead rabbit or somethin'. Not movin'. Jes lyin' there. Looked like he soiled his pants too."

Before Peggy could ask more about the man's condition or what happened to the girl, Stephen and Charlie Poole burst into the apartment.

"Sorry I dint show up fer work, Dad. That won't happen agin. I promise. I …"

"Never mind that now," Stephen said, out of breath, "You have to leave with Mr. Poole right now. Don't ask any questions. Charlie'll explain everything on the way."

Stephen hugged Carney and whispered, "You have to light it out of here. Away from this trouble," Stephen patted him hard on his backside, "When I was your age, I did some things I regretted too, Carney. Learn from it. That's all I can offer you now. I have a strong feeling you're going to grow up just fine. I see a lot of your Ma in you. If you just have a small share of her wisdom, you're going to be okay. Always remember what I'm tellin' ya. She was kind and she was wise. Now git."

Peggy kissed Carney. Charlie and Carney bounded down the stairs, several steps at a time. They ran out to the street where a horse-drawn wagon awaited them.

Peggy opened a bottle of malt in the kitchen. She and Stephen passed the bottle back and forth, taking turns slugging down the brew. "What was that all about," Peggy said, "Carney said he got into a fight and one of the fellas never got up. Is he in trouble?"

"He'll be safe for awhile," Stephen said.

"Where's Charlie taking our boy?"

"To the woods. That was the long-range plan for him, anyhow. This situation is making it happen sooner. Flaherty said Carney can do the heavy work up there. James'll teach him about the `tater patch and the work with the Lenapes."

"He already learned how to work well with one Lenape, that's for certain," Peggy said.

"This'll be a good move for him, helping his uncle. Flaherty responded immediately. Told me not to take any chances while Carney's in danger. He told Charlie and me that he needed a little time to work out a peace agreement with Minogue. That's all I know at this point."

"Who were those men in the park?"

"*Musk Rats*, Minogue's gang. He took 'em over from Billy the Butcher after Billy got shot dead. They all hang out at Morrissey's Saloon."

Peggy gasped. "Is one of them dead? Carney said he looked limp, like a dead rabbit."

"Even if the goon is dead, that's not Carney's biggest problem."

"Don't keep me in suspense."

"Minogue doesn't give a shite about his men. At least one of 'em gets killed every day. Either by a police bullet or a knife fight. It's the girl. She's the issue."

"Minogue's girlfriend, right?"

Stephen opened another bottle of malt. He walked to the front window, looking at the setting sun. "The girl's in more trouble than Carney at the moment. She's not long for this world if she gets pregnant. Minogue's got his harem, but this girl wasn't one of his whores."

"Jesus help us. Mary help us. Joseph help us," Peggy said as she held her head in both hands, "He's going to hunt Carney down."

"Flaherty will make a deal with Minogue," Stephen said, "But I have a whole lot of sorrow for the girl."

"Can't we do something for her, then?"

"Better to leave it alone. Let Flaherty handle it. At least Carney'll be safe."

"This is another entry in Flaherty's ledger," Peggy said, sinking despondently into her chair "We owe him more than we have."

The Callaghan brothers

The snow and biting cold quieted the hammer and saw. Uncut lumber stacked in steep piles and empty wheelbarrows sat outside the half-finished tenement. Taking advantage of the winter lull, Peggy and Stephen left the city for a rare holiday. They sojourned to the hamlet of Sing Sing to visit Peggy's surrogate mother, Emma Kennedy. This was the first time Stephen met the Irish widow who guided, protected, and sheltered Peggy when she was discharged from the clinic in Canada. While Peggy ventured into town to visit old friends, Emma used the time alone with Stephen to share what she knew of his wife's story: the unjust imprisonment of Peggy's father; the extreme hardship, suffering, and disease aboard the coffin ship; the waking up to an empty space beside her, unaware her mother had been tossed overboard; and the gruesome details of her sister's final hour on the beach of Isle de la Grosse Pointe. Emma's retelling of Peggy's life before Stephen truly humbled him.

After several days with the Kennedys, Peggy and Stephen crossed the river by ferry and travelled by carriage to visit Carney and James. They met Ginger, James's companion and nurse, at the cabin. A Lenape widow, Ginger also cooked for James and Carney.

Carney couldn't wait to show his dad and Peggy the improvements he made at Pine Meadow, utilizing all the skills he learned from them in the construction business. He took them on a tour of the storage shed he built and a small barn that housed a donkey, two goats, and a pig called Sammy that is more pet than candidate for bacon. Stephen saw that his son had picked up a lot of know-how while making a nuisance of himself with the workers. Next up, Carney proudly unveiled his latest project, a chicken coop, home to a promiscuous rooster and his hens that laid more eggs in one week than the family could eat in three months. Ginger, who helped organize the Lenape ladies with their basket weaving, seized upon this surplus and helped the Lenape women load their handmade baskets with fresh eggs whenever they went to market to sell their wares, generating additional revenue for their enterprise.

Since his Uncle James suffers from a severe arthritic condition and stomach disorder, Carney assumed the bulk of the workload at the homestead and took on odd jobs at the local quarries and iron mills. He worked as a sawmill woodcutter, team driver, ore washer, and coal hauler. Peggy and Stephen could readily see that living in Sloatsburg suited Carney, now a half-foot taller than his father.

"You're a mountain man now," Stephen said, putting his arm around Carney's broad shoulders, "Do you have your share of happiness here, son?"

"I sure do," Carney said, "I like the fresh air'n all the trees'n animals. Uncle's bin teachin' me how to fish. But I miss bein' around you 'n Miss Peggy 'n all the workers."

"Do you eat what you catch?" Stephen said.

"Yup. I know how to hook 'em, scale 'em, filet 'em, 'n throw the heads 'n guts to the buzzards. Ginger fries 'em up on the skillet. Them perch tastes real good. Um, um."

"You'll live a longer life right here, Carney," Peggy said, "You may never get to see the land you were born in, but the air you breathe here is as clean and fresh as anywhere on earth."

Peggy turned to Stephen. "Give Carney his share of good news."

"Flaherty made peace with Minogue. He gave his word to leave you alone."

"That's bin a heavy burden on my heart how I messed up life fer ya. I'm feelin' relief I gotta say," Carney said, "When I see Mr. Aubrey delivering his compost, he brings some rough lookin' men with him for the diggin' who're jes like the men in Corlears whose heads I introduced ta each other. That always makes me remember that event with that Injin girl I liked so much."

When they returned home, Peggy raised the subject of starting a family. In full agreement, Stephen used the rest of the harsh winter to reconfigure one entire side of the building's second floor, front to back, adding extra rooms. His crew created street level storefront space for a tenant, a purveyor of needles and threads, adding significantly to the building's profitability.

On June 21, 1874, Peggy and Stephen welcomed James Patrick Callaghan into the world. He weighed in at 8 pounds 6 ounces stretched over a 19-inch frame. James hardly slept at night and rarely napped during the day. Fatigued, Peggy confessed she might have quit the construction business too soon. Three months after the baby was born, Peggy invited Carney to meet the new addition to the Callaghan family. He jumped at the opportunity, anxious to meet his little brother.

Carney felt more like a proud uncle than a big brother as he looked at baby James propped on his father's lap. He was not quite sure what to make of this new phenomenon, a baby crying for his next meal, then spitting it up because he ate it too fast. He looked at Peggy and his father and said,

"I'm thinkin' of startin' a family of my own, but I don't know what kinda dad I'd be."

"Have you met someone, Carney?" Peggy said.

"I did. At the steel shop. She's a real good worker 'n tough like you Miss Peggy 'cept she's tiny. Minnie Mae's American born 'n ain't got the Irish history we got. We's gonna git hitched soon I'm guessin'. She'll be wantin' a lotta kids, just like this tot."

"Did you set a date?" Peggy said.

"For what?"

"The wedding."

"Yeah, the date," Carney said, stroking his chin, "Well the weddin' date might have ta come awful quick. Minnie Mae wants it to be Catholic like. She said we'd probably should stop doin' it 'til it's legal."

"Good girl," Peggy said.

"Anyways, my reverend friend up there'll do the ceremony. He ain't Catholic clergy but he's a real good carpenter 'n studied at night 'n git ordained along the way in a church group. He does funerals 'n baptisms 'n all that stuff. Minnie Mae likes him. He's teachin' me things ..." Carney laughed.

"What's so funny?" Peggy said.

"Like you, Miss Peggy. He's tryin' ta teach me to read 'n write. He wants me ta study the Bible he's always carryin' 'round but I'll be one foot in the grave by the time that happens. Anyhow, he comes ta the cabin 'n reads to us, tellin' us the good news, as he calls it."

"I hope we can all go to the wedding," Peggy said.

"It could happen any day. The reverend kind of roams 'round the woods 'n we never know when he'll show up. But Uncle James'll be there and Ginger."

"Carney, why don't you and dad talk for awhile. I need to get this baby fed," Peggy said.

"How's my brother doing?" Stephen said to Carney.

"He's sure glad I'm around. Not that Uncle James is lazy or anythin' like that. Fer some reason, I think he don't like the woods as much as me. By the way, when baby James gits a little older, maybe ya can let him stay with his big brother. I'll show him a thing or two 'bout the woods. I'll show him things like ya showed me, Dad. Sometimes I think I'm seein' things through yer eyes. When I start buildin' somethin' I say to myself Dad would do it this way 'n it winds up that's the way I do it."

"I wish I had been a better father to you Carney. Maybe I can do a better job of fathering with James. Not that it helps you any."

"Aw, don't say that. You're a good Dad. I unnerstand ya were busy a lot. Then I screwed up with the injin girl 'n caused a mountain of heartache fer everyone. Maybe some day if ya come up fer another visit we can talk some more father son stuff."

"I'd love that, son. Listen, Peggy and I would like you to meet someone special who moved in with us a little while back."

Stephen asked Carney to follow him and wait outside the bedroom for a few minutes. When Stephen opened the door, Carney saw his baby brother propped against a pillow on the bed. A dark-haired girl sat next to James, with one arm around his shoulders. Peggy picked up James and put him back in his crib. With a little coaxing, the girl bounded off the bed to meet the big stranger.

Carney bent over and took her hand into his. "Who might you be?"

"Wee Mum. I'm four years old," the girl said.

"She loves to hold James and feed him. She's a big help. Gives me rest when I need it the most," Peggy said, placing both hands on the girl's shoulders. "Mr. Carney Callaghan, it is our joy to say that you are already a father. Wee Mum is your daughter.

"We've been in negotiations for a long time and finally got guardianship right after James was born," Stephen said, "With the good news you've shared with us about Minnie Mae, maybe you can find it in your hearts to bring this beautiful little girl into your home. The city is not the best place for Wee Mum right now."

Carney dropped to one knee and wrapped his arms around the girl.

"This is your Papa, Wee Mum," Peggy said.

"Papa?"

"Like a chief, Wee Mum," Stephen said.

The little girl cocked her head to one side, "Papa Chief?"

"Yes, I'm your Papa Chief," Carney said, with a smile a mile wide, "I'm gonna look after ya real good."

The widow Vennell comes to dinner

The widow Vennell, with her pale face and rather large head topped with a mass of curly white hair, was last seen on a somewhat cloudy day in early spring tumbling 122 meters down Carrigblagher Cliffs, her black crepe dress and black velvet cape fluttering around her. With the coal black and snow-white contrast of her body integrated in flight, she at first looked like an Emperor penguin that lost its footing at the edge of a precipice. As she gained momentum in her descent, she appeared smaller and smaller in size. With her cape billowing in the wind, she resembled a clumsy fledgling magpie learning how to fly, bouncing off the nasty jagged rocks spread out along the slopes until she splashed into the welcoming waters of Lough Anscaul.

Thirty minutes earlier, the widow Vennell, stepmother to the precocious boy, Matthew, - whom she inherited from her recently deceased, and considerably younger husband - heard the traveling tinker and his son knocking on her cottage door. "Forks. Spoons. Water pitchers. Candle holders. For sale or repair," he called out in a voice familiar to the widow who purchased some items from him during his visit in the fall of the previous year. Having climbed the cliff's winding, rocky path, the tinker did not leave empty-handed as he slung a sack filled with several household items in need of repair over his shoulder and headed back to his wagon at the foot of the mountain. His son had asked to stay behind while his father did the repair work, as he had befriended the widow's stepson during the last semi-annual visit.

As the widow made tea in her remote cottage on top of Carrigblagher Cliffs, and the tinker banged the cold metal back into its original shape at the bottom of the cliffs, the widow's stepson opened a storage chest in the shed, revealing a secret treasure trove of frilly undergarments belonging to his stepmother.

It was a special time at this juncture in the lives of the pubescent boys as they shared a common interest in the three 'E's': explorations; erections; ejaculations. As the lads played dress-up, touching each other's private parts, the widow Vennell walked to the shed to see if the lads might be interested in a spot of tea.

What she found inside did not please her. Not one bit. She rushed back to the cottage to fetch the birch switch always at the ready on a hook near the door. Upon her return to the shed, she raised the cruel weapon high above the mound of white curls on her head and beat it severely upon the lads. The widow's stepson and the tinker's son raised their arms in a desperate attempt to protect themselves from the wicked sting of the switch. The widow's stepson having enough of this beating business, grabbed the switch from his stepmother and turned it upon her, swinging with all his adolescent might against her aghast face and upraised hands. She kept backing up as he kept swinging, her wild screams echoing throughout the valley below. After observing her maiden flight rather dispassionately, the widow's stepson hurriedly advised the tinker's son that he would be packing a few items to take on his voyage to Cork, with the intention of catching out the next available ship from there to America. He grabbed enough of his stepmother's money to pay for his transatlantic passage and handed more than enough to the tinker's son to pay for his silence on the matter of the stepmother's unfortunate trip down the mountain. He threw in additional funds for the repair of the household items, although not one of them would any longer be needed by the Vennell family.

The tinker's son suggested they not lose touch with one another since their intimate friendship was yet in its infancy. He put forth the idea that they should correspond once the widow's stepson settled in the new land and forward his letters in care of the General Post Office in Dublin, which he and his father customarily pass through at least four times a year on their nomadic tinkering journey around Ireland. While quickly packing his sparse belongings, the widow's stepson decided to pocket the remainder of his mother's household money, figuring that she no longer had any use for it.

It is a proven truth that Irish souls never die. It's not so much the traditional notion that they thrive as memories but as the true embodiment of living spirits housed within those who remember them most acutely.

In that respect, therefore, the widow Vennell was deemed present at a dinner hosted in a fine restaurant owned by Mr. Matthew V. Flaherty. Peggy and Stephen Callaghan were also invited to this dinner for an intimate celebration of the good life, and for the purpose of receiving firsthand an important announcement coupled with the opportunity to meet someone with brand new ideas for a richer life for all.

Years earlier, James and his caregiver Ginger moved in with Stephen, Peggy, and their two boys — young James and their second son, centennial baby William, born July 4, 1876. The Callaghans were left to guess what new announcement could top the year-end bonuses they received the previous two years. At the close of 1881, Flaherty bequeathed to the Callaghans the deed to 347 Cherry Street, granting them sole ownership of the property with all future rental income derived thereof. The next year, Flaherty gave them the Rockland County property, having surrendered plans to convert the woodland complex into 'Little Ireland'.

In the months prior to the dinner, a less than robust Matthew Flaherty was frequently spotted in one of his own clubs on Bond Street hosting the notorious leader of the ruthless *Musk Rats*, Paddy Minogue, owner of gambling resorts, casinos, dives, bordellos, and dance halls. There was gossip Minogue had a hold over Flaherty, using it as leverage to benefit from Flaherty's real estate holdings. It became common knowledge the two men subsequently planned to pool their resources, parlaying their combined wealth to acquire legitimate businesses in the city's better neighborhoods, including haberdashers, green grocers, and tobacconists.

With Ginger available to mind the boys, Peggy and Stephen accepted Mr. Flaherty's invitation to dine with him at his elegant *Plymouth Rock* restaurant. Peggy, resplendent in a billowy floor-length blue dress and Stephen dressed in a tweed suit, were led to the head table. Flaherty stood up to greet his guests. Two white-gloved servers eased back the upholstered chairs for the new arrivals. On this special evening, the round table was set for five.

The final guest arrived. "Peggy and Stephen Callaghan, I'd like …you to meet fellow Gael, Paddy Minogue," Flaherty said as he gripped both arms of his chair and pushed himself up slowly to shake hands with the much shorter man. Peggy and Stephen had learned a great deal about Minogue following Carney's tryst with the Lenape girl. "It is my pleasure to meet you, sir," Stephen said as he shook Minogue's hand. Peggy remained seated. By way of greeting her, Paddy tilted his head forward, fingered the top button on his Applejack cap, and lifted it slightly. Stephen pointed to the empty chair. "Will there will be another guest joining us, Mr. Flaherty?"

"She … she is here … Stephen," Flaherty said, breathing heavily, "This is the day … a tragic day many years ago, that life dropped … out of my Ma. It still pierces my heart as if it were yesterday. May she rest in peace. Her presence here tonight … this special night … gives me great comfort."

The server filled five water goblets. Minogue wore his cap throughout the evening. In the flash when he first tipped it, Peggy noticed the sparse patches of dark and light strands of hair spread in an unruly fashion across several bald spots irritated with a skin condition. Minogue had a prominent aquiline nose, and deep creases flaring out from that nose to the corner of his lips. Lips that were so thin they gave the appearance of being pencil-drawn. His skin was coarsely pockmarked with the marbleized grayish coloration of pigeon droppings. He spoke in an unusual way, every word hissing out of his nose in a high-pitched whistle. The wine steward came by and presented a bottle of champagne to Mr. Flaherty who nodded his approval. The cork was popped, and champagne poured into each flute, including the one set before the empty chair. Flaherty stood up slowly, bracing one hand on the chair. He raised his glass. "Here's to the Irish ... may they ever be kind ... and ... helpful to one another." The guests stood up and clinked glasses with one another. As more champagne was poured, Paddy Minogue moved his chair closer to Stephen and showed him sketches of his new project. Stephen looked at each one, and said, "Magnificent. Who drew these, the architect?

"No, I did," Minogue said.

"I tell you the truth," Stephen said, "You have a gift for drawing, Mr. Minogue."

"And you have a gift for building, Callaghan. That's why it's destiny we combine our talents."

While the two men were engrossed in the sketches, Flaherty invited Peggy, champagne flutes in hand, to walk with him up the winding staircase to the balcony. Resting their drinks on the top railing, Flaherty said to Peggy, "What do you see below?"

"Quite the busy place. All the diners, each one in a joyous mood. Eating. Talking. Servers, wine stewards and busboys slipping in and out of each other's way quite gracefully, so careful not to bump into each other,"

Peggy said, "Constant movement, yet smooth as silk I have a mind to say. Grand is as near a word as I can describe it."

"Ah … what else?"

"It looks like a wheel. Our table the hub with spokes spaced evenly around the outer rim, coming together evenly at the edges of a smaller circle."

"By design … came to me in a dream," Flaherty said.

"Brilliant, Mr. Flaherty. There is no other word. You are quite the restaurateur. Stephen and I have never been to a fine restaurant such as this. Such harmony. I have never seen tables set so elegantly."

"I don't want to keep you from your meal, Peggy, but … but just one more indulgence if it's no trouble to you. Look again, squarely down below."

"Mr. Minogue and my husband getting rather chummy," Peggy said, sipping her champagne. She noticed that Flaherty gripped the railing tightly, his other hand shaking again as he lifted his glass, having trouble finding his mouth.

"Are you all right then, Mr. Flaherty?"

"Give me a minute. I have these … moments of late. My mind is clear one minute, then I can't speak. Then …"

"Tell me. Why did you invite us tonight?" Peggy said.

"Ah … to meet Paddy Minogue. You might find him … to be an irritating kind of Irish. Then again …"

"I know who the man is," Peggy said, "It is no secret he's a gangster. When you brought the little Lenape girl to our apartment, I knew she was Carney's daughter. And I knew that Minogue was keeping her."

"If you and Stephen can … overlook his abrasive manner … his history in this city … you will be … very rich … much richer than you could ever be with me."

"At what price, then?" Peggy said.

"Same as mine. But he's on to something that ... you'll want to be a part of," Flaherty said, "Ah ... one more thing Peggy, before I go."

"Where are you going?" Peggy said.

"Keep a secret?"

"For certain I will do so."

"I'm not running ... for reelection. I am finished with politics."

"Doesn't surprise me. I never understood how you could handle government and business too. That's more pressure than most men can stand."

"No more ... real estate business either."

"What?" Peggy said as she gripped the railing.

"I'm thinking of turning over all my holdings ... to Minogue ... he's been my silent partner for many years. That's why I ... gave you the deed to 347 Cherry, knowing ... this day would come."

"What state of mind were you in to go into business with him? You are an elegant man, Mr. Flaherty. With fine manners."

"That man ... captivating your husband ... is your future."

"Not if I can help it," Peggy said.

"Think of your boys. Stephen will need ... your support. He will be getting the offer of a lifetime. I made it part of ... the deal that he be the first in line. That's the purpose of our ... get together tonight. Hear what he's got to say. You are under no ... obligation to accept it. Make no mistake, Minogue needs Stephen. This is ... the Callaghan moment right here. I suggest you seize it."

"Why should we link our lives with him?"

"Well, ... you invested quite a bit in me for how many years."

"That's diff ..." Peggy started to say. Flaherty turned from her, walking toward the stairs.

After catching up to him, Peggy placed her hand on his shoulder. "What makes you think Stephen will accept the offer?"

"Isn't it the dream of every man who ... comes from the other side to climb higher and higher up the American ladder? The Irish in him ah ... will keep pushing to the top rung."

"How did *you* get there?"

"Minogue and I are ah ... really no different. He flexes his muscles in the open. I ah ... do it in private. You know that. You're a smart woman, Peggy O'Rourke Callaghan. I'm sure you ah ... had me figured out all along."

"It couldn't be hidden from me what you do, Mr. Flaherty. It's greater the wish I knew otherwise than what I suspected all along. Why are you opening up to me now? Why are you telling me these things?"

"I know ah ... you're strong enough to keep another secret."

"I'll try to stand it," Peggy said.

Flaherty wiped his brow. "It's a little hot in here, isn't it then?"

"It is that."

"I'll be going ... up the road soon, Peggy."

"Are none of your plans grand enough to save yourself?"

"I'm ... dying, Peggy. I have been told ... by several doctors I have a brain disease. A rather large, malignant tumor. Soon I will be ... falling down stairs without even drinking," Flaherty said, finishing his glass of champagne, "That's why I ... am choosing this moment to tell you ah ... whatever you need or want to know."

"The best day was when you opened up to me," Peggy said, holding his arm, "You are humbling yourself now and I am deeply humbled because of it."

"Minogue will be ... bragging on his project the moment we sit down. Listen to him. Most of it will be true. Then you and ... Stephen talk it over when you get home," Flaherty drew closer to Peggy. "Whatever you and Stephen think of me, be so kind as to ... remember this. I tried my best to make it better for the Irish."

Peggy saw a different Matthew Flaherty. As she followed him to the table, he looked smaller and thinner. His broad shoulders sloped inwardly, shrinking in size. Once a strong, extremely confident, and private man, the larger-than-life Irishman met his match that bowed him to a low position. Uncharacteristic humility, Peggy thought, if only he knew earlier in his life how it suited him. The conversation during dinner was polite yet guarded.

"Ah … Paddy Minogue wants to share some exciting news and I … am going to let him do the talking from this point on," Flaherty said.

Minogue enthusiastically described the elaborate *Palisades Palace* project, mostly for Peggy's benefit. As Minogue handed rough sketches of the project to Peggy, she noticed that the nails on his short, stubby fingers were encrusted with dirt. "They will come from all over the world. Going to be bigger than The Crystal Palace. People will want to see it before they die," Minogue said, turning to Stephen, "A showcase of nations. Their cultures. Rides for the kids. Biggest and best casinos. A world-class zoo with monkeys, lions, tigers, and elephants. Swimming pools and fountains. The grandest hotel with elegant restaurants."

Looking around the room, Minogue said, "Like this one. No sawdust or peanut shells on the floor. Class. Music halls, pavilions, including Irish music. At night, firework displays. Everything for the family. Gardens you walk through like a maze. Here's the clincher! Musical spectaculars with casts of a thousand singers in a 15,000-seat amphitheater perched right on the cliff's edge. West 39th Street ferry to take you there. Access from the river in a giant 150-foot-high elevator connected to a train that crosses a trestle to the entrance at Liberty Place. People won't be able to see it all in a few hours, so they'll stay overnight or a week, even a month in our luxurious hotel."

Peggy noticed Flaherty slumping in his chair, his eyes half closed. "Hey waiter. Another bottle of wine. The best in the house," Paddy Minogue said.

"Stephen and I will consider your offer and get back to you next week," Peggy said to Minogue.

"Don't wait too long. You'd be crazy to turn me down. Seal the deal. Opportunity of a lifetime," Minogue said as the wine steward filled each glass. Minogue stood, holding his glass aloft. "To Weehawken. *The Palisades Palace*. The Eighth Wonder of the World!"

"Stephen and I want to thank you for giving Carney Callaghan a pass and for releasing the girl to us," Peggy said.

"Don't worry about it."

"But," she began as Stephen tugged her dress. She swatted his hand away. "Can you tell us what happened to the girl's mother."

"Of course. Don't worry about her," Minogue laughed and said, "We made damn sure she eats her vegetables." Looking over at Flaherty whose eyes were completely closed, he added, "Before the vegetables eat her."

Peggy took a long gulp of wine and sat down. Stephen said "Mr. Minogue, you haven't told us what part of Erin is in your heart and soul. Where are you from, if you don't mind me asking?"

"Me and my Da travelled all over Ireland, working together, himself and I," Minogue said.

"What kind of trade was belonging to your Da?" Stephen asked.

"Da was a traveling tinker."

"And you?"

"I tinker with this, and I tinker with that," Paddy Minogue said.

Tale of one household

What Peggy hoped to hear when they returned home from *Plymouth Rock* was that the boys behaved well and fell fast asleep hours earlier. However, while inside the bedroom, as Ginger helped Peggy change from her dress and crinolines into her nightgown, she got an earful of what actually took place.

Stephen waited in the front room, anxious to enlist his wife's unflagging support. He wanted Peggy to dream dreams of unimaginable riches, proposed to him by Paddy Minogue, the new Matthew Flaherty in their lives. Peggy often shared with Stephen that they were already blessed, living in an apartment with three bedrooms: one for themselves; one for the boys; and a third for Uncle James and his caregiver Ginger plus a well-ventilated front sitting room, a kitchen and dining room.

Sitting opposite Peggy, Stephen spoke breathlessly about the golden path that was opened wide before them this very night. Unmoved, Peggy said, "I married a man. His name is Stephen Callaghan. Are you the man I married or are you someone else?"

"I know who I am. A man whose ears were filled with wonders tonight. What I heard was not just for my hearing. They were choice words about dreams for the two of us. Maybe I should ask who you are … a lady who had more than her share of wine tonight."

"You know what I am referring to … who you're *trying* to be. First, it was Matthew Flaherty. Now it's Paddy Minogue. Don't play the innocent with me. I know you're a talented man. You can fix anything. Now, it is time to fix yourself."

"I don't want to be Flaherty or Minogue. I also don't want to answer to the likes of them the rest of my life. Once this project is over, I'll be on my own. *We'll* be on our own."

Peggy stood up, pointing in the direction of the boys' bedroom. "I've given you my body and my blood and from that body and blood I've given you two sons."

"And I have given you my heart in return. I truly have," Stephen said, "Maybe you expect too much of me, an Irish man from poor stock."

"I don't think it's too much to expect a man to be a man. Not just an Irish man. Simply a man who knows how to love his wife and shows that love. A man who is a proper father and sets a proper example for his sons. I want them to grow up to be real men. Is money the only thing that matters to you? We are not downtrodden. For the love of God, we own this building."

"What's so terrible about more money? It's a natural thing to look after," Stephen said.

"Do you *look after* your sons when you get up in the morning and go to work?" Peggy said.

"Keep your voice down, will you. Everyone in the building will know our business."

"I don't give a damn who hears me. I told you many times James is a trouble to me, and you ignore my cries for help. And he's difficult mean to William."

"William can take care of himself. He's a big boy."

"Size has nothing to do with it. William is weak and James picks on him. He needs a good whack on his backside. From his father! I can't raise them by myself. Paddy Minogue filled your ears with wonder? Ginger filled my ears with something well shy of wonder. James had a lip on him and spoke disrespectful to her. He talks that way to me too. His own Ma. You don't hear it because you're off to work before they wake. You come home when they're asleep. You told Carney you wanted to be a better father to our sons. Many a hard road we walked, Stephen. Dark and blighted were the homes we lived in before we came to America. But there was aways love where we came from. I know it. You know it. What happened along the way?"

"I love you Peggy, but I must let you know I need this project more than anything in the world. It is the opportunity we dreamt about since we crawled out of the darkness that was Ireland. We know where we came from. It was a dreary, unfriendly place," Stephen said.

"I always give affection and the love of my heart to you and our sons. But there came major changes in you. I need to talk to you about real life. Not dreams. *Our* life in the present. *Our* boys' lives. You say you don't want to answer to Flaherty or Minogue. How about answering to your wife and our sons? While you're off gathering riches, you leave us poor."

"It's awful your anger when it rises up," Stephen said, "Are you hearing just one sentence of what I'm trying to tell you? Minogue offered me twice what Flaherty pays. This is our moment to climb out of the lowest class. Listen to me."

"Listen to you? Listen to me! At what price with the likes of Minogue?" Peggy said, rising from her chair, "We have never been certain of Flaherty's ways because he lives in the shadows. But we know *for sure* about Minogue's. His gangs, brothels, goons, eye-gougers, tongue removers. You know full well of his payoffs to police and city officials for all his dirty business. It's out in the open. It's no secret he's a crook. Are you looking away from all of that?"

"Flaherty did us a lot of favors. Putting my name forward with Minogue tops them all. We have always made decisions together. I need you to be with me on this one."

"Look at the head of you lifted so proudly. I can't sign off on this one. Think of our family. Our future. Not in riches. But in genuine value. The price we pay as human beings. With our hearts, minds, and souls," Peggy said, "I have my share of guilt that I often looked the other way. But now. Right now! We have to look the *right* way."

Stephen stood. "I *am* thinking of our family. I *am* going to do this, and nothing will stand in my way."

Their loud, angry voices awakened the boys. James and William came into the front room, one behind the other. William, crying, rubbed his eyes with his blanket. He ran immediately to his mother, sat on her lap, gave her a hug, then crossed the room and snuggled with his father.

James sat down in the middle of the room, looked first at his father, then at his mother. "Will you two stop arguing? I'm trying to sleep."

A tale of the other

Paddy Minogue had boasted about the golden shovel groundbreaking to his daughters Helen and Eleanor when the girls were toddlers. He made a diorama for them. It was their dollhouse, replete with circus clowns, animal miniatures, tin toys, model trees, water-spouting fountains, and a working replica of a Ferris wheel. By the time the girls were teenagers, he had parceled together sufficient cliffside properties to accommodate his grandiose dream of building the *Palisades Paradise* Exposition. Minogue skimmed profits from his other businesses and acquired one parcel after another on the west bank palisades of the Hudson River. Ultimately, he amassed thirty-eight prime New Jersey acres with a clear view of Manhattan's west side.

Despite the stress of confronting unresolved issues common in his line of work, Paddy Minogue always reserved time for his girls. He rarely missed an opportunity to visit his Fourth Avenue brothel so he could tuck his daughters into bed. He sang sweet Irish melodies to them until they fell asleep.

When informed the girls were well behaved during the day, he read bedtime stories to them, classics like Grimm's Fairy Tales and original stories made up from the rich source material of his own experience, sometimes as current as that very afternoon. He told them tales of enemies being defeated, revealed in juicy, bloodthirsty terms, not sparing any gruesome detail of the gouging, biting, clubbing, and stabbing. Their eyes lit up when he read to them. They gasped, giggled, and begged for more. He rhapsodized about clandestine meetings with high-ranking government officials committing ghastly deeds in the moonlit alleys and foul-smelling, crime infested tunnels beneath the streets in forbidding neighborhoods. Paddy balanced dark stories with lighter fare, sprinkling colorful tales with elements of buffoonery and outlandish behavior, involving overstuffed, slow-of-foot police officers giving chase but never quite catching up to the bank robbers. He added scenes featuring courtroom dramas with their father as anti-hero defendant outwitting corrupt, witless judges dressed in white wigs and rainbow-colored robes, flanked by fancy-suited, silver-tongued attorneys.

The brothel had a homey atmosphere when the girls were little, a peculiarly domesticated scene, with a different surrogate whore mother each night preparing their meals. A pot of Irish tea was always ready when Paddy came home from a hard day at the office. Some enterprises required night shift duties but not a day went by without him spending quality time with his girls, whether at dinner or at bedtime.

Minogue's Fourth Avenue brothel was the most profitable of his various enterprises, yet it was clean and orderly enough to be a worthy domicile for his daughters. He had designated two different whores to be the mothers of his children, with the promise of additional compensation. One of the ladies, a blond-haired Norwegian, not especially attractive physically, had become his favorite. She was singled out for her capacity for endurance as Paddy was a prodigious and adventurous fornicator. This woman had given birth to Helen.

Around the same time Paddy lay with the blond, he recruited a dark-haired Jewess the moment she stepped off the boat. She had an aristocratic air about her that countered his rough looks and crude, abrasive demeanor. Paddy took the brunette beauty into his bed soon after her arrival. The fertility gods blessed their union. The woman subsequently gave birth to Eleanor.

Unlike Helen, who resembled the least appealing physical characteristics of both parents, it was not immediately apparent Paddy was the male who sired Eleanor. She was blessed with her mother's fine features and natural beauty. Neither whore turned out to be the nurturing, mothering type. The teenage girls did not suffer from lack of attention though, as the house was full of females assigned to attend to their needs.

If life for his daughters was swell when they were toddlers, it was grand when they reached their teens. They were terribly spoiled half-sisters, both thirteen, born within months of each other. Rarely did they compete to be father's favorite as he showered attention and gifts upon them equally. They considered themselves equal opportunity twins.

When the desire for sex with the intent of propagation with the Norwegian and Jewess had long become a thing of the past, Paddy found himself developing a sincere interest in a brand-new hire, a tall, flaming red-haired French woman. What distinguished her was that she was well educated and had worked as a teacher in her native country. Unable to find a school position immediately in New York City, she needed a place to stay and food to eat. She elected to make a living on her back until a teaching opportunity came along. Because of her academic background, Paddy asked that she consider becoming a personal tutor for the girls, who currently lacked formal schooling. He offered her a handsome bonus as an incentive in the decision-making process.

She accepted his offer. In addition to her tiny cubicle which had the dual function as the entertainment space for clients and her bedroom, she was given a nicely furnished office on the first floor with a desk and three chairs. The Frenchwoman agreed on set hours four days a week for lessons and the freedom to develop her own curriculum for reading, writing, arithmetic, and conversational French.

The sisters delighted in dressing up in the prostitutes' risqué outfits and were permitted by some of the working girls to use their powders, rouges, lipsticks, and jewelry. They always washed up before daddy came home though. They surmised he would be angry if he caught them playacting as cheaply made-up whores.

When Paddy was not available on Sundays, his personal bodyguard and brothel bouncer, Melvin Stein, got the unenviable assignment of chaperoning Helen and Eleanor to parks, playgrounds, as well as candy and ice cream stores. It was seldom an easy task as the girls were mischievous. One day, they ran down the block with Melvin in hot pursuit. He lost sight of them as they crouched down in an alley. When the sisters saw the disconsolate bodyguard sitting on a stoop, head in his hands, bawling like a baby, they approached the crestfallen man.

Helen tapped him on the shoulder.

"Where have you been? If I lost you girls your father would kill me."

"He would not. We'd tell Daddy we were goofing on you," Eleanor said.

The sisters did not know what Melvin knew. They remembered the bedtime stories, but never connected the romanticizing of criminal activities to the storyteller's actual life. Nor did the girls know their father had a stable of high-priced criminal lawyers working full time to keep him out of jail. Many of the charges against him were felony counts of extortion, robbery, even murder.

Soon after the girls turned fourteen, with his professional life fully immersed in the *Palisades Palace* and quite pleased with the progress his daughters were making with their education, Paddy decided to present a new offer to their teacher. He wanted a son and decided to try his luck with the Frenchwoman. Knowing that she still had a desire to secure a formal teaching position in the city public school system, he asked her if she would agree to bear a child. If she was successful in getting pregnant, he would guarantee her financial security by opening a bank account in her name and setting her up in a furnished, rent-free apartment in one of his buildings. She would be free to leave the prostitution business to pursue her teaching goals following the birth of the child, boy or girl.

The Frenchwoman became the third surrogate mother in the Minogue family, giving birth to a boy who, by the age of one, had a mop of red hair just like his mother. He was more spoiled than Paddy's daughters, not so much by his father, but by the doting prostitutes and even more so by his sisters. Paddy's daughters found that having a brother was quite the thing. Helen and Eleanor were totally devoted to him, proudly parading him throughout the Lower East Side in his baby buggy.

Not quite paradise

Minogue appointed Stephen Callaghan as Construction Supervisor of the *Palisades Palace* Exposition. With the breadth and scope of the project weighing down on him each passing day, Stephen came home less regularly. The pattern changed from every other day to twice a week by the end of the first three months. As the span between Stephen's visits became less predictable, Peggy abandoned the comfort of her bed. She wrapped a blanket around herself and waited for Stephen in a chair near the front window. Whenever she heard a man's voice rising up from the street below, she would gaze at the street below. When the silhouettes moved past, she settled back for another lonely night.

This ritual ended abruptly one night when Stephen returned home at three in the morning. Peggy heard the outside door open, followed by heavy steps plodding up the stairs. She waited as Stephen fumbled for his key. Peggy moved aside as he entered. Fueled with alcohol, Stephen staggered a few steps before finding his footing. He held up a wad of bills and attempted to hand it to Peggy. She let the money fall to the floor.

"It's so much money, I can't even count it. Himself's a good provider. Isn't he, then?"

Peggy scooped a few bills off the floor, crumpled them in both hands and threw them in his face.

Stephen sat down and laughed while stretching his arms along the edges of the upholstered chair. He threw his head back and continued laughing as he booted the scattered cash toward Peggy.

"This is the last night I keep vigil for you. The last night I miss the warmth of your body next to mine. The last time I meet the dead of night with tears shed for you, wondering if you will ever return. I've given you every piece of me there is to give. I've held nothing back," Peggy said, kicking the bills his way, "What have you given me in return? Dirty money? Are you now an Irish pig like Minogue?"

"Minogue a pig? You never said much before, did you? You looked the other way with the stuff Flaherty did. Am I right on that score? Tell me the truth before you get all high and mighty."

"It was never something we talked about much, was it?" Peggy said, "Forget Flaherty. Minogue is your god now. Seems like you made a deal with the devil himself. *You* tell *me* the truth now. If you don't, you can rot like Aubrey's compost. Whenever you decide to show up here, you're drunk. Unshaven. Filthy," she said, packing several loose bills in her fist and shoving them within inches of his face, "Did you get a big raise and forget to tell your wife about it? This money is more than your paycheck. Have you stooped to being a criminal? I don't need filth in our home. The home we built together. Taking bribes, are you? Have you found a way to disgrace our family name? Tell me, is this dirty money?"

Sobering up, Stephen stood and said, "You're getting your anger up at me because I have a big job? An Irishman clawing his way up from the bottom. Reading blueprints with gentlemen in fancy suits and college degrees. That's right. *Them and me* building Palisades P-A-R-A-D-I-S-E. Imagine. Me. *Equal to them.*"

"I don't know who you are anymore." Peggy said, going nose-to-nose, "What's worse, *you* don't know either."

"I know who I am. I'm the man who's given you a better life. A good provider. What Irish family do you know who's better than us?" Stephen said, taking a flask out of his back pocket.

As he started to unscrew it, Peggy swatted it to the floor. "A better life? A good provider? Are you a father to your boys? Did you forget you have a wife? Is providing dirty money your idea of love? There's love and then there's love in it. Which is it from you? I'll tell you what you're good for. You're good for shite."

Peggy grabbed another fistful of money off the floor, her strength giving way to tears. "Is this what you call being a good husband? Is this all there is to being a good father?"

"I don't tell you how to spend the money. Have I ever asked what you do with it? Have I? I've always wished the eye of no bad thing would ever see you."

"I'm *looking at* the bad thing right now. Tell me if I'm wrong. Before it's too late. Where are you getting this money?"

"Oh, stop being a cluckin' hen, will you. It's bonus money," Stephen said.

"Are you doing that well for Minogue? Tell me, Steven. I am your wife. I am the mother of your sons. I ask you this once and will never ask you again. Look me in the face and answer me with all of the truth."

"I'm looking," Stephen said as he picked up the flask and drank what was left.

"How did you get this money?"

"I work hard. Very hard," Stephen said, "Not like the rest of the Irish. Dumb and lazy, they are. I'm proud to be *real* Irish. Those others'll never get anywhere. I'm going somewhere. Somewhere grand."

"You're seeing the best of your Irishness through your liquor. You're not seeing the other parts. Maybe before. Not now. You're not facing the fullness of it. You lost the best part of you. You're at war with yourself. You want to fail, thinking you want to succeed. You never figured out the difference. It's some kind of perversion, dear man. Some kind of affliction. You can succeed without cheating. Without lying. You've done that already."

Peggy took the flask out of his hand, seeing that he was about to doze off. "You left me behind some time ago, husband. I thought maybe we could draw closer to each other. You and me. Love each other until death do us part. I ask you, are you any different than Flaherty? Have you any more morals than Minogue? Don't you see *I* am your success. *Our sons* are your success. Can you see that at last? I take my share of responsibility for what happened to us. I admit we were on the path to hell, but it looks like you want to get there before me."

Peggy sat down. Stephen struggled to keep his eyes open. "When I came to America, I was barely nine years old," Peggy said, "A strong Irish lad convinced me to go a little farther. He carried me on his back. I'll never forget that man. He never told me his name but forever his name will be Erin. I hope he is still alive and having his own success. He did for me what the Irish are supposed to do. Pick each other up. Carry each other on our backs. Not jump on the shoulders of a crook. I wanted you to be a strong man, Stephen, so I became less. I wanted to build you up. Not make something of you that you weren't but for you to fulfill what I knew you could be. If only you would look in the mirror. If only you would put aside what you think the Irish should do and just be a man. If you can be my man, I will always be your woman. Stay with me now or I will leave you forever."

Shaking off his stupor, Stephen stood over Peggy. "I did it for you ... not bad for a beaten down Irishman. I rise up. I am above."

"Don't give yourself too much credit. All along confusion's been your partner. A big share of 'oh, I come from such a poor place.' How you rose up out of the pit. I know Irishmen like you. Some of them get rid of their confusion. But I fear you're done. You'll always want to be someone else. As for me, I never missed one moment of agony in Ireland. But I've been waiting a long time in America for one moment of ecstasy. I'd have all my riches if I thought I had your love. I made up my mind. I'm going somewhere, husband. And I'm taking the boys with me. To get them away from you and give them a chance to grow up decent. I don't know what you're up to. But I have my suspicions."

"Aw, give me a chance, won't you? Can't you hear the angels whisper?"

"The liquor's talking out of you now. When you're sober, maybe you can think about the meaning of life before the next hearse rumbling down Cherry Street is yours. I'm finished with you," Peggy said, weeping.

"Don't unman me now," Stephen said, wiping his eyes.

"Go ahead, Stephen. Have your share of crying. It is a sad situation we are in. Brave men should not be ashamed to weep when they have to. This is a time to weep. Don't let me cry alone."

"You'll take me back," Stephen said, sniffling.

"I won't take you back. Going to push off to a different place. I've been on my knees to you every time you decided to grace me with your drunken self. Always beside you in the name of trying to help you. Tears would have to rain out of stones before I'd take you back. If only I heard one sincere word of love out of you, I might reconsider. Your soul left your body some time ago. I gave you affection. I gave you the love of my heart. You have a mind to gather off to riches, leaving us poor. I have to save my sons. It's out the door with me and the boys."

"I was born in dirt," Stephen said.

"And to dirt you shall return." Peggy said as she left the room, remembering the song Stephen had the band play the day he proposed.

Touching her hand gentle as a breeze bends the willow
The angels whisper once again before I sleep
At night I dream our two heads will share one pillow
And one life together is a promise I will keep

Reaching for the heights

The *Palisades Paradise* rose like a beacon on a hill, looming over the Hudson River, a fortress at the edge of impenetrable cliffs, a mighty rock formation that appeared out of the clouds, rising above the specks of cargo ships and fishing boats below. With the appearance of each new building along the skyline, what had been a natural landscape now resembled the unfolding of a multi-colored dream sequenced in serial installments.

The development dominated the view from Manhattan's west side. It was no stretch of the imagination that before long, the ferry terminal on the New York side would become a bustling concourse of shops with enterprising vendors barking prices for a vast selection of *Palisades Paradise* souvenirs. One could imagine an attraction with enough magnetic power to draw even the most dispassionate tourist. It would rival the record crowds that witnessed the building of the Brooklyn Bridge.

Major newspapers devoted front page coverage to each new addition to the complex, whether it was a fifty-foot fountain or yet another music hall. Future plans were shared with reporters: luscious botanical gardens; a zoo; a two-story casino; hotel suites with rooms boasting gorgeous views, booked long in advance of the expected finish date. Still to come were swimming pools, an aquarium, rides for the kids, six restaurants, and an ice-skating rink. Best materials. Best architects. Best engineers. No expense spared. Delivery trucks and building supply vendors were a constant presence at the site.

It was the fall of 1886. Five out of twelve stories of the main hotel were basically finished. Floors six through twelve had the main structural beams in place but were open caverns of concrete floors, elevator shafts, and stairwells. The pressure was on Stephen to keep pace with the tight deadline imposed by Minogue.

Palisades Paradise became Weehawken's biggest employer. Stephen had the heady task of scheduling different crews to work simultaneously on various projects spread throughout the 38-acre exposition complex. He orchestrated the flow and harmony of workers and suppliers. Millions in revenue hung in the balance. Minogue demanded perfection.

Window sash for the hotel's sixth floor was delivered at 6:30 one morning. When the laborer assigned to offload the sash failed to show up on time, Stephen took his place. Working in tandem with a worker on the ground whose job it was to load the sash to be hoisted, Stephen stood on the sixth-floor balcony facing east, with the wind whipping through the open space like a banshee. The sheer height of the cliffs and unpredictable weather created constant instability on the unfinished floors.

With the block and tackle affixed overhead, Stephen exchanged hand signals with the worker on the ground. When a load of sash was fully secured on the pulley system by rope and grappling hook, the man gave it a tug on his end, the signal for Stephen to ready himself to pull the load inside. Trying not to let the light metal blow wildly in the wind, Stephen would step near the edge of the open patio, grab the corner of the sash, and bring it home. Once inside, he would untie the load and lower the rope and hook to the ground. After several hoists, Stephen and the worker developed a rhythm to the cycle of loading, tying, and hoisting.

Whenever the pattern was interrupted, Stephen would peer over the edge, careful not to lean too far to avoid getting vertigo. The steepness of the palisades made him feel woozy. He made sure to keep a solid footing on the floor, respecting that the force of strong winds could suddenly put his life in jeopardy. It was extremely dangerous, working in an unstable, exposed-to-the-elements environment, which had already claimed the lives of several workers.

Stephen was in a crouch position, busy unwinding the grappling hook when he caught sight of Minogue coming out of the stairwell. The big boss was accompanied by his bodyguard and two other men. The visit came as a surprise to Stephen. He was accustomed to meeting with Minogue in the shanty field office located on the opposite end of the complex.

Stephen sorted the sash into a pile as the men approached, shoulder to shoulder, nostrils flaring, each stride kicking up concrete dust, like wide-eyed steeds charging into battle. Minogue moved along a straight path toward Stephen. His bodyguard veered to the left. The other men kept to the right. Stephen moved his head from side to side, keeping all four in sight. Minogue came upon him quickly and stood over him. "A little short-handed today, Callaghan?"

"No problem, sir. We're on schedule," Stephen said, standing up.

"I'm happy about that," Minogue said, as he glanced at his bodyguards.

"What brings you to the sixth floor?"

"I own the fucking place. I'll ask you the questions."

Stephen moved further back, trying to keep all four of them in view. He scoped the layout of the unfinished floor, littered with piles of debris, workmen's tools, sawhorses, bricks, pieces of metal, his mind fixed on locating an escape route, "I don't remember seeing you much on the floors. Just curious."

"I'm sure you are," Minogue said, "Relax. Everything looks good. I just thought we'd chat about a topic that has come to my attention."

"Can we meet after I haul in the sash?"

"This won't take long."

"How can I help you?"

"Help?" Minogue laughed, "As in help *yourself*?"

Minogue's minions moved toward Stephen, closer to the edge of the concrete lip with nothing but open space beyond, sky above, palisades and river below.

"What do you mean?" Stephen said.

"There are rumors floating around. From reliable sources. People I know. People who know me."

"I don't know anything about any rumors."

"Of course you don't. You're the *subject* of the rumors. I'm hoping for your sake you can help dispel these rumors."

The man to Stephen's right inched closer.

"How can I do that?" Stephen said.

"Start by telling the fucking truth."

"What do you want to know?"

"Have you been stealing from me?" Minogue said as the man nearest him on the left kicked the pile of sash out of his way while moving closer to Stephen.

"No! Why would I do that?" Stephen said, pointing to the sash, "What am I going to steal? Sash? Come on Mr. Minogue, I'm no thief. I don't need any of this shite."

"Maybe not stealing in ways you think are stealing. Maybe in other ways ... that go undetected for a while ... until people start complaining."

The thugs came to within two feet of where Stephen stood. Paddy Minogue stepped closer. Stephen backed up. His eyes searched for a clear line to the stairwell, a path getting narrower by the moment. He bent down and picked up a solid metal bar left behind by the wire lathers. He held it close to his leg, hoping he could knock one of them out of the way and make it to the stairwell.

"I don't know what you're talking about. I'm no thief."

"Aren't I paying you a lot more than Flaherty?"

"You are. I'm very grateful. But I'm no thief."

"Maybe thief is the wrong word. Maybe you're an extortionist."

"I don't even know what that means."

"Word's out you been working for tips from suppliers. The wood people. Steel people. Glass people. They tell me they can't make deliveries until your palm is greased. If they refuse, you threaten to get another supplier. I think that's what's meant by extortionist."

Stephen looked directly at Minogue, "What if I do? That's not stealing from you."

"Like I said, don't I pay you enough?"

"Sure, you do."

"Then why are you doing this shite behind my back? Flaherty said I could trust you. Turns out, you got your sticky hands out for bribes. Who gave you permission to do that? Are you so stupid? Didn't you think someone'd eventually rat on you?"

"I learned by watching you. What's wrong with me wanting to rise to grand heights? I'm not taking money out of your pocket."

"Guess you ain't learning much today, you defiant prick. Do you know how you got to America?"

"Flaherty paid my passage."

"How do you think Flaherty found out about you? Who do you think told him you had construction skills, making it worthwhile to rescue you from the hard times."

"He knew my family."

"Flaherty never stepped foot in Tipperary County. He lived at the edge of the world on Lough Anscaul in Kerry. The only time he left his home on top of Carrigblagher Cliffs is when he had to get the hell out of the country to save his life."

"What are you talking about?" Stephen said.

"You damn Irish fool. You know about construction but you ain't got any horse sense. He and I knew each other when we were lads. We wrote to each other for years and schemed to be in business together. Many a place I've been to in Ireland. I roamed all over the country with my Da, making note of anyone who could help our future business enterprise. Me and Flaherty had it all planned. The land of opportunity needed us. Skilled craftsmen were at a premium. Unskilled lugs we picked off the boat. I told him about you, and he made a grand gesture to bring you here. And *here* you are."

"I can get this place built on time," Stephen said.

"So can a lot of other people," Minogue said, "Time for you to shorten the road, Callaghan. You made it to the heights. Not everyone gets as far as the sixth floor. Question is, have you reached your limit?"

"I never killed anybody by making a few extra bucks. Who did I hurt?"

"You're not making a convincing case for yourself. Your mind is all twisted. You're right in the middle of a major confusion and you're too confused to know it. Would it help if my boys rough you up, so you get the message? To make it clearer what I'm attempting to explain to you?"

"I ain't afraid of nothing. I don't run away from anyone. You'll never catch a feather out of me. When it's my time to shorten the road, I'll be the first one to grab the divine hand that'll take me home."

"If you think today you chanced upon some danger, and you have any share of luck with you, you'll be safe. On the other hand, I don't see a soul around interested in protecting you on the day your life might end," Minogue said as the men moved closer. Minogue held up his hand. He walked to the edge, looked down, and signaled the man on the ground, saying to Stephen, "Looks like your man below is ready for the next load. Why don't you drop that rod and haul it in."

Stephen looked quickly over his shoulder. Sure enough, the rope was moving. He peeked over the edge as the wind twisted and spun the load around. When Stephen reached for the load, the slats of light sash went flying in the wind, sailing through the air in every direction. With the load flying off, the hoist raced toward Stephen. Within seconds, the grappling hook took dead aim at his face. It zipped into Stephen's right eye socket, lifting him to the edge of the open balcony. He desperately thrust both arms upwards, grabbing the air. His body wiggled helplessly on the hook. His weight sent him plunging, tumbling down to the ground.

Minogue and his men did not look down. Minogue spoke to Thug #1, "Get a hold of the coroner. Tell him to put cause of death as suicide on the death certificate. How unfortunate."

Thug #1, "But boss. He's got the hook in his eye. How're they gonna figure suicide?"

"Terrible way to die. He saw the hook coming and jumped on it," Minogue said.

"But boss ..."

"He jumped on the hook. It was the strangest thing I ever saw. Did us a favor, he did," the bodyguard said.

"Saved us a lot of trouble," Thug #2 said, "We didn't even have to touch him."

"Well, there goes another stubborn Irishman who'll live on in the hearts of no one," Minogue said to his bodyguard, "Just make it worthwhile for the coroner. The state doesn't pay him enough for what he's gotta do."

Storm clouds came quickly from the east, blackening the sky. A violent wind whipped the river's white-capped water into the height and fury of ocean waves, tossing commercial and fishing craft about as if they were toy boats in a bathtub. Moments later, the wind funneled dust and debris into wild dances on the ground. The gale roared in vicious twists, emitting eerie sounds, followed by successive crackling peals of thunder. Sinister forked lightning, like illuminated jagged edged swords, pierced sky and earth menacingly with a shattering noise that ripped the veil of peace. The rain poured down in torrents, causing instant flooding.

Paddy Minogue sent out word for construction workers to lay down their tools. He gave them the rest of the day off so they could go home early to be with their wives and children.

Paying respects

Sunday morning Mass at St. Mary's Roman Catholic Church on Grand Street had always reminded Peggy and Stephen of the days they grew up in Ireland. Although raised in different parts of Ireland, each Catholic church regardless of town, hamlet or parish was a place of universal familiarity and comforting sameness. Most priests at St. Mary's were Irish, the majority of parishioners were Irish, and the mysteries of liturgical Latin spoken during Mass sounded the same in America as it did in Ireland. The span of time since their childhood and the distance across the ocean did little to diminish their devotion to their faith. Faith in God and faith in the Roman Catholic Church were one and the same thing.

Peggy and Stephen took their two sons with them on Sundays to the same church where they got married. Father Donnelly was still there, though getting on in years and apt to boast that of all the couples whose weddings he officiated, one hundred percent of them were still married. Father Donnelly always told Peggy and Stephen their wedding was his favorite and they were the ideal husband and wife. Many suspected he told the same story to every couple.

James and William had been baptized at St. Mary's and received their First Communion there. The Callaghans were on friendly terms with every parish priest and the Monsignor. None of those connections mattered when Peggy, in the acute stage of bereavement, tried to make arrangements for a funeral mass for Stephen at St. Mary's and his burial in a Catholic cemetery. She was told in a handwringing, apologetic way by the Monsignor, that the Archbishop forbade Stephen's body to be interred in sacred, consecrated ground since the coroner's certificate listed suicide as the cause of death.

In her heart and soul, Peggy wanted to fight the Archbishop, the Cardinal, even the Pope, but she was too distraught. Needing to provide immediate emotional support for her sons, there was little fight left in her to tangle with the institutional stubbornness of the Catholic Church. Feeling conflicted about how their marriage ended, she needed to get the funeral and burial done respectfully.

Peggy accepted Carney's offer to arrange for a private service on the grounds of the Callaghan property upstate. The service would be conducted by a Protestant minister.

Carney was a nominal Catholic. After relocating upstate, he developed an interest in the Bible stories told to him by a part-time carpenter and roving missionary, Rev. Jeremiah Dooze. The minister endeared himself to Carney, Minnie Mae, and their children, as well as the Lenape who populated the woods in bark wigwams and rock-shelters. Rev. Dooze became the *de facto* family priest for the upstate Callaghans, as sacrilegious as that was for a Roman Catholic family to embrace the theology of a Baptist minister.

On a bit of a rise overlooking Pine Meadow Lake, Reverend Dooze gathered the mourners in a wide circle around the freshly dug grave. Those attending included: Carney, Minnie Mae; sons Mickey and Patrick; James, William, and their mother Peggy; and Emma Kennedy. Also included was Carney's half breed daughter, Wee Mum and her full-breed teenage Lenape female friends she called cousins, plus a few cats, a donkey, hens, rooster, goats, and the pet pig Sammy. Because he was ill, Uncle James stayed home with his caregiver, Ginger.

When the service was about to begin, Carney heard people whispering behind him. He clapped his large hands a few times. "We's in church now. Reverend wants to start the service."

The mourners listened respectfully as Rev. Dooze offered comforting prayers. With his heart full of compassion for the widow, he included the traditional Catholic *De Profundis*, providing some semblance of a familiar liturgy, hopefully mitigating the pain endured by the widow. Although the service lacked ceremonial pageantry, Peggy was comforted when she heard: Requiem aeternam dona Ei, Domine, et Lux perpetua luceat ei. Requiescat in pace.

And all God's people said AMEN.

The minister prayed in the Episcopalian tradition, thoughtfully choosing prayers from the *Book of Common Prayer,* many of them identical to the Roman Catholic tradition. Acting upon a special request made by Peggy, Rev. Dooze graciously invited Mrs. Kennedy to lead the group in a decade of the rosary.

Reverend Dooze invited Carney to say a few words of remembrance for his father. After Minnie Mae shushed the laughing goats and the oinking pig, Carney stepped forward, placed his hand on the pine coffin he made. He said, in a deep, scratchy voice, "I ain't no speechifier. Never been in govmint nor anythin' like that. Never did git any formal education, but I want ta thank everyone here fer comin' out today, payin' respects ta my dad." He stopped his tribute abruptly so Mickey and Patrick could chase the misbehaving pets back to the barn. After Sammy the pig was lassoed, Carney continued speaking. "I'm sorriest for Miss Peggy who had hardship all her life 'n lost many in her own family but is doin' such a nice task raisin' my two half-brothers, who I consider full brothers. 'N she was like a Ma ta me as I never did have a chance to meet my real Ma. I know Dad wuz a hard-workin' Irishman 'n he 'n Miss Peggy are a credit ta the Irish race.

Havin' survived the harsh times 'n all that ta come here ta America ta make somethin' of theirselves. I wish I spent more time with Dad. He teached me a lot 'bout craftin' things," Carney said, pointing to the cabin, chicken coop and the coffin, "Like me being able to build an addition ta our house seein' as Minnie Mae keeps wantin' more kids, she says ta eventually help around the house. I know Miss Peggy tried ta teach me ta read 'n write," Carney stopped for a moment and looked first at Rev. Dooze, then Peggy, "I think I told you Miss Peggy, that the Rev's trying ta teach me too 'n he's having about as much success as you. Maybe you can talk about that after we get Dad in the ground. Anyhow, I don't know what else ta say other than I guess I'm proud ta be Irish 'n American, born over there for a little while 'n now I'm here. I want Dad ta be proud of me for workin' as hard as him. Okay. That's enough."

Minnie Mae coughed, looking Carney's way. "Minnie Mae 'n me would like you all ta stay ta share a meal. You won't be disappointed. She's the best cook, spare none."

As Rev. Dooze prepared to say the final prayers over the coffin, Minnie Mae coughed again. Carney took her cue and said, "It's a sad time fer us, but seems the right time to say…," Carney took a handkerchief out of his coveralls and dabbed each eye before continuing, "We'd like ta invite anyone in the family, whether blood or … any family, that is … if ya get dead, ya can git buried right here. There's plenty of room. We'll push the tater plants aside if we haf ta. That goes fer everyone here. Also, Uncle James. He's not well 'n couldn't make the trip. He's the one give Minnie Mae 'n me the whole idea. He was my dad for a year after I was born. He brought me ta this country. He taught me things too. One of them being the fact family means everythin'."

Carney looked at the teenage girls, saying, "Even if you're not Irish. Uncle James told us this is where he wants ta be buried. Right here in this tater patch. It reminds him of the old country … during better times. He told me, 'Carney, just plant some heather alongside me grave 'n burn some of that sweet-smelling peat' That's what he said. Uncle James did say it exactly like that, dint he Minnie Mae?"

Minnie Mae said, "We gotta find us some peat."

"I think that's enough fer now. I don't want to talk no more. Thank y'all fer listenin',"

As Rev. Dooze placed his hand on the coffin, preparing to offer the committal prayer, Wee Mum tapped him on the shoulder, asking to speak to him in private. The minister took her aside and motioned for Carney to join the conversation.

"My cousins and I would like to pray to the Great Spirit in our tradition to honor Papa Chief's father."

Wiping his tears, Carney put his arm around Wee Mum, "My big girl, Papa Chief loves ya but the Reverend here is a Christian clergyman 'n ..." Reverend Dooze interrupted and knelt down beside the grief-stricken teenager and said, "Your Papa Chief told me that your grandpa and Miss Peggy took care of you when you were very young."

"I loved him too."

"Well, I can see why it's so easy to love you," Rev. Dooze said, "Do you want to pray for him right now?"

"We dance our prayers. Grandfather is in my blood memory just like it is with the ancient spirits."

"It's okay with me," Rev. Dooze said, "How about you, Papa Chief?"

"Is it just you 'n yer cousins, Wee Mum?"

"The boys know the dance too."

Rev. Dooze tapped Carney on the shoulder, indicating he was okay with the dance.

The boys formed a line parallel to the girls. Wee Mum and the others raised their right hands, and kept their arms extended throughout the dance. Wee Mum took the first step. They danced, hopping on one foot, then the other, dipping their bodies toward the ground, then rising, repeating chants as they moved in harmony:

He Ya Ha

He Ha Ya Ha

He Ya Ha

He Ha Ya He Ha

He Ha Ya He Ha

He Ya Ha

He Ya Ha Ha

He Ya Ha

He Ha He

He Ha Ya He Ha

After the dance, Rev. Dooze asked everyone to bow their heads: "In sure and certain hope of the resurrection to eternal life through our Lord Jesus Christ, we commend to Almighty God our brother Stephen and we commit his body to the ground, earth to earth, ashes to ashes, dust to dust. The Lord bless him and keep him, the Lord make His face shine upon him and be gracious to him, the Lord lift up His countenance upon him and give him peace."

And everyone said: AMEN

Reverend Dooze exhorted all present to console the person nearest them. The minister then played "Amazing Grace" on his harmonica. In between weeps and hugs, the mourners headed toward the cabin, enjoying a hearty feast of meat loaf with thick brown gravy, roasted wild turkey, rabbit, fresh peas, mashed potatoes, and corn bread.

Following the meal, Peggy and Mrs. Kennedy said their goodbyes and headed toward the road where a horse and cart would take them to the ferry. Peggy planned to return to the city, but she arranged for James and William to stay with Carney for a week, followed by a visit with Mrs. Kennedy in Mt. Pleasant. She reminded Carney to honor his father, raising an eyebrow for emphasis, encouraging him to resist teaching his little brothers anything she would have to spend years undoing.

After an overnight stay with her surrogate mother, Peggy took the train to New York City to attend to a multitude of issues at 347 Cherry Street.

Carney waited two days before he decided, despite Miss Peggy's raised eyebrow, that it was time to introduce his brothers to local customs and folklore. On the second night of their stay, James and William sat on a large boulder alongside Mickey and Patrick. They held long sticks speared with marshmallows over a fire. Getting their faces reddened at a campfire was a new experience for the city boys. They also got to taste something they never put their teeth to, delicious marshmallows charred black beyond recognition.

After consuming a half dozen roasted marshmallows each, Carney's eldest son Mickey jumped off the rock and said, "C'mon Pa, show uncles how to light 'er up."

Throwing a big log on the fire, Carney said, "Nah. I'd be in a big heap of trouble with Miss Peggy if I did."

"You won't tell her, will ya?" Mickey said to James and William.

"Not a word," William said. James nodded.

"Okay boys. This here is how ya light'er up," Carney said.

Mickey handed one of the sticks to his father. Carney put the stick in the fire until it flamed up, unbuckled his pants with his free hand and let them drop to the ground. He bent over, holding the flaming stick near his behind and let out with a loud, voluminous fart. As the flame from the ass-gas shot out three feet, the boys yelped, hooted, and hollered.

"Light'er again, Pa," Mickey squealed, convulsively dancing around in circles. Patrick joined hands with William, swinging him around several times. James smiled, staying on the sidelines. The city boys thought it was some kind of magic or a trick.

Laughing so hard he could hardly speak, Carney slapped his knee and said "I never git tired of doin' scientific spearmints. That's what I'll tell Miss Peggy if she ever finds out. What's more natural than natural gas?"

Mickey, Patrick and William danced arm-in-arm, while James sat off to the side holding a stick with a half-eaten marshmallow. Mickey exhorted his dad, "Blow it out yer ass again Pa. One more time Pa. Blow it out yer ass."

Mickey broke loose from the other two boys and spun around like a whirling dervish. Carney accepted his son's challenge, lit another stick, and put it close to his backside. He let loose a flamethrower, bright and spectacular enough to illumine the boys' faces. He buckled up his trousers and threw the stick into the fire. He looked at his younger brothers. "I doubt they'd ever teach ya that in yer school."

After some tales of the dark woods, the fire died down to glowing embers. With Carney leading the way, Patrick, Mickey, and William took out their willies and doused the fire in the most natural way.

When they were finished, James spat on the hissing embers.

Carney walked over to him and said, "Ya dint seem ta enjoy yerself like yer brother. We might hafta find somethin' special fer ya tomorrow."

James looked at Carney and said, "I heard that injin girl call you Papa Chief."

"That injin girl's yer niece. Older than you, but still yer niece. Blood related. Family. Not only that, she git her name lookin' after you when all ya could do wuz crap yer pants 'n upchuck yer dinner."

James sneered. "I got another name for you."

"What's that?" Carney said.

"Papa Chief Fartsalot," James said, finally laughing.

The checkered game of life

It was a damp October day. East River breezes blew the leaves helter-skelter in Corlears Hook Park, its ground covered with a soft layer of mist. Peggy watched the squirrels scramble, searching for acorns. She took a slow walk around Water, Madison, and Grand streets, listening to vendors haggling with customers, the whinnying of draft horses, and the excited sounds of children romping in the streets. When she arrived at 347 Cherry, she looked with admiration at the tenements, the sturdy structures she and Stephen helped build for Irish immigrants. She felt blessed that her good fortune enabled the next generation of Callaghans to rise above a life of poverty.

Standing at the edge of the park, Peggy gazed at the second-floor apartment window, aware it might be the last time she would ascend the stone steps, open the front door, and transport herself to the home that had claimed so much of her life. Stephen's brother James and his caregiver, Ginger, awaited her arrival.

Ownership of the building legally belonged to Peggy but woven into that security blanket was the fact Minogue owned every other Cherry Street tenement from Montgomery to the river. She knew the mobster would not hesitate to confiscate her property by any means necessary. Soon after Flaherty died, Minogue wasted no time evicting tenants whenever they fell behind in their rents. Whereas Flaherty accommodated the Irish poor, Minogue made no pretense for such largesse. Knowing this, Peggy hired an attorney to protect her interests, as Minogue's bribe chain contained no weak links.

Because Peggy witnessed firsthand the deterioration of Flaherty's mind, she never underestimated the potential for Minogue's underhandedness in taking advantage of his weakened partner. She did not put it past the mobster to have shoved fraudulent documents beneath the erstwhile Congressman's pen while telling him they simply involved mundane matters about their settlement. Peggy wanted James and Ginger to stay in the apartment as long as needed, without the worry Minogue might serve notice of eviction at a moment's notice.

When Peggy opened the door, James was stretched out on the sofa, covered with blankets. Ginger sat next to him. Peggy alerted her to Minogue's history and provided her attorney's contact information in case of trouble. Peggy said she planned to stay in the apartment for a few days to tidy up business affairs. She also needed to pack up all the boys' clothing and have St. Mary's transfer their academic records to their new school in Sing Sing Village.

When James awakened momentarily, Peggy gushed how lovingly Carney spoke of him at Stephen's funeral. When he dozed off again, Peggy took Ginger into the kitchen to inquire of her brother-in-law's failing health. "He has good days and bad days but today is a good day." Ginger told her. Peggy asked Ginger to continue collecting monthly rent from the tenants until a reliable agent was retained.

"You can talk in here," James's said, "Ginger, bring me the box from the bedroom."

When James opened the box, Peggy gasped at the contents of banded stacks of hundred-dollar bills.

"This is yours, Peggy. From Stephen."

"I won't take a penny, James. You keep it."

"If it's all the same to you, Peggy, I own no plan to reverse Stephen's trust in his younger brother. I must honor himself," James said, looking at Peggy, "Stephen told me if anything ever happened to him, I am to give this to you … for the boys' welfare."

Peggy shook her head. "You have a sickness upon you. You have no reason to be ashamed of what I offer you. The money is yours."

"Ginger and I have all the money we need, Peggy. This is yours. Take it. I've been hanging on longer than I deserve. You're raising the boys on your own. I hear the horses' hooves pulling my hearse closer to our door. With its black plumes waving in the breeze and the voice of Our Divine Lord showing me the way home. Got a mansion for me, He does, Peggy."

With Ginger's help, James removed his covers and sat up. "Ginger and I have been preparing for the day I will be buried alongside Stephen. It's just the two of us here. You can split this apartment in two. We only need a bedroom and a little kitchen. You will get good rent for a space with a window."

"I don't want this visit to be only about business. I need to share a personal issue with you James. Your dear brother was ashamed of his life," Peggy said, "There was something in him I could not reach. It vexes my heart."

"Ginger and I have ears, dearest Peggy. Whatever happened to him had nothing to do with the contents of this box. I understand your hesitation, gathering that this is ill-gotten gains. It is not the rotten money you think it is. Many times Stephen told me he did not know how to properly take care of you. Be assured, you were the only true treasure of his heart. This money he's been putting aside … for you … from the day you got married. He told me it was an insurance policy … for the woman who made his life worthwhile." James said as he handed the box to Peggy.

"What happened to him, James?"

"Listen to me careful now. Some men find the wonder of a woman fade over time. So that man finds another. Stephen never tired of the wonder of you. Not for one moment. He never looked at another woman. You were the world to him. Maybe the drinking got to him. Distorted his mind. Cursed he was by nothing on your part. Irish men have many things going on in their minds."

"It did not have to end this way. Why did he have to kill himself?"

"He did not kill himself," James said, "Minogue did the dirty deed."

"You know that for certain, James?"

"Workers fell off the palisades on a regular basis. Stephen told me these things, but insisted you not hear a word of it, lest you worry unnecessarily. Workers who got too mouthy got pushed by Minogue's thugs."

"Here's what I need to tell you," Peggy said, "Give a good listen. Minogue is the reason you and Ginger need to keep this money. To find a new place to live. He owns every building on this street, except this one. He made a deal with Flaherty. Part of that deal might be an opening for him to get this tenement. He would not hesitate to put you out on the street. He's ruthless. We both know that. With this money, you can find a safer place. You need to be careful, my loving brother."

"No more discussion, Peggy. The contents of this box is yours. I am comforted to know I honored me brother's final wish."

Parenting had become more challenging for Peggy as James and William got older. She made note of the boys' distinct personality differences and shared the information with Emma Kennedy. James was attentive in class. William often fell asleep. James was consistently defiant. William was slow and forgetful. Before she left for the city after Stephen's funeral, Peggy told Emma the boys liked to play board games yet warned her they often fought.

On one rainy afternoon, Mrs. Kennedy sat the boys down in her parlor and introduced them to the game of LIFE. She guessed James would win more games, as he seemed more disciplined and sharper. Yet on this particular afternoon, William got on a hot streak.

Suddenly, Emma heard William shriek. She ran inside the parlor and found William bleeding profusely from the nose. She grabbed a towel, held his head back and began wiping the blood off his face.

"What is going on here?" she demanded.

"He hit me because I'm winning," William said, "He's a sore loser."

"He moved into my square when I wasn't looking," James said, coming within inches of William while Mrs. Kennedy was trying to stop the bleeding.

She nudged James to the side. "Stand over there while I try to undo the damage you've done."

"You're a liar," William said, "You moved it when I wasn't looking. All I did was put it back in the space. You cheated at Life, James. Cheater. Cheater."

"You didn't read the number on the spinner. You put the dial on the wrong square." James said.

"I did it by mistake. Why did you have to hit me?"

"You should've known the rules."

Mrs. Kennedy put the bloody towel on the floor and pinched James's neck. "How would you like it if I hit you and gave you a bloody nose?"

"Why would you? I didn't break any rules," James said, pushing her hand away.

"I didn't know *all* the rules," William cried.

"You see. He just admitted it. He knows how to read. I read the rules. He didn't."

"Why didn't you read the rules out loud before you started? You're two years older than him."

"The rules are if you land in my square, you go to jail," James said, "That's what it says."

William, sobbing, looked up at Mrs. Kennedy. "He's still a cheater. When we started the game, he put me in the suicide square with a noose around my neck. Hanging from a tree."

"That was a joke," James said.

"That's cruel, James. And you know it. What you did is not a joke. Apologize to your little brother."

"I will not. There is nothing to apologize for."

"Do you think this is something your mother wants to hear?"

"If she believes in justice, she will side with me. William should go to a real jail," James said, pointing down the street in the direction of the prison.

The good priest

Although the church tower was yet to be constructed, plans were finalized to transport the 3000-pound bell on a truck drawn by a team of eight horses from the Sing Sing railway station to the site of St. Paul's Roman Catholic Church. Rain or shine, the date for the inaugural ringing was set; St. Patrick's Day, March 17, 1887. The giant bell would be paraded on a route that included every church in town until it arrived at St. Paul's. Adult males in the parish were asked to help transport the bell.

The day arrived as townsfolk came in large numbers from their workplaces and their homes. St. Paul's Pastor, Father Patrick J. Walsh rang the bell at precisely 2:30 p.m. He stood on a crate to greet local dignitaries, townsfolk, and school children. Peggy and her sons stood with other parents and children. A band played patriotic songs, familiar religious hymns, and Irish melodies. Cups of apple cider and shortbread cakes were passed around by church volunteers. Everyone was invited to get a closer look at the markings on the bell made by the Maneely Company in West Troy. Visible on one side of the bell were the raised letters 'St. Paul's Church Sing Sing, N.Y. 1887'. However, it was the simple "St. Patrick" stamping on the inside of the rim that drew the most interest and created the greatest source of pride.

Following the ceremony, Father Walsh worked his way through the crowd, shaking hands, giving hugs, and patting children's heads. He approached Peggy, flanked by James standing off to the side, and William, clinging to her dress.

"Good morning. I don't believe we've met," the priest said, extending his hand, "My name is Patrick Walsh."

"Good morning, Father. I'm Peggy Callaghan. Very lovely ceremony it was," Peggy said, accepting his hand, "You'll have to excuse me, though. I need to get back to work."

Father Walsh held her hand. "I won't keep you but a moment, Mrs. Callaghan. I wonder if you could spare a bit of time some day. I'd like to tell you about the parochial school we plan to build."

The priest released her hand, softly patted William's head, and nodded at James. "To give all the children in the parish a head start, we're opening up a voluntary weekly religious education class for them … I think it would be a blessing for your boys to get a Catholic education at St. Paul's. They won't get any of that in the public school. I'd be happy to show you the plans after church on Sunday."

"To tell you the truth, Father, I don't know if we'll be able to make it to church this week."

"I'd be more than happy to make a house call if that is more convenient. Is there any particular time that is good for you? I promise not to overstay my welcome. Is Saturday a possibility? I have Confessions in the afternoon but am free all morning."

"All right then. I imagine I could give you some time this Saturday," Peggy said, "How about eleven? We live on Dale. Emma Kennedy's house, near Glen."

"Eleven it is, then," Father Walsh said.

"There'll be a pot of tea and some cakes waiting for you," Peggy answered.

Peggy occupied the corner bedroom on the second floor of the two-story frame house. James and William shared a room, cater-cornered to their mother's. Three other rooms in the house were rented to boarders. On Saturday morning, Peggy helped set the table with Emma's best china, silverware, lace doilies and linen napkins.

When Father Walsh arrived, Emma escorted him into the front parlor. He settled in a corner chair. He went to push the footstool out of the way, but Mrs. Kennedy protested, "Father, put your tired feet up there and give them a rest."

The priest crisscrossed his legs on the ottoman. Emma noticed holes in both soles. "The Sodality of Our Lady will be getting you a new pair very soon."

Father Walsh planted both feet on the floor. "No need for that Emma. I have time to shop now that the bell is here."

"You must stop giving all your money to the poor. We have a mission for that. May I remind you, not everyone who knocks on your door is poor. There are some people take advantage of your good nature, Father."

"It's not up to me to judge."

"Father, you have to learn how to say no."

Emma stayed long enough to exchange a few more pleasantries, then headed upstairs. Peggy entered the parlor and invited the priest to join her at the dining room table.

"You want to ask me to join the church, don't you? Well, let me put your mind at ease," Peggy said, "I will join St. Paul's and I will send my sons to your new school. I will attend Mass in body only, yet my sons will see enough of a good example in their mother. They will see a Catholic woman who spends every waking hour doing the work of Jesus Christ. A servant who embraces the poor unfortunates living in the streets."

Peggy poured tea and pushed a plate of scones closer to Father Walsh. "I share this with you, and you only. After you turn your back to the congregation during Sunday Mass and take the Holy Eucharist out of the tabernacle, then turn around muttering Latin words, with your hands held high grasping the wafer embossed with a cross, you will see me with my sons, heads bowed all holy and devout. You will see a member of the ladies' sodality, a fervent frequenter of novenas to the Blessed Virgin. But you will know that I have less regard for you than I do for the fishmonger on Main Street who cheats me by twenty cents a pound for a filet of cod. For you will be looking at a skeptic who believes in nothing about church or religion. Yet I believe I am a spiritual person who might not have a holy book to quote, a cross or shrine to idolize, but who lives each day doing for the poor, the homeless, and the widowed while your most self-righteous parishioners march up the center aisle every Sunday bearing the gifts of the Eucharist, hosting malignant unrepentant sinfulness in their rotting hearts and souls. If you're okay with that father, I give you my sons to take under your wing to teach and nurture with your gentle, pastoral care."

Father Walsh took a bite out of the scone, "These are delicious. Did you make them? Or Emma?"

"I did," Peggy said, sipping her tea, "Don't you have any kind of comment about what I just said?"

Father Walsh placed the scone on his plate. "Oh, I'm sorry. Yes, I accept the terms you presented. And the challenge, Mrs. Callaghan. I welcome you, James, and William to St. Paul's."

"Finish that one and have some more," Peggy said, pushing the tray closer.

"Thank you no," Father said, patting his stomach, "I only recently had to punch another notch into my belt."

"I'll see you at Mass tomorrow. With the boys," she said, opening the front door.

"Will you permit me to say one more thing, Mrs. Callaghan?"

"Sure."

"If you ever feel burdened or just need someone to talk to … not confession … simply someone willing to lend a listening ear. Without judgment, mind you. I am available day or night. Don't hesitate to let me know."

"Must I be a parishioner?"

"Not at all. I'm sure Emma will tell you moments after I leave about many non-parishioners finding a home at St. Paul's," he said, reaching for the door handle, "The most important thing I learned at Seminary is this. I might have been assigned to a parish church, but God sends priests like me into the world. Into your world, for example. If that is where I can be of some help that is where I will go, obedient to His will. Serving Him by listening to you. I am here for you, Mrs. Callaghan. Whenever you need me. I neither judge nor accuse. That is God's domain."

Peggy held the door open for him, "Thank you for your time. You are everything Emma said you are."

Peggy did attend Sunday Mass faithfully as promised, at first in body but not in spirit. After a short time, she immersed herself in the good work of the church with the poor, the hurting, the lonely, working alongside parishioners she once despised. In the process, her spirit opened fully. Father Walsh kept to his promise and made his listening ear attentive to her need to talk or rant about the failings of everyone and everything except herself.

The day of trust arrived when she opened up to him, not in the confessional but at the dining room table. Over a pot of tea and his favorite scones, she spoke about the painful parting with Stephen "I never once cried, Father. Not one tear. He died a horrible death, and I did not bother to show any emotion whatsoever. I was dead inside."

"Do you still feel that way now?" Father asked.

"I'm not sure."

"What happened?"

"Something went wrong with *me*. I could not bring myself to scream or wail or … find any feeling whatsoever. That's not normal," Peggy said.

"Maybe you're delaying the grieving process," Father said, sipping his tea, "Did you love Stephen?"

"I did … at first. Then he changed."

"Not for the better I imagine," Father Walsh said, "Unfortunately that happens with some people."

"I feel responsible. He became such a weak man, in my opinion. I could not stand to see it. I wanted him to be strong. To hold me up. Not me doing all the lifting. Just when he was rising as a man, he let himself fall. For what?" Peggy said, folding her napkin so the corners matched precisely.

Father Walsh held out his hand. Peggy grasped it and said, "Will it always be like this? Will I ever be able to grieve like a normal person?'

"Give yourself some time and give yourself some credit. With every death of a close one, there is always unfinished business. No one has all the answers. Don't be so hard on yourself."

"But you cannot tell me how I behaved is normal, can you?"

"I imagine for strong people like yourself, it is hard to tolerate weakness in others. Especially those you love going about the business of self-destruction. You say Stephen changed, but he might have had those tendencies all along that had nothing to do with you," Father said, releasing her hand, reaching for another scone, "We can talk some more whenever you feel up to it. *And* try not to think you have to be normal. We all handle situations differently. The longer I live, the less I can figure out what normal is."

Over tea, Peggy let Mrs. Kennedy know she was making progress in her conversations with Father Walsh. "You know Emma, after I divulged more details about the situation with Stephen, he didn't let me off the hook about my share in the relationship."

"He has a certain way about him, doesn't he? Hitting the mark on the truth without making you feel guilty," Emma said.

"It's taken awhile but I'm beginning to sense some healing. Some measure of peace for my soul."

"He's helped many people in this parish, Peggy, myself included. I'm glad you warmed up to him."

"With his help, I'm learning how to grieve. Not just over the loss of Stephen, but I'm reaching back to Ma and Da. And the hardest of all, my dear little sister Colleen. Never did one tear flow from my eyes, Emma. Not until now. And now all the tears are flowing all at once. I cry so much each night I fear I must be waking up the whole household. I thought it was strength that held the tears back. I'm learning that real strength has vulnerability as its companion. I can't say this insight came from Father Walsh, but it came through him. It's allowed me to renew my faith in God, and the church."

All was going well with Peggy Callaghan and her sons until one Sunday in 1888 when she sat next to Emma Kennedy at the 10 a.m. Sunday Mass, while James and William were serving as acolytes that day.

Moments after, the parishioners heard Father Walsh say the words from the pulpit, "Do not let your hearts be troubled … I am going away, but …" midway through his homily based on the Gospel of John, Chapter 14, the impact of what he was preaching began to sink in. The awareness of it created an audible gasp throughout the sanctuary. Many parishioners had heard variations on the same theme about Jesus's parting words to his disciples but when it was revealed that the arc of the message shifted dramatically toward the revelation of the beloved priest's own imminent departure, the murmurs, moans, and sniffling became contagious. His work was done here he said. Ten years he pastored the church and led the flock: rebuilding the church; erecting a tower; the initial hoisting the 'St. Paul's bell that now resounds gloriously throughout the entire Sing Sing community every morning; and the opening of the St. Paul's parochial school in a little red schoolhouse with four classrooms, two up and two down, taught by the Sisters of Charity.

Many people wept openly. Each parishioner had a personal story with Father Walsh, but no one was affected more profoundly than Peggy. She listened when he encouraged everyone to lift each other up, to not be saddened, for a new shepherd would be arriving in a few weeks to take his place.

What distinguished the depth of Peggy's despair was the personal story Father Walsh shared which pierced her heart. The priest spoke passionately about several poignant events that took place in his life but none more transformative than when he landed on a beach in Grosse Point Isle after a long journey from his native Ireland, an eight-week passage by ship cursed with disease, hardship, and death. He told the crowded church how he prayed for a young girl who had crossed the same ocean in a coffin ship. When she was about to give up, he prayed more fervently. Saw her leave the dead body of her younger sister under a tree. As a fifteen-year-old lad, he placed this young girl upon his back and trudged to the clinic where she was placed in quarantine. It was that visit with God, he said, where he himself had considered giving up, but knew he had to save the girl. He underestimated the power of prayer until that very moment, believing that God brought the two of them together for His eternal glory. It was that experience, he told the congregation, that gave him the unmistakable sign for his vocation. That God Himself ordained him to study for the priesthood. God sent me on that ship. God landed me on that beach. God spoke to me through that young girl. God saved both of us that very day.

Peggy clawed the top of the wood pew in front of her, rocked back and forth, and collapsed in Emma's arms. Immediately after the Mass, Emma escorted Peggy into the sacristy. With bowed heads, James and William received Father Walsh's blessing, removed their cassocks and surplices, and followed Mrs. Kennedy into the sanctuary, leaving Peggy alone with her Pastor.

Peggy held her hands together in prayer, pleading before him on her knees, weeping. Father Walsh tried to lift her, but she was dead weight. She threw her head back and said, "I never knew your name then! Did you know it was me?"

"Only recently, Peggy. Emma told me what she knew. How our lives are intertwined. What a beautiful tapestry. It was God who brought us together when we were so young. And it is now God who reunites us. What a beautiful woman you have become."

"Reunited? You are leaving me," Peggy said, unable to control her tears, "That is so cruel. Please stay here with me. Never in my life have I needed anyone as I need you right now!"

"The archbishop has other plans for me, Peggy. Another church needs fixing up. Another school has to be built. We will always stay in touch," Father said, as he helped Peggy to her feet.

"Where are you going?"

"To a church only a few states away. Not out of reach," Father said, "Oh, how you've grown in your faith. I am so proud of you for never giving up. As brave as St. Patrick I have to say."

"You saved me twice, Father," Peggy said, "Twice! You carried me on your back when all I wanted to do was die. Then you taught me how to live again. To *want* to live. What am I going to do without you? Are you a man or an angel? Tell me, please."

"I am no more an angel than Emma Kennedy who invested more of her life in you than I did to help you survive. You are going to carry others on your back. You have your sons to love and to nurture. To help them grow in their faith," Father Walsh said, as he walked with her into the sanctuary.

Before he attended to other parishioners waiting in the narthex, Father Walsh offered God's blessings upon the lives of Emma, Peggy, James, and William.

"You are a good priest, Patrick J. Walsh," Emma said, "A very good priest. We will never forget you. Don't you dare leave before stopping by for a box of Peggy's scones."

Emma followed Peggy and the boys as they descended the large stone steps. When they reached street level, Peggy turned, and ran back inside the church. She came up behind Father Walsh as he stood before the altar of St. Paul, his hands folded in prayer. Her big blue eyes reddened with tears. Peggy cupped her hands over his and said, "No man has ever touched me as intimately as you. My body remembers being carried on your back. My soul remembers your righteous prayers. God bless you, Father. God bless you."

She rushed back outside, put her arms around her sons, took a deep breath and headed home.

Old Sparky

"Where is it?"

The guard turned around. "Who said that?"

James Callaghan stepped in front of his classmates "I did. And *you* know what I'm talking about."

The guard kept walking.

"Where is Old Sparky? We want to see Old Sparky!" James said, strutting like a rooster, trailing the keeper.

The High School field trip to the prison is organized by school officials each year to scare the seniors, to show them the grim consequences of living a life of crime. James liked the place. He interacted with the warden, the keepers, even some of the 'model' prisoners. After he asked about 'Old Sparky' the third time, the keeper pulled James out of the line, knowing full well he was talking about the prison's notorious electric chair. The keeper asked him if he was tired, did he need a chair to sit on, then promised he'd invite him back the next time 'Old Sparky' was all hooked up and ready for the deep fry.

The field trip represented an epiphany for James. He found his calling, deciding he wanted to be a keeper at Sing Sing Prison. He returned to the prison two weeks later to apply for their summer internship program. He was accepted into the Sing Sing Correctional Facility volunteer program to begin one week after receiving his high school diploma.

The yearbook entry for James P. Callaghan noted his yearly participation in the school's annual SONGfest. James had a pleasant tenor voice, not exceptional, yet good enough to sing in the chorus. He was never enthusiastic about the tedium of SONGfest rehearsals until one afternoon, standing high up on the risers, he heard the voice of an angel. He could barely see the top of her head. The Choir Director had selected a diminutive first year student to sing a solo part. The girl's sweet voice, an ethereal tone floating on air, wafted up to the top row where he stood, and lingered for several heartfelt moments in the hollows of the empty auditorium. The sound of her voice acted as an invisible aural magnet. The girl's singing drew James in like a siren call.

Rushing down to catch sight of her following the rehearsal, James found it hard to believe that such a big voice could be coaxed out of a tiny Irish wisp of a girl named Nellie Murphy. For several rehearsals, he tried to get close to her, memorizing beforehand what he would say to compliment her richly textured soprano voice. He waited for the right moment to approach when she was alone, but Nellie, painfully shy, stayed behind the shield of her girlfriends.

James got his moment after the final performance at SONGfest when the Choir Director presented Nellie with a bouquet of roses. James stepped forward, anointing her the Irish nightingale, and appointing himself president of her fan club.

Before the academic year ended, James invited Nellie to the sweet shoppe. Although she was impressed that a senior took an interest in her, she firmly said no. Determined, James asked if he could walk her home after school. She answered no. Her mother would not approve, claiming she is too young. Besides, she was busy with singing and step dancing lessons.

Just days before the close of the school year, James stopped Nellie in the hallway and said, "How can I get to know you better?"

"By winning over my mother."

"I want to date you, not your mother. Could you put in a good word for me so we can set things up in advance when I ask for your hand."

"You're a bold one."

"You're a sweet little bird. I want to hold you in my hands and listen to you sing all day. I want to run my fingers through your lovely hair," James said, blocking her.

"Aren't you a sweet talker," Nellie said, escaping under his outstretched arm, "I have a class and so do you."

"I'm not giving up on you."

"When you hold this little bird in your hands, will you let her fly away?"

"Never. I will take care of you. I will guard you with my life."

"Well, don't give up trying. You never know."

"You sure play hard to get."

After persisting for several weeks, James got to take Nellie to the sweet shoppe. They sat side by side at the counter sharing a ginger beer float. As she sipped on her straw, he leaned over, whiffing her hair. With his starstruck eyes still closed, he said, "I met the most beautiful girl in Westchester County, maybe in all of New York State, who is so pretty, delicate, so light and bright, and has the voice of an angel and ..."

"Has wisdom, discernment ..." Nellie said.

"Big words for a frosh."

"Wisdom to know I can never be too sure when listening to an Irish smooth-talker."

"And a handsome one."

"Well, don't you have confidence."

"I need to hear it from somebody."

After several secret dates over the summer, James took it upon himself to pay a call on the Murphy household, where Nellie lived with her mother and cousins in Mrs. McGuire's boarding house on Elizabeth Street. In an effort to build up his courage, he walked around town, trying to memorize the magic words that would sway her mother.

As he passed the Water Street Fanning Wire Company, the skies opened up and drenched him down to his underwear. Disoriented, he roamed the streets until he turned the corner of Clinton Avenue and knew he was close. He walked down Tompkins and headed toward Elizabeth.

James knocked on the front door. Mrs. McGuire stuck her head out of the second-floor window above the portico.

"Who's there?" Mrs. McGuire said, "And why are you so daft to be out in this rain?"

"James Callaghan, Mrs. McGuire. Respectfully so."

"Step into the street so I can see ya."

"It's pouring buckets, Mrs. McGuire. I'm quite wet already."

"So, come back on a sunny day, then," she said, slamming the window shut.

James knocked on the door again, quickly stepping into the street.

Mrs. McGuire opened the window and looked at James.

"I'm calling on the Murphy Miss," James said.

"Well, aren't you original. I doubt she'd be interested in a drenched fool like you. There are four Murphy misses up here. All live in the same room," Mrs. McGuire said, "Which one is of interest to you."

"The tiny one named Nellie is my particular interest. The one who sings like a nightingale, if you catch my drift."

"Oh, her. She's taking dance lessons with her cousins at the moment and not available," Mrs. McGuire said.

"Tell her I know how to dance, and *I* could teach her myself."

"You must be Irish, are ya? Anyhow, your little nightingale is with her mother."

"Tell'em both to come to the window so they can watch me dance. They won't be disappointed. My dad taught me. He's right off the boat from Tipperary."

Mary Murphy and daughter Nellie stood behind Mrs. McGuire, looking at James doing an Irish jig in the street. They thought his form was off a bit but gave him high grades for gumption.

Mrs. McGuire put a mat on the floor, opened the door and handed him a towel. Mrs. Murphy came down the stairs to have a closer look.

"If I wore a hat I would tip it to you, Ma'am," James said.

"You should see yourself in a mirror," Mrs. Murphy said, "State your business, young man."

"I got a promotion and earn a good salary with room for advancement."

"You're a volunteer in the prison office, helping the clerks file papers. You exaggerate like every other Irishman I know. Why do you men always have to make little things big things? Come back when you have a real job, young man."

"As the eldest son, I will one day have ownership of a nice house on Cherry Street in Manhattan. My brother William quit school and lives there now, taking up space after my dear old Uncle died. But he won't live there long. He's just holding the fort until I move in with my bride."

"And who would that be?"

"Your lovely daughter Nellie ... and you ... if you can stand to live with us. There's plenty of room."

"That's silly talk. What are you really after, Callaghan?"

"I would like to court your daughter."

"You want to marry my daughter?"

"I do and I will."

"She's too young."

"I can wait."

"You'll be waiting a long time, James Callaghan."

"When can Nellie and I start dating?"

"We'll let you know."

"When will that be?"

"When she's old enough," Mrs. Murphy said.

James left, fully aware that he did not get a yes. Although more importantly, he did not get a no.

When he was clear out of sight, Nellie said to her mother, "Oh Mom, isn't he handsome?"

"Yes … more so after he dried off."

"Oh Mom, isn't he funny?"

"That he is."

"Oh Mom, isn't he a good sport?"

"For certain."

"Oh Mom, I think I want to marry him."

"You can't marry that wet rag of a man. Aside from his good looks and his ability to put on a good show, you know nothing about him."

"But how will I get to know him unless you give me permission to date him?" Nellie said.

"There's a whole world out there, Nellie. You're very young. Right now, concentrate on your studies, your singing, and dancing. After a while, you'll find there are many fine young men who'll take an interest in you. The novelty of James Callaghan might wear off over time."

Nellie Murphy took her mother's advice. She had numerous suitors during the years following her graduation from High School.

James Callaghan immersed himself in his work as a Prison Keeper. He dated several different ladies on occasion but kept a soft spot in his heart for the Irish nightingale.

The Pilgrimage

James repeated the same graphic stories each night at dinnertime, not sparing any grim details about his work as Prison Keeper. Emma excused herself from the table. She did not need to hear ever again about the state electrician's step-by-step preparations for affixing the black leather straps, helmet, brine-soaked sponges, mask, and electrodes to the shrieking, wailing prisoner. He described the precise manipulation of the dials and switchboard levers, upping the voltage until the prisoner's body jerked forward, strained against the straps, smoke rising from head and leg, culminating in the scent of burnt flesh. He relished telling the whole grim story up to and including the doctor's pronouncement that the poor soul is dead.

Peggy was deeply concerned that James spoke in the same dispassionate tone about the splendid views of the Hudson River from Guard Tower No. 7, as he did about his observations of fresh fingernail grooves on Old Sparky's armrest etched by the latest anguished, convulsing electrocuted prisoner. When Peggy had finally heard enough, she pushed back her chair and told James it was time for him to find new living quarters. One week later, James packed his bags and rented an apartment two blocks from the prison. Emma and Peggy were now the sole occupants of the Kennedy home. The boarders were gone, and William had relocated to 347 Cherry Street three years earlier. He collected the tenants' rents and worked as a union organizer in the building trades.

"Do you think I was too hard on James, Emma? Throwing him out on the street like that?" Peggy said.

"There you go again with Irish Catholic guilt. He's a grown man. He can afford to be out from under mother's wing. Besides, he's courting that Murphy girl. He'll be free to ..."

"I don't know about her," Peggy said.

"What do you mean?"

"She's a wee bit soft. He needs a woman who can stand up to him. It's a difficult place where he works. I dread that he might become like the other men there ... I understand they have to be tough ... but I hear most are quite cruel."

"Even so," Emma said, "Not all of them take the job home with them."

Remembering a talk once given before the St. Paul's Sodality by Father Walsh about making a difference for Christ in this world, especially in one's own community, Emma and Peggy discussed transforming the virtually empty house into a mission. They wanted to make it a place of refuge for families that had to travel long distances to visit their loved ones incarcerated at Sing Sing.

After several attempts, Emma Kennedy secured an appointment with the warden. She had to convince him she was not there as a do-gooder social activist campaigning for prison reform. It was no secret he had his fill of those crusaders. As a fellow St. Paul's parishioner, she explained that she simply wanted to offer free lodging and meals for visiting spouses and their children. Once convinced of Emma's good intentions, the warden let the prisoners know about her offer and left it up to them to notify their families.

The Kennedy House had full occupancy year-round. The majority of visits lasted a few days, but provision was made for longer stays for families of prisoners on death row. Emma, Peggy, and other sodality volunteers kept a candlelight vigil for those distraught families on the evenings Old Sparky's lever got pulled.

As the Kennedy House mission grew, free clothing and laundry services were added. Word spread. More volunteers stepped forward. Peggy took charge of an ambitious fund-raising campaign, going door-to-door and writing to influential friends in New York City. Newspapers picked up the story. Despite significant backlash from local residents, wary about expansion of the prison's existing notoriety, donations poured in from the village and surrounding communities.

When the house behind Emma's became available, it was purchased and renovated, creating additional living space for destitute families. Paid staff was added when a nearby vacant factory was purchased. The commercial property was converted to accommodate a soup kitchen, offices and storage rooms for donated furniture and appliances. Mrs. Kennedy and Mrs. Callaghan became known in the community as Mother Emma and Sister Peggy.

Peggy and Emma corresponded regularly with Father Walsh, who praised their missionary work. His most recent letter informed them about an upcoming three-week Pilgrimage to the Holy Land, sponsored by his parish in Scranton, Pennsylvania. He hoped they could join him and the other pilgrims. Father challenged them to imagine the spiritual rewards gained doing the Stations of the Cross, not in St, Paul's, but along the *Via Dolorosa*, praying and walking humbly in the same steps Jesus Christ journeyed on his path from Jerusalem to Calvary, where he was tortured, sentenced, crucified, died, and was buried.

"It is a trip of holiness," Father Walsh wrote, "Where you will encounter God Himself."

"We must go," Peggy said.

"I agree," Emma said, "I would crawl on my hands and knees to follow the Way of Sorrows. We must buy Father new shoes. The only thing is …"

"The Mission will thrive and be grander when we return," Peggy said, "We have more than our share of volunteers and staff. Promise me you will rest before we sail."

Emma was closing in on eighty years of age. During the first few weeks leading up to the Pilgrimage, she agreed to conserve her strength. Yet Emma could not remain idle. One morning, while Peggy worked in another building, a volunteer saw Mrs. Kennedy at the top of the stairs holding a basket of laundry, piled high. The volunteer offered to help but was shooed away. As Emma began her descent, the tail of one sheet got caught under her slipper. Mother Emma tumbled down the thirteen steps, breaking her right hip and banging her head on the hardwood floor.

She was transported to St. Francis Hospital, unconscious and remained comatose for two weeks, with a tracheal intubation. Peggy visited every day. She prayed openly, read many Psalms, and quoted Bible passages about Jesus's love. Mother Emma never opened her eyes.

On the morning of the fifteenth visit, Peggy said, "Emma, have you heard any of my prayers about Jesus's love for you?" Emma opened her eyes at the sound of Sister Peggy's voice. A momentary distraction from death coaxed scratchy words from Emma's artificial larynx, "I love Jesus, Peggy."

Peggy fell to her knees. A mild breeze seeped into the windowless room. The pale blue walls softened the hospital's harsh sterility. Sweet alyssum and subtle hyacinth scents replaced the room's antiseptic atmosphere. The low murmurs of doctors' voices and the snap of clipboard reports devolved into silence.

"Our pilgrimage will be our mission, and the hope of the downtrodden, Emma," Peggy said.

Checking boxes

Carney rushed to the front of the cabin when he heard a knock. He swung the door open, bolting his large frame forward. He startled the visitor, a diminutive man dressed in suit and tie. The startled visitor backpedaled a few steps, stumbled, and fell to the ground, his clipboard and papers sailing in various directions.

Carney yanked the man to his feet. As he dusted himself off, the man beheld Carney, dressed in tattered coveralls and canvas shirt, a face weathered with craggy features resembling a shriveled russet potato. Carney's head was topped with a nest of grayish brown hair and stray whiskers poking haphazardly out of his deeply dimpled chin. As Carney bent down to help retrieve the scattered papers, the man caught a glimpse of two girls inside the cabin on their hands and knees, crawling behind a large pig.

"Who are you?" Carney said.

"I'm with the New York State Census Bureau," the man said, holding forth his credentials identifying him as Paul Ostrander, NYS 1905 Census Official.

"What's a cents us?"

"A survey. Every five years we identify and tabulate all the state's residents, Mr. Callaghan."

"Jes doin' your job, are ya? Howd'ya find me?"

"You're well known in these parts, sir. I followed the path to your cabin. It's on the map," Ostrander said, reaching into his coat pocket.

"Don't bother with that. I know where I live. I guess other folks in the county are easier to find. Folla me, fella. It'll be more relaxin' in the cabin. Minnie Mae'll make room at the table."

"It's kind of nice right here," Ostrander said, as he propped his clipboard on the fence rail. "If you don't mind, I'll ask a few questions. Do your best to answer them. We'll be done in no time. I'll start with this question: how many people live at One Pine Meadow Brook."

"I dint know we had a number one," Carney said.

"You're the only house on this side of the lake."

"That makes sense. We own the land. It's on our property, all legal 'n such."

"So, how many live in your house?" Mr. Ostrander said.

"Let's see," Carney said, counting on his fingers, "Got a coupla big boys 'n a coupla little girls," Carney said, then called out,

"Hey Minnie Mae, can ya git out here fer a minute?"

Minnie Mae stuck her head out and said, "I'm busy cooking right now. Ask that nice man to join us for lunch."

"She gets kinda cranky when I bother her," Carney said, "Let's see if I can do this myself. I got two sons. Two or three daughters."

"Two or three?"

"I wuz counting Wee Mum. She lives here sometime when she's not in her wigwam. She picked out a husband 'n got a growin' family of her own."

"What are the names and birthdates of your children?"

"Not sure of the exact day Mickey and Patrick wuz born but Minnie Mae'll help you with that after lunch. She's cookin' up somethin' good."

"The two daughters who live here ... did I see them inside the cabin?" Mr. Ostrander said.

"Twins. Consuela and Eleanor."

"How are you spelling Consuela?" Mr. Ostrander said.

"We call her Swell. Minnie'll give yer both spellins' when she's done cookin'. Swell's a sweet little girl. Eleanor's a wildcat. I might ask my friend Reverend Jeremiah Dooze to baptize her agin. It dint work the first time."

"Let me ask you about your wife ... Minnie Mae?"

"Okay, now we're talkin'. 'Nother man at the mill had serious interest in her but she chooses me. There wuz others too. A smelter, a miner 'n a logger. I wuz lucky she wuz attracted to a mountain man. She splained the difference 'tween me 'n them. They're varmits. I ain't droppin' my draws for none of them, she sez. She tells me that I wuz an animal too. More the domestic kind, like a dog, a cat, or a pig."

Mr. Ostrander positioned his pencil. "What is your nationality?"

"Chinese."

"Callaghan sounds like an Irish name," Mr. Ostrander said.

"We converted. That's a fact. Write it down. Might've bin Irish years ago. It wuz splained by Uncle James befer he git put in the ground. His grave's over yonder, 'neath the big red maple. Next to my dad. Anyhow, he sez all sorts of folks hated the Irish. So, we might as well be Chinese. Minnie Mae 'n I decided to make it official. Put it down on yer chart there," Carney said, stabbing the form with his forefinger.

Minnie Mae called, "Time for lunch."

"What are *you*?" Carney said to the census taker.

"What do you mean?"

"Irish? Franch? Italian?"

"Jewish."

"I knew Jewish people when I wuz a youngin' down on Cherry Street," Carney said, "All their names ended in stein or berg. Are you sure you're ..."

"I'm half …"

"Don't care if you're half, whole, or quarter. Makes no difference. I got a half too. My oldest daughter. Half-breed. She calls me Papa Chief cuz that's what I am to Wee Mum. She helped my dad 'n his wife Miss Peggy with one of my little brothers when he wuz a baby. It's an Irish thing when ya say wee. I find out Injins don't say *I* or *mine*. Only say *we*. We're kinda connected I guess, the Irish 'n Injins. Gettin' back ta the subject, they rescued Wee Mum from a bad criminal. By the way, I find you to be a very interesting man."

"I don't know how you find me interesting. I really haven't said very much."

"Let me ask you somethin'. Think you 'n I could be friends?" Carney said, "Do ya live around here?"

"Not even close."

"Not even close ta livin' around here? Or not even close ta bein' my friend?"

"I'm here on official business. I imagine you don't meet many strangers in the middle of the woods."

"I've bin out there in the world. Can I call you Mr. Os … Ostr…?

"Call me Paul."

"Settled. Call me Carney. No more Mr. Callaghan stuff. No one calls me that."

"I still have a job to do," Paul said.

"I 'preciate that. Fer certin'. Ask yer questions. I gotta tell ya it's much better here in the woods. You'll live longer. Fresh air. Live off the land. Git to know the birds 'n the animals. Partridges all over the place. Wild rabbits. Lakes 'n streams 'n ponds full of perch 'n pickerel. You like ta fish? Jes listenin' ta the sounds of the rushin' streams 'n brooks. Bleatin' goats. Hee hawin' donkey. Kicked me so hard one day give me a hole in my chest. I wuz madder 'n hell fer a while but we's friends now, the bastard. Oinkin' pigs. Lowin' cattle. You should consider movin' here. We gotta go in for lunch soon, else Minnie Mae's gonna be mad as hell," Carney said, placing his huge hand on Paul's shoulder.

"I don't know if I ..."

"You gotta. That's all there is to it. Once ya taste her soup, ya'll wanna come back fer supper."

"Well, I ..."

"Tell me, Paul, think ya might want to git baptized?"

"I'm Jewish, Carney. We don't get baptized. We get something else done."

"Even if you're half ..."

"The one half who mostly raised me is of the Jewish faith."

"I know what that somethin' else is," Carney said, placing both hands on his crotch, "OUCH! Well, I'm not gonna pry anymore but whatever the other half is that don't mind ya getting baptized, it could change ya."

"I'm still working on staying for lunch, Carney. I have to earn my pay."

Carney patted Paul's back. "Scuse me a minute. I'm gonna tell Minnie Mae to hold off lunch fer a little longer so ya can do yer job, I'll be right back."

Paul saw something odd in the field beyond the potato patch. He walked about fifty yards along the fence and waited there until Carney caught up to him.

"I got good news," Carney said to Paul who was leaning over the fence, staring at a fixed point, "Once I told Minnie Mae you'd have lunch with us, she sez she dint mind feedin' the kids first 'n chase 'em out of the house once you're ready. She likes company. She asked me to find out if there's anything you can't eat, 'cuz you're Jewish."

"I'll eat anything."

"Minnie Mae told me to stop scarin' ya wit baptizin' talk."

"She's a wise woman, Carney."

"That's what Rev. Dooze tells me too. He splained about the Israels 'n how we go way back together 'n Jesus wuz a Jew 'n all. He warned me 'bout tryin' to force Baptism on folk. Ya gotta have a talk first. He tells me the word conversion is inside the word conversation. He sez the best thing I could do is act like a Christian 'n then maybe people would want ta folla me. I tells him I hope not 'cuz I got some big sins in my history. He tells me they's ancient history 'cuz if I repent they's all gone. A sin I'm working on right now is not stranglin' the next govmint person comes knockin' on my door. I thought at first you wuz a govmint guy. But you sez New York State 'n that ain't the fedril govmint. Last fedril guy come here I tells him to git 'cuz they's plannin' to relocate us, knock down my cabin, barn 'n sheds 'n take my homestead away. Plans fer a park or some shit like that. Someone's gonna die before I let that happen. I got a deed. Rev. Dooze advises me to control my anger 'cuz I'm a Christian now 'n gotta act like one. I sez to Rev. Dooze sorry I cussed. Oh, I hear that kind of talk at the carpentry shop he sez. I tell him I worked at ironworks once 'n heard some choice words spoken all the time. Some new ones too I dint know befer … what the hell are ya staring at, Paul?"

Paul pointed to several crosses inside a fenced-in area. Carney stood behind him and looked. "Looks like another cemetery," Paul said.

"That wuz the original tater patch. You census folks don't count dead people, do ya?"

"Only the living," Paul said, "Why do you ask?"

"Some years ago the rain comes down heavy 'n some body parts popped up ta the surface. I tell Rev. Dooze 'bout the bones 'n you know what he did – a mass funeral fer the whole lot of 'em. That's why the whole bunch of crosses is there. I tells him my Uncle James suspected who 'n what wuz buried there but he never wanted ta talk about it much 'n never checked it out. I think jes parts of people are buried. Uncle mighta known more details – Minnie Mae 'n me think he git sick from the fumes or somethin' – anyhow I'm healthier than he ever wuz, 'cuz fumes dint bother me none. From what I unnerstand, there's a whole lot of bad people buried on these grounds 'n they wuz buried by badder people. Have an idea most of 'em never believe in Jesus on account of their behavior. I imagine the folks in there wuz not even sick when they died. Rev. Dooze buried them proper jes in case, both of us tryin' to figure out which head goes with which leg or other part. He's a very educated man 'n prayed some really nice words over their bones or whatever's left of them. Never hurt our tater crop though, 'cuz we relocated it. We 'n the Injins live off that crop as well as corn 'n we hunt deer 'n rabbit. That's why my boys is so big."

"Your uncle owned this land before you?"

"Never outright. My dad inherited it from that big shot Flaherty fella who he worked fer. When dad died his widow, my step-mom Miss Peggy, git it 'n signed it over ta me. Uncle James tells me when deliveries of compost wuz comin' ta jes let the men work 'n don't bother 'em. All he knew wuz what he wuz told when another load of eggshells 'n orange rinds 'n such were on the way. My uncle told me the men deliverin' compost would do all the diggin'. As it turns out all that food stuff wuz only code words. Compost dint do any good. Buried it too deep. Soil wuzn't worth shit when he wuz alive."

"They should declare this an official archeological site," Paul said.

"They must've been dumb cuz they dug too deep fer the taters 'n not deep nuff that's good for human remains. They made fumes from rottin' corpses. I don't know 'n Minnie Mae tells me she dint wanna know neither."

A cream-colored dove landed on Carney's shoulder as he spoke about the graves.

"I didn't know there were pigeons in the woods. I always thought they were a city bird," Paul said.

Carney held up his hand. The dove perched on his index finger. "When my uncle wuz buried Miss Peggy brought a few doves in a crate. Wanted ta release 'em durin' the ceremony. With the rosary 'n injins dancin' Rev. Dooze gits a little distracted 'n forgets 'bout the birds. Anyhow, the doves stayed behind 'n got fat 'n propagated. Ever now 'n then, a hawk comes down 'n picks off the biggest one. That's nature. Anyhow, this here one's my favorite. I put him on a diet."

"So, the other spot is like a family burial ground?"

"Uncle James buried next ta dad. He coulda been buried in a Catholic cemetery but got mad when they wouldn't allow that fer my dad. We started the family plot 'n kept it separate from those others."

"Carney, I know you must be really hungry by now, but I have a few more questions to ask."

"What do ya wanna know?"

Paul held up his clipboard and pointed to the words along the top of the form. "This is the word OCCUPATION. This is the word, EDUCATION. Here is EMPLOYMENT. INCOME, and so on. I have to fill in the boxes for each member of your family. Are you ready?"

"Shoot."

"I start with head of the household. What do you do for a living and how much did you earn this past year?"

"Well, I done a lot of jobs in my day. Right now, I git a few hens 'n we sell some eggs. Last year I made five dollars."

"The whole year?"

"Yep. Five dollars. Write it down."

"I'll put you down as a farmer."

"Fair enough. I don't feed any livestock. I don't harvest hay. I don't raise cattle. Not hogs neither except Sammy. We have some egg-laying chickens 'n every now 'n then I get a pair of matin' pheasants. I don't butcher or sell meat. We have a few goats who squirt some nice milk. Our donkey ain't worth his hee-haw. Too old ta pull a cart. Mostly, I grow taters but don't sell them. Whatever's left over from the family I give to neighbors."

"Neighbors? Paul said.

"Yeah. The Injins."

"That's not my department. Next category. EDUCATION. How far did each of you get to in school?"

"None fer me. Jes Minnie Mae. She'll tell ya 'bout herself later. Mickey git as far as the fourth then he git bored. The girls git their schoolin' from their Ma. She teaches 'em but gave up on me. Sez I got zero tention span 'n I'm unlearnable. Rev. Dooze is a little more patient with me."

"You can't read or write?"

"Nope. Rev Dooze teaches from the Bible. He sez he'll teach me ta read. I tell him a lot of people tried but no success, so he comes by every so often 'n jes read to me. I'm tellin' ya he must've read that book backwards 'n forwards ten times or more. He's a special man, very kind 'n a damn good carpenter too, jes like Jesus," Carney said, bowing his head at the mention of Jesus's name, "Rev. Dooze wears same pair of carpenter coveralls fer all the time we know him. Minnie Mae went to Sloatsburg 'n bought him a new pair. We give it ta him at Christmas. I thought he wuz gonna cry, he wuz so touched. Listen, I'm starvin 'n ya must be too. Let's go inside so we can talk some more."

As they walked toward the cabin, Carney said, "I'm not criticizin' yer work, Paul. Ya have a job ta do that I don't fully unnerstand. But ya sez the Injins're not yer department. I can take ya 'n show ya where they live. It's not on yer map. They don't have numbers on their tepees 'n rock shelters. When ya git some free time'n don't have any boxes to check, Minnie Mae'll make ya a feast, not just soup 'n a sandwich. Ya can git ta know some of the Injins. They're great people. They love the earth. Did you know they pray ta trees 'n animals? Thank 'em for givin' up their life fer our food? You gotta count Injins, Paul. They wuz the furstest here. Let's git somethin' to eat," Carney said, "I thank ya for visitin' today. It's not like we're lonely in the woods 'cuz we got a big family. Keep each other company. I hope ya come back agin when ya don't have so much work ta do."

"I got some vacation time coming up."

"I took up a lot of yer time today 'n maybe dint answer all the questions that'd help ya fill in those boxes. But I'm glad you came. I bet ya hear a lot of stories … the tales people must tell ya."

"Yours is the best one so far, Carney," Paul said, smiling "My job used to be kind of boring before I came here today. I don't know if I could keep a straight face if I asked you any more questions."

Life behind bars

Make boots. Make barrels. Ten-hour quarry shifts. Make marble. For churches. For government buildings. Return to twenty-square-foot brick cell. Silence. Reflection. Read the Bible. Work hard. Rehab. Obey the rules. No talk. Walk in lockstep. No writing. No whistling. No dancing. No jumping. No running. No visitors. Two eggs a day. Whippings. Isolation. Conditions cruel. Conditions brutal. Guards cruel. Guards brutal.

Not money. Not power. It was time that betrayed him. Time did him in. Time was everyone feared him: his rivals, his enemies, his employees. Time became his enemy. Now he has time in his cell, in the closeness, the suffocating atmosphere, with no light, no ventilation, to think and figure out which one of his lawyers ratted. *"Was the son of a bitch not paid enough? Didn't I always remember his kids' birthdays and give the little bastards extravagant gifts? The finest jewelry and furs for their wives and mistresses."* He envisioned the face of each employee. Not knowing tormented him. Which rat turned state's evidence that convicted Paddy Minogue for the crime of second-degree murder of a rival gang leader. Eight to twenty years. Might as well give him the chair.

Flaherty, Paddy Minogue's rival, protégé, and business partner died before he spent one night in jail. Flaherty told Minogue to pay his people

194

well and they won't turn on you. Minogue did exactly that. Some bastard turned on him anyway. He suspected it had to be one of his lawyers. They had the goods. Minogue had the authorities on the payroll like Flaherty, but his silent partner stayed in the shadows. Flaherty warned him that whenever he escaped conviction, he had better keep a close, suspicious eye on the underling who took the rap.

Minogue never pulled the trigger, thrust the knife, or swung the club that eliminated a rival. Nor was he the one who rolled a prosperous drunk, or extorted legitimate businesses, yet he alone gave the orders. On the rare occasion one of the crimes got as far as a court date, its jury would have been handpicked by Minogue's lawyers and the presiding judge would already be on the payroll.

Paddy owned the *Blue Chips* gambling resort on Bond Street with his partner, Flaherty. When the U.S. Congressman disappeared into the ground, what also disappeared was round-the-clock police protection guaranteed by Tammany Hall. Other casino owners, envious of the *Blue Chips'* wealthy clientele, decided to make their move, disrupting the club's reputation with muggings and bricks tossed through windows. Paddy located the source of the disruption and eliminated him. Someone in his organization was out to save his own ass and sang like a canary.

No one was better suited for Sing Sing's environment than James Callaghan, possessed of a ravenous appetite for the fulfillment of the law through the swift whack of his nightstick or a quick, well-placed kick with his boots. Likewise, no one on the wrong side of the bars was more hardboiled than Minogue. His official classification was incorrigible yet competent to work. It did not take long for the mobster to have a run-in with Keeper *Knuckles*. Callaghan customized the long list of Sing Sing rules by adding 'No hands on bars'. He would bellow, "Catch my drift?" as he used his baton to remind prisoners of his rule. Half the men in Cellblock 13 had deformed finger joints as a result of catching Keeper Knuckles's drift.

Sent upriver in 1900 to the stone fortress, Minogue began his sentence by ignoring most of the rules. He was not the meditative, Bible-reading type. He had a big mouth and loved to boast. He passed around notes replete with lewd cartoon drawings depicting Keeper Callaghan's parents. Owning enough hubris to think his indiscretions were safe among his fellow inmates, Minogue spread rumors about Callaghan's father, made believable by the fact Stephen Callaghan was once under his employ. He took credit for what role he played in Stephen's suicide at the short-lived *Palisades Palace*. He concocted tales detailing how Stephen Callaghan was not solely involved with Flaherty's construction business, but he and *Knuckles* Callaghan's mother were complicit in the sordid underground activities of the *Cherry Street Rotters*. He delighted in saying he knew where all the bodies were buried.

A fellow keeper intercepted one of the notes and gave it to Callaghan. It was written in Minogue's hand which was all James needed to pay an unscheduled visit to Minogue's cell. His family's name would be sullied no longer. Cellblock 13 Prison Keeper James Callaghan came upon Minogue's cell late one night and rapped his baton on the bars. Minogue stepped forward and could smell James's breath, made acidic from a rotting ulcer, combined with whiskey.

James opened the cell door. Minogue's cellmate Melvin crawled beneath the bottom bunk. Knuckles presented the note to Minogue, "Did you write this?"

"No."

James took a step back and rapped his baton across the prisoner's ribcage, cracking his bones. Minogue doubled over. James struck a second blow upon the gangster's shoulder blade. "You know the rules, Paddy boy. Guess which one you broke."

Now on his knees, Minogue tried to take a deep breath, but the pain worsened. James kicked the metal frame of the bottom bunk and summoned Melvin, "Hey Kike, get out where I can see your hooknose Jew face." Melvin stood, holding his crotch, "Open your mouth Jew." Melvin complied. James placed his baton inside Melvin's mouth, rattling the man's teeth. Callaghan then poked Melvin's chest with the baton. Melvin shook uncontrollably, "Are you a little sissy boy, pissing your pants?" James said, "Look at your buddy and tell him what rule he broke. Go on, tell him." Melvin lowered his head and shook it from side to side, placing his index finger vertically over his mouth.

"You're not stupid like him, are you? Get back on your cot."

James pulled Minogue to his feet, "No whistling. No jumping up and down. No dancing. No singing, and … no talking." Turning once again to the frightened cellmate, James said, "Which one did I leave out?" With his index finger, Melvin made the motion of writing on the palm of his hand."

"That's right. Minogue, I'll give you one more chance to come clean. Did you write this note?"

Minogue barely managed a whisper, "If I have to crawl out of my grave, I will kill everything you love. You are the devil himself." Minogue spit in Callaghan's face.

James wiped the spittle with his sleeve, stepped behind Minogue and held his baton against the man's throat, choking him. When he released his hold, Minogue's body slithered to the floor. James took a step back, gripped his baton with both hands and swung it across the side of the prisoner's head. Blood poured out of Minogue's ear.

Melvin backed into the corner of the cell. James grabbed his shirt and pulled him close. "You saw with your own eyes, Jew. I was innocently making my rounds, checking on the welfare of the inhabitants within, and your deviant mate here jumped up and spit in my face, cussing me up and down. I opened the cell door to take him to task and he raised his hand to strike me. That is when I defended myself. Understand? That's what happened. That's the story you tell if you value your sorry ass life."

Melvin shook. James patted him on the head, "Don't forget to tell the truth like I just told you. Or else the same will happen to you. Catch my drift?"

An hour later, Minogue was carried out on a stretcher, sent to the infirmary, then transported to St. Francis Hospital where he died three days later.

Paddy Minogue left behind three children he fathered with three different women, the thirty-four-year-old sisters Eleanor and Helen, and their twenty-year old redhead brother.

Concerned that news of the incident might leak to the public, the warden called James to his office, letting him know he was already under a lot of pressure, getting calls from Governor Higgins and Commissioner Johnson. They complained about some bleeding-heart do-gooder lawyers and reporters wanting to investigate what they characterized as cruel conditions at Sing Sing. "Can you believe they actually think we're going to let them talk to the prisoners?" the warden said.

Knowing the Callaghan family owned a building in Manhattan, the warden suggested James accept the transfer he arranged to City Prison which was located there. Effective immediately. James told his mother about his reassignment and planned to move into 347 Cherry Street, taking over from William all the affairs related to the supervision and maintenance of the tenement.

James also called on Nellie Murphy before leaving town. She and two of her former high school classmates found employment in New York City and planned to room together in Manhattan. James told her he got a promotion to City Prison, allowing their courtship to progress at a faster pace.

After performing the autopsy on Paddy Minogue, the County Medical Examiner submitted his report: cardiac arrest occurring during struggle and exertion due to underlying hypertension and atherosclerosis. No further investigation necessary. Melvin and the prisoners in surrounding cells remained silent.

Estrangement is a slow-cooked stew with hatred and fear, two of its essential ingredients. Estrangement from her son. Hatred and fear of Minogue. All thrown in the pot together creating a taffy-pull tug of war for Peggy. Conflicted, confused, angry, she knew what her son did to Minogue. However, she was not unhappy about his gruesome death, especially after what Minogue did to Stephen. She knew, "Vengeance is mine sayeth the Lord." Was it still possible to pour her spiritual self into the work of the Mission? Does doing good for others mitigate an impure heart?

No matter how much she tried to rationalize it, she found it impossible to reconcile that the bone of her bone and flesh of her flesh is a murderer.

James and Nellie

The mutual infatuation between James and Nellie blossomed into genuine romance. James endeared himself to Nellie's once skeptical mother and cemented their relationship by graciously inviting the widow to move in with them. Weekends for James and Nellie were spent painting, wallpapering, and negotiating the Roman Catholic rules regarding premarital sex. The specter of Mary Murphy's opinion on the subject loomed large. For Nellie. Not James.

Nellie tried explaining to James that her mother trusted her. Mary credited her daughter in advance to having enough self-discipline to keep a check on her sexual desires. James floated a counter argument to Nellie. Something to think about he told her. After all, we'll be married soon. Nellie resisted James's overtures at first, then weakened each time they were alone and responsible to no one other than themselves. Working together in close proximity became a bit too much to bear for James. The perfume on Nellie's neck quickened his pulse and set his heart aflutter.

Nellie was barely four feet eleven, close to a foot shorter than her future lifelong mate. Being a gentleman, James offered to help her extend the paintbrush further up the wall. As Nellie stood on the ladder and guided the brush, James guided his hands over her hips and her breasts.

She kept painting while his hands kept exploring the contours of her body. James continued to guide Nellie up each step of the ladder, boosting her from her bottom. Eventually, his hands found themselves inside her dress, feeling the heat source residing on the other side of her bloomers. The more the temperature rose the higher his hands explored her inner thighs.

One especially hot day, Nellie dispensed with her bloomers. That omission proved to be too much for James, as he nearly fainted when his reach did not exceed his grasp. Overexcited, they hurriedly bunched together drop cloths on the floor and went at it, clumsily at first, with premature ejaculations on the first, second, and third tries, the testosterone and estrogen aromas overcoming the smell of fresh paint and wallpaper paste. Prior to the occasion of the fourth attempt, they confiscated an old mattress from one of the vacant rentals on the third floor, threw a sheet on top of it and enjoyed smooth coitus. They kept at it day after day, being it was so thrilling and naughty. Very little painting and wallpapering got done during this transitional period.

On September 5, 1909 Nellie and James became Mr. & Mrs. James P. Callaghan at St. Mary's Church on Grand. William Callaghan acted as best man. Nellie's best friend and co-worker Sally Perkins was the maid of honor. Since theirs was a small wedding, the mothers, Peggy Callaghan and Mary Murphy, decided to sit together in the front pew. The marriage officiant, Father Patrick Corcoran took note of the contour of Nellie's stomach which the bride attempted to obscure with creative layering of frilly fabric. The priest let it pass as he had seen it all played out so many times before. He was satisfied the loving couple corrected a sinful situation by getting married in the church. During the Mass, Father Corcoran gave a short homily based on Ecclesiastes 4:10 and offered a blessing on their union, while he clasped his hands over theirs.

On March 5, 1910, James P. Callaghan, Jr. was born. Ten months following that big event, baby Raymond F. Callaghan joined the clan. Although the work of the Kennedy Home Mission expanded to include education and job training programs for prisoners' spouses, Grandma Peggy came down for both celebrations from Ossining, formerly known as the Village of Sing Sing, staying for several weeks each time in a nearby hotel. She visited the apartment while James was at work, delighted in fussing over her grandsons. Over the protestations of Nellie, Grandma Peggy showered the family with gifts of clothing, toys, and household items.

As the boys grew, the living arrangement in the less spacious apartment worked best when William was out of town. His big body bumped into everything whenever he returned from trips. Although he had a tendency to drink too much, his contribution to the family's monthly expenses was a welcome necessity. He often travelled out of state, stirring up trouble as a Union agitator, voicing the grievances of Irish laborers throughout the country. Whenever Uncle Bill did make it home, Jim and Baby Ray slept on the floor in their parents' room.

Double the pleasure

There was joy in the household on April 14, 1913, when Anna Teresa Callaghan was born. Big brothers Jim and Baby Ray were fascinated with the little bundle and stared at her for long periods, running to Nana and their mother every time the baby whimpered. Proud father James worked double shifts, accepting whatever additional assignments came his way, shuttling back and forth between City Prison and Blackwell Island assuring Nellie they would be able to keep pace with the food and clothing bills.

Whether leaving before sunrise or coming home in the middle of the night, James never failed to look in on Anna while she slept, tenderly touching her nose, whispering "You are my little button." Kissing his forefinger and softly placing it upon each eye, saying, "I kiss your eye, bluer than the sky." Then, with a finishing flourish, he traced the contour of her pursed lips, cooing, "Anna is Daddy's precious little girl." Sometimes, assured she was sleeping soundly, he would pick her up, hold her in his big hands and take a long, deep whiff of her neck. Made mush of him, little Anna did.

A fascination for brand new life took hold of the Callaghan family. Birth announcement telegrams were sent to Grandma Peggy and William. Uncle Bill, on special assignment with the Industrial Workers of the World union, replied he would be heading home very soon bearing gifts. Grandma Peggy sent a telegram stating she planned to purchase all available baby girl outfits on sale throughout Westchester County.

Nellie was touched that her husband wanted to spend every free moment with their newborn daughter. Mother and father sat on the sofa with the baby. "You fathers have a thing for the girls," Nellie said as James swayed Anna back and forth.

"You have given me a special gift, Nellie. I had no idea when we married that something this beautiful would come into our lives."

"Well, I'm glad at least one female in this household has won your heart,"

"C'mon wife, you know I love you."

"It would be nice to hear it once in awhile," Nellie said, sticking her face between James and Anna, "Hello. It's me, Nellie. Your wife."

James kissed Nellie on the side of her head. "I'll always love my little Irish nightingale."

"Maybe we could go out for dinner on our anniversary. What do you say about that?"

"It's not for several months."

"I have to plan these things far in advance with you."

"Will your mother watch three kids?"

"Of course. She loves her grandchildren. Each and every one."

"I catch your drift, smarty. By the way, the boys are starting to give me some lip."

"That's because they see how much you fuss over Anna. I swear you hear her voice through a brick wall. Wish you would give the boys a fair share of the affection you shower on her."

"They're Momma's boys."

"How about making them Daddy's boys?"

"You're nagging me now."

"And if I didn't, would anything change?"

Anna started to doze off. The humid summer heat and the warmth of the baby's body agitated James. "She's kind of hot right now," he said, handing her off to Nellie.

"I'll wash her down with some cold water. It'll cool her off," Nellie said, "I wish this heat would break."

"Won't that wake her up?"

"Little did I know you'd turn out to be such a softie. What changed you?" Nellie said, putting Anna in the crib.

"It's been all boys for three generations. Anna is the first girl. Hurrah."

"I told you Carney and Minnie Mae had twin girls, didn't I?"

"I'm not counting his kids."

"He's your brother, for God's sake," Nellie said, "I wish you'd pay more attention to Jim and Baby Ray. They need loving too. Spend time with them. Let them know they have a father."

James walked over to the front window and watched his sons play tag in the park. Nana monitored them. She leaned against a big Elm and kept a hawk's eye on the boys. Whenever they took a tumble on the grass, she ran over and brushed the dirt off their knickers. James turned from the window and said, "Jim looks a little like me, doesn't he?"

"He looks a lot like you. Same dark hair. Same big nose. Same full lips. Same droopy St. Bernard eyes."

"Thanks for comparing me to a dog."

"You're still very handsome. Who do you think Baby Ray looks like?"

"I don't know what side of the family he comes from. Kind of small, frail, blondish hair," James said, turning away from the window, "They'll both turn out all right just like me. My father wasn't around much either." He went into the bedroom to change his shirt, soaked through from the humidity.

Before he left for work, James went back into their bedroom for one last look at his daughter. He whispered into her tiny ears, and touched her nose, eyes, and lips. He stepped outside the room but quickly doubled back, leaned over the crib rail, and placed his forefinger gently on Anna's nose, "You're my little button," he said as he kissed his finger and placed it on her forehead, "Daddy will see you tonight."

Nellie held the door open for James, kissed him on the cheek, and listened to the familiar sound of knuckles being cracked midway down the stairs. She closed the door behind her, halved four lemons on the cutting board, and prepared to make iced tea for Nana and the boys.

It was normally a twenty-minute walk to work at nighttime for James but at least double that when he worked the daytime shift. Each street on the route to City Prison was jammed with men in skimmer hats and ladies in dresses made of dimity cloth. He navigated the tangle of screeching streetcars, vendors hawking produce off their horse-drawn carts, plus all the fuss and bother being paid to the ceaseless honks of brand-new Fords and Packards.

Before James got to work, he stopped at 144 Elm Street, just a few blocks from the prison. He walked up the stairs to the third floor. The washerwoman, Maggie Lenehan, left the door open for him. She knew his schedule. He was right on time.

He strolled inside, passed the table piled high with dirty laundry, and walked over to Maggie seated in a low-backed chair with her head thrown back. He kissed her on the forehead and placed his hand on her stomach. "Not much longer, heh?"

"Maybe two days, six at most."

"What do you think, boy or girl?"

"Who knows? Some of my lady customers say it's a girl," Maggie said, wiping her brow with a damp cloth, "From the way I'm carrying."

"I think so too," James said, looking at her stomach, "Can you still do me?"

"Yeah. Stay standing. I'm tired from all this laundry shit."

"That works for me."

"I'm going to need more money when your kid get's here," she said, undoing his trousers.

"I won't be sheddin' money like a moltin' canary, but don't worry. I'll take care of you. Extra bonus if it's a girl."

A boy's voice called out from the hall closet "Momma, let me out. I can't breathe."

"Shut up! I'll let you out when I'm done," Maggie said.

"I need to cuff his ear," James said, staring at a brownish water stain on the ceiling.

James took pleasure in buying new dresses, shoes, and hats for Anna, parading up and down Cherry Street, pushing the little princess along in her brand-new baby buggy gifted by Grandma Peggy. He started attending Sunday Mass at St. Mary's with the family and made sure everyone in church got a chance to ooh and ahh over his pretty little daughter.

James's second daughter was born six days after Anna's arrival. James and Maggie named her Rose.

Double trouble too

Having served two thirds of his sentence for racketeering, Melvin Stein was released from Sing Sing prison June 16, 1916, two months shy of his sixty-sixth birthday. The guards escorted him out of the building where he had been austerely sheltered, poorly fed, and frequently beaten. With a bundle of personal items tucked under his arm, he walked forward and never looked back.

Once outside the barbed-wire gate, he inhaled the fresh air of freedom. He loosened his rigid stride, gave his body a shake and walked confidently as a man empowered, assured that a brand-new chauffeur's uniform awaited him at the penthouse apartment at 1 West 72nd Street, New York City.

Helen and Eleanor Minogue kept up a steady correspondence with Melvin throughout his incarceration, often making special mention of how grateful they were for the years he looked after them growing up as bordello brats. The ladies had promised to send a car for him on the day of his release and there it was, only a few steps away. With the choppy river behind it, the fancy vehicle was a bright sight for his weary eyes. This was no ordinary car. The luxury Locomobile Model 48 Sportif Touring Car idled on the gravel path, dust blowing against its emerald chassis and canvas top.

The driver insisted Melvin take a seat in the rear, acting on instructions from the Minogue sisters, wanting their old friend to exchange his brand from ex-convict to King Melvin for a day.

Two ladies sat on a bench facing the white-capped waters and tossed bread to the ducks. They looked skyward when the mandrakes and buffleheads quacked excitedly, flapping away from the three high school boys tossing stones in the water. The boys dropped their ammunition when the women threatened to notify the principal of their truancy, and they wandered over for a closer look at the showy Sportif.

"Swell automobile, Pops," said the head truant, bending down to examine the fancy wheel spokes, his eyes roving over the vehicle's sleek body, taking in each dose of excessive opulence.

"I'll tell you what's swell, Sonny Boy," Melvin said, "When you're released after a long stay and get driven home in a deluxe vehicle."

"I ain't got no plans to go to prison like you, Pops," the boy said as the Sportif kicked up gravel, leaving the truant in the dust.

In just a few hours, Melvin would get to see Helen and Eleanor, whose acquired knowledge of brothel economics provided them with a lucrative prostitution business in the city's Tenderloin district. Melvin asked the driver to make an extra stop in Manhattan before they arrived at the Minogue sisters' residence.

When they arrived at 144 Elm Street, the driver parked across the street. Melvin stayed in the car and looked out the window, catching a glimpse of the people sitting on the stoop.

Melvin got teary when Helen and Eleanor welcomed him into their spacious penthouse duplex, featuring eighteen-foot-high ceilings, luxurious velvet drapes, a marble fireplace, antique vases, sculptures, elegant Victorian sofas, Chippendale chairs, and every comfort fit for prosperous entrepreneurs. He hardly recognized the ladies, still picturing them as mischievous teenagers.

The three friends sat on the balcony overlooking Central Park, drinking tea. When Eleanor noticed the teacup in Melvin's hand rattle on the saucer, she said, "You're safe now. No one's going to hurt you anymore."

"I was there and … did nothing to save your father," he said, crying.

"Don't do this to yourself. We know the whole story," Helen said, "It's not your fault."

"We didn't tell you in our letters, but we have a few surprises for you," Eleanor said, "This is your home now. With your own bedroom."

"I don't deserve this," Melvin said.

"Nonsense. We've always considered you a member of our family," Helen said, "In a little while you can a take a nice long nap on a big, soft bed with big feather pillows." Eleanor summoned the maid with the tinkle of a little bell and instructed her to make up Melvin's bed with fresh linens.

"Do you know how long it's been since I slept in a real bed?"

"When you wake up, we have another treat for you," Eleanor said.

"What is it?"

"Filet mignon. Baked potato with butter and gravy. Fresh peas."

"My favorite meal. I can't believe you remembered. You two are spoiling me. And I love it," Melvin said, "By the way, is your brother still around?"

"You remember him?" Helen said,

"Of course. Does he still have all that red hair?"

"Everyone calls him Red. You know he's a cop now."

"No."

"He works on the east side. We almost disowned him. But he's still our baby brother, all six foot four of him."

Eleanor excused herself and headed to the kitchen to check with the cook about preparations for dinner.

"I know something you ladies don't," Melvin said to Helen, "Found out from an inmate who did time in the city system. Callaghan's got a second daughter. Same age as the one on Cherry Street. Knuckles is very fond of her. Had her with a washerwoman. There's also a boy in the apartment. But I don't think Callaghan's the father."

"Where does the little princess live?" Helen said.

"144 Elm Street, around the corner from the prison."

When Eleanor returned, Helen said to her, "Guess what?"

"Another surprise for Melvin?" Eleanor said.

"No. Melvin has a surprise for us."

"Ooh, tell me. I love surprises."

"Callaghan's got two daughters he's crazy about," Melvin said.

"I had no idea. I only know of Anna, the Cherry Street girl," Eleanor said, "What's this one's name?"

"Rose," Melvin said.

"Rose and Anna. Twins like us!"

"I'll be damned," Helen said.

April 14, 1918

Before the sun came up, James slipped out of bed and put on his uniform. The boys were asleep in Uncle Bill's room, having guessed correctly he was not going to make it home after a night of heavy drinking. James knelt beside Anna's bed. The light from the small candle he held softly illumined her curly black hair and long eyelashes. Most of the baby fat on her arms and legs had disappeared except for one pinchable roll on her neck. James zeroed in on that spot and inhaled deeply. He brushed her hair back and kissed her forehead. He placed a box wrapped with a big purple bow next to her pillow. It would be the very first thing she would see when she awakened. It was a special present, a Kewpie Doll that Anna wanted more than anything in the world. The doll's dress was made by Nana out of the same cloth she used for Anna's birthday outfit. James tripped the jumper wire to the gas line he rigged before he left the building, remembering Nellie planned to give Anna a hot bath before church.

With the sun glistening on the East River, prison keeper James Callaghan boarded the East 26th street ferry headed to Blackwell Island.

"Hey men, listen up. Today's your lucky day you get to meet the legendary 'Knuckles' Callaghan," Sergeant Anthony Costello hollered as the keepers in the midnight-to-eight shift got ready to head home, exchanging war stories with the groggy eight a.m. crew. The keepers grabbed their coffees and sat at the long rectangular table in the locker room.

As James extended his hand to greet Costello, the sergeant put his hand forward, but quickly withdrew it. "Oh no you don't Callaghan. Last time you gave me a stink palm. I ain't falling for that trick again,"

"Thanks, Sarge. Good morning fellow keepers of the Blackwell Zoo. I'd like to say it's good to be back here, but I'd be a lyin' toad if I did," James said, "I'm filling in for that lazy ass, Angelo. He called in sick or is it that his old lady is sick and needs him to look after her, if you catch my drift."

One of the keepers defended Angelo, "Hey Knuckles, Ange was puking his brains out yesterday. Cut the guy some slack, will ya."

James looked around the room. "Oh sure, my heart bleeds for him. He musta got sick locking up all those smelly Yids. Catch my drift?"

Sgt. Costello said to James, "Tell these suckers about your happy times at Sing Sing."

"I know some of you guys gotta catch your ferry, so I'll make it short. Seems like Sarge never gets tired of hearing the story."

Costello smiled and sat down, all eyes and ears on James. "Ossining ain't a big city. So, when it happens, every family sittin' around the dinner table in my old hometown all of a sudden can't see their dinner in front of them. And their little brats spill their milk all over the floor. It's the same thing in every house - at the same exact time whether they're eatin' I-talian or franks and beans. It's the same thing I'm tellin' ya. Catch my drift?"

"What're ya yakking about, Callaghan?" one of the keepers said.

"Every time they throw the switch on Old Sparky, another murderin' son of a bitch gets fried and every single light in the city goes black."

"The whole city?" another keeper said.

"That's right. The whole fuckin' city. They use all the juice they got while the S.O.B. wiggles in the chair and expires. Boo hoo." "That's bullshit about the lights, Callaghan. I heard the prison's got their own generator," Angelo's friend said.

"I was there, sucker," James said with authority, "I watched the whole fuckin' show. Many times."

At eight o'clock, Jim, Baby Ray and Anna sat in a small circle in the front room. The boys couldn't wait to let Anna in on a big secret. Anna waved her new doll in the air, made it hop on the floor, calling out, "Kewpie, fly like a bird. Kewpie, hop like a bunny."

"That's so-, so-, so dumb," Baby Ray said, "Her name isn't Kewpie."

"Kewpie. Kewpie. Kewpie," Anna insisted.

"That's not a-, not a-, not a name, dummy," Baby Ray said, "That's a k-, k-, kind of doll."

"I named her Kewpie."

"It's her doll. She can name it anything she wants," Jim said, "It's her birthday."

"But-, but-, but-"

"Let's take a vote," Jim said, "All those in favor of naming the doll Kewpie, raise your hand." Jim and Anna raised their hands. Baby Ray folded his arms across his chest and stared at the floor. Jim grabbed Baby Ray's hand and lifted it for him.

Excited, Anna pressed her nose against the doll, "Kewpie, it's namamus."

Baby Ray asked Jim, "Can-, can-, can I tell her about the big-, big secret?"

"Wait just a minute," Jim said, "First, I have to give her something. Anna, close your eyes."

Anna complied while Jim fetched a card and a paper bag from behind the couch.

"Open the card first," Jim said.

Anna unfolded the hand-made card illustrated with a big red heart and the words, 'Happy Birthday, Sis. From, Big Brother Jim.' She ripped open the bag from Cheap Charlie's candy store. Her favorite goodies tumbled to the floor. She scooped up a handful of chocolate covered cherries. "Just eat one or Momma will get mad," Jim said.

"Okay," Anna said, stuffing her mouth.

"I got you a pres-, pres-, present too, Anna," Baby Ray said.

"Should I close my eyes again?"

"I left it in school. To-, to-, tomorrow."

"What is it?"

"A po-, po-, poem."

"For me?"

"Just for you."

"Okay. Tomorrow."

"What's the big secret?" Anna said.

Baby Ray looked at Jim for approval. Getting the nod, he said. "A racing cart."

Anna squealed, "Where is it?"

"At Mr. Nico's. But you gotta wait for us to get back from First Communion class," Jim said, "We gotta be the first to give you a push."

"Pr-pr-promise to wait," Baby Ray added.

"I promise," Anna said.

"Gotta, gotta, gotta. Gotta go first ... gotta," Baby Ray said, dancing in circles.

Nellie came into the front room, took Anna by the hand, and led her into the kitchen for her bath. After a good scrubbing, Nellie dried her off, wrapped her in a big white towel and handed the bundle to her mother who waited in her rocker. After Nana helped her get into her undershirt and bloomers, Anna snuggled close, and they recited a rhyme together.

Plum cherry quick
Give the girl a candy stick

Let her lick it before the dog kicks it
To the floor. I want more I want more
The little girl cried
Until Nana and Anna tried to march
The naughty doggie out the door.

"One more, Nana. Please."

"I have to think for a minute, baby girl."

"I got one," Anna said:

Nana banana smells like pickles
That's why she gives me lots of tickles.

Nana tickled and Anna giggled. Nellie came in and said, "You can't go to church dressed like that, can you?" She held out her hand, but Anna clung to her Nana.

"Five more minutes. No more," Nellie told her daughter, pinching her cheek.

As Nellie returned to the bedroom, Nana whispered to Anna, "That was silly."

"What was silly?"

"You called me Nana banana. How can I be a banana AND smell like pickles?"

"Momma told me you work there," said Anna.

"That was a long time ago. I worked in a pickle factory," Nana said, "But I don't smell like pickles anymore, do I?"

"I guess not."

"What does your Nana really smell like?"

Anna planted her nose on Nana's neck, took a deep breath and said, "You smell like a thousand hugs."

Nana squeezed her. "Well, here's one thousand one."

"And a million cuddles."

Nana rocked her back and forth, "Here's a million and one."

"I love you, Nana."

"I love you too."

"I love you three," Anna said.

"Silly."

"Can you keep a secret?" Anna said.

"Your secrets are always safe with your Nana"

"Jim and Baby Ray made me a racing cart for my birthday."

Nellie returned and led Anna into the bedroom. "Can I wear my new dress Nana made?" Anna said.

Nana made Anna's black and white checked dress out of woven cotton material. It was trimmed with red flannel bands and strappings, the bottom one third of the dress pleated with wide panels and finished with gilt buttons. With enough fabric left over, she made a matching outfit for Anna's Kewpie doll.

"Of course, you can wear your new dress. But you have to change after Mass if you want to play outside," Nellie said.

"I don't want to," Anna said.

"Then you'll have to stay inside. That would be a shame because it's such a nice, sunny day."

"Please Momma."

"That's not a good idea," Nellie said as she held the dress against Anna's body, "This will look so beautiful on you. You don't want to ruin it now, do you? It could get ripped while you're riding in the cart."

Jim and Baby Ray walked down the block to the Nicoletti tenement at 357 Cherry. Salvatore Nicoletti, his wife, and brood of six children were the only Italian family on the block. He made chairs and dressers for several neighbors, including the Callaghans. A master carpenter by trade, he promised the boys he'd build the push-mobile in time for Anna's birthday, provided they gathered the necessary parts. Working off his list, Jim and Baby Ray spent their after-school hours scavenging in railroad yards, alleys, empty lots, and dumps.

Mrs. Nicoletti opened the door, holding 8-month-old Salvatore, Jr. in her arms, with two-year-old Sofia clinging to the bottom of her dress. Jim tipped his cap. "We're sorry to bother you, Mrs. Nico, but we want to pick up Anna's cart."

"Papa issa notta here righta now."

"Mr. Nico told us we could take it any time." Jim said.

"Needsa braka, no?"

"No br- braka, It's a p- p- pusha," Baby Ray said, making a pushing motion with both hands.

A dish crashed to the floor behind Mrs. Nicoletti, followed by a child's piercing cry. "Scusi," Mrs. Nicoletti said as she rushed into the kitchen.

"Prego. Ciao," Jim said, closing the door and running down the hallway with Baby Ray. They took the cart out of Mr. Nicoletti's shed, carried it through the hallway, down the stoop, and pushed it along Cherry Street.

Helga Nilsson was sweeping her steps and waved to the boys as they approached. "Is that for Anna's birthday?"

"Yep," Jim said.

"She's going to love it," Helga said.

"I hope so" Baby Ray said.

"Where are you going to park it?"

"I dunno. Bottom of our stoop, I guess." Jim said.

"Aren't you afraid someone might steal it? Just last week, Timmy Dooley's new bike got stolen right outside his house. He left it on the sidewalk when his mother called. Five minutes later, the bike was gone. You don't want Anna's cart stolen, do you?"

Jim and Baby Ray looked at each other for a moment and pushed off. "We gotta get ready for church."

Helga walked over to the boys, placing her hand on the cart. "Don't worry. I'll mind it for you. I'll take it inside my house where it'll be safe. You can pick it up after Mass."

"We have to go to First Communion class after church. Anna's coming home with Momma and Nana and she's gonna want to ride it right away. We made her promise to wait for us," Jim said.

"I'll be looking out the window. I'll bring it down when I see you," Helga said, patting Baby Ray on the head, "You boys sure are swell."

"Are you sure it's no trouble for you, Miss Nilsson?" Jim said.

"No trouble at all. You boys just run along. It'll be safe with me. I won't take my eyes off it."

"Geez, th- thanks," Baby Ray said as they ran home.

Nellie opened the closet door and stood before the mirror. She tried on a new camisole corset cover, knowing it was several sizes too big. Aware her bust size was keeping pace with her expanding waist, she hoped the undergarment with an elastic waist would have a lifespan deeper into her pregnancy. She fingered the silk red ribbon draw. She frowned when she looked in the mirror, turning left, then right to examine her profile on each side. She squared up to the mirror, considered her own Irish face, fuller now, yet still pretty, she told her reflection.

William Callaghan reached Corlears Hook Park after an all-night binge; his work pants soaked in urine. He had fallen down several times, trying to navigate uneven ground on wobbly legs. He made it as far as a park bench, plopped down and fell asleep.

As Monsignor Patrick J. Corcoran emerged from the sacristy, Nana, Nellie, Jim, Baby Ray, and Anna stood up in their regular pew, three rows back from the Blessed Virgin's altar. Monsignor Corcoran took a deep bow before the crucifix on the main altar. The church was full, the ten o'clock Mass began right on time.

The first ride

It was a breezy day on the Lower East Side. Enterprising boys needing change for the cinema fetched ladies' hats blowing helter-skelter down the street. Over on Grand, a curious crowd gawked at Ginger, an old peddler wagon horse, her massive carcass spread out in the gutter, having gasped her last breath from exhaustion three days earlier. Some of the older boys pitched pennies in an alleyway off Orchard near Hester. Others played marbles for keeps. Kids flooded the streets, kicking cans while dodging autos, horse drawn wagons and pushcart peddlers. Children played stoop-ball, punchball, and stickball, launching the respective rubber spheres over imaginary home run fences. They ate red hots, spent change on dice and dime novels, swigged soda at two cents a pop at Ziggys on Delancey, tried to outdo each other telling the latest dirty joke, and snuck on street cars and trolleys, skipping the five-cent fare that was better spent at the penny arcade.

The diverse ethnic communities shared the common thread of poverty. They all struggled to survive. Mothers bonded together, looking out for each other's children, scanning the busy streets from their windows and vigilant perches on the stoops. Sometimes, peaceful bonds were breached, evidenced by ugly ethnic slurs made by one group against another. James

Callaghan, passionate about his Irishness, warned his sons to avoid making friends with anyone identified as a Coon, Kike, or Kraut. Cherry Street was predominantly an Irish block, with the Callaghan name etched in the street's notorious and violent past when Irish gangs and waterfront thugs ruled the neighborhood. Jim and Baby Ray ignored their father's threats. He was never around the house long enough to carry them out. No family member questioned where he went or what he did before or after his shift. Nellie trusted him, knowing he was a stickler for the rules.

James 'Knuckles' Callaghan lived up to the reputation he earned at Sing Sing. His nickname accompanied him downstate. Veteran inmates warned the newbies about keeping their hands off the bars. 'Knuckles' disfigured inmates' hands with a lightning-fast flip of his trusty nightstick. The sight of fleshy knuckles grasping steel bars was too inviting for him to ignore. James never missed. He swung his weapon by its leather strap, slipping it back and forth under each armpit like a champion baton-twirling leader at a Fifth Avenue parade. He pranced along the cells, clanking his weapon across the bars, ready to bang it upon unsuspecting bone and flesh. James Callaghan was considered a star employee in the city system, commanding the respect of his fellow guards and fear among the inmates.

From her perch at the front window, Helga Nilsson heard melodic voices rising up from the street below. She opened her window to have a look. Sure enough, the joyful singing came from the Callaghan ladies. Nana and Nellie wore their big hats and best Sunday dresses. They each held one of the birthday girl's hands as she skipped along. Anna yanked their hands, her signal for another swooping lift off the ground. The three of them sang together:

> *I'm always chasing rainbows*
> *Watching clouds drifting by*
> *My schemes are just like all my dreams*
> *Ending in the sky*

Believe me, I'm always chasing rainbows
Waiting to find a little bluebird …

Helga ran down the steps into the front hall, grabbed the push-mobile and dragged it into the street. By the time she got to 347, Nellie and Anna had already made it through the front door. Helga caught Nana taking a breather on the stoop. "Here's Anna's cart. Can you keep an eye on it, Mary?"

"Will you look at that," Nana said, admiring what her grandsons made, "Why don't you sit down a spell."

Helga parked the cart on the side of the stoop and sat down. As Nana listened to her neighbor speak rapid-fire about war news, she became intrigued with certain features about Helga's countenance, as if seeing them for the first time. Nana's eyes drifted to the hair framing Helga's triangular shaped face. Lighter strands weaved haphazardly in and out of the darker ones. She studied the woman's left eye, noting it was considerably larger than the right, musing what two creatures created this woman.

Nana stood and said, "Excuse me. It's naptime for this old lady. Don't feel you have to leave. Nellie and the little one will be down any minute."

Nellie changed into a more comfortable outfit and tried to convince Anna to change into her play clothes. Singularly focused on the importance of the push-mobile launch, Anna argued she must stay in her brand-new birthday dress since Nana made a matching dress for her new doll. After all, what would Kewpie wear if she changed her dress?

At eleven thirty, Nellie closed the apartment door. She walked quickly into the hallway trying to keep up with Anna, who slid down the bannister, bounded out the front door, hopped down the stoop, and came close to spilling into the street. Nellie dragged her back to the front steps. Anna squealed when she caught a glimpse of the cart. "I know you want to hop right in. But you have to wait for your brothers." Anna's eyes were riveted on the cart.

Nellie sat down next to Helga, a newcomer to the Cherry Street community. Helga Nilsson moved into her apartment a few doors down only a few months ago and very soon afterwards made fast friends with Nellie. She tapped Helga on her shoulder and pointed to a young, uniformed soldier on the other side of the street. "Look, there's Obie, Eddie O'Brien's boy. Haven't seen him since he joined the Army. I wonder why he's home now."

As the soldier drew near, the ladies noticed his right arm was missing, his crisply pleated uniform sleeve pinned at the shoulder.

Helga stood up as he approached, "Hello Obie!"

Obie tipped his hat. Nellie started to rise. "Don't you trouble yourself Mrs. Callaghan," he said, winking at Anna, her eyes diverted from the cart, now fixated on the empty sleeve. "You're gonna be a killer when you grow up, little girl," Obie said to Anna, "That black hair, long lashes, and them blue eyes are gonna turn lots of boys' heads. You wait and see. Better keep an eye on her, Mrs. Callaghan. Don't let her out of your sight."

"What's that poor boy going to do now with just one arm?" Nellie said to Helga.

"Aren't you proud of our boys overseas?"

"I am but it frightens me, Helga. I have two boys and maybe a third one on the way."

"The war will be over soon."

"I hope so," Nellie said, noticing Anna inching closer to the cart, "Anna, get back here … still, we know neighbors who lost their sons. Or they come home damaged like Obie. War is a terrible thing."

Anna slid closer to the cart, decorated with a big purple ribbon and the letters of her name painted in tropical orange around the top edge.

The boys stayed in church an extra hour after Mass to attend the religious instruction class regarding Baby Ray's First Communion. Jim had already received the sacrament the previous year, but Nellie had asked him to stay with his brother. At first, Jim was resentful that he had to sit through the classes all over again. It was cruel and unusual punishment he told her. Nellie explained about the dangers on the streets for any child walking alone. "You're his protector," Nellie said, "That makes me so proud of you."

Nellie kept calling Anna back to the stoop whenever she wandered off, encouraging her to play with Kewpie while she waited for her brothers. The anticipation was too much for her. Nellie compromised. "I'll let you ride up to Mr. Nicoletti's stoop, and no farther. Is that understood young lady?"

"Yes, Momma," said Anna, as Nellie pushed her off on the cart's maiden voyage.

Nellie was the only neighbor who tolerated Helga. She was good at small talk, which took pressure off Nellie to keep the conversations going. Everyone else on Cherry Street despised Helga, calling her a Kraut behind her back, despite her claim to be of Swedish stock. Nellie and Helga looked up as a strange woman approached. She was dressed in an out-of-season full-belted corduroy coat and a velour hat accented with rich silk velvet. The coat's chin-chin fur collar covered her neck completely. A large canvas bag was slung over her shoulder.

"Look at this one, will you. A bit overdressed, wouldn't you say?" Helga said as she eyeballed the woman up and down. Nellie kept one eye on Anna.

The woman stood close to the ladies, and handed a pamphlet to Helga, who crumpled it immediately and threw it to the ground.

"That was rude, Helga," Nellie said.

"So, what! I bet she's connected with Emma Goldman, another Yid," Helga said.

"Who's she," Nellie said.

"Ask your husband about Goldman. She spent some time in his jail."

Anna saw the woman's intrusion as an opportunity to venture past the Nicoletti tenement.

The breeze blowing in off the East River picked up. The woman distributing the pamphlets ducked into the tenement where Helga lived. Gaining access to the roof, she blithely tossed the mother load of propaganda into the Lower East Side's blustery atmosphere. In a matter of minutes, the Cherry Street sky was awash in pamphlets, hundreds printed in Yiddish and hundreds more translated into English. The anti-American Bolshevik rants rained down on windowsills, stoops, and heads. Mixed in with the pamphlets were scores of one-dollar bills and a handful of five-dollar notes. Up and down the street, men tipped their straw hats, hoping to catch the money. Women and children ran amok, snatching papers out of the air as if they were manna from heaven.

A woman screamed, "I got a dollar!"

"I got a five!" A little boy yelled, as his mother yanked it out of his hand.

Word spread quickly that real money was pouring down on Cherry Street. A feeding frenzy kicked into high gear. Crowds exited Corlears Hook Park to join the melee. Paper blew all over the street. People shoved, squealed, and jumped off their stoops to catch whatever the wind blew their way.

A Yiddish version of the pamphlet smacked into Nellie's face. She lost sight of Anna, tripped, and fell to the ground, bruising her knee. She hobbled into the street, hoping to see Anna near the Nicoletti tenement. Frantic, she screamed her name over and over again, veins popping out of her neck as she limped in and out of the crowd. Helga joined Nellie in the search but moved off to the side, saying she needed to catch her breath. Nellie kept pushing through, stopping to ask neighbors if they had seen Anna.

Unaware of her mother's fright, Anna took off full speed ahead. She darted in and out of what looked like a sea of legs, short, squat, thin and long, calling out, "Push me! Push harder!"

Rolling past the tenements in a blur yelling "Whee!" Anna leaned forward in her cart and thrust her body forward, gaining momentum. Anna raced past a cluster of people, then bumped down the curb to the less crowded street level. She rolled past the O'Learys, O'Dwyers, Monaghans, O'Briens, and Fitzgeralds, approaching a bit of a rise with enough oomph to get over it. She began her easterly descent toward the confluence of Cherry and Grand, two streets that merged at the riverbank. It was a dangerous intersection. One week earlier, two autos collided at full speed, the impact sending one of the vehicles crashing into a light pole, knocking it to the ground.

There was a long stretch of pavement between the river and the end of tenement row, mostly on a downward grade. Not obstructed by a mass of humanity, Anna's cart picked up more speed, reaching the last building on the street. No longer darting around crazed people catching flyers and dollar bills, Anna was free to see how fast her cart could go.

A large man, a lumbering figure unsteady on his feet, crossed over from the base of Corlears Hook Park heading toward Cherry Street, stumbling around trees and park benches, nearly falling at times. At the same moment, a uniformed police officer raced around the corner with the propaganda flittering down upon his head. A canvas sack landed at his feet.

Anna kept rolling down the grade. She saw the large man as he approached unsteadily. She yelled to him with all her might, "Push me! Faster!"

The cart picked up speed. It tilted back and forth, twisted wildly, never righting itself, hitting the curb near what was left of the lamppost. The pram wheel on the left rear caved inwards on its axle. Wheel bearings on the front skate came loose and spilled onto the street.

It was 12:16 p.m., high tide on the East River. The wind picked up considerably, kicking up whitecaps on the choppy water.

The sack in the back of the meat wagon

The 'Tub of Misery' steamboat to Blackwell Island, loaded with lunatics, liars, and paupers, pushed against the East River tide. The latest cargo of convicted criminals guarded by corrections officers would soon be outfitted in freshly laundered black and white stripes. Shackled together at the ankles, one prisoner said, 'I did nothing wrong'. 'Me too' his partner in crime decried in a song of innocence on the lovely boat ride to their new living quarters.

Closely guarded by burly men in white jackets, the lunatics talked to themselves incessantly, scratched themselves continuously, and rocked back and forth in a beat counter to the rhythm of the river.

The poor and sick were scattered about the ferry, with no one to guard them except a nurse or two. These poor souls were one month, one week, one more cough away from Potters Field.

Also on board, a tiny lady, dressed in black hat, black shawl and long black dress sat alone, paying no mind to anyone and no one paying any mind to her. She set a big basket upon her lap filled with edible goodies and a single long stem rose. The goodies were for a friend enduring a long stay in the hospital. The single rose with accompanying sealed note was to be delivered to Keeper James Callaghan at Blackwell Prison.

The lady dressed in black made the prison her first stop. Sgt. Costello summoned Callaghan into the visitor's room, informing him that a lady was waiting to see him.

"Who are you?" James said to her.

"Good day to you sir," she said, handing him the rose and envelope, "Before I boarded the ferry, a very kind police officer asked me to deliver this note to you. The lovely lady with him gave me this beautiful flower and said it would mean a lot to you."

James put the flower on the bench. He read the note:

> ### A RIDDLE
> *There's a musk rat in the burrow*
> *Bleeding from the ear*
> *If you get there before tomorrow*
> *There's a rotted pit in the cherry dear*
> *Five feet south under the southerly side*
> *Enter from the street and step inside*

"Who gave this to you?" Callaghan said.

"The police officer, sir,"

"What's his name?"

"I do not know," she said, backing away, "I was rushing to board the ferry and he asked me to bring it to you. Excuse me. I need to visit my friend. The poor dear is waiting for her goodies."

"What did the copper look like?" Callaghan said, blocking her exit.

Hearing Callaghan's angry voice, Sgt. Costello entered the room, "What's going on?"

James handed the note to Costello and said to the woman, "Were you paid to deliver this?"

"I tried to refuse, but he insisted," she said, offering the ten-dollar bill to James, "Maybe he meant for you to have it."

"Did you ever meet the officer before?" Costello said.

"No."

"Ma'am. Keep the money," Costello said, "We know most of the police officers who work near the dock. Any chance you remember his badge number?"

"I do not."

"What did he look like?" James said.

"Very tall."

"What about the woman?"

"She was tall as well."

"Anything special you might have noticed about the copper?" Costello said.

The lady put her finger to her chin, and said, "He had a shock of red hair."

"Notice anything different about the woman?" James said.

"I'm not sure, but ..."

"But what?" Costello said.

"She seemed overdressed for this time of year."

Costello took James aside, whispered to him, then turned to her, "I'm sorry we've delayed you Ma'am. In our line of work, we're trained to ask questions."

As she was leaving the room, James gave her the rose, "Give this to your friend."

"I'm not one for riddles, Callaghan," Costello said, "But I remember the *Musk Rats*. You had trouble upriver with their boss, Paddy Minogue. Right?"

"I gotta catch the next ferry out, Sarge" James said, "My mother's in trouble."

"Why?"

"Remember *Palisades Palace*?" James said.

"Yeah, Weehawken. What's that got to do with your mother?"

"My father worked there and fell to his death. Word is Minogue arranged it. My mother went after him with lawyers. Maybe …" James said, "… I gotta get to Ossining. She's old and sick. Don't want any creeps bothering her."

"How you getting there?" Costello said, "Never mind. Who's the mechanic at City?"

"Georgie," James said.

"Get your ass on the ferry. I'll tell Georgie it's a family emergency. He can gas up a wagon and meet you at the dock."

"Can you call Nellie. Tell her I had to take care of my mother."

Georgie drove a green and black 'City Prison' meat wagon to the dock. He gave the keys to James who got in and took off. Having immediately decoded the riddle, he drove straightaway to the Cherry Street bulkhead, *Five feet south under the southerly side.*

James crawled under the bulkhead deck and spotted the sack on a mound of dirt. Heart pounding, he peeled back the flap and saw the distinct pattern of Anna's birthday dress. He closed it. Feeling faint, he lowered his head between his knees, took several deep breaths and vomited.

He opened the flap completely and vomited again.

He put the sack under the prisoner's bench and drove north. He stopped at Emma's Bake Shop on the east side of Route 17 in Sloatsburg, parking the wagon near the front door.

James sat at the counter, drinking coffee. The waitress stared past him through the large window, taking in the wagon's stippled gilt lettering 'City Prison'.

"Do you know Carney Callaghan?" James said.

"Everyone knows Carney. He's a legend in these parts … he's not in any kind of trouble, is he?" she said.

"No. Carney's my brother … my older brother. Haven't seen him in a long time. Thought I'd surprise him with a visit. Can I leave the wagon here for a few hours?"

"Sure. Do you know how to find his cabin?"

"Point me in the right direction. It'll come back to me."

James followed her outside. "Go a quarter mile that way," she said, pointing south, "Follow the markers for Pine Meadow Trail. Not the shortest way but it's got fewer rocky ledges."

When the waitress went back inside, James opened the back of the wagon, and stared at the sack. He shut the door, returned to the bakery, and stood at the register. Beads of sweat rolled down his forehead.

"Are you feeling okay?"

James pointed to the phone on the wall. "I should let him know I'm coming. It's been some years."

"They don't own a phone. Their cabin's in the middle of the woods."

James stared at the wall. "I might call someone else … my wife ... my mother ..."

"Call anyone you want. Central will patch you through."

"I got kids too. Two boys. Two girls."

A customer walked in and stood in front of the display case, eyeing the breads and cakes. James lingered at the register, staring blankly.

"Give me a minute. I'll make the call for you," she said.

While the woman was busy with the customer, James walked out. He took the sack out of the wagon, crossed the road, and headed into the woods, to a place he had not visited since his father's funeral. He stopped several times along the path to catch his breath, sweat soaking through his uniform, creating a map of broad, moist splotches on his jacket. He came to the clearing within fifty yards of the cabin, and spotted Carney splitting logs near the storage shed.

Carney waved when he saw James, whom he had not seen since Nellie and James's wedding. When Carney attempted to embrace him. James waved him off. "I'm full of dirt and sweat. I smell like a pig."

"That's sweetness around here brother. Ya don't smell any worser than me." Carney leaned over to pick up the sack.

"Leave it. I'll carry it," James said, wiping his mouth on his sleeve.

"Come ta the cabin. Minnie'll git ya somethin' cold ta drink."

"Later. Let's talk in the shed."

Once inside, Carney put his boot to a crate, sliding it across the straw-covered floor. He brushed it off for James. Still clutching the sack handles, James sat down, removed his cap, and covered his face with his forearm. His whole body quivered, his knees banging together and head swaying back and forth.

Narrow shafts of light entered the shed through two eye windows. Carney stared at the sack, noticing fresh stains along the bottom edge. "I put my pet pig Sammy in the ground a few weeks ago. What ya got in that sack smells worse 'n that pig. Ya gonna show me what's in there or not?"

James released his grip on the handles. He covered his face with both hands. Carney placed the sack on a workbench. When he opened it, he jolted back several feet. "Fuck me!"

James covered his face with his cap.

"What trouble ya in, brother? Tell me befer I hafta start guessin' the worst."

James stood beside his brother, weakened by the sight of Anna's mangled body, "My little girl!" he said, holding the sides of his head, stomping his foot on the plank floor.

"She ain't nobody's little girl no more," Carney said as he gently placed a loose eyeball into its empty socket, "She belong to Jesus now."

James took deep breaths, staring wide-eyed at his brother.

Carney scooped out a fistful of blood-soaked propaganda flyers matted on the bottom of the sack and threw them on the floor. He closed the flap and cradled the sack in both arms.

As he started to walk toward the door, James said, "Where are you going?"

"Open the door fer me, will ya. Minnie'll clean her up."

"No. Don't let her see the body!"

"Minnie's tougher than you 'n me combined. She guts the jackrabbits 'n big bucks we eat, 'n skins their hides fer clothing."

"No lady should have to see ... I ... I touched her nose this morning. It's her fifth birthday."

"We ain't gonna leave her like this. Minnie's got some nice soaps, some spices 'n a nice clean sheet ta wrap her in. I bet there's a nice dress fer her in one of the trunks. Jes wait here 'n then we'll talk," Carney said, shaking his head, "Damn. I feel sick."

Carney told Minnie it was James's daughter and that's all he knows. He washed his hands in the sink. With her back to her husband, Minnie went about her business. She laid Anna on a side table and worked silently. She wiped her tears with the edge of her apron. Carney came up behind her. She turned around and fell into his arms. They wept together.

Carney returned to the shed and handed James a cup of whiskey, "Ya probably need this more than water. Ya up to talkin' now? Start anywheres ya like."

"Can we go outside?" James said as he gulped the whiskey.

They walked about fifty feet and stopped at the railing with a view of the old tater patch.

"When Bill and I came up here, you said any Callaghan family member could get buried here."

Carney pointed to a spot further east. "The offer still stands. We'll find a special place ta bury Anna. That's the family plot over there. While you're here, ya can pay yer respects to Dad 'n Uncle James."

As they walked toward the gravesites, James told Carney about the note delivered to him at Blackwell and its connection to the beating he gave Minogue years earlier at Sing Sing. He added that he never went home after picking up Anna's body. He has no idea what Nellie does or does not know.

"She's frightened to death. That's all ya gotta know. Her girl's missin' 'n ya ain't there ta give her the strength she needs. You're her husband. She be dependin' on ya in a terrible time like this. Ya gotta get back in town 'n call her. Let her know yer comin' home right away. Ya gotta protect her. Wimmen are fragile."

"I need time to think this through. Nellie can't see Anna's body. That'd haunt her forever."

"She must've called yer prison to tell ya a terrible thing happened. Wantin' ya to come straight home."

"I asked the sergeant to call her. Say I had to visit my sick mother right away."

"Why'd ya go 'n do that fer? Miss Peggy ain't sick. I unnerstand the pressure you're under but yer makin' some strange choices in this situation," Carney said, scratching his head, "I know ya bin strangers for a long time. But ya can't lie 'bout yer own mother. That ain't right. Take my advice. Git into town. Call Nellie first. Let her hear yer voice. Then, befer ya head home, visit yer Ma. This way, you won't be a liar. She's bin terrible missin' her grandkids growin' up. Ya gotta let her know now there's one less. Minnie Mae 'n me paid a visit 'bout a month ago. She's as healthy as a hog. Better git yerself a hotel fer the night. She's got some orphan kids stayin' in yer old room. Turned the house into a Mission place fer poor folk."

"I might do that but there's more to the story."

"Jes tell me the whole damn thing, will ya fer God's sake."

"The lady who brought the note to the prison gave me a rose. Telling me it has special meaning," James said, "So whoever told her to say that knows I have another daughter. Name's Rose."

"Ya got twin girls?"

"I had Rose with another woman."

"You're in a whole pile of shit right now, brother. Ta tell ya the truth, if it wuz me I wouldn't know what ta do next. How you'd wind up with another woman?" Carney said, looking at James, "You're white as a ghost. Better sit awhile. I'll get a refill on yer whiskey 'n join ya myself."

The brothers leaned back against the tree and drank.

"Nellie and I have been drifting apart for a while."

"Don't ya take care of her?"

"I give her money every week. Without fail."

"It don't surprise me ya think that's all there is ta takin' care of a wife. Dad thought handin' money over ta Miss Peggy made everythin' okay. She's still mighty troubled by it. Maybe Dad wasn't takin' care of her in ways important ta a woman. I got some of his habits, too. I guess we inherit the good 'n the bad 'n some shit all our own. Ya still with that other woman?"

"It'll be over as soon as I get back," James said as they stood and finished off their whiskey.

"Ya gotta warn her too. Don't ignore it. Maybe yer other daughter is still alive. Ya owe her that much," Carney said, attempting to embrace his brother again.

Carney picked up the log he had been working on. "Let me show ya somethin'. When yer in the middle of sawing a log 'n the wood starts ta bind, it means it's tryin' ta come back together."

"What're you trying to tell me? Just shoot straight."

"You 'n Nellie still got a chance. Ta be one whole piece of one another agin. Don't cut her all the way through. There's oppertunity ta repair yerselves."

"I get your drift."

"We'll git word ta ya on the funeral. I'll git my minister friend who'll say some mighty prayers fer this angel."

"Don't wait on me," James said, "Find a nice spot for her. Will you do that for me, Carney?"

Carney put his hand on James's shoulder. "I'll do it. It was me who started this shit with Minogue. I'll tell ya the story some day whenever ya come back with what's left of yer family. Rev. Dooze'll do a memorial or somethin' like that."

"I don't know if anybody knows anything. Maybe they think Anna's just missing, and need to keep looking for her," James said as he walked inside the shed and picked up the bloodied clump of papers off the floor.

"What're ya doin' with that garbage?"

"Evidence. Someone killed my little girl. They're gonna pay for it. I'll track 'em down."

"Ya got some healin' to do befer the trackin', brother. Ya know a lot of police from bein' in prison work. Why dint ya talk ta them 'bout your suspicions?"

"I got my reasons."

"I'm guessin' ya must've made enemies along the way in yer line of work. Am I on the right track?"

"Can't say."

"Ya got a whole lot of shit to straighten out. Talk to yer brother Bill when ya git home. Maybe he can help."

"He's no help."

"What 'bout yer boys?"

"What about them?"

"What're ya gonna tell 'em 'bout their little sister? Death's a delicate thing fer little kids."

"I don't plan to tell nobody nothing for the time being."

"This terrible thing could make ya harder or softer. What's it goin' to be? Could go either way with ya. Have a heart, brother. Be a man 'n tell yer wife 'n yer sons the truth. Tell'em we're gonna find a special burial place fer their little angel. Tell Rose's mother what she needs ta know. Nellie 'n yer boys need comfort 'n strength from ya. Ya gotta let them know they no longer have a sister. Else they'll be sick the rest of their lives. They'll find peace knowin' she's in heaven. 'N ya need to git care fer yourself too."

James turned around and started to walk away.

"Minnie Mae! Can ya come out here quick 'n give my brother a hug," Carney yelled, "Someone's gotta give this hurtin' man a hug. He ain't takin' none from me."

Minnie rushed outside the cabin, but James had already hit the Pine Meadow Trail. Carney put his arm around his wife and said, "Minnie, kin ya write poor Nellie a letter. My brother ain't goin' ta tell her nothin'. Jes be gentle n' soft with yer words. Tell her she n' the boys should come fer a visit. Tell her we know where Anna is but gotta tell her in person. Tell her to stop at Emma's on Seventeen n' they'll show her where the trail starts. I'll take the letter ta the Post Office when yer finished writin' it."

When James got back to Emma's Bakery, he called Costello. Sarge told him he had terrible news. Nellie's mother said there was an accident when Anna took a ride on the cart. The Coast Guard and NYPD Harbor unit have their boats out looking for her. Hopefully, she's still alive. "Oh God, Knuckles, I'm sorry. Let me know if there's anything I can do. Hope your mother's okay. Tragic. That's all I gotta say. Tragic."

James crossed the river. When he got to within one block of his old house in Ossining, the street was roped off, blocking all traffic. He parked the wagon and walked up to a man standing at the edge of a large crowd. "What's going on?" James said to him.

"Mayor's on his way."

"What's the big occasion?"

"Ribbon cutting. Renaming Dale Street."

"Why?"

"Honoring Mission work."

"What kind of Mission?" James said.

"Started out taking care of prisoners' families. Home for orphaned kids. Soup kitchen. Clothes for the poor. Good things I guess," the man said, lighting a cigar, "Not everyone likes the element coming in though. Know what I mean?"

"I know exactly what you mean. What the hell are they gonna call it now?"

"Mother Emma Kennedy Way."

"What kind of name is that for a street?"

"First they were going to name it after Peggy Callaghan. She told the board all credit goes to Emma …" The man stepped closer to James, putting on his spectacles to read the name tag on James's jacket, "Hey … you from around here?"

"Nah," James said, backing away, "I made a wrong turn."

A rose for Rose

The woman Margaret Lenehan, more familiarly known as Maggie, lives in a small apartment at 144 Elm Street. She is broad and stout with big bosoms and a wide behind. She walks with a gimpy gait and takes in laundry to pay the rent. So busy, she does not look after her children so much. Not proper like. A man comes by once a week for some special favors and helps out whenever he can with whatever money he finds in other men's pockets, mostly from gents recently incarcerated and who are required to change out of their street clothes and into prison uniforms which are kept pressed and neatly stacked in the storage room.

Maggie bore a son eight years ago. The boy was named Edward after his father with whom Maggie was once engaged but neglected to marry. Said father got crushed by a truck one teetering tottering whiskey hoisting afternoon.

Maggie also had a daughter named Rose whose fifth birthday was about to be celebrated in just a few days. Rose's father is the aforementioned gentleman who kindly provides supplementary monetary sustenance for Margaret Lenehan. Rose smells so sweet and is highly favored by her father who showers her with many gifts that give her much delight. He bounces her on his lap and runs his fingers through her curly blond hair. She giggles a lot.

Edward is mostly ignored by his mother's male visitor except on those occasions when the boy misbehaves and does not listen. At these unfortunate times Edward is subsequently disciplined in a rather severe manner. A sudden crack across his face is never applied by his mother but often requested by her of the man for whom she provides special (ahem, sexual) favors. As it turns out, Edward only hears out of his right ear, as a result of so many direct strikes to the left side of his face.

Edward helps his mother with the nasty recurrence of household expenses, collecting scrap wherever he finds it or is able to steal it, selling the metal to the scrap man who puts the pieces on his scale and pays Edward by the pound. Edward does not attend school and when he is not busy collecting scrap, it is his responsibility to safeguard his little sister from harm whenever she ventures outside to play.

On this lovely day at roughly 1:30p.m. Edward and Rose sit on the front stoop of 144 Elm Street while mother busies herself washing other people's dirty undergarments and sheets. A very wealthy lady who is also very pretty and very tall, comes by in a big fancy automobile, a Locomobile Model 48 Sportif Touring Car driven by her chauffeur who wears a uniform cap and coat. The chromium nickel chassis boasts a huge interior with ample seating for seven adults. The front fenders follow the contours of the bright yellow-painted-spoked wheels. The vehicle possesses long running boards, a cape style top, and luxurious leather upholstery throughout. There is glittering brass outside mirrors flanking both passenger and drivers' sides, and a gleaming emerald exterior all befitting of the vehicle's owner. The automobile commands the attention of all eyes capable of withstanding such wonder.

More than a few people are of the opinion this woman possesses a natural beauty. She has a high forehead and big brown eyes, accented by subtly arching eyebrows and long eyelashes. She must have very long brown hair because it is pulled back over her ears and tucked beneath her black satin hat causing the hat to sit rather high upon her head. The fashionable headpiece she wears has a matching ribbon band stretched over the hat's small peak, which in turn is adorned with a fine cross-shaped diamond pin. This latter article of jewelry matches the brooch pinned against the piece of black ruffled lace cloth which rises up from her shoulders and delicately, though unevenly, surrounds the entirety of her slender, quite elegant neck. The pins closely match the centerpiece of a beaded necklace, which sits under the ruffled lace collar and drops in a V-shaped pattern, just inches below the brooch. The woman has a fine nose with perfectly rounded nostrils and a subtly dimpled chin.

Edward and Rose look up from their play when the woman leans her head outside the window. With the forefinger of her right hand, she beckons Edward to come hither. Edward takes a few sideways steps toward the Touring Car, never removing his eyes from his sister longer than a second or two. The young protector of little sister circles the Touring Car with his big brown eyes wide open, which never before beheld such a splendid sight, a motorized chariot fit for the gods. When Edward comes close to the Touring Car's rear window, the woman hands him a red, long-stem rose and says to him, "Give this bloom to your sister for her birthday. Tell her to be mindful of the thorns."

Edward walks back to the stoop and hands the rose to Rose, placing her hand on the part of the stem that bears no thorns. "This is from the lady. Go over and say thanks." Before Rose could say anything, the woman opens her window wider and holds up a box with the lid removed, displaying a brand-new doll and motions for the little girl to come to the Touring Car which she does, with Edward close behind.

"Do you like this doll?" the woman says, removing the kewpie from the box.

"It's a Kewpie!" Rose squeals as she hands the flower to her brother so she can grab hold of the doll, that wears a very pleasant little dress fitted exactly to her little body.

"Yes, it is and it's yours … for your fifth birthday," the woman says.

"Her birthday ain't till the end of the week," Edward says.

"I know that" says the woman softly, "Would you like me to come back later in the week?"

"What fer?" Edward says.

"To treat you and your sister to some ice cream. How would you like that?" the woman says, looking at the curly-haired girl with chubby cheeks and chubby legs.

Edward looks at the woman, "How'd ya know it wuz my sis's birthday … who are ya anyway, lady?"

The woman laughs and taps the chauffeur's window, "Melvin, tell these children who I am."

The chauffeur turns his head, looks at Rose and says, "This grand woman is your father's sister. They grew up together in Ossining."

"We can't go. I hafta watch her," says Edward.

"I want ice cream now," exclaims Rose.

"Why don't you both come along with me. We'll have a party for Rose's birthday," the woman says cheerily, "Celebrate early. I bet you know the ice cream parlor around the corner."

"Depends on whether Ma tells me I gotta hunt down some scrap," Edward says.

"I have a question, Edward," the woman says as she opens her purse, "How much do you make in one whole week collecting scrap?"

"Sometimes three bucks," Edward said.

The woman hands Edward a five-dollar bill and two one-dollar bills.

"Wow!"

"Give your ma five dollars, then spend the rest on yourself. *I'm* paying for your ice cream."

"That's a good deal, son. I would take it if I were you," Melvin says, "You can go to the arcade *and* the cinema."

Edward stares at the five-dollar bill, not paying any attention to the driver. None at all.

"And we can go for ice cream on my real birthday, too," says Rose.

"We'll see about that," Edward says.

Edward and Rose go back to the stoop. Edward stares at the money in his hands while Rose plays with the kewpie doll.

Edward puts his arm around Rose. "You really wanna go for ice cream today, don't ya?"

"Please. Please."

"Ma won't let us go with a stranger," Edward reasons.

"She's no stranger. She's my daddy's sister."

The lady heard what Edward said and motions for both children to come closer to the auto. As they come up to the rear window of the fancy coach, the lady says to Rose, "Your big brother is right to get permission from your mother. She needs to know where her children are at all times."

"Aw. I want ice cream," says Rose.

"What's your favorite ice cream flavor, Rose?" the woman says.

"I like strawberry."

"How about you, Edward?"

"Chocolate."

Got 'em. Got 'em! The woman smiles at Rose and Edward. "How about we get a double scoop of strawberry and a double scoop of chocolate *today*."

"Yay," says Rose.

"I gotta ask ma," Edward says, "I don't think she'd mind, seein' as you're Rose's aunt and all."

"I want to be your aunt, too, Edward. Your *favorite* aunt."

The woman leans her head and long, elegant neck out the window, nearly losing her fancy hat, "Here's an idea. Rose, why don't you put the kewpie back in the box so your brother can take it upstairs. You really shouldn't play with it until your actual birthday."

"Okay," Rose says as she hands the doll to the lady, "It's still okay to get ice cream today, right?"

"Of course." she says to Rose.

"Edward, here," the lady says to him, as she opens the car door and hands over the box. She then slides sideways on the plush leather seat, patting the space just vacated.

"Rose, come sit with me while your brother goes upstairs and asks for your Ma's permission."

When Edward heads toward the door, Melvin puts his head out the front window and says to the boy, "Hey sport, how would you like to ride up front when you come back?"

Edward looks at the big Touring Car. "You bet, mister!" then runs up the stoop with Rose's Kewpie and long-stem rose tucked under his arm.

Almost there! All our planning. Stay on it! Oh Daddy, it's working. Go inside, little boy. Close that door and go to Momma. Hurry now! It's almost done!

As Edward closes the front door to the tenement, Melvin turns around. "Are we good to go?"

"Certainly," the lady says, patting Rose's head, "Start her up, Melvin. We're going to transfer this precious little girl to a finer whorehouse."

The chauffeur gets out of the driver's seat. He closes the back door as the woman puts her arm around the little girl's shoulder and draws her closer to her side. Melvin gets behind the wheel and speeds away.

When Edward gets upstairs, he sees freshly folded laundry piled two feet high on his mother's worktable. Just a few feet away, Maggie Lenehan is asleep on the living room sofa. Edward puts the flower and box with Rose's doll next to the laundry so that his mother will see it as soon as she wakes.

When Edward returns to the street, there is no fancy auto in front, up, down or across the street. He walks around the block to the ice cream store on Leonard. He waits and waits. The big fancy Touring Car is nowhere in sight. He knows he is in trouble and also knows that his mother will ask Rose's father to give him another crack on the side of his head. And, he realizes, this time he deserves it. Then, sensing this incident is far more serious than any of his previous infractions he takes the seven dollars out of his pocket, looks at each one of the bills, and starts walking in the opposite direction of where he lives.

He never did return home.

Visitors

A pall was cast over Cherry Street. Anna drowned, most neighbors supposed, whispering in the darkness that shrouded the Callaghan family. It was the void of the unknown, a cruel time of in-between. Not a death, but rather a disappearance. Hope was still alive yet with the narrowest of margins.

How could a five-year-old survive East River currents? Was her body swirling around on the bottom, being torn by shards of broken bottles and the ragged edges of cans littering the river floor? Or was Anna roaming the streets, unsure how to get back home. Police were on the alert, investigating every possible lead.

Despite the concern that the family needed privacy, three individuals took it upon themselves to visit the stricken Callaghans.

The unbearable weight of the troubling matter affected everyone on Cherry Street, none more so than Salvatore Nicoletti. Salvatore's pain was raw. He took full responsibility for this tragedy.

The police called on the Nicolettis early Monday morning. They revealed disturbing evidence related to Anna's disappearance, which Salvatore felt obligated to share with the Callaghans. Salvatore struggled to climb the stairs. He gripped the railing with both hands, taking a breather on each landing, mouthing the words he planned to say. When he reached the second floor, he removed his cap, holding it tightly to his chest and combed back his curly black hair with his fingers.

He knocked on the Callaghan's door. Nana opened it, stepping halfway into the hallway.

"Escusa, Missa Nana. I am so sorrowful for your Anna. Such a preciosa girl. May I pleasa see Missa Nellie?"

"I'm sorry Salvatore. Mrs. Callaghan's not taking visitors today," Nana said, wiping her eyes with the tip of her apron, "There is little comfort for her right now."

"And you, Missa Nana?"

"I've seen much and suffered much. But this ..."

"Hard. Issa so hard."

"How is Mrs. Nicoletti?" Nana said, breaking the silence.

"Shesa mad at me today."

"Why, Salvatore?"

"She come after me witha the pan. Hitta me on the head. Seza to me stoppa making things for neighbors. We needa the money. No more free," Salvatore said, hanging his head, "I so sorry for builda the cart, and-"

Nana placed her hand upon Salvatore's forearm. "There's no need to apologize Salvatore. Everything you do is made from a pure heart. Whatever happened had nothing to do with your work."

Salvatore wiped his eyes with his handkerchief.

"Please don't blame yourself. What can I tell Nellie for you?"

"The polizia. They come to my house and tella me they found a small piecea Anna's cart in the river."

"How did they know it was her cart?"

"It hadda orange and parta Anna's name on it."

"I wonder why they told you and not us,"

"They say they knewa I build it."

"How did they know?"

Salvatore looked at the floor, then at Nana. "I dunno," quickly adding, "Maybe they gonna finda Anna too." He excused himself, put on his cap and hurried down the stairs.

A few minutes later, Helga knocked on the door, wearing a black dress, and a small black hat with a veil pinned at the top.

Nana opened the door. "Hello Helga,"

"I am so sorry. This is horrible! Can I speak to Nellie?"

"She's fast asleep."

"Poor thing. I am so sorry," Helga said, sobbing.

"We all are. Anna is the heart and soul of our family."

"How are the boys?"

"I don't think it's sunk in yet. Shocked doesn't even describe it."

Helga removed the hatpin, letting the veil drop over her face. "I just wanted to say how sorry I am. Will you tell Nellie I came by and ..." in between sobs, she said, "I should have never left Nellie's side ..."

"It's no one's fault. It was a tragic accident. No one's to blame." Nana scrutinized Helga's face through the veil, "Why are you wearing black?"

"I didn't know what else to do." Helga turned and ran down the stairs, sobbing.

Ten minutes after Helga's visit, there was another knock. Nana opened the door and tilted her head back to make eye contact with the tall police officer. He removed his cap, revealing a mop of curly red hair, "Sorry to bother you Mary, but is Mr. Callaghan about? He wasn't at the prison this morning. I'd like a word with him."

"He's not at home."

"Any idea when he'll return?" the police officer said, looking over her head, peering into the apartment.

"He's visiting his mother upstate. She's not been well lately."

"Sorry to hear that. Okay, thanks." The policeman turned toward the staircase.

Nana called after him, "Is this about Anna?"

"No news yet."

"Can I tell Mr. Callaghan the purpose of your visit?"

"It can wait until he gets back."

He was halfway down the stairs when Nana called after him from the landing, "How did you know my first name?"

"Everyone knows the Callaghans, Mary."

"Everyone who knows the Callaghans calls me Nana," Nana said as she came down a few steps. "What's *your* name so I can tell Mr. Callaghan who called?"

"Everyone calls me Red."

"I've never seen you on Cherry Street before. Are you new with the seventh?" Nana asked, as the front door shut.

Maggie

James parked the wagon in the prison garage. Georgie ran outside. "Hey Callaghan, sorry about your daughter." James kept walking, heading straight to 144 Elm. He used his own key to enter the apartment. As soon as he crossed the threshold, Maggie rushed him with a knife in her hands, "Where are my kids?"

James sidestepped her as she lunged at him. She kicked the door shut, trying to corner him. "I'll put this pig sticker in your fat gut."

Keeping his back to the wall, James wormed out of the corner.

"I'd stick it in your heart if I thought you had one."

James smelled her whiskey breath, looked at her wild eyes, then grabbed hold of a small wood chair. "Put that down, you drunken bitch," James said as he upended the chair. He pressed its four legs against her chest.

With her hair askew, dark sacs under her eyes, neck laced with protruding veins, and drool dripping out of the corner of her mouth, Maggie grabbed a rung of the chair and pushed him away. She gripped the knife with both hands, thrusting the weapon at him, grazing his hand. James threw the chair at her feet. She stumbled, recovered her balance, and came at him again with renewed fury. James grabbed a pillowcase and wrapped it around his hand. When Maggie thrust the knife again, the blade penetrated the fabric, drawing more blood. Lifting his arm high over his head, he swung full force on her wrist, knocking the knife to the floor. As Maggie scrambled to retrieve it, James wrapped a towel around her neck and yanked her backwards. She rolled over and rose to her knees, but James punched her squarely on the side of her head, and she fell to the floor, moaning.

James looked at the piles of unfolded, unwashed laundry lying side-by-side with empty whiskey bottles scattered on the floor. He sat on an upholstered chair, breathing heavily, heart pounding. Out of breath and bleeding from the mouth, Maggie rose to a sitting position.

James used his teeth to tear several strips off a dirty sheet. He used two pieces to stop the bleeding of his hand and threw a few strips of cloth at Maggie. "Wipe your mouth."

"I went to the coppers about my kids. Won't rest till they find them. Bullshit. Maybe they ran away. More bullshit. They got boats on the river searching for another kid. Open season on five-year old daughters, huh?" Maggie wiped her mouth, and said, "You in trouble, mister prison keeper?"

"Shut up," James said, winding the strips around his hands.

"I went to the prison. They told me you took a few days off. Didn't think to let me know, huh? By the way, I know where you live; 347 Cherry. As soon as I clean up, I'll make a social call on your wife. Have a nice, little chat with her. Seems we have a lot in common."

"You'll regret it if you go near my house. Catch my drift, Maggie dear?"

"Suppose I do. What the hell are you going to do about it?"

"It'll be your last day this side of heaven."

"Not sure I'll make it to heaven. But it's a short trip to hell for you ... Lucifer. I wish I never laid eyes on you and never did any of the disgusting things you made me do. I shouldn't a been so desperate for money. Look who I got mixed up with."

James glared at Maggie as she wiped the blood from her mouth. "Fair warning, bitch. Don't go near my wife. You don't belong in the same building together. She's a lady. You're a fat, useless sow."

"I'm sure she's a right proper lady. But I was good enough for your perversions, wasn't I?"

"I coulda done better on Seventh Avenue for less dough. You're a washerwoman whore taking care of customers' dirty laundry. Your job is soaking, boiling, scrubbing, hanging out to dry, ironing, sucking, and blowing. Sometimes you catch a break on your back, spreading your legs like a hard-up beetle. That's who you are. No more. Often a lot less. Catch my drift?"

"This whore is the mother of your daughter," Maggie said, rising to her feet.

"That's the only thing to your credit. Taking a good dump gives me more of a thrill than laying down with you."

"By the way, there's a present for you under the table. Have a look."

James lifted the lid off the box, never taking his eyes off Maggie. He looked inside and saw a rose broken at the stem and Anna's Kewpie doll.

Maggie took a note out of her dress pocket and said, "This came with it. Let me read it to you. 'To James. Love from your sister, El Yid'."

"I don't have a sister," James said as he grabbed the note.

"I always knew you were a Jew lover."

"Clam up. Or I'll give you another whack."

"You only told me about your fat slob brother. He's better off than you are right now, isn't he? You pissed on some bad people and now they're putting their stink on you. Why did you have to drag me along? Are my kids still alive?"

"I have no idea."

"You better find them. Bring them back here. Then, get the hell out of my life."

"I'm done with you, sow."

"I'm not nearly done with you," Maggie said as she hawked up phlegm and spit it in his face. James wiped it off, raising his hand to strike her. Maggie stood still. James lowered his arm. He opened the door and left the building, his hand bleeding through the cloth.

James walked into the apothecary shop on Centre Street frequented by prison employees. The pharmacist led him into the back where he held James's hands over the sink and poured a liquid antiseptic over his wounds. He then wrapped them with gauze. James offered to pay him, but the pharmacist refused.

Back Home

Jim opened the front door a crack to listen in on his father who was having a conversation with a policeman. The men's voices barely rose above a whisper.

He heard the police officer say, "No cop named Red in our precinct."

Jim also heard the policeman say that a piece of Anna's cart washed ashore near Catherine Street. It was a small piece with the letters "AN' painted on top of what looked like the outer edge of an orange. People he knew in Sanitation told him other pieces might show up further downriver. He also mentioned there were bloodstains on the ground near the broken lamppost.

The two men moved further down the hallway. A few more words were exchanged that Jim could not decipher. As the policeman walked down the stairs, Jim closed the door behind him and joined the rest of the family, gathered together at his father's direction.

When James came inside, he went into the bedroom and emptied the drawers and closets of all clothing, bedding, dolls, coloring books and toys belonging to Anna. He shoved everything into two large sacks and put them in the hallway. He entered the front room where Nana, Nellie, Uncle

Bill, Jim, and Baby Ray waited. Nellie and Nana sat on the sofa. Uncle Bill sat in a wood chair while the boys sat next to each other on the floor. Standing over them, hands on hips, James forcefully instructed his family to never mention Anna's name again. There would be consequences if they did not follow his orders.

When his father's voice throttled to its most fearsome pitch, Baby Ray cowered in a corner, fingering his rosary beads. After more angry words bellowed out, Baby Ray wet his pants. Jim stared at the floor the whole time his father barked. Nana held Nellie, mother and daughter dissolving into one body. Nana's embrace never loosened throughout James's harangue.

Bill stood up and announced he had to meet a friend.

"Sit down. You ain't going nowhere," James said.

"Wadda you want with me?"

"Let's review this again," James said, "You were coming out of the park when you saw Anna, right?"

"I said I saw a girl in a cart."

James grabbed Bill's shirt and shook him violently, "Who the hell did you think was in the cart? You don't know your own niece, you idiot?"

"I was tired from working all night."

"Correction. Drinking all night."

Bill pried apart James's grip and stood. "Maybe I had a few."

"Did you see anyone?"

"I told you I saw a girl."

"Anyone else?"

Bill thought for a minute and said, "A woman. And a copper."

"What did the woman look like?"

"All's I saw was her back."

"What was the color of her hair? What was she wearing?"

"I didn't look at those things."

"What about the copper?"

"He was in uniform."

"Was he tall or short?"

"I don't know. He was bending over, picking something up."

"What color was his hair?"

"He had his hat on," Bill said.

"Wait for me in the hall. I'll need help with the sacks."

Nana stroked Nellie's cheek and said to James, "What happened to your hands?"

"I cut myself … helping my mother move some stuff around."

"Oh, is that where you were?"

"Yeah. That's where I was."

"I'm only asking because we weren't sure. We were worried."

"Didn't Costello call?"

"I spoke to him. I don't remember exactly what he said. We were all hysterical," Nana said, "Sorry to hear Peggy's sick. We grandmothers aren't getting any younger, you know … wiser maybe."

Over thirty hours without sleep, James stared blankly at the wall behind his mother-in-law, wincing whenever he rubbed his bandaged hands.

"We had visitors this morning," Nana said, "A few neighbors stopped by to pay their respects."

"Who?" James said.

"Helga and Mr. Nicoletti."

"The Kraut and the Wop."

"Salvatore's a good neighbor," Nana said, "There's not a room in this apartment without something he built for our family."

James leaned close to Nana. She could smell his cigar breath. "Did he ask me if it was okay to build the cart? Look what happened."

"Salvatore said he mentioned it to you once. Maybe you forgot. The boys wanted it to be a surprise. They thought you'd be proud of them for helping him build it," Nana said, smiling at the boys. She looked up at James, "I almost forgot. There was a third visitor."

"Who?"

"A police officer."

"From the seventh?"

"I have no idea where he's from."

"What do you mean?"

"He didn't tell me his name. Said everyone calls him Red."

James whispered, "What did he want?"

"He said he'd discuss it with you, acting like he knew you."

Nana placed one hand on Nellie's head and the other on her stomach. "Do you want to lie down?"

Nellie wrapped both arms around her mother's waist. Jim held on to her leg.

When he had awakened that morning, Jim found his mother sitting on the kitchen floor beneath the breakfast table, her legs splayed, her arms limp, and her eyes fixed on the opposite wall. He tried talking to her, shaking her at times, but her whole affect was numb, her stare vacant. He knelt in front of her, put his face close to hers, blinking his eyes, hoping she would blink in return. "Momma, it's me, Jim," he said, kissing her forehead, "I love you Momma."

The only occasions Jim saw his mother up and moving were the trips she made to the toilet. He waited each time for her return. He pulled out a chair for her, hoping she would finally speak. Yet, each time it was as if he was invisible. Each time she rested her back against the wall and slid to the floor.

Nana was the only person Nellie responded to following Anna's disappearance. She stayed up most of the night, pacing, looking out the front window every few minutes until Nana coaxed her back into bed. Mother and daughter curled up together. Nana holding her until she fell asleep.

It startled Nana when Nellie suddenly jumped up in bed, letting out with a painful moan.

"What's the matter, Nellie?"

"My back. A sharp pain," Nellie said, perspiring. She fell back asleep, but it was a fitful sleep, waking up every fifteen minutes.

James stopped bellowing for a minute as Nana got up and led Nellie into the bedroom. The boys followed. James tapped Jim on the shoulder and pointed him back to the front room. Jim looked at his father and said, "I saw it too."

"What are you talking about?"

"I heard what he said about the blood. I saw it myself."

James slapped Jim full force on the right side of his head. "That's for not minding your own business." James slapped him again, knocking him to the floor. "That's for skipping school." Jim had difficulty hearing much of what his father said afterwards.

Inside the bedroom, Nellie complained about the pain in her back again. She told her mother she'd been spotting her underwear.

"When did that start?"

"Right after … it happened," Nellie said.

In the front room, Jim started seeing double. His father's face and the ceiling above his head swirled in a dizzy mix of nose, eyes, mouth, and plaster. The clamor of his father's angry words reverberated in his head.

"Don't say anything about the blood, again. It's none of your business." With his father's wild-eyed, red face pressed so close to his, Jim saw the detritus of a chewed cigar, tiny bits of brown matter stuck between his father's crooked yellow teeth. James put his face close to his son's face again, a hairbreadth away. Jim was repulsed by the cigar breath and felt the bile rise in his throat. Each time his father's mouth opened, more bits of dark brown tobacco joined the spittle rolling over his moist lower lip.

Jim's head pulsated in an agonizing thrum. With the maniacal look in James's fierce eyes, and the angry, cruel words he spewed forth, Jim focused on his father's teeth, worn down from years of chomping on cigars.

Back in the bedroom, Nellie stood up unsteadily and held her stomach with both hands.

"What is it? Tell me exactly what's happening," Nana said.

"I'm having contractions … they're coming …"

Nana escorted her down the hallway, praying that the toilet was not occupied.

Nearly delirious, unable to defend himself, Jim absorbed his father's breath, so close and rank it nearly overtook Jim's ability to breathe. He felt his heart beating faster, a fearful and furious pounding on the wall of his skinny chest.

Finally, James backed off and joined Bill in the hallway. They each carried one sack of Anna's belongings. James put his load down and lit a cigar. Bill, the uncle, and James, the father, hauled off every material trace of Anna as they transported her garments and toys to the dump. There, the brothers watched five years of Anna's life disappear in a vapor of smoke and ashes.

With Nana's hand on Nellie's shoulder, the embryo Nellie carried for close to two months dropped from her womb into the toilet, gender undetermined.

The Confessional

"If either of them falls down, one can help the other up," Nellie said as she sat across from James at the breakfast table. Sitting sphinx like, with weary, swollen eyes, he stared at the framed prints on the wall: Pope Benedict XV; an Irish blessing; and the blond hair, blue-eyed Christ, whom James referred to as the Danish Jesus.

Nellie knelt at his side, placing both hands on his arm. "But pity anyone who falls and has no one to help them up. Remember our wedding when Father Corcoran shared that verse with us. We exchanged our solemn vows. Promised to hold each other up forever."

James withdrew his arm from her grasp. "Our daughter probably drowned. That's all I have to say."

It was late Saturday morning, three weeks after Anna disappeared and one week after Baby Ray made his First Communion. It was confession day for the Callaghans. The boys waited for their mother in the front room, looking out the window, watching neighborhood friends playing stoop-ball.

Nana kept the family from falling apart. She stayed close to Nellie, got the boys off to school, and took over the cooking and cleaning. She was

Nellie's sole support, carrying her through the dual crisis of Anna's disappearance and the miscarriage.

Jim stopped questioning his mother about Anna. The depth of her sorrow frightened him but when she crawled out of her blank-eyed abyss, his despair turned to hope.

James camouflaged his sorrow. He focused intently on his work. He relished the opportunities to break the spirits as well as the knuckles of the prisoners that made New York City an unsafe place. These outcasts needed to be reprimanded for their crimes and reminded that they were worthless human beings. To James Callaghan, the keeper, his prisoners needed to be defanged, declawed, and kept in manacles, until they lost their bite.

Nana suggested that Nellie take Jim to the doctor as he does not hear well out of his right ear. He complains about severe headaches. Poor sleep causes him to doze off in class.

"We're both hurting so bad," Nellie said to James, "What are we going to do?"

"I don't know," James said.

"Is there anything you can tell me?"

"Like what?"

"You said she probably drowned. Will we ever know for sure?"

"Maybe. Maybe not. They're still looking for her. They found more pieces of the cart. That's all I know."

"James, look at me," Nellie said, "I need you to talk to me about how you're feeling. I know you're hurting. I'm hurting. I'm trying to get through this with you. I need to be able talk to you about our lost child," Nellie said, "And please, please talk to Jim."

"About what?" James said.

"Anything. For God's sake, he's your son. You slapped him so hard he's having trouble hearing. He wants to know about his sister. He's only eight. It's perfectly natural for him to ask about Anna."

"He's gotta learn to obey me."

"The boys and I are going to confession. Why don't you come with us?"

"I went last week."

"Who did you see?"

"You know damn well who I go to."

"Father Flynn?"

"I've known him for years."

"He's totally deaf."

"That's a lie."

"No, it isn't, and you know it," Nellie said, "Father O'Brien is our family priest. Why did you stop going to him?"

"Everybody loves Father Flynn."

"Three Hail Marys and two Our Fathers Flynn. That's his penance for everyone. It doesn't matter if you killed someone or told a little white lie. That's why I need to go with the boys. All the children know the trick. Go to Father Flynn. His line is long, but the visit is short. You should know better, James, a good Irish Catholic like yourself."

"Father Flynn is a good priest," James said as he got up from the table.

"How would you know?" Nellie said softly, gazing at the now empty chair.

Once they stepped inside St. Mary's, Nellie escorted her sons to the short line outside Father O'Brien's confessional. She said a prayer at the Blessed Virgin's altar and lit a candle for Anna. She stood in Monsignor Corcoran's line, with only two people ahead of her. Father Flynn's line stretched to the back of the church.

When his turn came, Jim knelt on the pew. Father O'Brien opened the sliding panel. Baby Ray was waiting his turn on the opposite side of the box.

"Bless me Father, for I have sinned. It has been three weeks since my last confession." After listing a few venial sins, Jim said, "I hate my father."

"You should love your father," the priest said.

Jim leaned the left side of his head closer to the screen. "He beats me."

"A father's discipline is a good thing. It's a sign of love, like Our Heavenly Father correcting those He loves. Do you have any other sins you want to confess?"

"Yes. A mortal sin. I want to kill my father."

"Son, you must not …"

"I don't really want to kill him. I want to hurt him."

"You must ask God for forgiveness …"

Jim interrupted, speaking rapidly, "He beat me and won't let me talk about my sister. When I get bigger, I'm going to hit him as hard as he hit me. I asked him where my sister is. I want to know if she's really dead. One day I'll push that smelly cigar down his throat while it's still lit. Hope it chokes him. Before that I'll break his yellow teeth."

Jim lost control. He had thought of nothing else for weeks, and let it all out, "I want to watch him run around the room, knock over chairs because it hurts so much, and he can't even talk because the lit cigar is stuck in his throat. It'll teach *him* a lesson. The pain'll be so bad it'll make him faint on the floor." After a moment of silence, Jim said, "I'm sorry Father but that's how I feel. I don't care so much that he hurt me. I want to know about my sister!"

"Who are you talking about?" the priest said.

"Anna, Father. You baptized her five years ago. You baptized me and Raymond too. For all the good it did."

"I want to offer you absolution for your sins."

"Do you know where Anna is, Father? Can you tell me?"

"I can't help you."

"Does my father come to you for confession? Did he ever say anything about Anna? My mother says you're like a member of our family. You're the baptizer. Like John the Baptist."

"Ask your mother these questions," Father O'Brien said. Before he closed the panel Jim said, "My mother's not allowed to say Anna's name, either."

The priest took his hand off the sliding panel. "I must say your penance and offer my blessing."

Crying, Jim said, "I'm doing penance already ... and I don't want your blessing."

"God forgive you. Five decades of the rosary. Ten Our Fathers," the priest said and slammed the panel shut. He opened the panel on the other side where Baby Ray waited.

Nellie was next in line for Monsignor Corcoran. She spotted Jim across the sanctuary and motioned for him to sit in the front pew.

This was Baby Ray's first confession following his First Communion. Father O'Brien prompted him, "Do you have any sins to confess?"

"I wr- wr- wrote a poem for my sister."

"Is it a naughty poem?"

"No. It's a n- n- nice poem. Want to hear it?"

"Some other time. Can you think of one sin you committed this past week."

"I saw a girl who looks l- l- like us."

"That's not a sin."

"My friend t- t- told me to go to Elm Street and l- l- look for her. She sits on a st- stoop a lot ... with a man."

"What are you trying to tell me?" Father O'Brien said.

"She looks a lit- little like An- An- Anna and Jim and me. The same k- k kind of voice, too. I met her once b- but didn't say who I was."

"I'm not sure I follow."

"I w- w- went over there before my sister f- f- fell in the river. Miss Hel- Helga told me about the girl. I know her name. I know her m... mom ... mommy's name. She washes sh- sheets and d- dirty un- underwear."

"I'm not ..." the priest said.

"Ro- Rose," Baby Ray blurted out, "I for- forgot her mommy's name."

"Rose is a lovely name."

"Like the fl- flower. The g- girl got a older br- brother. But he doesn't look li- like us." Baby Ray noticed Father O'Brien's hand moving to close the panel, "I d- did a sin."

"Yes?"

"I spy on my f- father."

"Why would you do something like that?"

"He works on W- White Street, near Ro- Rose's house. I saw him on her st- stoop eating."

"He was probably on his lunch hour and needed a place to sit," the priest said.

"But he … he had … had his han- hand round … round Rose."

Father O'Brien shut the panel.

Nellie's turn came for Monsignor Corcoran. "Bless me Father, I am not sure if I have sinned."

"Excuse me?" Monsignor said.

"I need to know the difference between penance, punishment, and prayer for forgiveness."

"Do you have sins you want to confess? This is not religious instruction class."

"Can't I ask a question first?"

"This is not a negotiation," he said, "Are you seeking absolution for your sins?"

"Like I said, I am not sure whether I sinned or not."

"You can make an appointment at the church office. Maybe, one of the priests can answer your questions."

"I'm not sure whether I sinned," Nellie said.

"Did you want me to tell you what you did or did not do in the eyes of God?"

"Then, you decide if I sinned?" Nellie said.

"God decides."

"Then, should not God be the one who decides what the penance should be?"

"He does, through me, your priest."

"I am not educated in theology like you. Yet I listened to my mother when she told me that there are some religions that impose a severe penance. That you must actually live another life if what you did is so terrible."

"That is what repentance is in our Catholic tradition," Monsignor said, "To turn your life around. Admit your sin. Ask God for forgiveness. Accept His grace and willfully say that you will not commit that sin again."

"That's just it. There is no *again*. It's something that happened that is lost forever. The other religion makes you take a vow of silence for the rest of your life, or serve the poor, a penance not for the length of the rosary but for the length of your life. That's a real penance. Intentional. Severe. Maybe that's what I need to forget my pain."

"I want you to have peace with what happened, Nellie."

"You don't know what happened and you don't have the authority," Nellie said.

"I beg your pardon."

"You have been most helpful, Monsignor. Thank you." Nellie said in the middle of his absolution. She exited the confessional, closing the door behind her.

She wrapped her arms around her boys as they walked along Grand Street. They passed pushcarts brimming with a variety of merchandise for adults and children: umbrellas, stockings, whistles, overcoats, ribbons, shoes, and more. Nellie idly examined the goods, trilling her angelic voice above the squeaking wheels and noisy vendors. Rows of fruit and vegetable pushcarts were lined up, side by side, offering bananas, oranges, baked goods, and sweets. The boys' eyes opened wide. Nellie knew what they wanted most. She led them into the sweet shop and let them choose their favorite ice cream.

They reached the river where Grand meets Cherry at the riverbank. A dense fog painted a haze over the river, washing its mist over their faces. The river's gauze veil obscured their visibility but did not disguise the sounds of river commerce, the toots from tugs pulling barges, or the blast of tanker horns from halfway uptown. The breeze off the river swept aside a few strands of Nellie's long brown hair, as she looked to the sky.

"Is heaven up there, Momma? Jim said.

"It's all around," Nellie said, drawing her sons close to her side.

"I don't see nothing, Momma," Baby Ray said, looking skyward. He cast his eyes at the river, "Is hell d- down there?"

"Hell is very close, sometimes," Nellie said, staring into the distance.

"What are you looking at, Momma?" Jim said.

"Just looking …and listening," Nellie said.

"To what?" Baby Ray said.

Nellie hummed. "The sea. Can you hear it?"

"I hear water splashing," Jim said.

"What do you hear, my little Baby Ray?" Nellie said.

"Not much. But I- I *smell* the wa- water. Some days it doesn't smell so g- good but today it smells g- good. Do you smell the wa- water, Momma?"

"I do. It smells fresh and clean."

"The fog makes it hard to see anything," Jim said, "Are you still hearing something, Momma?"

"I hear the water singing," Nellie said.

"That's sil- silly. I don't hear any mu- music," Baby Ray said.

Nellie pointed upriver. "Look. This river flows toward the sound, a bigger body of water and the water in the sound flows into the ocean which is even bigger. You boys learned about the ocean in school, right?"

"Very big." Jim said.

"B- big … b- bigger … b- biggest!" Baby Ray said.

"Bigger than all the lakes and rivers," Nellie said, "You can't see the ocean from here even on a clear day. But there's land on the other side of the ocean where our family comes from."

"You're our family. And Nana is our family," Jim said.

"That's right. You can't see it but across the ocean is where my mother and my father come from. A country called Ireland. They're from counties Mayo and Sligo."

"Where's your father?" Jim said.

"Over there. Buried many years ago."

"I'm glad Nana is with us," Jim said.

"So am I," Nellie said.

"Was your father a good man?" Jim asked.

"Yes. You would've loved him. And he would've loved both of you more than anything. He'd be bouncing you on his knees and telling you silly jokes. He was funny. And kind. I want you boys to grow up like him. Work hard. Be kind. Be loving. Do all that, and heaven will find you and hell won't have a chance."

"Will we ever see Anna again, Momma?" Jim said.

"I'll never stop looking for my little girl."

"I'll never stop looking for my little sister," Jim said.

Nellie started singing as the boys took the last licks of their ice creams:

> *"There's a land far away in the Somewhere of time*
> *Which, by faith, in the distance I see;*
> *There beauty and loveliness only are found*
> *What a wonderful land it must be!*
> *I'll be there by and by. I'll be there by and by*
> *For my Savior has promised me*
> *If His will I obey …*
> *Some sweet day, some sweet day*
> *In this wonderful land I shall be*
> *There are millions of souls in that land far away,*

And from sorrow and pain they are free

"Momma you have s- such a pretty voice. It's … it's s- soft like the b- breeze."

"Baby Ray," Nellie said, squeezing him, "I think you're going to be a poet."

"We love you so much, Momma," Jim said.

"I love both of you so much too. Always remember if you ever need me, I will be there for you."

"What ab- bout Dad?"

"Your father's family? Well, you've met your other Grandma. I wish you could see her more often. She's such a beautiful woman. I'll try to get your father to make the trip. I don't know a lot about the others on his side. But I hear music from over there. I hear singing. Some of it happy. Some of it sad." Nellie put her arms around the boys and walked west on Cherry Street.

Biggest fight of his life

End of Round One. Stop the f- fucking fight. He's going to k- kill him! Says Baby Ray. All's I see is Knuckles says Jim. Spits out mouthpiece. Cotton ammonia tubes shoved up his nostrils. Cut man: I've got my rent on this. Ya gotta hang in there 'til the fourth. Extra C-note for you. Ref: you heard the bell. Get him out here. The Hammer waited. Relaxed, arms at his side. Bouncing up and down on fresh legs. Quite a specimen. Healthy son of a bitch. Mismatch. Waiting to uncoil a haymaker. Not going to lose to this sucker. Just another wild Irishman. Doesn't know shit about boxing. I'll finish him this round. Scorers gave first round to Drummond.

Brother Lambertus, Jim's Math teacher at LaSalle Academy, an amateur boxer prior to getting the godly call, watched Jim in the schoolyard. Fearless brawler. Always had to prove himself. Always angry at someone. Anyone. Brother gave him his own pair of boxing gloves. Needs technique. Defensive skills. You got length. Guy coming at you can't judge your reach. Jab more. Wear him down. No wild punches. Don't leave yourself open. Next thing he knows is leather smashing his face. Jim saw himself as the next great Irish boxer. Jack Dempsey no less. Magazine cover of Dempsey in night table drawer. Standing over sucker he knocked out cold. Pound the shit out of anything that moves. Wants a name like 'Mannassa Mauler' or 'Gentleman Jim'. What should I call myself? 'Jungle Jim' Callaghan. That's it.

September 1929, two years, and three months out of high school. Twenty-five prize fights. Dives, saloons, dingy basements. Decent record: 18-2-5. Jim: they bet on us like it's a cockfight. Eddie 'The Hammer' Drummond, Jim's first meaningful fight. Legitimate boxing arena. Elks Lodge Downtown Brooklyn. Huge underdog.

Round Two. Listens to corner man. Bobbing. Weaving. Middle of round. Jim scores a few jabs. Employs some defense. Drummond measures him. Be patient. Wait for the opening. 'Jungle Jim' never fought a ranked opponent until ... seconds before the bell rang ending Round Two, a body blow took the wind out of Jim. Probably cracked a rib. Drummond came close. Smells Callaghan's fear. Hungry lion. Round Two ends in a draw.

Twenty bucks a fight. Not this night. A grand for the winner. Three fifty for the loser. Got the break when Drummond's scheduled opponent broke his toe kicking a chair during weigh-in. Put poster of himself and Drummond on the inside of his closet so Knuckles wouldn't see it. 'Jungle Jim' Callaghan vs. Eddie 'The Hammer' Drummond. Jim wrote the word 'Knuckles' across Drummond's face. The arena smells. Cigar smoke. Sweat. The stink of underarms passing money to bookie in the middle of the row. Classy dames cling to arms of cigar-chomping front row big shots. Tempers. Curses. A few bucks missing in the passing through sleight of hand. Fistful of cash got to bookie short. All thefts noted. Pay-back later. Stealing fingers broken after the fight. Jim loved boxing. Listened to the big matches every week on the radio. Nellie suggested James share that interest with his son. Said he's proud of Baby Ray. Did summer internship at New York Life. Good job waits for him after graduation. Moving up the ladder ever since. The other one doesn't have his brother's brains. What little he has going to mush.

Jim had ten straight victories. Started to get noticed. Began to make more than $25 in winnings. A few managers liked his brawling style, wild at times, but always moving forward. Never retreat. People said he fights like an animal. Ergo the moniker 'Jungle Jim' Callaghan stuck. Without father's consent, Jim started to make a name for himself.

Round Three. Getting schooled. Wild punches missing. Drummond's haymakers closer to the mark. Down two times. Up at nine. Getting brains beaten. Make it to the fourth. Big money. Jim to Baby Ray: That's his face. I gotta smash it one more round. He's a bl- bl- black man. Qu- quit now! T- take my brother out. Have a death wish, brother? He's getting k- killed!

Jim wasn't much of a student at LaSalle. Dreamt all day about his real ambition. Become heavyweight champion of the world like Jack Dempsey. Got the idea during junior year when Brother Lambertus said he could make a decent living as a boxer. With proper guidance and training. His fearlessness and aggression could translate into a successful career in the ring. Brother worked with Jim after school a few times a week.

"First of all, forget about the heavyweight division. You're six one and skinny. But you have a long reach that'll fool a lot of opponents. Put on a few more pounds. You'll be a decent middleweight."

"I'll just knock 'em out with one punch," Jim said.

"That's the spirit. But if you lack fundamentals, you're the one getting knocked on his ass."

"Can you teach me?"

"I teach Math. You need a place to train. Someone to work with you every day. In a place with heavy bags and speedball rack. The sweat and smell of the ring."

"All I have to do is imagine my father's face and I'll destroy him."

"None of my business. First things first, pass algebra so you can graduate."

"I don't get math. I get boxing."

"Listen to me. You can have Dempsey's aggression, his savagery, his scowling disrespect for his opponent, but you need finesse too, like Tunney. You have to know how to bob and weave and defend against uppercuts, roundhouses, jabs, hooks, and haymakers. You have to see your opponents' weaknesses, anticipate what's coming next from different situations. Look for openings."

"Why can't you teach me?"

"I'll give you the names of some boxing clubs. You got the piss and vinegar part down. You'll get noticed by a trainer when you show talent in the gym. You'll need him, otherwise you'll wind up like other pugs with a flat nose, gnarly knuckles, cauliflower ears and hash for brains. Want to be a punching bag or a real fighter? Listen and learn. You have to earn the right to step into the ring. It's hard work. There's skill involved."

Commotion before bell. Baby Ray rushed the corner, wormed his way through the bottom rope, and grabbed the towel off the cut man's shoulder. He lifted his arm to give it a toss. The manager reached over and grabbed Baby Ray. "Throw this jerk outta here," he told security. Jim, bent over, arms crossed over his midsection, got off the stool, turned to his brother and said, "This is for Anna." Two guards escorted Raymond into the tunnel. "You w- want to k- kill my b- brother?"

Round Four. Just answer the bell. Jim walked to the center of the ring, touched gloves with Drummond. He knew his ribs were broken. He lunged at 'The Hammer'. Eddie moved his head to the side, avoiding the punch. He unleashed a vicious right-hand uppercut that landed with unrestrained force. With lightning speed, Eddie swung his left hand over Jim's right arm, grazed his forehead, opening a small cut over his eye. Jim landed on the canvas in a lump. He was taken out on a stretcher. The ref held up Eddie 'The Hammer' Drummond's hand, declaring him the winner by knockout in the fourth round.

A lot of fight fans made money that night, even Jim.

Baby Ray followed the men bearing the stretcher into the dressing room. He looked at his brother, flat on the trainer's table, unconscious, barely breathing. He watched the doctor dab the wound and clean it with antiseptic.

As the doctor drew the needle through Jim's skin, he said, "He'll be unconscious for a while and won't feel a thing. When he wakes up, he'll be in a whole world of hurtin'. Anybody got whiskey? Give him the good stuff when he wakes. Make sure it's not bootleg hooch. He's sick enough."

"Is he g- going to be all right?" Baby Ray said.

"He'll be all right if he never fights again. His brawlin' style is passé. He'll lose to boxers like Eddie every night. Quit while you still got half a brain is my advice. No offense, Raymond, even though your brother acts tough, he's too soft for a fighter. His aggression is too random. Needs to be focused. Get totally fixed on being mean. Mean to the bone. All the time. Like your old man. Just telling you the truth in case Jim has any delusions about making this a career."

"How do you k- know my father?" Ray said.

"I do some work at City. Patched up a few boys over there. The keepers get aggressive at times. Know what I'm saying?"

"My father?"

"It's the culture. Not as rough as Sing Sing. But rough enough to keep criminals in a behaving state of mind. If you know what I mean."

"I get your dr- drift," Baby Ray said, watching the men unwrap the tape on Jim's hands.

"He's got a couple of cracked ribs, a broken nose, a cut eye, maybe internal bleeding. A trip to the hospital's probably a good idea. He took quite a pummeling from the Hammer. My bookie told me to bet on a knockout in the fourth, so I'm happy. Jim's not in Drummond's class. Money people needed a punching bag like Callaghan to prop up Drummond. A lot of the Guineas are moving up in class. They're the ones to watch. Pushing the brawling Irish out of the way in all divisions. I'll make money on the I-talians … more than I do in medicine."

The doctor wrote out a prescription for medicinal alcohol and handed it to Ray. "There's no prohibition on medicinal. Don't hesitate to get it refilled. Your brother will need it to get through the next couple of weeks. Do him a favor. Steer him into a different profession. He'll live longer. Good night gents."

Jim Callaghan had his big chance. He thought he was on the verge of making a name for himself, but his career ended that September night. His consolation prize: three hundred fifty bucks, a flattened nose and a scar that cut through one eyebrow, giving him rugged good looks.

The crash

The *Brooklyn Daily Eagle* sports reporter waited an hour outside the lodge. He got usable quotes from Drummond and needed a few from 'Jungle' Jim Callaghan.

"Think you were outclassed tonight, Callaghan?"

Barely able to walk, Jim said, "Drummond's a great fighter. He'll be champ some day. I fought my best."

Ray hailed a taxi on Flatbush Avenue. Standing room only in the ER at half past midnight. The sick and wounded with black eyes, broken bones and bleeding flesh spilled into the white antiseptic halls of Bellevue Hospital in Manhattan. The hospital's emergency unit bustled day and night, more so on weekends, with rotating teams of doctors, nurses, medical students and orderlies in their white hats, shoes, frocks, smocks, and scrubs. They all gave their best to treat the wounds and listen to complaints.

The bleeders got attended to first. Porters mopped the floor continuously. Nurses moved about, escorting patients from waiting room chairs to chairs at the nurses' station to stretchers in the hallways lined on both sides with the wounded and the city's downtrodden seeking a warm place for the night. The blend of disinfectant and antiseptics opened everyone's nostrils.

After two hours of trying to keep Jim's head upright, Ray stood when the nurse approached. She wore an apron stained with a full night's work. She led the Callaghans to her station. They sat while she recorded causes of injuries and medical history. She leaned over to get a closer look at the wound over Jim's eye. She arched one eyebrow, looked at Baby Ray, and said "Where'd your brother get this done – the ladies' sewing circle?"

Seeing that Jim was quite faint, the nurse and Ray got him onto a stretcher and into the hallway queue. Ray stayed by his side. After an hour passed, an attendant wheeled Jim into a room with a team of doctors and nurses working on a constant influx of patients. "What the hell happened to him?" the attending physician said, carefully removing the fight doctor's crude stitch-work, applying fresh antiseptic. He laced the two flaps of flesh closer together, put one bandage over Jim's eye, another on his broken nose, and wrapped tape tightly around his ribs.

"He's a prize fighter," Ray said, helping Jim down from the gurney.

"More like a punching bag," the doctor said as he moved Jim along, awaiting the next ER casualty.

The brothers took a taxi crosstown to Ray's apartment on West 18th Street between 8th and 9th, a one-bedroom walk-up over a butcher shop, furnished with a sink, toilet, kitchenette, an iron post bed, a two-seat sofa, one hard backed chair, and one cushioned chair.

Ray coaxed his brother's limp body to the second floor one step at a time. Once inside, he removed Jim's shoes, shirt, and pants, and lay him down on the bed. Ray fell asleep on the sofa his parents gave him, a present for getting promoted to Assistant Manager in the Underwriting Department at New York Life Insurance Company.

The first light of day poked through tiny holes in the window shade. Ray listened to Jim's faint moans. He dampened a washcloth and pressed it against Jim's forehead. He made tea and toast, propped Jim into a sitting position, and fluffed the pillow. He put the steaming teacup under Jim's nose.

"What's this?" Jim said.

"Tea. Drink it," Ray said, taking a sip before handing it over, "It's good. You need to replace the fluids you lost."

"I lost?" Jim said, opening his one good eye.

"Just barely. It wasn't so much you lost as the other guy won. You gave him one helluva fight."

"How long did I last?"

"A min- minute into the fourth round," Ray said, handing him a slice of toast.

"Good," Jim said.

"Why's that good? You lost the fight."

Jim grabbed his pants and pulled out a wad of cash. He handed it to his brother. "Count it."

Ray unfolded each note, stacking them in piles of twenties, tens, and fives. "Three hundred fifty," he said. "Your best payday."

"Sure about the total?" Jim said. He inched forward on the bed, attempting to count the money himself. He felt a sharp pain in his ribs and leaned back against the pillow.

Ray counted again. "Three fifty."

"I answered the bell for the fourth. I expected ..." Jim said, looking around the tiny room, "Where the hell am I?"

"My place."

"Why didn't you take me home?"

"Momma can't see you like this. I can take care of you until you're stronger."

"I don't want to be a bother," Jim said, holding his ribs as he swung his feet over the edge of the bed, "I was happy when you moved out. First time I didn't have to share a bedroom."

"What are your plans?"

"All's I know is I don't want to go down from three fifty to twenty-five a fight."

"You're done as a boxer?"

"Got a mirror?"

"You don't want to look."

"I'll look for a job," Jim said, searching through his pants pockets.

"What are you looking for?" Ray said.

"The prescription."

"I got it right here," Ray said, patting his shirt pocket.

"Well, I need it right here," Jim said, pointing to his mouth.

"The doctor said you should only take it if you're in pain."

"I hurt all over."

"It's medical hooch."

"I don't care what the hell it is as long as it works."

The hollers of merchants from the street below, the blasts of bus horns, car beeps, and the dings and screeches from the crosstown trolley signaled the start of another day.

"I bet a lot of the people down there are experts at something," Jim said, "Let me tell you what I'm good at."

"Tell me," Ray said.

"Never mind," Jim said, "What day is it, anyway?"

"Saturday."

"You don't work Saturdays, right."

"Right."

"Lots of people do, I guess. Help me to the window, will you. I hear her screeches."

"That's the streetcar."

"Anna's calling us from the grave. If someone doesn't die natural, their soul's never at rest."

Ray walked his brother to the chair. Jim rested one hand on the armrest, holding his ribs with the other. "I'd trade places with anyone down there. Looks like they're just going back and forth. Doesn't matter. They're going somewhere."

"Hey brother, you'll get your chance. You have time to think about your future. While you recover."

Jim looked up at Ray, "Know what I noticed?"

"What?"

"You're not stuttering so much."

"I do when I'm under stress. Like last night. My boss told me I'd go further if I get help."

"Someone wave a magic wand?"

"Speech therapist. The company paid for it."

"I really fucked up this time, Ray."

"You're twenty years old. You got lots of time ahead of you." Noticing Jim's body sagging a little bit, he walked him back to the bed. Before he lay down, Jim started to cry.

"What's bothering you, brother?"

"There're only two people, and ..." Jim started to say.

"And?"

"Don't know how to say it… without sounding sappy ... they're only two people in the world I admire."

"Who?"

"You and Momma."

"You're right on one count. She's the greatest mother in the world."

"She's so proud of you Ray."

"Yeah, but you're still her favorite."

"Bullshit. I'm an embarrassment. If Anna were here, you'd have to compete with her. Not me."

"Anna's gone. Long time. We've got to move on. Or else ..."

"That fucker father knows what happened."

"She drowned. Never found her body," Ray said.

"My gut tells me that bastard hid something from us. I used to think Momma knew. I kept asking her. Thought she was protecting us because we were kids. But she would of told us. She's not cruel," Jim said, doubling over.

"You all right?"

"Get my shoes, will you," Jim said.

"Where do you think you're going?"

"I need the medicine."

"Stay here. I'll drop it off, then go home and get the rest of your clothes. The prescription'll be ready by the time I come back."

"Thanks," Jim said as he fell back on the bed.

When Ray got to Cherry Street, he told his mother Jim was going to stay with him until he found his own place.

"Tell him to get a job," the father said from the other room.

"Can *you* get a job for Jim?" Nellie said.

"They're always hiring in the Claims pool. I'm only a junior executive but I'll give it a try."

Before Ray left, Nellie took money out of her private stash so Jim could buy a decent suit in case he got an interview.

Jim got the stitches and tape removed at the hospital. He could breathe without wincing. The bridge of his nose was flattened, and his eyebrow had a permanent scar. Otherwise, he looked presentable enough for an interview.

"I don't want to be a paper pusher the rest of my life," Jim said.

"It's a start. Give it a try. It'll make Momma happy."

One bright Monday morning in mid-October, Jim Callaghan, dressed in a brand-new double-breasted suit, stood on the sidewalk, leaned his head back to look up to the very top of New York Life headquarters at 51 Madison Avenue, a 34-story skyscraper designed by Cass Gilbert. He felt self-assured that morning, having been well coached by his younger brother, right on time for his 9am appointment in the Claims Department.

Jim got the job and used prizefight money to pay for an apartment on 14th Street near Fourth Avenue. He joined the army of paper pushers in the Claims pool, a vast, open room illuminated by banks of Arts and Crafts drop lights. The transition from boxer to desk jockey was less difficult than anticipated. He adjusted to a routine that included lunch every day at a local cafeteria with veteran clerks sharing stories of clients' outrageous claims. He especially enjoyed the 10am coffee break when one of his pool buddies slipped some hooch into his cup from a pint he kept in his desk. Much to his surprise, Jim liked pushing paper. He cashed his first paycheck and treated his brother and mother to dinner at a neighborhood restaurant.

Everything was going swell, until October 29, 1929, when newspapers across the country headlined the grim story …

WALL STREET IN PANIC AS STOCKS CRASH!

AVP Raymond F. Callaghan kept his job. Jim was furloughed. Ray pleaded with Jim to hang in there. He was not being fired. Even as the crisis worsened, Ray explained to Jim what was told to him by upper management that there was no reason to panic at New York Life. Jim panicked.

Later that year, New York Life's assets survived the crash. State regulation and company investing policy led them to invest in government bonds and real estate, not common stock. It was too late for Jim. He decided he could not afford to wait it out.

Ray called on Tony LaLota who owned a steak joint on 9th Avenue that he and his buddies frequented. Tony needed a cook immediately. Ray recommended Jim for the job. With a cigar stub hanging out of his mouth, Tony stood alongside Jim in the small kitchen. No longer functioning as a bar, Tony's still had a following for his restaurant. The food is good and easy on the wallet.

The long bar became a shelf for plates, flatware, and napkins. Twelve tables seating four lined the wall the length of the bar. Another four tables seating up to six were on the landing. Two bathrooms and a tight kitchen filled out the small space. Tony waited on tables along with long-time employee Mike, the former bartender. Tony wore the same outfit every day: thick horn-rimmed glasses; black slacks; short-sleeved white cotton shirt bearing brown sweat rings where shirt meets neck; and a clip-on bowtie that dangled from one side of his unbuttoned collar.

Tony shoved an apron against Jim's chest and gave him the noon to 10pm marching orders. "Four things we serve here. We don't need a menu or a blackboard for specials. New York strip steak, a bowl of boiled jumbo shrimp, fresh peas, and mashed potatoes. That's the four. And a spicy cocktail sauce for the shrimp that I make myself. You just dish it out into the little bowls that're right over your head. Got it?" Tony said. "Don't come out of the kitchen unless you gotta piss or take a dump. And don't forget to wash your hands. Otherwise, stay in the kitchen and cook. By the way, you look like shit. I don't know why your brother's company hired you. Ray said you got your ass kicked in the last fight," Tony looked Jim square in the face, studying the former boxer's scarred eyebrow, and flattened nose, "He says you're dependable, though. You better be or that's it. I run a tight ship. People come here for the food, and they don't like to be disappointed. If you're the reason for their disappointment, it's going to be a short romance. Any questions?"

"Nope," Jim said.

Jim stayed in the clear lane for six straight days. Customers were happy. Tony wasn't unhappy. Ray came one night with some of his New York Life buddies. They gave Jim a thumbs-up before they left.

Near closing time on Saturday night, Tony counted the night's take. He sat at a table on the landing, with his back to the bar. Jim spread out utensils that he needed for Sunday but couldn't find the peeler. It wasn't in the dishwasher. Rather than disturb Tony, he looked inside the cabinets behind the bar. He saw what must have been Tony's private stash of booze. Several bottles of gin, rum, and rye all lined up on the bottom shelf behind a cloth. While Tony made entries in his notebook, Jim put on his overcoat. He stuffed an unopened fifth of Seagrams Gin in one pocket and a three-quarters full bottle of Rye into the other. He opened the front door. "Good night, Mr. Lalota."

"Good night, Callaghan," Tony said, without looking up.

Jim walked a few blocks and ducked into a storefront doorway. He twisted the cap off the whiskey and took a long drink. He got to his room around eleven p.m. and continued drinking until the bottle was empty. He woke up at 3pm Sunday, with head pounding. Hair-of-the-dog gin came next. Down it went. He went back to bed and woke up at 9am Monday morning. Dressed in the same clothes he slept in for two nights, he slicked his hair back and walked to the restaurant. He opened the door and headed straight for the kitchen. He saw another cook working the stove. Tony came from behind and smacked Jim on the back of his head with a rolled-up magazine.

"I'm sorry. I was sick," Jim said, turning around.

Tony poked the magazine in Jim's gut and pushed him the length of the bar, out the door and into the street. "Get the fuck out of here and never come back," Tony said, spitting at him, "No call. No nothing. I lost customers, you stupid bum. I got customers ten years. Cooks always showed up. Your brother said you were dependable. He didn't tell me you're a bum. I don't want to see him around here either."

When he returned to his room, Jim drained the last few drops from each bottle. Since he failed to show up for work, he lost the entire week's pay. He paid his rent with cash from the fight, leaving $100 to his name. He asked his neighbor down the hall where he could buy decent booze.

Early the next morning, Jim walked into the back room of a florist shop on 27th Street, near 6th Avenue. He walked out with a bag containing several bottles of hooch. On the way back to his room, he bought a loaf of bread and a bunch of bananas from a greengrocer. One week later, the bread got moldy, the fruit rotted, and the bottles were empty. When he returned to the florist shop, no one working there knew anything about selling liquor.

Contraband booze is a movable feast.

Happy days are here again

"How'd you find me?" Jim asked as he broke off another piece of Italian bread, smeared it with butter, and glanced at the menu.

"Some detective work and a little luck," Ray said, "You didn't make it easy for me."

"How're you doing?" Jim said.

"Fine."

"Still with the same company?"

"Yes. Maybe not much longer, though."

"Why, didn't they make you president, yet?"

"I'm moving up the line, but I found someone."

"Someone?"

"A beautiful woman."

"What's her name?"

"Dorothy."

"What's Dorothy got to do with your job?"

"Her uncle owns several businesses. Could be a bigger opportunity for me."

"You going to marry this girl?"

"That's a long way off. We just started seeing each other. I think she's the one for me, but …"

"But what?" Jim said.

"She's got a long line of suitors."

"Good luck."

"And yourself?"

"I've had a string of bad luck."

"You made bad choices, Jim."

Jim threw the menu down on the table and pushed his chair back. "See you around Baby Ray. Thanks for the bread and seltzer."

Raymond grabbed Jim's arm. "Sit down, Jim. Please. I told Momma I was going to see you today. She's afraid something happened to you. No call. No letters. It's been rough on her."

"No lectures, okay. I get enough of them at the Mission."

"I promise," Ray said, "You get lectures at the Mission?"

"They feed us. Give us a bed. *Suggest* we show up for preaching and prayer time. Kind of shame us."

"Like a sermon then?"

"I guess. Some of them are funny though."

"How so?"

"Last week, the preacher man warned us about sex. Watch out for the harlots. What the hell! We all laughed. All's we want is another drink. Can't remember last time I was with a woman."

"I'm sorry. Staying sober's got to be the hardest thing. How are you doing with that?"

"Off and on. Today's a good day."

"It is for me, too. I miss you brother."

As the waiter took the order of meatballs and spaghetti for Jim and linguine in white clam sauce for Ray, a burst of raucous singing caught everyone's attention.

"What the hell is that?" Ray said.

"Sorry about the noise," the waiter said, "Houlihans. Or, as we like to say, Hooligans. It's like these people never drank before."

"I don't remember a bar next door," Ray said.

"They had a speakeasy in the basement. Now they're legit. The landlord rented out the top floor. Happy days are here again."

"More bread when you get the chance," Ray said.

"Sorry I got so touchy. This is swell. Can't remember the last time I had meatballs and spaghetti," Jim said.

"Never had a bad meal at Angelo's."

"Momma's meatballs are the best. I'll be a happy man if these come close."

"Remember how Dad taught us how to curl spaghetti on a spoon, saying I-talians think it's a sin to use a knife on pasta."

Jim cut his spaghetti into bite-size portions.

"Our old man retired. They moved to Queens or Brooklyn. I'm not sure which. They bought a house on the county line. One side's in Queens, the other side's in Brooklyn," Ray said, "I'll give you their new address and phone number. Try to visit. Or at least call. Momma'd love to hear your voice."

"Meatballs are pretty good. Momma's are still the best, How'd you find me?"

"A Bowery copper helped me."

"Someone I know?" Jim said.

"Said he knows you. Told me he moved you along at times. Didn't want you to die in the street. Had me looking for you in some of the hotels. I kept checking until Red suggested …"

"Red?"

"The copper. Everyone calls him Red. Last name Murphy. Know him?"

"Might have seen him around. Not mean like the others."

"Red told me to check the Bowery Mission and here we are. I'm glad I found you."

"So am I, Ray. I mean that. Sorry I'm leaving half the meal on the plate. It was really good. But my stomach can only handle so much."

"Why don't you come home with me. I'll find another job for you."

"You forgot about LaLota's?"

"I never went back there. Didn't appreciate the way he treated you."

Ray paid the check and wrote down his telephone number and his parents' address and number on a napkin. "I'll tell Momma you're okay. Give her a call. She'll be the happiest woman on earth."

The singing upstairs grew louder. Jim turned to Ray and said, "I have to use the men's room."

"I'll wait. We'll taxi to the Mission."

"Nah. It's not that far a walk."

Ray stuffed cash into Jim's pocket, "Just take it. Call me if you need more. Stay in touch. And don't forget to call Momma. She was crying all Christmas Day. Couldn't stop talking about you."

"Thanks for lunch," Jim said as Ray took off.

When Jim stepped outside a few minutes later, a Newsie kid handed him a card.

"What's this?" Jim said.

"Read it, Mister," the boy said as he handed cards to other passersby. Jim read it: "First drink FREE/Houlihan's."

Jim followed the noise and spotted the entrance fifty feet from the corner. He climbed the stairs, making his way through the crowd, a democratic gathering of the downtrodden whooping it up. The patrons were FDR-infused rising middle class, even some well-to-do slumming rich, all packed together four deep at the bar. Jim squeezed through. A dandy dressed in top hat and three-quarter coat, blocked Jim with his extended arm. "Excuse me," Jim said, trying to maneuver around him.

The man lifted his arm. "Let me buy you a drink, buddy."

Jim hesitated. "Thanks but the kid outside gave me a card for a free drink."

"Throw it away. That's a trick to get you in the door. All that coupon's worth is a short beer. I can tell you're the kind of man who enjoys a real drink. How about a sidecar, a French 75, or the Bee's Knees."

The man shook Jim's trembling hand. "My name's Bill Fletcher. And yours?"

"Jim Callaghan."

"Another fine Irishman. Well, Jim Callaghan, now that we know each other. How about that drink?"

"I guess one drink won't hurt."

"The first one never does. But the fifth can sting a little," he said, bending over in laughter, "The morning after, that is. Name your poison, Jim."

"I'll have a rye and soda, if you don't mind."

"I don't mind one bit," Bill said as he waved a twenty at the bartender. "Seagram's and soda for my friend Jim Callaghan and another Bee's Knees for me." The two men clinked their glasses and toasted the end of Prohibition and the coming New Year. The raucous chorus rang out again, Jim chiming in with the rest of the Houlihan's crowd:

Happy days are here again

Jim insisted on treating the next round. He reached into his pocket for the money his brother gave him. He peeled off a twenty. As he attempted to put the cash back in his pocket, someone bumped into him, and the cash fell to the floor.

A woman behind him scooped it up. She tapped Jim on the shoulder and said, "Is this your money, handsome?"

"Thanks," Jim said, "I should give you a reward."

"You can buy me a drink. I'll be sitting right over there at that table for two waiting for you."

One week ago, the Mission preacher man preached a proverb:

> *Keep my commands and you will live;*
> *They will keep you from the adulterous woman,*
> *from the wayward woman with her seductive words.*
> And the jolly patrons kept singing:
> *Happy days are here again*

Bill said to Jim: "Beware, my new friend Jim Callaghan. Just yesterday I saw that very same woman lift a wallet out of a drunk's pocket."

"She just handed me money that I dropped on the floor. She could of kept it and I never would of known the difference."

"A word to the wise. She's a grifter. One of the best."

"The least I can do is buy her one drink," Jim said, as he looked over at the woman. She blew him a kiss.

"I need this, Bill."

"She's all yours. Happy New Year, Jim. Hope it's a good one for you. See you around," Bill said, waving another twenty at the bartender.

One week ago, the Mission preacher man preached a proverb:

> *She is unruly and defiant,*
> *her feet never stay at home;*
> *now in the street, now in the squares,*
> *at every corner she lurks.*

And the jolly patrons kept singing:

> *Happy days are here again*

When Jim inquired of her cocktail choice, she said the waiter was already familiar with her favorite drink. He'll have it ready in the spare coatroom so we can enjoy some privacy. She took Jim's hand and led him through the glass-beaded curtain. The drinks were set on a small table on either side of a lit, pine-scented Christmas candle.

The woman lifted both drinks, handing one to Jim. They touched glasses and sipped. She placed his hand on her breast, and cooed, "Hey, big fella, my name is Ella. I want you to know I have a big heart," She lifted her dress above one knee, "Isn't this a pretty garter belt holding up my stockings. There is much more to see."

Jim finished his drink.

"You want me?" Ella said.

"No thanks," Jim said.

"Why not?"

"I'm looking for someone … a little less available … naughty girl."

One week earlier, the Mission preacher man preached a proverb:

> *Come, let's drink deeply of love till morning;*
> *let's enjoy ourselves with love!*
> *My husband is not at home;*
> *he has gone on a long journey.*

The music from the bar faded into the background.

"Question is are *you* ready to be a *naughty* boy?" she said, holding her bounteous breasts with both hands, "You don't have to play it cool with me."

"You do have a lovely rack, Mademoiselle Ella," Jim said, "And I would like very much for you to …"

Ella pressed her body against Jim, grinding against his groin, kissing him with an open mouth. She moved her hand slowly down his stomach to his pelvis.

"I think I could stand another drink, Ella."

"If you have one more, you won't be able to do what needs to be done."

"I need to pull down your silks and drive it home."

"I'm not wearing any silks, silly man."

"Are you pay for play?"

"What kind of woman do you take me for? My other lips moistened the moment you walked into the bar. I'm a goner for tall, handsome men like yourself," she said, kissing her index finger and placing it on his eyebrow, "Especially ones with battle scars. Did you get that fighting for a woman?"

"No, I got …"

She placed her hand on his mouth, "Shh. Not interested in details. Just the finished product. I guess it's my lucky day you dropped that money on the floor."

Kissing him again, Ella said, "Heard tell there is nothing softer than the inside of a woman's thigh. Do you agree?"

"I'd have to say yes." Jim said.

"You married?" She asked.

"Never," Jim said, "And you?"

"Off and on. Mostly off," she said, "Been with many women I bet. Might be a few of your kids making mischief in the world."

"Maybe," Jim said.

One week earlier, the Mission preacher man preached a proverb:

> *All at once he followed her*
> *like an ox going to the slaughter,*
> *like a deer stepping into a noose*
> *till an arrow pierces his liver,*
> *like a bird darting into a snare,*
> *little knowing it will cost him his life.*

"I can't stand idle chitchat," Ella said, "Come home with me so we can do it all night long. I have better hooch than this place. Whadda ya say, big boy?"

One week earlier, the Mission preacher man preached a proverb:

> *Now then, my sons, listen to me;*
> *pay attention to what I say.*

Do not let your heart turn to her ways
or stray into her paths.
Many are the victims she has brought down;
her slain are a mighty throng.
Her house is a highway to the grave,
leading down to the chambers of death

She called her driver and within minutes, the car was parked outside Houlihan's. Ella led Jim into the back seat. The driver took a zigzag route to her apartment. Ella playfully blindfolded Jim. She rubbed the inside of his legs.

One week earlier, the Mission preacher man preached a proverb:

He was going down the street near her corner,
walking along in the direction of her house
at twilight, as the day was fading,
as the dark of night set in.

When they arrived at her apartment, Ella led Jim into her bed, which was covered with colored Egyptian linens, perfumed with myrrh, aloes, and cinnamon. After the first penetration and release, Jim was anxious to enter her again.

Ella persuaded him to save some for later. "You never know what might come of it," she said, "Just relax and drink the finest whiskey the world has to offer."

Jim took the drink and passed out a few minutes later. Ella relieved him of what was left of the two hundred dollars Ray stuffed into his pocket. She opened her door. The burly driver carried him outside, being told by Ella, "Big boy won't remember where he was. Drive a few blocks. Put five bucks in his pocket so he can find his way home."

Jim shared a stoop that night with a Christmas tree tossed out of a window. Straggling bits of tinsel decorated his head. At daybreak, he struggled to gain footing on the stoop and tripped on the bottom step, stumbling into the street.

"Now here's a whack on your ass to remember me by," said the redhead copper, helping him to his feet, "Keep moving. Next time it'll be your thick Irish skull."

"Where can I get a drink?" Jim said.

"You're asking the wrong person, Callaghan. If you stay in the gutter, the teenagers around here'll piss on your face for the fun of it."

Jim walked a few steps. The copper turned him around and pointed. "The Mission's that way."

After a few blocks heading south, a hand-painted sign for liquor and wine drew Jim inside. With the five bucks in his pocket, he bought a pint of Five Star Twister, leaving him three bucks and change to his name. He walked south two blocks, ducking into several storefronts, twisting off the cap, and taking swigs at each stop.

He fell into the gutter when there were no swigs left.
New York City is so lovely in a snowstorm. Flakes like crystals pass by under the lamppost lights. Up and down the streets. Across the avenues. Glistening. Shimmering. Serene. Picture perfect. Streams of hot cocoa swirling this way and that.

Angels on a train

Static sounds like those from a shortwave radio buzzed in his bad ear. The noises tormented him.

The conductor called, "All aboard!" Dazed, Jim stood on the platform. He almost missed getting the last train out, if it were not for a considerate fellow who extended his hand and yanked him aboard. Jim fell backwards when the long choo-choo, chuff-chuff whistled out of the stack. The steel reins of the iron horse's flaring nostrils cranked, pulled back, jerked forward, with the smoke and steam pouring out its mighty power. Steady on his feet now, he found an empty seat and settled in for the ride.

He searched his pockets for his ticket. A man took the seat next to him. Jim looked through the sliding windows, seeing the cityscape of tall buildings and gray streets turn into a blur of green fields leading to the west end of all things.

"Where you headed?" the man said.

"Weehawken."

"You're a long ways off. That's in Jersey. We're almost in Idaho. Gonna get off and pick some taters for 5-cents a bushel and a free lunch. Got a good bakery in town. The sweet baker ladies is kind. Gives us yesterday's leftovers. Go to the back door. Give a little knock on the screen. She comes out with a platter. I make the trip every year."

"I was told this is the train to Weehawken. I got family there. My half brother Edward invited me. Same father, sort of. Not sure."

Edward came by and said, "Hey Jim. Long time never see. Listen, I'm in the next car forward. We'll catch up later. Enjoy the ride."   Another passenger sat on Jim's other side.

"No train goes where you want to go. You need a ticket to the 39th Street ferry on the west side. You hear me? I'd like to go there some day. Got a big Ferris Wheel. Popcorn by the bushel. Right on the Palisades. Used to be a big palace there. This train don't go there."

The man going to Idaho got off. A distinguished looking man took his seat. Nicely dressed yet smelled like moldy potatoes.

"This train might crash. Some people are train wrecks. Their lives destroyed through no fault of their own. Commonly called accidents. For others, it's their own doing," the malodorous man said, "They live lives hell bent on destruction."

"Are you a religious person or something?" Jim said.

"Where are you headed, Jim?"

Jim listened to the conductor, "Weehawken next stop. Gather your belongings. Doors open on the right."

A different passenger slipped into the seat next to Jim. "Don't listen to him. Doesn't know what the hell he's talking about. Weehawken is the stop after next."

A man standing over them said, "There is *no* stop after the next one. The next one *is* the last one."

"I have family in Weehawken," Jim said.

"I ask you again, Jim. Where are you going?"

"How do you know my name?"

"You look like a Jim, Jim. All Irish look the same."

"No, they don't. The people who say that put up signs No Irish Need Apply."

The smelly man and the other man disappeared.

A different passenger slipped into the seat next to Jim. "So, you're Irish, huh?"

"American Irish."

"Ever been to the other side?"

"Other side of what?"

"Other side of the world. Where you think you see a straight line. Then you get on it and it wiggles this way and that. The road rises up and you fall off the edge. That's the other side I'm talking about," the man said, his eyes growing wider, glowing in a greenish Klieg light phosphorescence, "Ever been to Ireland?"

"No and I don't plan on ever going there," Jim said, shielding his eyes.

"Everyone, regardless of education, is capable of having a philosophical outlook on life. It's based on experience. If you live long enough, you'll have a wealth of philosophical viewpoints."

"You sound just like the last guy. How'd I wind up in this seat?" Jim said, "Viewpoints are someone else's ideas you agree with."

"I see your point. I know passive people simply go through the motions. Biding their time. Waiting for someone to stick TNT up their ass. Or draft them into the army. Put 'em in a foxhole and some bastard fixes a bayonet in your face and cuts you a new nostril. It don't matter. Someone to wake you up. Make you do something on your own. Then, you'll have a real point of view. Self-preservation's a good clarifier but not the only one. Looks like *you* need someone to wake you up, Jim. Where you headed?"

"Home."

"Where's that?"

"Gravesend." Jim said.

"Maybe I'll visit someday."

"For the harvest?" Jim said.

"Is that where you're headed, Jim?"

"Aren't we all?"

Jim walked to the next car to meet up with Edward.

"Let's get somethin' straight, we got opposite good ears. Talk into this one," Edward said, pointing, "Not sure we have the same father. Never stayed around long enough to find out. Do ya know if you're ridin' the cushions or the rails, Jim?"

"What do you mean?"

"See all these stinkin' bags of bones smellin' like stale piss? This ain't the Pullman Express."

"I try to keep to myself."

"Here's a question for ya. What's the difference between a hobo and a bum?"

"Not sure." Jim said.

"I be the hobo. You be the bum. Ho hum. Ho hum. Get it?"

"Hey, watch it. I fought Eddie Drummond and almost won."

"I'm not tryin' to pick a fight. Just want ya to know the difference. I follow the harvests. Strawberries on Long Island. Tomatoes in Jersey. Wheat in Kansas. Corn in Oklahoma. Peanuts in Georgia. Get the picture?"

"I'd like to do that too. I don't want to be a bum."

"When you're ready, I'll give ya the whole plan. Good part is when ya don't need your Hoover blanket no more. Map it out. Pick the right season. In the right part of the country. Hear what I'm sayin'? Ya wanna pick oranges and grapefruits in Florida and California. There's a way to do both. But you gotta love the rails, Jim," Edward said, "Interested? Then, get your bindle stick and let's go."

"I picked a watermelon out of the trash once," Jim said, rubbing his face, "I hadn't eaten for days. Maggots all over it. Thousands. They got on me. Eating my eyes. Crawling up my nose. In my ears. Tunneling into my brain. A whole army of them... see them now? Get them off! Get them off!"

Edward left the car. The brakeman, fireman, and engineer stood alongside the conductor. The brakeman and fireman lay a stretcher on the floor. The conductor and engineer hold up a jacket. The four of them in white uniforms. Stiff starched. Sparkly clean.

The engineer said, "You're causing quite a commotion, Callaghan."

"Leave the light on! Get the maggots off my face!"

Frightened eyes bulging, writhing on the floor, a whirling dervish shaking all over, picking at his face. Pick. Pick. Pick. The fireman says to him, "Some men get beat up on the train by other hobos. Or the railroad bull gives them a licking with his truncheon. Sometimes they actually shoot a man if he keeps running. Target practice. You need to jostle for space on a crowded train. You need to give me everything that's in your pocket. I'll take care of them for you. Often things get stolen without recourse, recovery, or restitution."

"They're crawling up my legs!"

The brakeman and fireman pick the maggots off Jim's face and legs. A woman dressed in white enters through another door. She sticks a needle into his jelly-like flesh.

The prodigal son

In the waning twilight before dawn, Jim Callaghan strayed into the center lane of Park Row. He staggered on the walkway that ramped up to the Brooklyn Bridge. He stumbled several times. A driver approaching the bridge saw Jim fall and parked his auto several feet behind him. He helped Jim to his feet and lifted his limp body into the front seat. He glanced at Jim's glassy eyes, his unshaven face, and the bruises on his hands. He winced at the penetrating stench of urine that soaked Jim's trousers.

"Hey buddy, you trying to get killed?"

"Trying to get home," Jim said, his head bobbing.

Jim struggled to keep his eyes open. When he leaned his head back, the man saw bloodstains on his collar. "Want me to take you go to the hospital?"

"Home," Jim said, "Trying to get home."

"What's the address?"

"Not sure."

"Neighborhood?"

"What?"

"What part of Brooklyn?"

"Uh, Bushwick, I think."

The driver pulled alongside the curb when he crossed into Brooklyn, "Listen, buddy. I'm heading to Queens. Give me some idea of where you live."

"Want to get home."

"I understand that. I'm trying to get home too. Where's your home?"

"Where Momma lives."

"You live with your mother?"

"I want to. Momma makes it a home."

"I hear you, buddy. What street does she live on?"

"Cooper."

"Cooper Avenue or Cooper Street? One's in Brooklyn. One's in Queens."

"Thanks for taking me home," Jim said, coughing into his handkerchief.

"I'm trying to buddy. Maybe your folks can help you get back on your feet."

"I hope so. Just want to get home."

"Cooper Avenue or Street"

"Street, I think … yeah, Street."

"What's the house number?"

"Not sure."

"Near a cemetery?"

Jim jerked forward. "Who died?"

"No one died. I'm asking if the house is *near* a cemetery. This area's full of them - some near Cooper. I know one is Trinity - Most Holy Trinity Church Cemetery. Near Cooper Street."

"Never been there."

"How about if I drop you off near Trinity cemetery? Would that help?"

"You're very kind."

"You need to be careful. I don't want you to get run over."

The man drove to the Most Holy Trinity Cemetery, and helped Jim get out of the car. Jim stood still, looking around. The man rolled down the window. "Zip your fly," he said and drove off.

Jim vaguely remembered what Ray wrote on the napkin: an address in the 100's. Not sure of the exact number but remembered his brother saying it was the only house on the block with a green canopy over the front door. Jim walked a few paces and sat on the ground outside a small grocery store. He leaned against the door and fell asleep.

Cars passed. Buses passed. People passed without noticing Jim until the store's proprietor approached with his arms full of loaves of Italian bread. He fumbled for his keys, nudging Jim with his foot. The grocer put the bread on the counter and stepped outside. "Get out of here or I'll call the cops. This ain't the Bowery."

Jim struggled to his feet. "Sorry. Is this Cooper?"

"You're on Central. Cooper's that way. Now, get lost."

Jim walked in the direction the man pointed, bumping into railings, knocking over trashcans. He reached the corner, turned around and saw the grocer talking to a cop, gesturing with both hands, pointing his way. Jim turned the corner and hid in a basement well. Sweating, feeling feverish, he took the whiskey out of his overcoat and drank what remained.

The streets in Bushwick were alive with workers boarding buses, and children being escorted to school by parents and grandparents. When he tried to cross Central, he forgot which way the grocer pointed. He slipped to one knee in the middle of the street. Cars honked. Drivers cursed as they drove around him. He made it across and approached a pedestrian. "Cooper Street?" Jim said as the man swerved in a wide arc around him.

The man pointed. "One block that way."

"Momma's house," Jim muttered.

Both sides of Cooper were lined with cookie cutter two-story attached houses. Near the point of collapsing, Jim stepped into the middle of the barren street, swiveling his head from side to side, trying to make sense of the addresses. He spotted a house with a green canopy and saw a big 'FOR RENT' sign in the middle window on the second floor. He gripped the iron railing, climbing seven steps to the first-floor landing. He saw a few broken chairs and empty window frames lying on the cement outside the basement window. He stood under the aluminum canopy, trying to peer into the window but the shades were drawn. He saw the name Callaghan printed on the mailbox.

Jim banged the brass Claddagh doorknocker. He heard the inside chain lock being released. The doorknob turned slowly. Nellie looked through the peephole.

James heard the knocking and said, "Who is it?"

"I think it's Jim."

"Momma?" Jim said, sliding into a sitting position, his feet splayed, head lowered, his back propped against the railing.

Nellie turned the doorknob again.

James rushed out from the kitchen. "Get away from the door."

"It *is* our son. I know his voice."

James placed his hand on top of Nellie's and pushed her out of the way. He put the chain back into the slot and opened the door slightly. He shut it immediately. He pulled Nellie into the kitchen, forcing her to sit while he dialed the operator. Nellie fought him, screaming, "Get out of my way. Let me see my son."

"Give me the police …" The connection went through.

"Hello Sarge. This is James Callaghan on Cooper. Can you send one of your men over? A drunk's asleep on our stoop … I have no idea who it is. Just need him removed."

"I never knew you could be so cruel. Until now. I hope to God you die," Nellie said.

"You wanted me to die when I had my heart attack. But I'm still here."

"I *want* you to die right now," Nellie said, pulling at her hair, weeping.

James raised his hand to strike but let it fall to his side.

"Go ahead. Hit me. You couldn't hurt me anymore if you tried. You *are* the devil himself."

"I supported you all these years. What did you do? Never worked a day in your life."

"I raised two sons without any help from you. When they left, you kept me caged up like an animal. You're a poor excuse for a husband and father. You sold *our* house. Kicked your brother out. You should have kicked me out too. I would've been better off."

"You couldn't even do the *only* job you had. Keeping your eyes on Anna. She wouldn't have drowned if you hadn't yak-yak-yakked on the stoop with the Kraut. I'm a man who provides for his family. I had a tough job. Never missed a paycheck. I worked extra shifts. Never stopped working until the heart attack. Now we got my pension."

Nellie tried desperately to get around him. "I am pleading with you. Let me have two minutes with my son! I carried him inside my womb. He needs me now! I promised him I'd always be there for him. I beg you. Please open the door so I can hold him!"

"Stay right where you are, wife. This is a police matter now."

"You only think you were a good provider. Every penny you earned working extra shifts you spent on your slut! You filthy, disgusting pig."

"Shut up. As long as I'm alive, you'll do as I say. Do I make myself clear? I'll persist like a fly on shit," James said, hearing some commotion outside.

Nellie took a deep breath and said, "Order your cemetery plot yet?"

"What are you yapping about?"

"St. John's Cemetery."

"That's a stupid question. You know I bought it years ago. For both of us."

"When you croak, your fat body is going into that ditch by itself. I had to spend most of my life on top of the ground with you, but I'll be damned if I spend one moment with you in the grave."

"You're talking nonsense."

"*I* want to die right now. To put an end to my miserable life. I wish you killed my body the same time you killed my spirit," Nellie said, covering her face in her hands, "Dear God, have mercy. Restore my son, Lord."

James relaxed his grip for a moment and Nellie made a run for the front door. James yanked her by the hair. She got to her knees. "Just for one moment, let me see my son. I beg you." She collapsed on the floor, her small body twitching and flailing with uncontrollable spasms.

James opened the door and walked down the steps into the street. He looked in both directions. Jim was nowhere in sight. He returned to the house, closed the door behind him and slid the chain lock in place.

He bit off the end of a cigar, spit it out, and lit his long Perfecto.

On a mission

Cheery as hell in her saddle shoes and apron dress, armed with a degree in Social Work from the College of New Rochelle, the indomitable Dorothy Jenkins took a field trip to the Bowery with her fiancé Raymond Francis Callaghan. She gamely followed Raymond into the Holiness Mission. She stood behind him in the large room with row upon row of docile men sitting shoulder to shoulder in what had all the makings of a church sanctuary furnished with simple wood benches on either side of a center aisle.

The men, ranging in age from late teens to early forties, sat four across, stretching back twenty rows. Full occupancy. The men stared in silence at the floor and ceiling. Several slept. The Mission provided their clothing, spectacles, underwear, and meals.

A man entered from a side door. "My name's Bill. Can I help you?"

"I hope so," Ray said, "I'm looking for Jim Callaghan."

"And you're..."

"Ray, his brother." Dorothy stepped forward. "This is Dorothy, my fiancé."

"Nice to meet you both."

"Jim probably won't be here today. His regular days are Tuesday and Thursday."

"Regular days?" Ray said.

"Jim volunteers. Does the dishes. Serves meals. Mops the floor. Good therapy. Makes him feel good about himself."

"Are the men waiting for church service to begin?" Dorothy said.

"The chapel's upstairs. They're waiting here for the lunch bell."

"How's Jim?" Ray said.

"He's had a few visits to the hospital. Detoxed. Then back on the street again," Bill said, "Vicious cycle but he's got a lot of fight. So far so good, lately. Been sober about three weeks and counting. He talks about you a lot. And his sister."

Dorothy squeezed Ray's hand.

"Any idea where we might find him? He hasn't met Dorothy yet. We're anxious to tell him about the wedding."

"Try the Jefferson Hotel," Bill said, "He'll be delighted. You make a beautiful couple."

"Thank you. Do you know the address?" Ray said.

"The Jefferson's on President's Row ... a little joke ... right between the Washington and Madison hotels. There's also the U.S. Hotel on the same stretch. You can't miss them. Walk three blocks north."

"Thanks so much, Bill ... Bill?" Ray said.

"Lincoln."

Ray laughed and said, "You're kidding."

Bill handed his card to Ray. "Bill Lincoln at your service. Call me if you want to check up on Jim. If I'm not in, any one of the managers can help."

Ray shook his hand and said, "I can only guess their names."

"Anderson. Fontini. Spiro."

Bill escorted Dorothy and Ray to the door. "I hope your brother gets to the wedding. Good news never hurts anyone."

"We're going to do everything we can to make him part of our lives," Ray said.

Bill looked around the room. "Sometimes it's touch and go. They have the best intentions and then … they slide back. Some of them pick up again. It's tough."

Dorothy handed an envelope to Bill. "This is for your Mission, truly a blessing for these men."

Dorothy and Ray held hands as they walked through the Bowery. A face-to-face confrontation with the poverty, disease and despair of the area's denizens manifested itself viscerally for Dorothy in the sounds, smells and palpable sadness surrounding them. It empowered Dorothy beyond lectures and textbooks. Upon hearing the sad tale of Anna from Ray, Dorothy insisted on meeting Jim. She knew of his struggles with alcoholism, his obsession with the loss of Anna, and was determined to embrace him. To her, Jim was already family.

On the three-block trek to 'President's Row', Dorothy stepped over drunks, encountered man after man foul smelling, unshaven, and unclean. Some of the men had genitals fully exposed. Several were sprawled on park benches, malingering in doorways, their emaciated bodies draped over stoops, pulling pints out of overcoat pockets, fighting over pennies. Dorothy had stocked her pocketbook with bills and coins to give to the needy, determined to come home with an empty purse. Ray warned Dorothy that giving money did more harm than good for Skid Row residents. The money simply procured another cheap pint, another trip to the gutter, another visit to the hospital.

Ray loved Dorothy fully. Here she was in the flesh, unconstrained in her generosity, never condescending, full of heart and spirit and love for the least of these.

They reached the first of the 'President's Row' hotels, the Washington. Dorothy observed the malingerers on the front steps, smoking, drinking, cursing, fighting, so unlike the passive men she observed at the Mission.

One glassy-eyed drunk closed to within an inch of her face, "Hey, rich bitch, slummin' today? Nice shoes. I got holes in mine. Gimme a few bucks, will ya." Unprepared for an aggressive encounter, Dorothy recoiled at the stench of his breath and the threat in his beady eyes focused so hatefully upon hers.

Ray stepped between them. Dorothy gently pushed Ray aside and spoke to the man, "My name is Dorothy, sir. You need to treat me like a lady. Do you have a mother? A sister? Would you behave as rudely with them? I'm sorry you're not doing well and need to beg for money. But I demand your respect, sir!"

The man walked away. Dorothy studied his bent over frame, his threadbare suit, and his shuffling walk. Much to Ray's fright, she chased after the defeated man and stuffed a fistful of cash into his pocket. Despite his foul odor she hugged him and said "God bless you sir. May you be spared any further sorrow in your life."

When they reached the doorstep of the Jefferson, Ray said, "Please let me handle this," He took loose change and bills out of his pocket and distributed the cash evenly among the men. Dorothy held Ray tight as they approached the desk. The clerk sat on a stool perched inside a cage, fortified with metal bars and a lock. A broken clock hung on the wall and rows of room keys dangled from pegboard hooks. At the front of the cage, there was a slot wide enough for taking payments and the distribution of keys for the residents able to afford a room with a bed and locker.

"Is Jim Callaghan here?"

"Who's asking?" the man said.

"His brother," Ray said, slipping a ten-dollar bill through the slot.

"Yeah, he's here. Upstairs, third hole on the right."

"Can you keep an eye on the lady?" Ray said, spotting him another ten.

"Don't worry about it," the clerk said, putting the bills in his shirt pocket, "Try not to be too long."

When Ray entered the narrow room, Jim gripped his hand and said, "Found me again. You ever give up?"

"Hey, big brother, you're going to meet my fiancé today. She's waiting downstairs." Ray noticed Jim's hair was speckled gray, a significant change in the two months since he visited him in the hospital. Ray stayed in touch with his contact at the local Police precinct, allowing him to keep his mother informed. Over a period of several years, Ray visited every flophouse, fleabag hotel, mission, YMCA, and hospital Jim occupied on his journey to the bottom. He was keenly aware of the toll alcohol took on Jim's mind, body, and spirit. As each day, week, month, and year went by, there was less of Jim. Ray tried to rescue his brother, give him money, set him up with a simple job, and pay for an apartment. All efforts failed. On one visit to the hospital, thinking it was the last time he would see his brother, he fell to his knees and begged Jim to stop drinking. His dire supplications worked. Until they did not.

"Nice to meet you," Jim said as Dorothy extended her hand, "When Ray told me he found someone, I didn't believe him. But here you are. Sorry he dragged you to this place."

"Jim, Dorothy and I want to take you to a few special places today. Are you willing?"

"I don't know. Did you check with my secretary?" Jim said.

"First stop. Herald Square. More surprises to follow after that," Ray said, "Grab your coat and let's go."

"All right then. I'm game. Dorothy looks like someone I can trust. Not sure about you."

When they got out of the taxi and entered Macys, Jim was overwhelmed by the opulence. He looked around with a child's wonderment. It was the first time in his life that he stepped inside a department store. Dorothy marched Jim to the Men's Department. She asked him to pick out a suit and try it on. "I might panhandle on the Bowery for my next pint, but I really don't want any handouts from family," Jim said.

Dorothy took Jim aside. "First of all, I want to thank you. Only meeting me less than an hour ago, you already consider me family. That being said, can we get something straight before we lose the day?" Dorothy said, "Please let us give of ourselves today. I want to be part of your life. Not only giving monetary things. I want to give my heart to you. You might not think so now but one day you'll be able to help someone less fortunate than yourself. What do you say?"

"To tell you the truth, Dorothy, I really don't need a fancy suit living at the Jefferson. Know what I'm saying? Every time I fall asleep, some other bum steals from me. I'm better off just keeping whatever I got on."

"I'm begging you, Jim Callaghan, make that the last time you refer to yourself as a *bum*. We're going to shop now for a nice pair of trousers, a shirt, socks, underwear, overcoat, and shoes. If you want to sleep in what you got on after we're done here, that's your business."

"Okay, Ma'am," Jim said, and with that Dorothy grabbed his hand and led him to the men's casual wear department. At the end of the spree, Jim wound up with several wool sweaters, socks, drawers, slacks in brown, navy and black, a new pair of shoes and a camel hair overcoat. Ray told Jim that whatever article of clothing did not fit in his locker, he would store in his apartment. With Ray loaded down with shopping bags, they hailed a cab outside Macy's and headed uptown to the Waldorf Astoria Hotel.

Ray and Jim stayed in one room of the suite and Dorothy bedded down in the other. Jim got the hot towel treatment and a lathered-up shave in the hotel's barbershop, followed by a massage, a hot bath, a one-hour nap in the suite and off to an early dinner in one of the hotel's restaurants.

Jim searched for something simple on the menu, explaining that his sensitive digestive system would not tolerate rich foods. The waiter said he would ask the chef to make him a special meatloaf with mashed potatoes. Dorothy and Ray ordered the same. Dorothy brushed back several locks of her raven black hair, looked straight across the table at Jim, and with her expressive blue eyes said, "Well, Mr. Callaghan, do you feel like a million bucks?"

"I could get used to this lifestyle."

"Hold on to this moment, Jim" Ray said, "Dorothy and I don't do this every day. But today is special. We have something special to share with you which requires the right atmosphere."

"Can I say something first?" Jim said.

"Sure," said Dorothy, noticing that Jim's hands were shaking.

"I don't want to forget the manners Momma taught me. I want to thank you for today. For the nice clothes you bought," Jim said, gripping his glass with both hands, "I also want to thank you for paying for my room and locker at the Jefferson. It's a fleabag hotel but better than trying to sleep in a big room full of other men, all stinking up the place."

Dorothy nodded to Ray, who said, "I have no idea what you're talking about, Jim. Dorothy and I had no idea you were at the Jefferson. It was Bill Lincoln who suggested we might find you there."

"Who's paying for my room, then?"

"Beats me," Ray said.

"Enjoy it while it lasts," said Dorothy, "You must've made a good impression on someone. Doesn't surprise me one bit."

"Damn. I'm not going to rest until I find out. Anyway, what's your big news?"

"Jim, you're not only my big brother, you're my best friend. Would you honor Dorothy and me by being my best man?"

"Correction. I've been a terrible brother and a lousy friend," Jim said, dabbing his tears.

"Will you do it, then?" Dorothy said, handing her unused napkin to Jim, "My sister Veronica is going to be the Matron-of-Honor. Growing up, I always wanted a big brother. You'll make a handsome couple. Better not steal my spotlight!"

"I should've taken your offer to get the fancy suit."

"We'll do better than that," Ray said, "All the groomsmen will have tuxes, top hats, spats, and walking sticks. Now that we got your measurements, you'll be all set. I'll arrange car service for you from Manhattan to New Rochelle."

"New Rochelle?"

"That's Dorothy's hometown. Eleven a.m. wedding at Church of the Redeemer, followed by the reception at the Glen Island Casino."

"Well, ain't that hoity toity!" Jim said, "Except you left one thing out."

"What's that?" Dorothy said.

"When's the big day?"

"March 24," Ray said.

Jim closed his eyes, put his index finger to his forehead, and said, "I just checked with my brain and found out I'm available. I'll do it."

"Thanks for being a big part of our lives, brother. You'll be sitting at the head table with Dorothy's Uncle George. He's owns the place plus Westchester's largest limousine company, plus, plus, plus. One of his chariots will be taking you to New Rochelle on the day of the wedding. Uncle George got his finger in a lot of pies and will be taking me into the company fold. Going to be opportunities for you too, brother."

"I'll take the tux and the limo ride but don't give me any money. All those Jefferson bums- … I mean men … steal. Every fleabag and flophouse I was ever in, someone stole from me. Never had much but they'd steal anyway. Except the Mission. They look out for you there. No overnight stays anymore, though."

The meal was served, enjoyed all around, followed by coffee and a chocolate soufflé.

"Momma will be at the wedding, right?" Jim said.

"Probably not," Ray said, "We have alternate plans to make sure she's a part of the wedding."

"Is she all right?" Jim said.

"Momma had a bit of a breakdown."

"I'm such a lousy son. I can't remember the last time I went to Cherry Street. Has to be years."

"She lives in Brooklyn," Ray said.

"Where?" Jim said.

"I guess you don't remember I told you sometime back. Cooper Street. in Brooklyn."

"What happened to Cherry Street?"

"Dad sold it."

"The prick," Jim said, then looked at Dorothy, "Oops. Sorry about that. Did Momma agree to the move?"

"That's a long story for another day," Ray said, "I have another piece of bad news."

"What's that?"

"Dad passed away a year ago."

"Shit! That's good news," Jim said, "Oops again Dorothy. Sorry. There's a long …"

"That's all right, Jim," Dorothy said, turning to Ray, "Why don't you tell Jim more about our plans for Mom."

"She was sick, so we got her a very caring personal attendant to help her out at home with cooking, cleaning, that kind of thing, then …"

"Then what?" Jim said.

"She had another breakdown. After that, we got her placed in a wonderful facility where she gets twenty-four-hour care. Dorothy and I plan to visit her the day after our wedding. I'll be in my tux with a fresh boutonniere. And Dorothy will be dressed in her beautiful wedding gown – so everyone has to be careful not to spill anything on her at the reception."

Jim stared at the crystal chandelier, musing, "What do you mean by breakdown? Was it like the time … was it anything like … after Anna took her ride on the cart? I hope she wasn't that way? She never should've blamed herself."

After dinner, the brothers and future sister-in-law retired early to their rooms. They enjoyed a good night's rest and ordered room service for breakfast. As they waited for a taxi outside, Jim coughed into the napkin he had removed from the breakfast tray. As Dorothy and Ray got into the taxi before him, Jim glanced at the napkin. It was stained with blood.

Red to the Rescue

They're all sick. Beyond repair. TB the big killer. Lifestyle of the down and out. Exposure to rain, blizzards, wind, hot sun. Doesn't matter. Don't know what day it is. Drunk out of their minds. It's surprising that some live as long as they do. Better off diving off the top floor. Get it over with. Mercy! Lack of cleanliness. No soap. No shower. Bodies in need a commercial disinfectant. Vermin all over them. Contagion from one to the other. Infection in every part of the body. Ill-clad. Undernourished. Eat out of trash cans. Donated clothes never fit the next day. Beat up on each other for coats and gloves. Beg a buck. Get a jug. Toxic pus oozing out of mouth and anus. Lips dry with sores, heavy head, stomach hard as walnut. Day-to-day struggle. Gain an inch on Sunday, lose a mile on Monday. Flop houses three, four stories high. Waiting room, chipped lead paint. Never vacant. Narrow halls. Horse stable stalls. Single bed. Metal locker. Bugs. twitching on curled-up flypaper dangling from single flickering bulb. Urine-soaked mattress. Top floor bargain price, nothing but ropes catch the flopping drunks. Slippery puke, piss smelly floors morning to night, night to morning. No difference. Smell big enough to make a horse vomit. Reasonable upgrade YMCA 40-cents a day.

317

Where are you now in the ancestry of blood and bones, the strings from heaven frayed into splintered light, a jail arrayed between the bars?

What were you afraid of young man   when you bottled to the bottom   before the ground hit your head?

"The same nightmare for the last twenty-two years, Callaghan. I held your sister's eyeball in my fucking hand! Today it ends. I can't take it anymore. Not another day. Do you understand?" Lieutenant Thomas J. (Red) Murphy picked Jim out of the gutter and propped him against a lamppost. Jim's pint of Five Star Twister fell to the cement. The last few drops spilled into the sewer. Jim's boxer legs thinned to a whooping crane's stalky limbs.

"You again?" Jim said, eyes half opened, dribble spooling out of his mouth.

Just the day before, Jim called Raymond like he promised. He was on his way to pick up his tuxedo at Steckman's Formal Wear on 14th. Dorothy got on the line and told him about their meeting with the minister. The big event was only a week away. Jim tried on the tux. It fit. The tailor packed it in a fancy box and tucked it under Jim's arm. He walked south on 2nd Avenue. He passed a liquor store, then another, but kept walking. He picked up his pace, keeping his eyes focused on the street ahead. He stepped into a storefront alcove to catch his breath, his acidic stomach churning and growling, his mouth tasting what transported him out of this world. Jim put the box on the ground. He needed to blow his nose. The bloody handkerchief had a faint smell of his last drink. He looked across the street and saw the sign, CHRISTOPHER T. HARDEN FUNERAL DIRECTOR. He walked into the building, perfumed with memorial flowers. Mr. Harden invited him to have a seat. Jim remained standing. He put the box on Harden's desk. "What'll you give me for this?

Mr. Harden examined the contents: collapsible top hat; spats; studs; shirt; tie; vest; jacket and pants. "Ten bucks."

"That's all?" Jim said.

"It's second hand," Mr. Harden said.

"It's brand new. I just picked it up at Steckman's."

"Did you try it on?"

"I had to see if it fit," Jim said.

"Did it?"

"Yes."

"It touched your skin. Touched your underwear. It's used merchandise. I'll give you ten bucks. Take it or leave it," the undertaker said.

Jim took it. He doubled back to the liquor store and bought three bottles of Five Star Twister. He put the change in his pants pocket. He took a long drink in the next available doorway. He wiped his mouth, coughing up more blood.

"I put your sister's bloody body in a sack and hid it under the docks. Got driven by my sister's chauffeur to 26th Street. Eleanor sat next to me in the back and wrote a note to your father. Got a nice little lady to give it to him at Blackwell. The two of them left me there and hunted down your father's other daughter. Do you hear what I'm telling you, Callaghan?"

A patrolman walked over. "Hey Loo, need any help?"

"Nah. I can handle this. He just needs a good talking to," Red said, "Go back to your beat."

The patrolman took a close look at Jim. "Not much left of him. You know how many times I whacked his sorry ass. I'll give him another one if he's bothering you."

"Here's what you can do. Face the other way and keep the gawkers moving along. I need ten minutes with his guy."

"Sure thing, Loo."

Jim struggled to keep his head erect and eyes open. Red gripped his jacket. "I didn't know my father like my sisters did. I was shuttled from one whorehouse to another. I have nightmares every night. Your sister's eyeball in my hand. Jesus have mercy! I hate my sisters. I hate what happened to you and your mother. Your brother. Grandmother. My sisters planned the whole fucking thing. I don't give a shit what your father did to Minogue. My *own* family set me up. They told me they only wanted to scare your father. Teach him a lesson. I've been wanting to tell my side of the story for twenty-two years."

Jim fixed his eyes on the big cop. Red loosened his grip. "Your Uncle Bill kicked the cart your sister rode in. When it hit the curb, her body went flying, landing on a broken lamppost. Tore her face apart. Jesus! The cart went sailing. Helen kicked it into the river. Eleanor ran out of the building and picked up the doll. She screamed at Helen to get back in the crowd. She screamed at me to put your sister in the sack with all the Commie propaganda shit. I hid it under the dock. She was dead already. Do you understand what I'm saying?"

Red let go of Jim's jacket and stepped back a half foot, seeing that Jim peed his pants. "I'm making my peace with you now," Red said, crying, "I take responsibility." With his free hand, Red patted Jim's face, "Look at me Callaghan. Your brother doesn't know what I'm telling you. He knows me as a cop who keeps tabs on you. I promised him that you'd get to his wedding. Do you hear me? You need to get sober. Oh, Jesus. I'm so sorry, Jim. I'm asking your forgiveness. You. Your brother. Your mother. Forgive me."

"I forgive you," Jim said, eyelids closing, "Her name's Anna. She's calling me from the other side."

"Your old man had Anna buried at your Uncle Carney's place in Sloatsburg."

Red tapped the patrolman on the shoulder. "I'm done here."

"What are you going to do with him?"

"Take him home," Red said as he lifted Jim up and straddled him over his shoulder.

"Need help?"

"Nah. Doesn't weigh any more than either one of my kids." Holding Jim aloft, Red walked two blocks to the Jefferson. He placed Jim on a bench inside and banged on the cage. The clerk stepped out. "Hey Lieutenant, what do we have here?"

Red put his hand on the man's shoulder and said, "Listen Joe, you've got to do something for me." He handed the clerk a hundred-dollar bill.

"What the hell is this for? You putting him up for a year?"

"Listen. I don't have much time."

"Shoot."

"Take twenty out for his room. Another twenty for a decent suit he can wear to his brother's wedding."

"What's the rest for?"

"That's yours. Don't let me down. On Sunday, make sure he's dressed and at the Mission by ten. Walk him there if you have to."

"That's it?"

"Call Lincoln on Friday. Make sure he knows a limo is coming for Callaghan. Make sure he's sober and gets there on time."

"No problem. Consider it done. Thanks for the cash."

"I'm counting on you," Red said, "I gotta take a piss. Give me the key."

"Don't use that toilet. Wait 'til you get to the precinct."

"Give me the fucking key. Or I'll piss on your shoes."

Red walked down the dark hallway, illuminated by a single bare bulb hanging on a frayed cord. The stench of urine assaulted his nose when he came to within ten feet of the bathroom. He locked the door behind him. Inside, the malfunctioning radiator hissed. The small tiles on the floor were cracked. Black grime filled the spaces where grout used to be. The porcelain sink had been ripped out of the wall. The toilet seat was missing. Caked feces encrusted the bottom of the bowl.

Lieutenant Thomas J. (Red) Murphy took the snub-nosed .38 revolver out of his ankle holster. He placed the snout of the gun against his temple and pulled the trigger. He fell to the floor, blood pouring out of his head.

The sun sent a harsh light through the dust of the stippled glass window, casting an irregular shadow over the police lieutenant's body. The noise from streetcars drowned out some of the gun's discharge but a fair number of the rowdies in nearby beer gardens and pawnshops heard the shot. It was the first and only bullet Red Murphy fired in the twenty-two years he served in the New York City Police Department. He left behind his wife, an 11-year old son and 13-year old daughter.

The wedding

Joe said Red is dead. Amos the janitor quit. He ain't cleaning no blood squirts and brain bits splattered on the walls. Does something to you. You got to scrub that stuff hard. Don't come off easy. Not getting paid extra. Amos does floors, not walls. After the coroner and police inspectors did their work, the condition of the bathroom remained the same. Who cares? They piss in their pants most of the time. They don't bend over a grimy toilet when bile rushes to the surface. They're pretty loose with all their orifices. Let it flow. Let it hurl.

Sunday mornings are quiet in the Bowery. Dorothy's Uncle sent his Rolls Royce to Holiness Mission. The driver got there on time, but Bowery bums got their own time. Time's an abstraction. It's not like anyone wears a wristwatch. Items like that get pawned for a pint. Time's wasted on them. By the way, Jim's not in his room. Hasn't been seen for a day or two.

Joe at the Jefferson called Lincoln at the Mission. I'm not his keeper. Joe made no mention of the money Red gave him to make things happen the morning Jim's baby brother gets hitched to the rich girl from New Rochelle. Joe bought the suit, a few sizes too big but it looked decent enough. He bought him a white shirt, dark brown tie and a pair of shoes, no holes in the soles. Jim had been dropping about a pound a day. By the end of the week nothing fit. Coughing up blood took its toll. Bill Lincoln hopped into the back of the Rolls and told the driver where to go. He's done cowboy round-up before, lassoing the paper-bag-in-a-bottle rancheroos. He knew their habits and hangouts. He gave up trying to get Jim to church on time. Let's shoot for the reception. Jim thought the wedding was at St. Mary's. Everyone named Callaghan gets married at St. Mary's. Baptisms, First Communions Confirmations, weddings, and funerals. Bill found Jim at Second and Ninth, getting a five-cent shine. The Rolls pulled up to the curb. Bill hopped out and grabbed the pint midflight to Jim's thirsty mouth. Go straight to the reception, he tells the driver.

A man in uniform opened the reception hall door for Jim. He walked past the table holding place cards. Only a few left, including 'James P. Callaghan, Jr. Table #1'. He got there after a groomsman made the toast. Jim heard someone at the mic, blessing the food.

A variety of food on trays passed by, held aloft by waiters attired in shirtwaist tuxedo jackets, Scotch plaid cummerbunds, matching bowties and handkerchiefs peeking out of jacket pockets. They were clearing the cocktail hour leftovers. Jim grabbed some rolls off a tray, stuffing them into his pocket. Other waiters carried fresh drinks en route to the ballroom. Jim grabbed a glass off one of the trays as the waiter tried to outmaneuver him. The man explained these were special order drinks. An elegantly dressed woman whispered in the waiter's ear. He headed back to the bar but not before Jim grabbed a second drink off his tray.

The woman wore a light blue, floor-length gown, decorated with sparkly colored glass stones stitched in a swerve pattern on a layered bodice undergirding the woman's considerable bosom. She approached Jim, who held a drink in each hand. The woman placed her gloved hand on her chest when she caught Jim staring at her cleavage. She mentioned that the cocktail hour was over and drink orders were being taken at the tables.

Would he like to follow her to Table #1? Oh, I'd like to do more than follow you he said.

The ballroom thrilled to big band music. It don't mean a thing if it ain't got that swing.

Instead of following the kind lady's directions, Jim headed straight to the bandstand. The gorgeous, radiant, effervescent bride headed him off at the pass.

Dorothy hugged Jim.

"Oh my, how beautiful you look," Jim said, "Sorry I'm late. Is Ray mad about the tux?"

"He'll get over it. Probably not the best time to talk to him though," Dorothy said, "You're here and that's the important thing. How I wished you had come into my life sooner."

"Then you would've picked me over shorty."

"Ray and I were meant to be husband and wife. That means I'm your sister. Well, technically Sis-in-law. No one will ever replace Anna but I'm going to love you as a full-fledged sister. Will you be my brother?"

"Most certainly."

"We'll be so happy as one big family. Maybe some day you'll move in with us."

"I'd be a third wheel."

"This is a day for dreaming dreams, isn't it, Jim?"

"This is the greatest day of your life. Don't worry about me."

"Can I show you to your table?" Dorothy said as she held Jim's face in both hands, "See. It's right over there. Come meet Uncle George. I bet he'll have work for you."

Jim took a crumpled dollar bill out of his pocket and handed it to Dorothy. "Why thank you, Jim," she said.

"It's not much. But it's the first dollar I ever earned. I saved it. Long time ago, I ran some errands for my neighbor, Mrs. Nicoletti. She was poor but gave me a nice tip. And I delivered newspapers for a week or two. Made twenty cents. Sold some scrap iron after we finished Anna's cart. Took all the pennies, nickels, and dimes to the candy store. I said, 'Give me a crisp one-dollar bill, Mr. Candy Man'. That's it. My first dollar. I want you to have it forever."

"You're making me cry. This is the nicest wedding gift ever."

"It's everything I have. It's the first and the last dollar I own," Jim said.

"Not the last one, silly man," Dorothy said.

Jim took a yellowed, crumpled envelope out of his pocket and handed it to Dorothy, "Here's something else," Jim said, as Dorothy stuffed the dollar and envelope into her satchel. "There was a letter from Aunt Minnie came one day. Arrived about a week after Anna disappeared. The Postman handed it to Momma. My father grabbed it right out of her hands. Told her we don't want anything to do with them rubes. He tore it up and threw it in the garbage. I went to take it out of the pail. The son of a bitch pushed me out of the way, and stuffed the pieces in his pocket and went off to work. I got a few pieces he missed and hid them … it said something about Anna … like she's with them … the piece with directions is right here… Sloatsburg. Park at Emma's bakery on 17. Follow markers Pine Meadow Trail." Several guests surrounded Dorothy, pulling her away to the dance floor. Jim said "Maybe you and Ray can take me …"

The music drowned out the last few words Jim spoke as a group of Dorothy's friends guided her to the dance floor.

Jim wandered over to the bandstand. "Hey, play something by the Ink Spots, will you?"

The bandleader looked down, pointing his baton at Jim. "You're Ray's brother, right?"

"That's right. I'm the best man."

"You're the best man who missed the toast. For your information, we don't play their music. Why don't you run along, now."

"Did you know the Ink Spots sing Irish songs?"

"Listen, take a seat at your table like a good boy. We're about to play the couple's wedding song."

Jim burst out singing, "My Wild Irish Rose, the sweetest flower that …".

Jonas, Uncle George's right hand man, grabbed Jim and escorted him to Table #1. Jim spotted the lady with big breasts crossing the dance floor. He stooped to have a closer look.

"Mind your manners," Jonas said, firmly holding Jim's arm, "That's the pastor's wife."

"Priests don't have wives."

"Come along now," Jonas said, "Meet the boss."

Uncle George stood up to greet Jim. "So glad you could make it," Uncle George said, "There's your champagne. I can't drink that bubbly stuff. Gives me a headache. I like Whiskey. Something tells me you do too. How do you take it?"

"Straight up," Jim said.

Uncle George snapped his fingers. A waiter came running. "Get this man the finest whiskey we have," Uncle George said, then turning back to Jim "Dorothy tells me you're looking for work."

"Sure am. I'll do anything."

"Take a piece of bread with that drink. Lines the stomach so the liquor doesn't land so rough, know what I'm saying? So, Jim, ever play golf? Got Ray into our Club. Gave him a set of clubs as a wedding gift. Woods, iron, putter. Putt. Putt. Putt. You know Jim, Raymond was a nobody from nowhere. But he's going places now."

"I never played golf. But I'll do any kind of work."

"Will you? Okay, so maybe now's a good time to give you an interview."

"Right now? Maybe tomorrow I can come to your office."

Uncle George snapped his fingers again. The waiter brought another fine whiskey to the table. Straight up in a glass, instead of a bottle Jim was used to drinking out of. His hands shook as he lifted the glass to his mouth.

"Easy there, big man. Sip it. Tastes much better that way. About the interview. You're here. Right next to me. The groom's brother. The best man. Although you missed the church, and you missed giving the toast. So that's why now is the perfect time for an interview. On Dorothy's big day. Swell gal, isn't she?"

"She certainly is."

"You know Jim, you more than disrespected her. Lucky for you she's a most forgiving type. Your interview won't take long. Drink up," Uncle George said as he snapped his fingers. Jonas came to the table. "This is my right-hand man. He knows talent when he sees it."

"I'll do anything," Jim said.

"I know you will," Jonas said, "Follow me."

"Here we are, Jim," Jonas said, "Tile floors that lead into stalls made private with cherry wood swing doors. Urinals, each topped with heavy, circular blue-gray Carrara marble ashtrays. Have a smoke."

"What are we doing in here?"

"Your interview."

"In the men's room?

"Why not? Have you ever seen a more elegant bathroom? Isn't it swell? Look overhead. See the slow turning ceiling fans with wide cherrywood blades. Finely etched sconces," Jonas said as he turned to the men's room attendant, "Wilbur, open one of those stalls, would you? Jim, take note of the tongue-in-groove mahogany trim on the wall, the brass fixtures, the smooth cedar seats. Did you ever? Look at those long sinks with the finest selection of talcs, colognes, masculine musk-scented soaps, and terry cloth towels. Steaming ones if you prefer. Wilbur 'Black Pepper' Williams is your personal attendant ready to take care of your every need. You might remember him. He was Eddie 'The Hammer' Drummond's sparring partner. Subsequently, a rival. A big-time contender, weren't you Wilbur? Don't be modest. Wilbur was supposed to fight 'The Hammer' the night you took his place. At the weigh-in, Wilbur lost his temper and broke a toe, kicking a chair too hard. A publicity stunt gone wrong. That's where you stepped in. Brave man. I seemed to remember you lost that night. A little above your class, I think. Anyhow, Wilbur was in Eddie's class. Would have kicked his ass. Had quite a boxing career. His foot's all better now. He can dance, too."

The music of Duke Ellington was piped into the men's room.

Just give that rhythm everything you've got ...   t

"Here's twenty bucks, Wilbur, do a little Bojangles for us, will you," Jonas said.

"Prefer not to Mr. Jonas if it's all the same to you," Wilbur said, "Lost a few steps, I'd rather ..."

"Clean toilets? C'mon, take the twenty and tap a little for 'Jungle Jim'. It'd take twenty flushes to earn this much."

"I'd rather not," Wilbur said.

"I won't force you," Jonas said, turning to Jim, "How about applying for ladies room attendant? It'll be easier than Wilbur's work. Ladies have better aim, know what I'm saying? Wait! I have a better idea. Jim, Pepper. Take your shirts off. You guys are prize fighters, right? Twenty for the winner. Ten bucks for the loser."

Jonas pushed Jim close to Wilbur.

In a clinch with the attendant, Jim whispered, "Let's take this sucker out."

"I need the job, man."

Jim turned around, and removed his shirt, exposing a clear outline of each rib; a sunken abdomen; loose, wrinkly skin; hollowed, saddened eyes; an already defeated posture. A nobody from nowhere stuck in nowhere.

"I'm game but I need a corner man," Jim said.

"You mean *cut* man," Jonas said, doubling over, eyes closed by habit whenever he laughed. Jim reared back and tried to sucker punch the closed-eyes man with everything he had. He missed.

It don't mean a thing if it ain't got that swing.

Deeper into the woods

Jim's last moments in the men's room unfolded randomly in his mind: the side of his face flush with the white tile floor, eyeballing the tips of shiny black shoes. The last words he heard came from the bride's uncle, "I think you've done enough damage for today, Jim. Two of my men are going to help you get home. Tell me where you're living now."

"Home … to Anna …Dorothy's got directions," Jim remembered saying as he crawled into daylight from under the rock-shelter, getting as far as a bed of cinnamon fern. He studied the piece of pottery in his hand. Curious, he scraped away some of the black soil encrusted in the etched lines of its textured surface. It revealed a design resembling an ear of corn. He put it in his pocket. As he grabbed the branch of a nearby mountain laurel, a ruffled grouse burst out of the bush. Startled, Jim boosted his sore body into a sitting position.

The drum roll of spring made him fully alert.

He absorbed the sun's rays that dried the damp film on his skin. He looked to the heavens, seeing the bright blue sky and puffy white clouds through the treetop canopy. Seated on the soft loam of the forest floor, he was surrounded by the distinct scent of pinesap, and the fresh, sweet, earthy smells of every green thing around him. He could see the rich earth colors of the surrounding woods. A landscape of pitted rocks and massive twin boulders loomed ahead of him. The beauty of the plants, trees, and wildlife introduced him to a world he never knew as a city boy.

Here, he did not ache for the next handout at the mission pantry, the abased begging for loose change, or the reach for the next swig of Five Star Twister. Jim's life up to this point was measured moment to moment by being just a cap twist away from another fall into the gutter, and another nightstick poke in the stomach. The awakening of his senses, the inhaling of fresh air, the sight of a clear sky and the songs of birds distracted him from the realization of his status as a *bona fide* Bowery bum.

Jim made it to a nearby stream. He cupped his hands and drank several mouthfuls of fresh, cold water. He then crawled over a log that abutted a rock outcropping. He grabbed a fissure in the rock and boosted his body to a standing position. Exhausted, he leaned against the boulder. His aching bones told him he was many years older than thirty. He managed a few tentative steps, feeling his way along the rock. Encouraged, he continued without support, stepping slowly along a well-travelled footpath. The fresh air invigorated him.

Random scenes from the wedding reception continued to flash through his mind: a waiter wearing a white linen vest and black slacks, skillfully holding in one upturned palm a tray of mixed drinks, green olives, pearl onions, maraschino cherries; the bride's bouquet; and the ample cleavage of a woman he stared at much too long. He reached into his pocket and found the souvenir matchbook, imprinted in gilded letters: Glen Island Casino: Raymond & Dorothy Callaghan, married March 24, 1940. He remembered Dorothy, the sweetest, kindest, most beautiful bride.

Jim reached a clearing. He rested on a flat boulder and raised his hand to his forehead, shielding his eyes from the bright sun. Suddenly, a baby deer moved into a shaft of light no more than fifteen feet from where he sat.

Not wanting to disturb the gentle fawn, Jim lowered his hand slowly, resting it on the sun-warmed rock. The animal's big, soulful eyes, moist black snout, unsure, spindly legs, and the white dots on its brown fur blended with the sun, trees, and earth. The curious fawn tilted its head toward Jim, its big eyes making contact with his.

Jim remained still for fear the animal would leave. When the fawn's curiosity waned, it turned around quickly, hopped up and down, then scampered off into the woods on its skinny, wobbly legs.

No sooner had Jim momentarily tilted his head to see where the fawn was headed, a full-size doe suddenly appeared, just six feet in front of him, sniffing the ground the fawn had just vacated. The doe looked intensely at Jim, a prominent vein jutting below her eye, to within an inch of her snout, pulsating as the animal moved her jaw up and down. The doe kept one eye on Jim, alternately clenching her teeth and raising her head, with the protruding vein becoming more prominent. The doe sniffed the ground once again, then bounded off into the woods in pursuit of her baby, with her short, striped tail bobbing up and down.

Jim followed the trail markers. A crudely painted red arrow on a wood plank nailed to a tree pointed the way. He was acutely aware his weak body would soon fail him. Exhausted, goose bumps rising on his forearms, he began to sweat profusely. He took a soiled handkerchief out of his back pocket, unfolded it until he found a spot unstained by blood. He coughed into the cloth, his whole body convulsing with each effort to clear his throat. He then heard the voices of several people approaching.

Four men and a woman not thirty yards distant headed directly toward him. He fingered the sharp edge of the potsherd in his pocket. The woman in the center of the group appeared considerably older than the men. Three of the men were tall, broad-shouldered and strode with shirts unbuttoned, exposing thick necks and muscular physiques. The fourth male was much shorter than the others and less physically imposing. He was naked to the waist. His fingernails were painted and his hair appeared to be streaked with tricolor strands drawn into a bun, with a large feather poking through it. A large loop earring dangled from one ear.

Drawing closer, the woman spread her hands wide, halting all movement to within ten yards of where Jim stood, his body shaking. She pointed in Jim's direction. One of the men broke ranks, picked up a large rock off the forest floor and lifted it over his head. Jim took the sharp-edged potsherd out of his pocket and held it against his leg.

The man hoisted the rock higher as he approached. The man's eyes widened. He advanced a few more steps. Jim froze.

The man lifted the rock to the full extent of his outstretched arms and thrust it at Jim's feet, hitting a spot, inches from Jim's shoes. Jim looked down to witness the twitching death throes of a rattlesnake, seconds from delivering a venomous strike to his lower calf. The man bowed and returned to the group. Another man put the dead snake inside a burlap sack.

As it became apparent that the emaciated stranger might collapse at any moment, the man who killed the snake came back to Jim and lowered his body to the ground, cradling him in his arms. The woman took a cloth out of her dress pocket and wiped Jim's brow.

"My name is Wee Mum. Don't be afraid. These men are my grandsons."

Wee Mum turned to one grandson and said, "Hurry. Give him water." The slightly built man unhooked a hand-hewn wooden water flask from his belt and held it up to Jim's mouth.

Jim took a few sips, and said, "Thank you," then turned his head to look at the man holding him, "You saved my life."

Wee Mum pointed to each grandson, introducing them, "Crooked Nose, Two Spirit, Soft Paws and Rabbit Tail. We're Ramapough Lenape. Indians. Members of a nation. A tribe."

"I never met anyone with interesting names like those."

"It's one of our customs. Parents look for what's special about a child before naming them," Wee Mum said, "I'll show you. Turn around, Rabbit Tail. Show this man your big bushy backside. Hold up your hands Soft Paws. See how soft and smooth they are. And can you see which grandson was born with a crooked nose."

"What about Two Spirit?" Jim said.

"He has two spirits. It's as simple as that. What's your name?"

"Jim … what would my name be … if I was in your tribe?"

"Let's see … this'll be hard because we don't know anything about you yet. We'll give it a try. Boys, what do you think? Remember to be kind to our new friend."

"Black Eye," Rabbit Tail said.

"Scarred Brow," Soft Paws said.

Crooked Nose leaned his head over to get a better look at Jim. "Broken Nose."

"And you, Two Spirit?"

Two Spirit looked over every inch of Jim's face and body, examining his eye, nose, blood spots on his shirt, then took a few steps back, turned to his grandmother and said, "Only two words?"

"Two words," Wee Mum said.

Two Spirit looked at Jim and said, "What Happened?"

The brothers laughed.

Wee Mum bent down and examined Jim's face. "That eye looks very bad. Does it hurt?"

"Everything hurts," Jim said, coughing violently, holding the bloodied handkerchief to his mouth.

Two Spirit left the group for several minutes and came back with several leaves he pulled off a low-hanging Sassafras branch. He cupped the leaves between his hands and whispered into them, "Release your healing powers. Make our friend a new man." He placed the leaves gently against

Jim's eye. He then lifted Jim's hand so he could hold the leaves in place by himself.

"See if he's able to stand," Wee Mum said, "Hold his head straight." The grandsons worked together and got Jim to his feet, holding him. Jim looked at the grandmother and said, "Wee Mum, what about you, won't you find a name for me?"

Wee Mum placed her hand gently upon Jim's face, chanting a prayer in her native tongue. Her grandsons joined in the prayer, calling upon the Great Creator spirit.

When their chanting ended, Wee Mum said to Jim, "The spirits have spoken. You are *New Man*."

Wee Mum bent down and picked up the potsherd Jim dropped. She reverently wiped away the remaining soil with the hem of her dress. "Where did you find this, New Man?"

"Back there," Jim said, pointing, "Under a big rock. Near other big rocks. I used it to help me crawl out. So many rocks."

"Did you see anything in the distance?" Wee Mum said.

"Two mountains," Jim said, "And a flat space between them. I woke up under a big rock. Close to a stream."

"Split Rock," Soft Paws said, "Where the devil dropped big rocks out of his apron."

"Did you make that up?" Jim said.

"We have legends passed down to us from our ancestors, New Man," Wee Mum said, "We tell the story to our children. And they tell their children. It is our history."

Wee Mum lifted the potsherd skyward and said, "We know the place where you slept. It is sacred ground for our people. We have to bring this back to its home. Nothing belongs to us. We must leave everything in its place."

"I didn't mean to take it."

"That's okay, New Man. You didn't know. It was made by our ancestors many, many sunsets ago. It was made with the purest intentions, sacred to our people," she said, softly touching the bridge of Jim's broken nose, chanting another prayer.

"I have ancestors too. My Grammy Peggy told me once that my Grandpa Stephen told her he used to visit a special place called Devil's Bit Mountain in Ireland. The way she described it sounded like Split Rock."

"Can we help you find your way?" Rabbit Tail said.

Jim held the handkerchief to his mouth, coughing. "You saved my life," Jim sobbed, looking at Crooked Nose, "Why did you bother? I'm a stranger to you."

"All life is sacred to us," Wee Mum said, "You are a stranger no longer."

"Is Anna here?" Jim said.

"Who is Anna?"

"My sister."

"Is she lost?"

"I don't know. Someone brought me here so I could find her. I want her to know I never stopped looking for her."

"What is your family name, New Man?" Wee Mum said.

"Callaghan."

The mother and four grandsons looked at one another, lowering their heads.

"Would you let us help you find your sister?" Wee Mum said.

"Yes. Please."

"How long have you been looking?'

"All my life. She just disappeared one day."

"My father lives deeper in the woods, New Man. He can help you," Wee Mum said, "We'll take you to him."

Crooked Nose and Rabbit Tail made a cradle with interlocked hands and placed them under Jim's bottom. The man with the black eye, scarred eyebrow and broken nose weighed no more than a child.

Soft Paws placed Jim's arms around his brothers' shoulders and walked behind the three of them, holding Jim's head upright.

Wee Mum turned to Two Spirit and said, "Run. Tell Papa Chief we found a man named Jim Callaghan. Then gather the medicines. Quick. Go!"

Wee Mum led the way deeper into the woods. Jim said to her, "Your grandsons are very strong."

"We dig out canoes from fallen trees, New Man," Rabbit Tail said.

"I've never been in a canoe."

"When you get stronger, we'll take you for a ride," Soft Paws said, gently massaging Jim's neck.

Wee Mum and the brothers were deeply saddened at the sight of the frail, wounded man, knowing his extreme weakness signaled the nearness of death.

"Hold on to us, Mr. Jim," Crooked Nose said, "We'll get you there very soon."

"I hear her voice. Her silly laugh," Jim said.

Knowing immediately Jim was his nephew, Carney told his great grandsons to put him in the spare bed. He then dispatched the four of them to find Rev. Jeremiah Dooze and alert all family members - whites and Lenape - to come immediately for a gathering as his nephew Jim is gravely ill and wants to go home.

Carney wept.

Wee Mum removed Jim's clothing and bathed his body in warm water and soap. She gave his feet a deep rub with a creamy mixture of aloe and pitch pine. She placed cold cloths on his feverish head and covered him with sheets and blankets when the chills caused him to shiver. Jim drifted in and out of consciousness, answering her sporadically. To Wee Mum's eyes, her patient seemed to be comfortable, though delirious at times.

With his eyes closed, Jim called out the names Edward, Rose, and Ella. Don't you see them holding hands, dancing around the bed … leaning in close to me … smiling. They look happy to see me.

Rose: I got a Kewpie doll for my fifth birthday too. Anyhow my mother went nuts when I disappeared. Eleanor and Helen kidnapped me and raised me in a whorehouse. Oh, I see you're staring at the scar on my face. That's a dog bite. I took his food bowl away and he bit me. Lie! It was a human dog. One of my tricks didn't pay, so we had a little disagreement. He lost. I used a corkscrew. I wasn't sure if he had a heart. I had to dig around to find which side it was on. Went upriver for a few years. Our father would have been proud, but he croaked before I got sentenced. Have you seen Edward yet? Here he is. Talk to him. He's a swell brother.

Edward: Remember when father said whadda ya goin' to school for. Member when ya asked the conductor to punch yer ticket. You git punched too many times in the ring I bet. I dint think you wuz made fer the hard life, Jimmy boy. When Rose went fer her ice cream I knew I wuz in deep shit. I dint want to git hit no more and Ma be goin' mad as a hatter so I jes keep walkin'. Dey puts me on a orphan train. I hopped off when I had the chance 'n catched out on anudder train to Hooverville 'n picked up all de oranges in Florida 'n ate a lot of dem til I git sick 'n dey eat up my stomach wit all de acid, ya know 'n them taters in Idaho. I git sick a dem too but dey dint eat up my stomach. I think we mighta caught da same train to Weehawken but where you wuz comin' from woulda bin da ferry. Jes kiddin' ya wouldn't abin cut out for dat fleeing a broke home stuff. It wuz more adventure for me. I dint want to beg. Sorry fer callin' ya a bum. My workin' wuz nothin' ta brag about.

Ella: Where ya been big fella? Here's a wink wink just for you. When I was a teenager and feeling my hormones I got together with this available fella. My parents had a clean basement that they locked their soiled daughter in. When the baby came out they gave *my* daughter away or sold her. After that, I always wanted a child I could call my own. Anyhow, you and me have a son! Congratulations! He looks just like you, handsome. I wish you could be around to watch him grow up. I'm a little nuts and not much of a mother but I love him and promise to do my best.

After a few hours' rest Jim woke up and said he felt stronger. He asked Wee Mum if he could sit outside in the sunshine with Uncle Carney.

When Papa Chief put out the urgent call concerning his nephew's condition, everyone on all sides of the family dropped everything, got dressed in their finest and headed to Pine Meadow. Mickey and Patrick owned homes and a riding stable in Sloatsburg. They called the twins, Eleanor and Swell, who lived with their families three towns north. When the Lenape grandsons tracked down Rev. Dooze, he promised to get there before sunset. Paul Ostrander, the retired census taker who became Carney's neighbor and best friend, gathered his family, and rowed across the lake. He wanted to be with the man who inspired him to stop checking boxes and start asking poignant questions.

Wee Mum refused to leave Jim's side. She sorted through the men's clothes brought over from family and found a decent outfit for him. The grandsons carried two easy chairs out of the cabin and placed them side by side under the big elm tree near the open field where the tater patch used to be, so Uncle and nephew could have some private time together.

Mickey's wife Phoebe and Patrick's wife Sara took the deceased matriarch Minnie Mae's place organizing all hospitality and food preparation. The Callaghan brothers and their wives got plenty of help from their children and grandchildren. When the Callaghan brood arrived, they hauled out every available barrel, crate and chair stored in the cabin, sheds, and barn, dusted them off and set them up in an area near the brook, a spot Papa Chief selected for Rev. Dooze's service. The Lenapes prepared their own special ceremony.

The Callaghans, Ostranders and Lenapes poured onto the property, including granddaughters with flowers in their curls, wearing pink and green pastel dresses and grandsons dressed in suits and ties, with hair slicked back. They were all asked by Wee Mum to leave Carney and Jim alone, until she gave the signal.

Closing in on his 90th year, Carney was hard of hearing in one ear but otherwise his same vigorous self. When Jim explained to Crooked Nose and Rabbit Tail that he also had one bad ear they placed his chair on Papa Chief's good side.

"You might not want to hear this but I gotta fill you in on some family history," Carney said to his nephew, "You know how my daughter Wee Mum got her name?"

"I know it had to be something special," Jim said.

"Well, the day your Grammy Peggy and Grandpa Stephen plopped yer father on my knee, I meet my daughter I dint know I had. I think she wuz 'bout three or four at the time 'n she helped my stepmother Miss Peggy look after yer father right after he wuz born. She had a natural instinct fer motherin' so we named her Wee Mum. A little Irish 'n a little Injin mixed together. Listen, your old man wuz a stinker. I know you got worser names fer him, but he ain't 'round to torment you no more." Carney tapped Jim's knee and said, "I know ya followed a rugged road to git here today, Jim, but I gotta tell ya how blessed I am to finally meet ya."

"You and Wee Mum and the boys are the kindest people I ever met in my life ... excluding my Momma and my brand-new sister-in-law, Dorothy," Jim said, crying, "I should of made the effort to meet you sooner. I really fucked up."

"Listen careful, Jim. We all fuck up at one time or the other," Carney said, putting his arm around Jim's shoulder, "I'm the worst offender. I made so many damn mistakes it could fill a book if I knew how ta write."

Wee Mum came up to the two men, carrying a large basket. She unbuttoned Jim's shirt to apply some medicine to his aching body. She created one poultice containing skunk cabbage root, slippery elm, rattlesnake oil, and salt pork for his chest and placed a smaller, more aromatic pitch pine poultice on his neck. She replaced the sassafras leaves that covered his eye and put a quilt across his lap.

Two Spirit came by and took the empty basket from his grandmother. "Will you be leading the ceremony, Wee Mum? We're almost ready." Wee Mum took her grandson aside. "I can't leave New Man. Ask Oxeye Daisy to take my place. The reverend sent word we do our ceremony first. Ask the Callaghans to hold off the food for now," Wee Mum said, looking over her shoulder at Jim, "He can't hold anything down."

Two Spirit walked around Jim's chair and whispered to Carney, "Should we tell him now, Papa Chief?"

Before Carney could answer, a seven-year-old boy and his towhead four-year old cousin came running out of the woods ahead of their parents. The children belonged to Carney's twin daughters, Eleanor and Swell. They gave their grandfather a kiss on either cheek as he nudged them along to stand in front of Jim. He told them to give him the gifts they were hiding behind their backs.

The little boy stood in front of Jim. "This is from all your cousins," the boy said, placing a big cut-out red heart on Jim's lap, "See. We signed it. We love you, Cousin Jim." The little girl put a bouquet of wildflowers on top of the card. She whispered something to Wee Mum who lifted her up so she could kiss Cousin Jim's cheek.

"Thank you, children," Jim said to the little ones, "You look so beautiful all dressed up."

Carney asked Two Spirit to help him out of his chair. Papa Chief, Wee Mum, and Two Spirit stood in front of Jim. "New Man," Wee Mum said, "We had a meeting of the elders. We are honored to tell you it was decided to make you a member of our tribe."

"And they got a little ceremony for you," Papa Chief said.

The Lenape filed into the open field with the Callaghans gathered nearby.

What did I do to deserve this?" Jim said.

After awhile, Two Spirit came by with fresh medicinal dressings for Jim and handed the basket to Wee Mum.

"Jim, there's no one better at nursin' than my daughter," Carney said, "Jes come natural ta her. Anyhow, we're goin' ta see a special ceremony by the tribe. Jes for you, young man. When they're done payin' their tribute, we'll all gather down by the water. The Reverend will come by with some special prayers and some singin' for you."

"A priest?" Jim asked.

"Yep, the bestest priest I know."

Jim inched his way up in the chair. He pointed to a spot in the open field. "Look Uncle Carney. The Momma deer and baby deer found each other."

"Ain't that a beautiful sight!" Carney said.

"Do you think they're the same ones I saw this morning?"

"I bet they are, Jim."

The doe and fawn ran off together as the men, women and children of the Ramapough Lenape Nation entered the field in large numbers. The Lenape women wore beaded moccasins, leggings, and deerskin ribbon dresses. Oxeye Daisy added a single feather headband to her outfit. The men were bare-chested with body and face paint and wore buckskin loincloths and leggings.

Crooked Nose and Rabbit Tail built a fire. Oxeye Daisy handed prayer sticks to each child instructing them to light them and hold them up with their right hands, so the smoke will rise as prayers to the Creator. Two Spirit and Soft Paws joined their brothers in a single line with other male Lenape. The women formed a parallel line led by Oxeye Daisy. Three men sat on the ground ready to beat the drums. A Lenape woman played the recorder. The elders smoked pipes.

When Oxeye Daisy lifted her right hand to the sky, the children lifted their prayer sticks, rocking back and forth as the two lines started dancing and chanting in synchronization, accented by the drum and recorder beats:

He Ya Ha

He Ha Ya Ha

He Ya Ha

He Ha Ya He Ha

He Ha Ya He Ha

He Ya Ha

He Ya Ha Ha

He Ya Ha

He Ha He

He Ha Ya He Ha

Jim touched Wee Mum's hand resting on his shoulder. She leaned over and said, "Is there anything else we can do for you, New Man?" Jim nodded.

"Can I see Anna … and ride in the canoe?"

One of Mickey's sons waited for Rev. Jeremiah Dooze's car on the main road. He held the reins of one of the stable ponies. When Rev. Dooze emerged from his car, the young man made him aware of Jim's rapidly weakening condition. He boosted the elderly minister onto the saddle and walked the horse along the trail to Pine Meadow. The mourners were in their seats near the stream and some of the Callaghan and Lenape children had climbed onto tree branches overhanging the water,

Wee Mum removed the medicinal wrappings from Jim's body. Her grandsons carried Jim down to water's edge on a cot bolstered with several pillows. As soon as Rev. Dooze dismounted he was greeted by Carney who introduced him to Jim, "This is my nephew, Jim, Reverend Dooze. Isn't he a fine-looking Callaghan?"

"He sure is," Rev. Dooze said, kneeling down, holding Jim's hand in both of his, "What an honor to meet you, sir."

"Thank you, Father," Jim said, his eyes barely open.

"Do you know where you are going today, Jim?"

"I do," Jim said, "I am going home ... home to be with my Lord ... and Anna. Wee Mum said I will see Anna today."

"I have a prayer for you right now, Jim. Would you like to hear it?"

"I would. Please pray for me," Jim said, as he tried to raise his hand to touch Rev. Dooze's face.

"Are you trying to pull my beard, Jim Callaghan?"

"No ... I ..."

Wee Mum wiped Jim's forehead with a damp cloth. She leaned over and Jim whispered in her ear.

Wee Mum turned to Rev. Dooze and said, "He is ready... wants you to know that he is sober today."

Rev. Dooze anointed Jim's head with oil, and prayed, "Almighty God, look upon this your servant, lying in great weakness. Comfort him with the promise of life everlasting, given in the resurrection of your Son Jesus Christ our Lord. And all God's people say ..."

"Amen."

"We know our time is short today, so I want to offer just a few verses from Psalm 139," Rev. Dooze said.

> *If I say surely the darkness will hide me*
> *And the light become night around me*
> *Even the darkness will not be dark to you*
> *The night will shine like the day*
> *For darkness is as light to you ..."*

Rev. Dooze stopped at that point and motioned for Carney to come forward. Papa Chief got out of his chair, accompanied by his friend Paul. The Reverend handed the Bible to Carney and pointed to the spot where he should continue the reading.

Paul stood close to Carney and held the book open for him. Carney read slowly:

"For you created my inmost being

You ..." Carney struggled to mouth the next word.

Paul whispered, "The 'k' is silent. Start with the next letter, the 'n' sound."

Carney continued, *"You knit me together in my mother's womb. I praise you because I am fearfully and wonderfully made."*

Carney handed the Bible back to Rev. Dooze. He then kissed Jim on the forehead. "Those words wuz written fer you, Jim. See ya on the other side. We'll all be together soon enough."

As Crooked Nose, Rabbit Tail, and Soft Paws carried Jim to the canoe, Two Spirit lined the inside with pillows. Wee Mum, knee deep in the stream, held the canoe steady as her grandsons gingerly placed Jim inside.

Rev. Dooze played the harmonica and invited everyone to sing *Amazing Grace* together:

> *Amazing Grace, how sweet the sound   That saved*
> *a wretch like me*
> *I once was lost, but now am found*
> *Was blind but now I see*
> *Was Grace that taught my heart to fear*
> *And Grace, my fears relieved*
> *How precious did that Grace appear*
> *The hour I first believed*
> *Through many dangers, toils and snares*
> *We have already come*
> *T'was Grace that brought us safe thus far*
> *And Grace will lead us home*

Two Spirit steadied the canoe as Wee Mum leaned over, whispering to Jim, "You can't see it from here but there is ahead of you a corridor of reeds in the marsh, appearing low and sparse at the opening, then taller, thicker, and darker as you drift farther along. The entrance is wide at first, but the path narrows as the reeds close up. They will have different colors, textures, layers, and sizes, sometimes looking like they're woven together. You will float through them going with the movement of water. You will see Anna in the light as you come through the opening. She waits for you there, on the other side. There is no turning back, Jim. You won't want to turn back because your journey will be warm and welcoming. It is time to go now. Do not be afraid, New Man. You might get some scratches from the reeds snapping back as you go forward. Maybe some animals and birds will startle you, popping up out of the reeds without warning. But you will get there safely."

Jim turned his head to look at Two Spirit and Wee Mum, and said, "Won't you come with me?"

"You must take this part of the journey on your own," she said.

More Callaghan and Lenape children climbed into the trees overhanging the stream. As the canoe started to drift, Rev. Dooze asked for a call and response for the final hymn, *As It Is in Heaven*:

> *When sorrow comes near,*
> *You wipe away every tear,*
> *For yours is the Kingdom*
> *As it is in heaven,*
> *When I break into pieces of clay,*
> *You make me whole again today,*
> *For yours is the Power*
> *As it is in heaven,*
> *When all I see is darkness and fright,*
> *You open the veil to let in the light,*
> *For yours is the Glory*
> *As it is in heaven*

EPILOGUE

Well, I'm still half of this and half of that. Fully aware I'm no expert on the last knowable thing before one leaves this world, - that transitional moment when we step across the threshold into the next part of our journey, I withhold all judgment on the matter.

I'm glad I took Carney's advice and started listening to each person who needed to tell his or her story beyond what fit into the blank spaces on preprinted forms. Thanks to him, I decided to retire to this beautiful part of the state, take up the pen and jot something down more meaningful than one's yearly income and current occupation.

I have to say Carney was one pain in the ass neighbor, showing up at my cottage whenever the hell he felt like it, always unannounced, saying it's time for another reading lesson, Paul. I made a note to myself to visit the library in town and borrow some kiddie books to share with him. We can't read the Bible every single time, I told him. But let me tell you, no one could treasure a more faithful friend than Carney Callaghan.

I decided to write this tale about three generations of the Callaghan family, with the mountain man himself being my main source of information. Who else? He was there throughout all three generations. He told me as much as he knew and introduced me to others who lived through some part of it or personally knew others who did. I scoured mountains of family documents, letters, and miscellaneous papers to get all the background stuff. Hopefully, I pieced together an account that's close to the whole truth.

As far as Carney's nephew Jim is concerned, I can report as an eyewitness to what I saw several years ago on Jim's last day on earth. I have no way of knowing whether or not Jim beheld God's Glory as Carney is so certain he did. Or that he's now in heaven with Jesus as you read this. I found out for certain, however, Jim Callaghan did not see much of heaven on this earth. But he had one hell of a day on that particular Monday.

It was just a few days into spring on March 25, 1940, and everything that was dead started coming to life again. I did my best to tell the Callaghan story. Since I'm the author of this tale, I get to say the last word.

Shalom

Acknowledgements

My deepest gratitude goes to three dedicated volunteer editors, my wife Carol Donahue, our dear friend Joan Lehnert, who has since passed, and my nephew Matthew Garvey. These three people read and reread my numerous drafts more times than I can count. They continually suggested changes to the story, both minor and major. They told me when something did not work or simply fell flat. They questioned and acted as copy and story editors, informing me about overwritten sentences, muddled paragraphs and impossibly dense prose. They did this arduous work with love and persistence, all the while carrying on with all their other tasks in life. Without them, this novel would never have seen the light of day.

Also, I want to thank my son, David Donahue and son-in-law Mark Daley, for cautioning me about the importance of specifically tying together language/dialect with character.

I also want to thank the author Stephen King for the invaluable advice he imparted to me through his book, ON WRITING. Although I never met him personally, I met him through his book. Not one word of boastfulness appears within its pages, but what does permeate the master's work is his generosity of spirit. In it, I learned about his humble beginning as an author and the absolute commitment to the daily discipline of writing. In it, I heard the voice of a master storyteller, telling me, a fledgling novelist, "Jack, I want you to succeed'.

Last but certainly not least, is the grateful acknowledgement of the extraordinary contribution to this work made by my professional Willow River Press editor, Penny Dowden. She is not only an astute grammarian, but a stickler for historical accuracy. Even though my novel is a work of historical fiction, the history part of it has to be right. Penny made it right when I got facts wrong. She is truly a gifted editor and made many suggestions, most of which I adopted, significantly improving what I hope is the quality of my own prose.

Numerous short stories and poems written by Jack Donahue appeared in journals and magazines alongside literary luminaries such as Pablo Neruda, Margaret Atwood, and Tennessee Willams. His literary work has been published around the world in North America, South America, Scotland, U.K., Austria; Cyprus, Ireland, New Zealand and India. His book of poems "InsideOut" was published in 2020.